Contents

Chapter Seventy-One

EPILOGUE

Other books by Carlene Havel:

Books by Carlene Havel and Sharon Faucheux:

Chapter One

At precisely nine o'clock Saturday morning, Lacy Chapman parked in her usual spot behind Pearl's Roadhouse. Tall pecan trees and spreading oaks arched over picnic tables on the side of the dark green building, partially shading the blacktop parking lot. The trees helped dampen the ceaseless hissing of automobiles speeding by on the highway. Soaring above the treetops, a lighted sign advertised "Home Style Cooking".

Leonard's old red pickup was wedged into a barely-big-enough spot between the smokehouse and the dumpster. A curl of smoke told Lacy the faithful old man was already hard at work, preparing choice pork, beef, and turkey breast. Pearl's little white compact sat in its designated parking space, earlier than usual.

Since Pearl was on the premises, Lacy put away her keys. Pushing aside the heavy wooden back door, she flipped on the kitchen lights and began her daily routine. As soon as she slid the bread trays into the oven, she poured herself a cup of coffee and made her way to the dining room.

Pearl's seventy years were memorialized on her well-lined face and confirmed by her silver-white hair. She looked up and smiled at Lacy. "Good morning, Sunshine."

"Morning, Pearl. How are you this fine day?" Lacy eased into a sturdy wooden chair as her mother-in-law's smile faded. "Is something wrong?"

"Nothing the Lord and me together can't handle." Pearl wrapped her hands around her coffee mug. "I have to make a few changes, that's all."

Lacy fought an uneasy feeling. "What's going on? Are those corporation people after you to sell this place again?"

"They never stop pestering me, but that's not it." Pearl drew a deep breath and lifted her eyes to meet Lacy's. "I don't know how to say this except to spit it out. I have cancer."

"Oh, Pearl. No." Suddenly Lacy realized why Pearl missed several days of work during the last few weeks. "Have you seen the doctor? It may not be what you think."

"I'm sure." Pearl lifted a palm, fingers spread. "I've known for a while, and I've done a lot of thinking."

Lacy puffed her cheeks and exhaled noisily. "You're the strongest woman I've ever known. You can beat this thing."

"Maybe. I'm sure going to try." Pearl took a sip of coffee. "Like my daddy always said, I'll hope for the best and prepare for the worst."

"Have you told Monty?"

"He wasn't answering his phone. I'll try to call him again tonight." Leaning back, Pearl combed three fingers through the side locks of her luxurious white hair. "I've decided to sell you the Roadhouse."

It took Lacy a moment to process what she'd heard. "Pearl, I don't have that kind of money."

"For the sum of one dollar," Pearl interrupted. "My attorney assures me since you and Monty are divorced, my son will have no claim on the place if I sell it to you. I want my granddaughters to be taken care of, and I've decided this is the best way to make sure that happens." Pearl smiled. "I'm having the papers drawn up."

"I can't manage like you do." Lacy chewed her bottom lip. "And, besides…"

"Nonsense. You run things just fine when I'm gone. All you need is a little stiffer backbone, and that will come with time. I hope you'll keep everybody who's working here now, but that will be your decision. To be honest, I'm kind of looking forward to easing off a little. God willing, I'll get through this cancer ordeal and maybe do some traveling. If He has other plans, well, I'll just be taking a longer trip than I expected." She scooted her chair away from the table and stood. "I'd better get busy if I don't want the new boss to fire me."

Lacy swirled the remains of her coffee. "Pearl, there's something I need to tell you."

"Honey, it don't matter to me if you want to get married again, or dye your hair purple, or start smoking cigars. As long as you take care of the girls—and I know you will—whatever floats your boat is fine with me."

"I'm not sure Monty and I are divorced," Lacy whispered.

Pearl slowly sank back into her chair. "But you went to court. Me and half the town wrote statements saying you should get sole custody of the girls."

"I know, but I'm not sure the final decree ever got done. You remember, Judge Wilson was ailing when we had our hearing. Afterward he was sick for a long time and then he passed away. I don't know if the paperwork got lost or what. I decided to let it go because I knew I would never remarry."

Pearl shook her head. "Good grief, girl. I'll check with Darrell and make sure he makes that deed transfer airtight. I remember he said something about making sure the Roadhouse is your separate property, with Monty being my only child and all." She rose, resting one hand on the back of her chair and using the other to point a finger at Lacy. "And you'd better get a copy of that signed divorce paper. Don't you know Texas is one of them community property states now? I love my son, but you sure don't want him owning half of your house or deciding to take off for parts unknown in your car someday."

Chapter Two

With her daughter's high school graduation only two weeks away, Lacy was too busy to think about the status of her divorce. She'd put the whole mess behind her long ago and hesitated to reopen the old scars crisscrossing her heart. For two years after Monty left Polson's Crossing for Nashville, she'd prayed he'd come back to her and their two girls. Finally, she filed for divorce in the hope he'd wake up and realize what he was sacrificing to his dogged ambition. To Lacy's disappointment, Monty agreed to her terms without putting up a fight. Obviously, chasing after a career as a singer meant more to him than their marriage. As far as Lacy knew, Monty had not been back to Polson's Crossing since the day he grabbed his guitar and walked out of their home ten years ago.

Lacy brought pecan pies from the kitchen and carefully slid them into the display case. She glanced across the dining room where Pearl sat on a high-backed stool near the cash register. She knew her mother-in-law—or should she say her *ex*-mother-in-law?—used to fly to Nashville occasionally to see her only son. Pearl always came home deflated and quiet, taking days to recover her characteristic optimism. After her last return from Nashville, Pearl said Lacy ought to go ahead and divorce Monty.

Noticing customers waiting, Lacy took a pen and order pad from her apron pocket and approached the nearest table. As soon as school was out, her teen-aged daughters would join the wait staff. Meanwhile, the summer rush was starting, and the Roadhouse was short-handed. "Hello," she greeted the couple in booth number one. "How are you folks doing?"

"Very well, thank you." The man closed his menu. "We both want the chicken fried steak and a glass of sweet tea." He tapped the nickelodeon wall box. "Does this thing work or is it just here to give the place atmosphere?"

"It works like a charm. Pearl's handyman keeps the sound system running." Lacy scribbled the simple order on her pad. "It used to play three songs for two bits, but now you have to put in a quarter to hear one selection." She stuck the ballpoint pen behind her ear and grinned. "That's progress, I guess."

"I suppose so." The woman sat her handbag on the table and dug out a coin purse. "I haven't played a juke box since we moved to Dallas."

Ordinarily, Lacy would linger longer in conversation with the couple, asking them where they had been and where they were going. However, she didn't want to keep other customers waiting too long. Therefore, she turned in the couple's order to the kitchen, delivered two glasses of sweet tea and moved to another booth.

The Good Eats Café had been a popular restaurant in Polson's Crossing for three generations. Locals laughed when Pearl's father sold his cotton farm to finance moving his restaurant away from Main Street. Nevertheless, Jack ignored his banker's advice and built a big building alongside the highway. He renamed the Good Eats Café to Pearl's Roadhouse, in honor of his daughter. When Pearl was almost sixteen, her mother died suddenly. The teenager quit school the following day and had worked full time in the family business ever since. "We had some tough times in the years before the interstate was finished. Everybody did." Lacy remembered Pearl saying, "But Daddy was dead right about the move."

Although the kitchen had been updated several times in the ensuing years, the public area of Pearl's Roadhouse looked about the same as it did when it was built. The stuffed deer head still dominated one wall of the rectangular room, facing a big silver cross at the other end. Original rusty signs and expired license plates graced the cedar plank walls. Maintaining the status quo suited Lacy. Years ago, she'd hoped to go to college, but marriage and motherhood changed her plans.

"Treat your customers like family" was the first thing Lacy learned from Pearl when she came to work at the Roadhouse as a new bride twenty years ago. It took considerable effort at first to overcome her natural shyness, but she enjoyed hearing the stories of travelers and imagining the places they'd been.

After Monty left, Lacy worked hard to make a living at the Roadhouse. In the process, she learned the ins and outs of the food business and became her mother-in-law's right arm. "I always thought my boy would take over the Roadhouse someday," Pearl said once, in a pensive moment. Then she shook her head and wiped down the already-clean counter.

"Hey, Patty. Coffee?" Lacy offered the frequent customer a menu, which she did not accept.

"Always."

Lacy filled Patty's cup and took out her order pad. "Have you found me a house yet?" Her question was a form of greeting, since both women knew Lacy wasn't in the market for a new home.

Patty smiled. "No, but I'm keeping my eyes open." She tapped a well-manicured nail on the table top. "I'll have my usual, a BLT, no mayo."

Chapter Three

After scanning through the document, Monty Chapman asked, "Where do I sign?"

"Right there in the middle of the last page." Carson Henry accepted the signed contract. "Congratulations. This is the best deal I've ever negotiated for a song writer."

Rubbing his chin, Monty said, "I hope I didn't sign my life away."

"You only agreed to a few minor concessions for the sake of public relations." Carson slipped the paperwork into a dark blue folder. "And, of course, you have to keep turning in three good songs every year."

"After all this time, it still seems like a dream." Monty extended a hand. "Let's shake on it."

"If you like." Carson grasped Monty's hand briefly. Then he then tapped the folder. "But in this town, a signed contract is a lot more reliable than a handshake. I'll shoot you a paper copy this afternoon."

"That reminds me." Monty took a card from the pocket of his shirt. "You can start sending my mail to this address."

The agent stapled the card to the blue folder. "In care of Pearl Chapman, Polson's Crossing, Texas. A relative?"

Monty answered with downcast eyes. "Pearl's my mother. I just found out she has cancer, and I'm going home to take care of her." He rubbed the back of his neck. "Maybe I'll mend a few fences while I'm at it."

"Commendable," Carson murmured. "You can write songs anywhere, I suppose." He plopped the blue folder into a wire basket. "Remember, the music business loves you as long as you're hitting the charts. Start missing your deadlines, or quit submitting songs that sell, and they'll drop you like at hot potato." Without smiling, he added, "And so will I. Nothing personal. That's just the way it works."

"I'll keep that in mind." Monty took his agent's rising from his chair to be a dismissal. He likewise stood, tucked in his shirttail, and picked up his guitar. "It's a pleasure doing business with you, Mr. Henry."

"I'm sure you want to go out and celebrate." Carson Henry looked over the rims of his glasses. "But don't do anything foolish. Nothing, for example, that will get you locked up."

"Don't worry," Monty said with a smile. "My wild days are all in the rearview mirror. I've been born again, and I intend for my life to show it."

"Right." Carson sat behind his desk and picked up the telephone receiver. "Stay in touch."

Monty closed the door softly and stood in the hallway of his agent's office building. Celebrating sounded like a fine idea, but how and with whom? On the street, he tilted his Stetson hat back on his head, folded his arms, and watched people walk by. They all seemed to know where they were going, and most of them scurried along as if they were in a hurry to get there.

The only place Monty knew where he could find acceptance and not be tempted by alcohol was a rescue mission a mile or two away. He wandered down the street in that general direction, stopping to buy a pencil from a street vendor. Instead of dropping the requested dollar into the battered coffee can at the man's foot, Monty took a twenty from his wallet and let it fall into the nearly empty can.

"Thank you, sir," the ragged man said, touching the brim of his battered baseball cap. "That's right generous."

Rather than walk on, Monty squatted next to the man. "Can I talk to you?"

"Be my guest." He nodded toward the guitar case Monty balanced with one hand. "You a musician?"

"I have been known to play a tune now and then."

"My daddy was a banjo player. He tried to teach me, but I never got the hang of it." The man pursed his lips. "I could make a lot more money out here on the street if I'd learned how to pick and grin." Shooting Monty a sidelong glance, he said, "Why don't you break out your guitar and hit a few licks? People like to be entertained. I'll split whatever we take in with you, fifty-fifty."

"That's okay." Monty snapped the case open and put the guitar strap over his shoulder. "I've already made a little money today." After settling cross-legged next to the street vendor, he played a chord, adjusted a string, and then sang "Home on the Range".

A group of people stopped to listen. At the end of the song, they applauded and dropped bills into the coffee can. "Man, you can sing," the street vendor said. "You ought to get a job in a bar or a nightclub. Nashville has a million of them."

Monty smiled, continuing to strum his guitar. "I chased down that road for ten years. Folks like the songs I write, but they seem to want someone else to sing them."

"You're a singer and a songwriter, too? Why don't you play something you wrote? The crowd might like it."

"Can't." Monty laughed. "I signed a contract that says I can't sing my own songs in public. The bigwigs want their young heartthrobs to have exclusive rights to perform my work."

"It's a crazy world." When a woman dropped a folded bill into the can, the old fellow said, "Thank you kindly, ma'am."

After singing "Home, Sweet Home" and "Lord I'm Coming Home", Monty turned toward his companion. "Tell me something, buddy, do you know Jesus?"

The man scooted an inch or two away from Monty. "You're not some kind of holy joe, are you?"

"Nah." Monty opened the case and laid his guitar inside as gently as if he were putting a baby to bed in its crib. "I'm just a no-good, two-timing drunk that God took pity on."

After sorting the bills from his coffee can by denomination, the street vendor put a hand on Monty's shoulder. "This is the most money I've ever made in one day. How about I buy you a whiskey at a little place I know down the street? You know, to show my appreciation."

Monty shook his head. "No, thanks, man. I gave up booze when I met the Lord." He snapped the guitar case shut and stood it on end. "Alcohol can get hold of you like a demon if you're not careful. I ought to know. Running wild cost me everything, including my family." He stood. "I'm on my way to a downtown rescue mission. Want to come along? They'll give you a hot meal, and some clean clothes and a place to sleep if you need it. All you have to do is let some guy like me tell you what God has done for him."

The man stuffed the day's earnings inside his shirt. "Maybe some other time." He struggled to his feet, accepting Monty's help. "Can you come back again tomorrow? We could go into business together."

"No, thanks." Monty grabbed the handle of his guitar case. "I'm heading home to Texas in the morning."

"I kind of figured something like that was on your mind, since every song you played had something to do with home."

As the two men shook hands, Monty said, "Think about visiting a rescue mission sometime. Or go find a good church, or just sit down and read the Bible. You'll be amazed at the peace the Lord can give you."

"Maybe I'll do something like that someday." The man ambled away.

"I'll pray for you." Monty wasn't sure whether the man heard him or not.

Chapter Four

As soon as Lacy walked through her front door, she had an unexplained feeling something was amiss. Her younger daughter Cindy strummed her mandolin softly. Monica seemed to be absorbed in a magazine. Normally they would be watching TV at this time of night, but what Pearl called the idiot box was turned off. When Lacy asked what the girls were doing, they replied "nothing" in unison, with neither of them making eye contact with her.

Instead of retreating to her recliner, she dropped her handbag on the coffee table and sat between her daughters on the sofa. Lacy spread her arms to embrace both girls. "How was school today?"

"Cindy broke up with Jerry," Monica volunteered.

Lacy wasn't surprised. Cindy discarded boyfriends like last week's leftovers. "What happened?"

"Nothing in particular." Cindy struck a chord on her mandolin. "He's just so boring."

"Right," Monica said, turning a page in her magazine. "He got that way immediately after he bought you dinner at *Le Colibri* and took you to the prom in a limo."

Cindy giggled and plucked a few strings. "Monica and I were just talking about education. You know, how some of it you get in school. And some of it comes along other ways."

Cindy's comment struck Lacy as peculiar. What did education have to do with dating? "I'm not following you."

"Cindy's making the point there are things we learn outside of the classroom," Monica commented. "They say travel, for example, broadens our horizons."

Lacy nodded and wrapped her bottom lip over the top one for a moment. Although her daughters seemed to think they were clever, she detected a conspiracy. So, what was the objective of the scripted conversation? A pitch for a vacation perhaps? "It's wonderful to go places," she agreed, "if you have the money."

"I think life itself is a great teacher." Monica laid her magazine neatly in the rack. "You know what I mean? Having a variety of experiences stretches us, and makes us grow."

"Could be." Lacy was too tired to play a game. "I think I'll take a shower before the news comes on."

Monica put a hand on her mother's forearm. "Mom, wait. There's something we need to talk about."

Cindy sprang from the sofa. "I'll be in the bedroom."

"Subtle," Lacy said as Cindy made her escape. She turned to face Monica. "What is it, sweetheart?"

"Philip has asked me to marry him."

Lacy paused to take in this information. "That's wonderful, Monica, if Philip is the one you want to spend your life with. After you finish school—"

"He has an overseas assignment, to England, reporting in September. He wants us to get married now so I can go with him." Before her next words, Monica took a deep breath. "I said yes."

"But you're all set for the fall semester at the university. You can't opt out now."

"Mom." Monica's voice was calm, but firm. "I know how much you've always wanted me to go to college. I've gone along because I didn't know what else to do. But that's your dream, not mine. I want to marry Philip."

Lacy had the feeling she'd already lost the argument, but she couldn't stop herself. "You can have it all, honey. Get your degree, and then get married."

"Philip doesn't want to wait four years, and neither do I." Monica leaned her head against her mother's shoulder. "Please try to be happy for me. For us."

Doing her best to hold back tears, and not totally succeeding, Lacy gave Monica's knee a pat. "We'll talk about this tomorrow, after a good night's sleep."

"Okay, but I'm not going to change my mind."

"Goodnight, Cindy," Lacy called out as she passed by the open bedroom door.

"Night, Mom."

Lacy could hear the padding of Cindy's bare feet behind her, receding toward the living room. She felt betrayed by being excluded from her daughters' plans and thoughts. How long had they kept this secret from her? The unspoken reality that Monica was old enough to marry without permission gnawed at her gut. She closed her bedroom door and leaned against it for a long moment.

Almost automatically, Lacy gathered her things. She heard the girl's low voices as she zipped through the hallway into the house's one bathroom. She could have bought a bigger house or built onto this one if she hadn't squirreled away every extra penny for the girls' college funds. And now, after all the sacrifices, Monica was throwing away her chance to get an education. As soon as Lacy turned on the water, she loosened the grip on her self-control, knowing the noisy pipes provided the perfect cover for a good cry. She crouched in the corner of the shower and wept disappointed tears until her hot shower cooled to tepid.

The following morning, trying to avoid saying things she would regret later, Lacy ate an early breakfast and scampered off to work before either of her girls emerged from their bedroom. She suspected they were awake, waiting until she left the house to show their faces. She took some satisfaction from knowing in another week the girls would start their summer jobs at Pearl's Roadhouse. At least she would know where they were and what they were doing every day.

As she sat having her morning coffee at the roadhouse with Pearl, Lacy fussed, "Last night Monica told me she wants to get married."

"Most girls do, sooner or later."

"Monica's opting for sooner," Lacy growled, disappointed by Pearl's lack of outrage. "She wants to ditch all of her plans to go to college and marry Philip right away."

Pearl stirred her coffee. "Maybe you could talk her into waiting a while."

"How?"

"Oh, suggest taking time to plan a nice wedding. The thought of wearing a beautiful white dress carries a lot of weight with a young woman."

"Maybe I'll try that." Lacy glanced toward the kitchen.

"One thing I've learned in my seventy years of living." Pearl sipped and stirred again. "If there's a runaway freight train, you won't stop it by throwing yourself on the tracks. You can stand back and watch the train go by or go and get yourself run over. Either way, the train moves on."

"Wanda probably needs help in the kitchen," Lacy said. She flew through the swinging double doors without a backward look. Why couldn't Pearl show a little indignation at Monica's foolishness?

26

Chapter Five

Monty parked his aging auto and the rented trailer against the curb in front of Pearl's house, relieved he'd made the drive from Nashville without a mechanical breakdown. He'd assumed his mother would be home in the middle of a Sunday afternoon, and the sight of her car in the driveway confirmed his expectation. A few years ago, he'd found life in Polson's Crossing confining, but now he realized there was comfort in the town's predictable rhythm.

It felt strange to knock at his mother's front entrance instead of walking in. However, the locked door left him with no choice.

Pearl's eyes grew wide and a smile overtook her wrinkled face. "Monty! What in the world are you doing here?" She bear-hugged him with more strength than he knew she possessed. "Come on in this house. You should have let me know you were coming so I could bake you some goodies." She stepped aside and held the door open.

"I didn't want you to go to any trouble." Monty stepped into the living room, somewhat surprised to see the old familiar furniture had been replaced.

Pearl stood gazing outward for a long moment before closing her front door. "How about a glass of tea?"

"I'd love something cold to drink." Monty stepped toward the kitchen. "I'll get it. You sit down and rest."

To his surprise, Pearl settled into a platform rocking chair without argument. "You know where everything is.

There's cinnamon rolls on the stove, too. Help yourself if you want one."

The kitchen was at once both familiar and strange. A fancy refrigerator occupied the niche where the noisy old-fashioned model used to stand. Although the drinking glasses were exactly where Monty remembered his mother storing them, the cabinets themselves had been replaced with newer, nicer wood. The wall separating the kitchen and dining room was gone, and an area that used to be the back porch was now part of the inside living space. Monty raised his voice to carry into the next room. "Do you want a glass of tea?"

"No, thanks." Pearl answered. "I just had some."

Monty hadn't planned to have a cinnamon roll, but they smelled so yummy he couldn't resist. After pouring cold tea into a glass full of crackling ice cubes, he returned to the living room. "The house looks nice. You've made a lot of changes."

"Thank you. I thought about moving out to one of the new subdivisions, but Lacy talked me into staying and having this place fixed up the way I wanted it instead."

Monty took a bite of his warm cinnamon roll. "Mm-mm. Nobody can bake like you, Mom." He drank a sip of tea. "Is my room still the same?"

"It's still up there." Pearl rocked back and forth while Monty ate. "I hope you're not thinking about moving back into your old bedroom."

The stainless-steel fork clinked against Monty's now empty plate. "Well, yes, that's what I have in mind. After you called and said you were sick, I decided to come home to take care of you." He set the plate aside. "I could live somewhere else and look in on you every day, but the logical thing is to be in the same house."

"Son, I can see you're down on your luck." Pearl closed her eyes and leaned against the back of her rocker. "I'll help you get a new car if that's what you're after."

Monty had brought his glass to his lips, but set it down without drinking. "A car? Mama, what are you talking about?"

"I saw that old jalopy you parked out front, and I'll bet everything you own is in that there little trailer you're hauling."

"Well, yeah, I was able to get my clothes and things in the trailer." He leaned forward. "I don't need money from you, Mama. I thought about buying a new car in Nashville, but I really wanted to wait until I got home. You know I went to school with Jimmy Glassman. I thought it would be good to give him my business instead of spending my money with a stranger in another state."

"So you drove all the way from Nashville to buy a new car from Jimmy Glassman."

"No, Mama. The car is secondary. I came home to help you. To take care of you. To do anything and everything you need me to do."

At last Pearl opened her eyes. "I've been taking care of myself ever since they came and told me your daddy was missing in action. I reckon I can keep on doing it."

"You're tough, Mama, but even you can use a little help to face down something as nasty as cancer."

"We'll see, but I just can't let you move into my house." She put a hand to her forehead. "While we're on the subject, you may as well know I'm selling the Roadhouse."

"I don't care about—"

Pearl held up a hand. "To Lacy. And I've fixed up my will to leave everything I have to your daughters."

"That makes sense to me. I don't understand why you think…" Monty stopped talking and stared at his mother for a moment. "Of course. Why wouldn't you assume I'm here to get instead of give? That's the way it has always been with me, isn't it?"

Monty squatted on the floor in front of Pearl and took her hands in his. "Mama, remember all those years you spent trying to teach me about the Bible? Well, it finally soaked in. I'm not the same man who walked out on my family ten years ago. I've accepted Jesus as my Lord and Savior, and He has changed me."

Pearl shook her hands loose and folded them in her lap. "You're my son, Monty, and I'll always love you. But I have to say, it breaks my heart to think you'd lie to me about something as precious as my faith."

Sitting back on his heels, Monty whispered, "You think I'm making this up? What a rotten son I've been."

Chapter Six

After checking in at the first motel he spotted, Monty took a shower, put on clean clothes, and laid across the bed watching television. He had plenty of cash in his wallet. Plus, there was more money than he knew how to spend in his Nashville bank account. Tomorrow, he would head out to Glassman's Auto World and get the new car he'd been itching for. As near as he could remember, most locally-owned Polson's Crossing businesses, including Pearl's Roadhouse, were closed all day on Sunday. Never mind tomorrow. His immediate challenge was getting through a lonely evening.

It occurred to Monty he was slipping into a danger zone. He was hungry, tired, alone, and starting to feel sorry for himself. Based on a book he read at the Nashville rescue mission, he knew what to do. He had to pray for strength, find something to eat, and mingle with people. Afterward, a good night's sleep was essential. Fighting a strong desire to remain prone, he sat on the side of the bed looking at his feet and praying hard. In a few minutes, with his body not nearly as determined as his spirit, he grabbed his guitar case and left the motel room. Polson's Crossing had a minimal crime rate. Nevertheless, he wasn't going to leave his favorite musical instrument with only the flimsy lock on a cheap motel room's door to protect it from a thief.

After unhitching his trailer, Monty drove by a decent-looking restaurant, wary of the flashing neon sign advertising beer on tap. Perhaps another time he could withstand that temptation, when he was with friends. He let out a sigh that sounded more like a groan. What friends? It wasn't long before he found himself at the center of

Polson's Crossing. He drove around the town square twice before choosing to go north. In a few blocks, he spotted a burger joint and pulled in to a parking space. Although everyone else appeared to be taking advantage of the drive-through service, he took his guitar and went inside.

Monty placed his order at the counter and took a seat at a booth in the small eat-in area. He chuckled as the speaker system serenaded him with one of his own compositions. "Barely Hanging on in Old Nashville Town" was the first song he'd sold, and it accurately described the state of his emotions at the time.

The young woman who'd taken Monty's order brought his food to the booth instead of summoning him to pick it up at the counter. Perhaps that was because he was the only person eating inside, or maybe because he was twice the age of her typical customer. "Don't you just *love* that song?" she asked as she slid the large strawberry malt in front of Monty.

"It's one of my favorites," Monty agreed.

"Me, too." She wiped a table with a rag that would never have passed inspection at Pearl's Roadhouse. "It makes me want to cry and laugh at the same time." After gazing at the ceiling for a moment with a rapturous look on her face, she retreated behind the counter.

Monty took his time to enjoy the smoky flavor of his oversized burger. Plentiful chunks of real strawberries in his thick malt suited him just fine, too. He gave up on the soft, greasy potatoes, spoiled by memories of his mother's crunchy French fries. He paid scant attention when two teenagers came inside. However, when the dark-haired girl turned away from the counter, he almost choked. She looked so much like Lacy, he almost called out to her by that name. He swept his hair back and rested his forehead in a hand. Maybe he was losing his mind. That pretty young woman wasn't Lacy. She was young enough to be her daughter.

Monty stared down at the remains of his meal while reality penetrated his mind. He looked up again to meet the taller, blond girl's eyes. "Monica?"

"Daddy?"

Leaping from the booth, Monty gathered his daughters into a hug. The return hugs were less enthusiastic than his, which Monty attributed to surprise. "Come sit with me."

Moving his guitar case aside, Monty sat next to it, leaving the seats across from him for the girls.

Cindy slid into the booth first. Monica looked around as if searching for something, and then joined her sister. "What are you doing in Polson's Crossing?" she asked.

"Your grandma is sick. I came home to check on her. I'm planning to stay a while."

"How long is a while?" Monica unfolded a napkin.

Before Monty could answer, Cindy chimed in. "Wow, Mom is never going to believe we just ran into you by accident here at Bob's Burger Barn. I mean, what are the odds of that happening?"

"Speaking of your mother, how is she?"

Monica and Cindy exchanged a look Monty could not interpret. "Fine," Monica answered. "She didn't feel like going to church with us tonight. That's where we're headed after we have something to eat."

"Mom and Monica had a big argument," Cindy said.

Monica's face reddened. "Hush, Cindy."

"Well, you did. That's why we decided to get out of the house instead of fixing dinner at home. You know it's the truth."

"Even if it's true, you don't have to tell everything you know, Cynthia Pearl. How many times has Mom told you that?"

Monty was curious, but he resisted the impulse to ask about the reason for his daughters' disagreement with Lacy. "So, you're on your way to church. Do you think it would be all right if I go, too?"

"Everybody is welcome at church," Monica said without enthusiasm.

When her sister left her seat to collect the food order, Cindy leaned forward. "Monica is getting married, and Mom is mad because she wants her to go to college first." While the older girl was occupied gathering condiments, Cindy cupped a hand beside her mouth and continued, "This afternoon Monica said she and Philip—that's her boyfriend—are going to elope the day after

35

graduation. I guess he's really her fiancé now. Mom said the least they could do is get married in church. Fluffy and I hid in the bedroom while they yelled at each other. Fluffy's my cat. Are you coming to Monica's graduation Friday night?"

Chapter Seven

Lacy felt for the alarm clock and shut it off without opening her eyes. She lay in bed mentally going through her plans for the day, wishing she'd built extra time into the schedule to luxuriate in bed. After cleaning house and picking up her dry cleaning, she and the girls were meeting Pearl for lunch. Then she was taking her daughters to have their hair and nails done. The four of them planned to eat dinner at the Roadhouse before the formal graduation ceremony this evening. For years, her focus had been on her daughters, and suddenly they were almost grown. Now what? With Pearl facing a serious illness and Monica getting married, Lacy knew changes were afoot, both at home and at work. She yawned and stretched before swinging her feet onto the floor.

Cindy was humming and putting plates on the table when Lacy wandered into the kitchen. She gave her daughter a side-arm hug and a light kiss on her cheek. "Good morning. Something smells good."

"Cinnamon toast. I tried to outwait Monica so she'd make breakfast, but she's still in the bathroom trying to make her eyes look like she hasn't been crying. So I gave up and decided to make my specialty."

While filling the carafe with water for the coffee maker, Cindy's remark registered. "What was Monica crying about?"

Cindy removed a baking sheet of toast from the oven. "She's all torn up because Philip isn't going to be at graduation. I told her, everybody's going to wear that same funny hat and choir robe. All the senior girls will look pretty much alike from the bleachers. Well, except Carlotta Simpson, maybe, with her purple hair. If Philip was there, he wouldn't know Monica from anybody else walking across the football field until they announced her name on the loud speaker. And she couldn't see him because you know she's too vain to wear her glasses. So what's the big whoop? I mean, she can pretend he's there and send him pictures. Besides, they're going to get married pretty soon so it's not like she's never going to see him again."

Standing over the coffee maker, Lacy slid the glass carafe aside, simultaneously positioning her mug to catch the stream of brown liquid directly. "Philip probably can't afford another plane ticket to come home twice this summer."

"Try explaining the economics of the situation to Monica." Cindy rolled her eyes. "At least she can't tell you that you've never been in love, like she did to me. You and Daddy were in love once upon a time, huh?"

"Yes." After a big gulp, Lacy closed her eyes. "Mmm, that's good. There's nothing like that first cup of coffee in the morning."

"Was it exciting and romantic and absolutely *comme il faut*?"

"For heaven's sake, Cindy, it's just coffee. It beats me where you come up with some of the words you use." Taking a seat at the table, Lacy hunched over with her head in her hands.

"Not the coffee, I mean you and Daddy. I found those words in my French dictionary. They mean the two of you were as essential as breathing to each other, or something like that. Is that how you felt?" Cindy arched her eyebrows expectantly before returning to the scrambling eggs.

"That was too long ago to remember." Lacy sat sipping coffee while her older daughter silently slipped into the kitchen. How could she explain how consumed with each other she and Monty were once upon a time? Against her will, memories began to bubble. The song he wrote asking her to marry him. Moving into their house together. How excited he was when she told him she was pregnant. Lacy shook her head, hoping to stuff old pictures back into the locked album of her mind.

"Good morning, Monica. I hope you're feeling simply marvelous on this, your high school graduation day." Cindy placed the full toast rack on the table.

"Morning," Monica mumbled, receiving a nod of acknowledgement from Lacy.

Cindy stood with hands on her hips for a moment. "I must say it's challenging to be a normal person in a house with two anti-morning night owls."

Without responding, Monica poured herself a mug of coffee and gulped from it. She topped off the mug before taking a seat across from Lacy at the table.

While Lacy and Monica sat in silence, Cindy put plates of eggs and bacon on the table with a flourish. "There you have it, folks. A magnificent breakfast, if I do say so myself. Which as a matter of fact is the only way much of anything gets said around here before ten o'clock."

"You know how talking before breakfast irritates me," Monica said without making eye contact.

Cindy said, "It's a gorgeous morning, bright and sunny. This is the day the Lord has made so how can anyone be in a grumpy mood? Listen to the sparrows, singing their little hearts out."

Monica glanced toward the window. "Stupid birds, chirping like they have good sense."

"Girls, please." Lacy noticed a wad of gold foil on the table. Pointing toward it with her fork, she asked, "What's this?"

"I sampled your candy. I hope that was okay." Cindy grabbed the tiny ball and tossed it into the trash. "It's top of the line stuff, in a metal box no less, with a real ribbon around it. All of the pieces are individually wrapped in different colors of foil. It's almost too pretty to eat. Notice I said *almost*. There are lots of nuts, too, not just a bunch of cheapo cream centers."

"Cindy, what are you chattering about?" Lacy took a slice of cinnamon toast.

Cindy covered her eggs with ketchup. "When I got up this morning, there was a box of candy and a bouquet of roses on the porch. I brought them in and put them in the living room."

Monica looked up from her coffee cup for the first time. "Where did they come from?"

"Wow, at last a spark of genuine interest from sleeping beauty." Cindy grinned and batted her eyes at Monica. "I don't know. There's a card but I didn't open it. I didn't think I should since it's not addressed to me."

Monica stared at her sister. "You felt it was all right to open the candy but not the card?"

Cindy nodded. "The envelope was attached to the roses. Now the box of chocolates could, conceivably, have been left on the porch for me by a secret admirer. Then, through a remarkable coincidence, someone else happened to send Mom flowers on the very same day. I mean, it could happen. We don't know for sure it didn't." She pushed her chair away from the table. "I'll go get the card."

Lacy yawned. "She ought to go into politics."

Cindy returned and put a vase with a dozen red roses on the kitchen table.

After glancing at her name on the small envelope, Lacy slipped it into her robe pocket. "I'll look at this later."

Cindy's eyes widened. "Why, Mom? Don't you want to know who sent you roses?"

"They're from your father. I'd know his handwriting anywhere."

"But—" Monica's hand on her arm stopped Cindy's protest.

41

The older girl stood and cleared the table. "Let's go get dressed."

As their voices trailed down the hallway, Lacy ripped open the envelope and read the card's message. "*Congratulations. Monica and Cindy are fantastic. You've done a wonderful job raising them. Always, Monty.*"

This is not like Monty, Lacy thought. *What kind of scheme is he up to?* She hoped the florist didn't get a hot check for the roses.

       ***

That evening as graduation was about to begin, Lacy settled onto the bleacher next to Pearl. "I wonder why I wore shoes with heels," she muttered.

Pearl grinned. "So you'd look good, and you do."

"Thank you, Pearl." Although she knew she was not the only single mother present, it did feel as if every family she saw sitting nearby included a dad. That was one more thing Monica and Cindy would not experience, having their parents attend their high school graduation together. Lacy remembered Monica saying she'd invited Monty to her graduation, but Lacy knew he wouldn't show up. He was probably at some honkytonk, singing or getting drunk or both. If he was still in town.

"I sure hope the weather holds out." Pearl pointed toward a dark cloud. "That big old thunderhead is going to dump buckets of rain somewhere."

"I hope not here," Lacy answered. "At least not until the graduation ceremony is over."

Pearl gestured toward the athletic field and offered her binoculars to Lacy. "I see Cindy. Even in that band uniform, she looks like a doll. That trombone is as big as she is. Why in the world does she want to play that big old horn?"

"The mandolin is her first love, but she wanted to be in the marching band. I think she decided to take up the trombone because the brass section is mostly boys." Lacy adjusted the field glasses' focus to get a clear view of her younger daughter's face. "She is a cutie, isn't she?" She scanned the block of graduating seniors already occupying folding chairs on the well-manicured grass. "Monica told me she's in the second row. I think that's the back of her head, there in the fourth, no fifth seat, right on the forty-yard line."

"Beats me." Pearl accepted Lacy's return of the binoculars. "Like everything else in this old, worn-out body, my eyes aren't what they used to be." She dabbed at her forearm. "Is it starting to rain?"

Lacy was about to disagree, when she felt a drop of moisture hit the tip of her nose. Then another spattered on her shoe. After glancing up at the darkening sky, she rolled her eyes toward Pearl. "There's no way the rain is going to hold off long enough."

"Yeah." Pearl leaned forward and looked up at the press box. "They'd better get the kids off the field before it comes a gully-washer."

A sudden clap of thunder ushered in a steady sprinkle. As raindrops fell harder and closer together, the public address system crackled to life. "Ladies and gentlemen, the graduation ceremonies are being moved to the gymnasium."

A low murmur swept through the crowd in the bleachers before people began to move toward the field house. Meanwhile, the band quick marched indoors. Each robed senior took a folding chair and ran for the gymnasium doors.

From the depths of her ample handbag, Pearl produced an old-fashioned plastic rain bonnet and slipped it over her head. With people jamming the aisles, there was nothing for Lacy to do but wait patiently. She took Pearl's arm to keep from getting separated in the crowd. Meanwhile, she attempted to protect her hair with a graduation program.

As the people ahead funneled through the field house doors, Lacy became aware of an umbrella partially sheltering her and Pearl from the intensifying rain. When she turned her head to thank their benefactor, she was shocked to see Monty's face smiling at her. She managed to mumble "thank you" before being squeezed through the entrance by the wet mob. The logjam thinned as the crowd fanned out to find seats on either side of the basketball court. Lacy glanced behind her, but the good Samaritan was now lost in the sea of people. Most likely he only looked like Monty. Surely it couldn't have been him.

Chapter Eight

Pearl spoke before Lacy sat down for their Tuesday morning coffee break at the Roadhouse. "Monty's in town."

"I know. The girls ran into him by chance, or so they claimed. He went to church with them." Lacy decided not to mention he'd sent her roses and may even have been at graduation.

"Can you imagine that? Monty inside a church without being roped and hogtied? I didn't tell you last week, but he wants to move in with me." Pearl stirred her coffee the way she always did when she was thinking. "I hated telling him no."

Lacy winced. "He probably doesn't have any other place to go, but I can't blame you."

"I also told him you're buying the Roadhouse, and that I cut him out of my will. He acted like he didn't care."

"Maybe he doesn't. You know Monty. He has his faults, but he's never been concerned about material possessions beyond a collection of good guitars." Lacy studied her manicure. "Here's what I can't figure out. Monica and I had a big row Sunday afternoon about her getting married. Later, she said she'd talked things over with Monty and decided to wait and have a church wedding in July. How do you suppose he convinced my bull-headed daughter to do that?"

Pearl shrugged a shoulder. "He's always been pretty good at persuading people to come around to his point of view.

"True enough. I don't know what Monty said to her, but Monica and I actually had a civil conversation about her wedding. She set a date, and I gave her a budget to work with."

"Let me know if you need any financial help."

"Thank you, Pearl." Lacy patted her mother-in-law's forearm. "You've always been more than generous with the girls and me, but this wedding is coming out of the money I set aside for Monica's college education. Which she has suddenly decided is unnecessary."

"A lot of folks do all right without all that higher learning." Pearl brushed imaginary crumbs from the table. "This will be her third summer working here at the roadhouse. She can always get a job in a restaurant if she ends up having to make her own living."

"I wanted her to have something easier than waiting tables," Lacy said. "But like you've said so many times, kids do what they're going to do. We follow along and clean up behind them."

Pearl nodded and stirred. "Now don't wig out on me, but I'm thinking about offering Monty a job."

"Monty? Work here at the Roadhouse? Do you think he would do it?"

"Well, I expect he's dead broke. He's not likely to get a job, not with the reputation he has in Polson's Crossing. At least I can feed him and keep an eye on him. But you're the new owner, or will be before long. What do you think?"

Lacy hesitated. Could she tolerate being around Monty and not fall victim to his considerable charm? Then again, she was certain he would never put up with regular hours for very long. "I can't stand to think of him going hungry."

"Good." Pearl rotated her left shoulder and massaged it with her right hand. "I don't know how to get in touch with him, but I reckon he'll drop by for a free meal before long."

***

On the other side of Polson's Crossing, Monty strode confidently into the showroom at Glassman's Auto World. As soon as he opened the door of a sporty convertible, a well-dressed man appeared at his side. "Hi, I'm Mike Freeman. What can I do for you?"

"Monty Chapman." The men shook hands. "I want to buy a new car today, and I'd bet you're just the man to sell it to me."

"Yes, sir. This one is a beauty, isn't she?" Mike ran his hand across the convertible's shiny red fender.

"Sure is," Monty agreed. "But she needs a younger man to drive her around. I'm looking for something more conservative, with four doors to haul a family." He leaned against the convertible. "By the way, is Jimmy Glassman around? We were pretty good friends in high school. I'd like to say hi to him."

"Mr. Glassman normally doesn't come in until later. He always goes by his boat and camper lot first thing in the morning." Mike straightened his tie. "Now what general price range are you considering?"

"I haven't given it much thought," Monty answered. "What have you got?"

Three hours later, after two test drives and kicking innumerable tires, Monty sat sipping a cold soda in Mike's tiny, glassed-in office.

"I just need to get a little information." Mike pulled a pad of forms from his desk drawer.

"I'll save you some trouble." Monty smiled. "My trade-in is a pile of junk and my credit history is your worst nightmare."

The cordial smile Mike had worn all morning faded instantly. "Is there someone who will co-sign for your loan?"

Taking his checkbook from his shirt pocket, Monty answered, "Fortunately, I won't be needing a loan. I'll give you a check."

"For the full amount?" Mike clicked and unclicked a ball point pen. "Will you excuse me for a moment? I need to speak with my manager."

Monty chuckled and wrote out a check payable to Glassman's Auto World. As he signed his name, Jimmy Glassman came to the door of the office. "Monty."

"Hey, Jimmy." Monty jumped up and shook hands with his old friend, clapping him on the back at the same time. "I was hoping I'd run into you. Long time no see. You don't look a day older than the last time I saw you."

"You always were a smooth liar." Jimmy laughed, and Monty joined him. "Come on over to my office. We'll have more privacy there."

Monty followed his friend to a larger enclosure, equipped with real walls. Instead of sitting behind the desk, which was approximately the size of an aircraft carrier, Jimmy plopped into one of two overstuffed chairs and motioned for Monty to sit beside him. "My salesman tells me you need a car."

"Yep. I picked out a honey, with electronics that would be the envy of a spacecraft. If it doesn't cause you any problem, I'd like to drive it home and leave my car parked out back until I can arrange for a junk dealer to pick it up."

Jimmy accepted the check Monty offered and stared at it.

"Did I use the wrong date?" Monty asked.

"This bank is in Tennessee."

"Yeah. You can call them and verify my balance if you like."

49

"I can't let you do this, Monty." Jimmy ripped the check into small pieces. "You can get away with a small hot check here and there, but this amount is a felony offense. You could end up in prison."

"But Jimmy, I have more than enough money in that Nashville bank to cover my check."

Jimmy made a steeple with his hands. "I'll tell you what. I'll get a mechanic to fix up that old car you drove in here. It may take a while because it looks like it needs a lot of work. Meanwhile, you can have one of my loaners to get around in."

"Jimmy, you don't understand my situation."

"Sure I do. You don't need to explain anything to me. This is the least I can do for an old friend. Check back in about ten days. By then we should have your car in good enough shape to go another few thousand miles." He stood. "It's been good seeing you, Monty. I have to run now. Take care of yourself."

Monty sat in stunned silence for a few minutes after Jimmy hurried away. When he emerged into the show room, Mike handed him a set of keys. "Your courtesy car is the white station wagon parked out back.

"Thank you." Monty put his guitar into the station wagon and drove away wondering if Jimmy Glassman had lost his marbles.

Chapter Nine

"Thank you for making time to see me." Monty set his guitar in a corner and shook the pastor's hand.

"My pleasure." Sprinkles of gray in his dark hair gave Tom Gillespie a distinguished appearance, although he was much younger than Monty expected. Late thirties or early forties, perhaps. The pastor gestured toward a pair of easy chairs. "Make yourself at home. Would you like something to drink? I've got water, sodas, and iced tea."

"Tea sounds good, if it's no trouble."

"No trouble at all as long as you don't mind it coming in a can. What's on your mind?"

"My personal life is a mess, and it's my own fault. I lived selfishly for lot of years, despite my mother and later my wife's attempts to get me to straighten up. A few months ago, I gave my heart to Jesus." Monty rubbed the back of his neck. "I made amends to everyone I know of that I wronged in Nashville." He stopped to pop the top on his can of tea. "My mother is sick. I've come home to help her and try to patch things up with my wife and kids. I don't know if they can forgive me for the way I've neglected them, and I wouldn't blame them if they don't."

The pastor rested his elbows on his knees and his chin on his clasped hands. "You were here at the Sunday night service with the Chapman girls, weren't you?"

"Yes, Reverend Gillespie. They're my daughters, but I hardly know them."

"Why don't you call me Tom? Or Pastor Tom if you prefer. So Lacy Chapman is your wife."

"Ex-wife actually, but I'm hoping and praying to remove that ex part. Here's my problem. My mom will come around, and I think my daughters will thaw out eventually also. But I don't know how to go about getting my wife back. I'm hoping you can give me some advice."

"Folks sometimes think preachers are experts in matters we know very little about. I'll pray with you, but my best recommendation is to walk close to the Lord and live the way the Bible says. I've witnessed failing marriages put back together that way, but I have to tell you we've also had some heartbreaking divorces in this very congregation." Tom leaned back in his chair. "How did you and your wife meet?"

"The two things I've loved as long as I can remember are music and Lacy. This may sound nutty, but the first time I saw her, I knew she was the girl I wanted to marry."

"When was that?" Tom asked.

"Second grade. She was passing out crayons from a cigar box. She gave me purple, green and gold ochre. Those are Mardi Gras colors, although I didn't know that then. I drew a heart and printed her name inside it, and then I took the picture home and hid it in a drawer. I didn't tell Lacy how I felt for five or six more years. We went steady from middle school on. Then we ran off and got married the summer between our junior and senior year, just a couple of crazy, headstrong kids. She quit school and started working at my mom's restaurant, but I went back to high school for one more year and graduated."

Tim swirled his glass of tea round and round. "Your mother is Pearl Chapman, and she owns Pearl's Roadhouse, right?"

"Yes. Mama was all for us getting married, but she wanted us to wait another year or two. You know how mothers are."

"Miss Pearl, as everyone around here calls her, has stuck with this church through thick and thin. Looking back, do you think she was right about waiting?"

"No doubt about it." Monty shifted in his chair, crossing his legs. "But I didn't listen to anybody back then, least of all my mother. Lacy and I had big plans. We were going to save up our money and move to Nashville as soon as I finished high school. Naturally I was going to be the nation's number one country singer." He paused and took a deep breath. "By graduation time, Lacy was pregnant. We stayed in Polson's Crossing another year so we would have some help when the baby was born."

Monty took a long drink of tea. "We were about ready to take Monica and go to Nashville when we discovered another baby was on the way. Less than a year after Cindy was born, Lacy lost her mom. We seemed to encounter one delay after another. All this time I was singing with a band. The other musicians drank, and I wanted to be one of the boys. So I joined in. My wife and I began to argue a lot. I guess it was about ten years ago, when the girls were maybe seven and eight that things came to a head."

After a brief silence, Tom prodded, "What happened?"

"One evening I got way too drunk, and we argued. I threw some clothes into a suitcase and told Lacy I was going to Nashville. I gave her the choice of going with me or staying in Polson's Crossing, and said I didn't really care which one she picked. She told me if I walked out the door that night never to try walking back in."

"Do you think she meant what she said?"

Monty took a napkin from the side table and wiped condensation from his tea can. He kept at it after all of the moisture was absorbed. "I honestly don't know for sure. I haven't spoken with her since that night."

"Not at all?"

Shaking his head, Monty whispered, "No." He cleared his throat and continued, "I'm sure you've read the story of the prodigal son, which is about as good a description as any of my life in Nashville. Even after I started selling the songs I wrote, the money didn't help the emptiness inside. One night I was walking around downtown feeling low when the sound of music drew me into a rescue mission. Monty brushed away tears with the back of his hand. "I can't help but get emotional when I think back on that night. Sorry."

"Don't be." Tom nudged a box of tissues toward Monty. "That probably means the memory still touches your deepest feelings."

"That's true," Monty agreed. "I would have bolted out of there if someone had started preaching. Instead, a fellow sat beside me and starting telling me how accepting Jesus as his Savior changed his life. I mean, he wasn't a minister or anything. He was just a guy, and the more he talked the more I wanted what he had. I don't know if anybody in Polson's Crossing will believe this, but I walked out of the mission that night a different man." Monty snatched a tissue.

Tom smiled. "What the Bible calls a new creation."

"For sure." With a grin, Monty pulled another tissue from the box. "I won't say I haven't *wanted* another drink of alcohol, but since that night I've never touched the stuff again. To tell you the truth, I'm scared to death to be around it. Plus, I've given up cussing, lying, messing with women, and writing worthless checks. Well, mostly. Now and then a curse word spouts out of my mouth before I can stop it." He uncrossed his legs and leaned toward Tom. "I've made up my mind to live here in my home town, helping out my mother and doing whatever I can for my daughters. More than anything else, I want to be a good husband to Lacy. If she'll let me, that is."

Tom's eyes bored into Monty's. "Why is that? Is it out of a sense of duty?"

"Partly," Monty admitted with a fidget. "I believe it would please the Lord to put my family back together. But it goes beyond all of that. I love my wife more than I can ever tell you. I always have and I think I always will. She's had it rough, and I want to take care of her and make her happy for the rest of our lives. So how do I convince her to give me another chance?"

"You can't control how Lacy feels," Tom said. "Concentrate on your own actions. Jesus told us to treat other people the way we want to be treated. I'd start trying to do that, with your family and basically everyone." He reached for the Bible on the table next to him. "There's some very specific advice in the book of Ephesians, which you probably read in your younger days."

"You mean that thing about wives submitting themselves to their husbands?"

"If I were you, I wouldn't worry about what wives are supposed to do. Your responsibility is to fulfill the husband's role. I'm thinking about the passage that instructs husbands to love their wives the way Christ loves his church. Meaning you have to love Lacy sacrificially. You're supposed to put her needs, desires, and welfare ahead of your own, even to the point of dying for her if it comes to that."

Monty was quiet for a moment. "That's a tall order, Tom. I'll give it a try, but I can't promise I can live up to your requirements."

"Not mine." Tom held up the Bible. "His. Let's read from the word together, and then we'll pray."

Chapter Ten

Monty woke up after dreaming he and Lacy were teen-agers again, dancing to the juke box music at Pearl's Roadhouse. How good it felt to hold her in his arms, even if it took place only in his mind. He stared at the ceiling, thinking about the one person he knew would never walk away from him permanently, his mother. Sure, she hadn't welcomed him into her home. He couldn't blame her, since he'd let her down so many times before. Nevertheless, he knew she loved him. Checking the time, he made a mental note to eat a meal at the Roadhouse. He'd be able to visit with Pearl, and maybe catch a glimpse of Lacy if she was still working there.

The loud hum of the motel room's window air conditioner reminded Monty to look for a decent place to live. He stumbled to the bathroom sink and splashed cold water on his face. One day at a time he reminded himself. Sampling the unappetizing free breakfast at the motel restaurant reinforced his resolve to relocate. When he put coins into a newspaper dispenser, the machine banged open and belched out a double handful of quarters. Monty sighed and went to the front desk to give the bewildered clerk the money. Back in his room, he leafed through the real estate ads, wondering how so many new neighborhoods sprang up in ten short years. He folded the paper, deciding to drive around until he found a real estate office.

For old times' sake, Monty drove by the little house Pearl gave him and Lacy as a wedding present. Mature trees now shaded the small dwelling. A few of the surrounding houses needed paint, and an occasional yard was somewhat overgrown. Overall, however, the old neighborhood was holding up well.

Monty turned south toward his mother's house. He wanted to be as close to her as possible when she needed him. Driving up and down the streets where he'd spent his boyhood brought back a flood of memories, but there was not one 'for sale' sign. Disappointed, he meandered toward downtown until he spied a real estate office. After pulling into the strip mall's parking lot, he grabbed his guitar case from the back seat and went inside Chesterfield Realty.

Two large desks dominated the cramped space. One was unoccupied, while a well-dressed, attractive blonde woman sat at the other. She looked up with a smile when the bell attached to the glass door signaled Monty's arrival. "Good morning."

"Good morning," Monty replied, leaning his guitar case against the wall. "I'm Monty Chapman."

"Patty Chesterfield." Bracelets tinkled as she waved a hand dominated by brightly lacquered nails toward a plastic chair. "What can I do for you, Mr. Chapman?"

"You can call me Monty." He sat next to the desk. "I'm looking for a place to live, and I'd like to be as close as possible to Shady Oak Elementary School."

"That's a very desirable, older neighborhood. Let me see what we have." Patty lifted the glasses hanging from a chain around her neck and perched them on her nose. "Are you looking to rent or buy?"

Monty shrugged. "I'm open to either one."

Patty scrolled through listings of houses on her computer screen. "Can you tell me how many bedrooms and your general price range?"

"None of that matters." In response to Patty's surprised face, Monty said, "My mother lives half a block from the school. I want to be close to her. If she has an emergency in the middle of the night, it's important that I get to her house in a matter of minutes."

"I see. Do you have a home you're planning to sell?"

"I've been away from Polson's Crossing for a number of years. So, I don't own a house. I'll be living alone." Monty studied the office while Patty continued to tap the keys of her desktop keyboard. "I went to school with some of the Chesterfields, Gilbert and Charlie. Are you related to them?"

"I'm from Arizona." She doodled for a moment in the margin of a pad she'd been writing on. "Gilbert is my *ex*-husband. He lives in Fort Worth now."

From the emphasis Patty put on "ex", Monty suspected he had touched a nerve. "I'm sorry," was all he could think of to say.

"Don't be. I got the house, the car, the kids, and the business, and all he got was the girlfriend. Anyway, that was another life." She looked at him and smiled. "There's a nice garage apartment for rent, only fifteen minutes from Shady Oak. I'll have to arrange an appointment for you to see it, since the current occupants aren't moving until next week."

"That's quite a distance." Monty frowned, as he often did when concentrating. "I'd really like something closer."

After scrolling more, Patty tapped the screen and wrote a number on her scratchpad. "Tell you what. I'll make some calls and see what I can come up with. How can I get in touch with you?"

With a scrunched-up face, Monty replied, "I'm in between cell phone companies at the moment. I'm staying at the Highway Motel, but I don't spend any more time there than I have to. I'm planning to eat lunch at my mom's restaurant, Pearl's Roadhouse. Do you have that number?"

"The Roadhouse is one of my favorite places. Why don't I meet you there, say elevenish? We can discuss available houses over lunch. If I find something by then that meets your requirements, we can go take a look at it."

"Great." Monty stood. "I'll see you there."

When he grabbed his guitar case, Patty asked, "I hope that's not a machine gun."

Monty chuckled. "No. I hear guys carry those around in violin cases. This is my favorite guitar, another reason I'm in a hurry to find a place to live." He slung the carrier strap over his shoulder. "I'm afraid it will get stolen if I leave at the motel, and I sure can't leave it sitting in a hot car."

"Oh." Patty let her glasses fall back to their position as a necklace. "Bummer."

Monty sat in his loaned station wagon with a phrase assaulting his mind. Not in the mood to return to his motel room, he navigated to the main public library. He hurried inside with his guitar, attracting curious looks from the few patrons. At an old wooden table, he sat and dashed off the words to a new song. "Three Generations of Trouble" summed up the difficulties he felt in dealing with his mother, wife, and daughters. When he wrote the line 'And I think they'll be the death of me', he hoped his words would not prove to be prophetic.

Chapter Eleven

Lacy poured herself a cup of coffee and sat near a front window overlooking the front parking lot at Pearl's Roadhouse. "Have you heard anything from Monty?"

"No, not a peep," Pearl replied. "I have a feeling in my bones he'll drop by here sometime today, though." She looked toward the window for a long moment. "I have to go to Austin next week to see an oncologist. I've asked Leonard to drive me over there."

Taken by surprise, Lacy sputtered, "Pearl, I'll go to the doctor with you, or we can ask Monica to take you."

"We have new people coming in for summer jobs first thing Tuesday, and who knows what would go on here with you and me both gone? As for Monica, that girl scares me to death with her driving, especially out on the highway. Everything works out better if Leonard is my chauffeur." She peered over her glasses. "There's no need to get all discombobulated. Stay here, keep the Roadhouse running smooth, and pray for me every time you think about it."

Try as she might, Lacy could not keep from thinking about Monty later as she and Pearl prepared peach cobblers. As soon as the head cook Wanda removed the day's bread from the industrial ovens, the desserts went in. During the wintertime, baking in the big ovens gave things a homey warmth. Now, in early June, the kitchen felt uncomfortably hot to Lacy—despite the powerful air conditioning unit Pearl had installed.

As soon as the cobblers were done and set aside, Lacy escaped to the main dining room. While folding napkins near a front window, she saw Monty get out of a car, retrieve his guitar case, and walk toward the front entrance. She'd tried to prepare herself for this encounter, resolving to be calm and detached. However, her racing heart and dry mouth refused to cooperate. Monty's blond hair caught the sunlight like a halo, and Lacy smiled in spite of herself at the association of an angel with her wayward ex-husband.

Not wanting to be the one to greet Monty in the nearly-deserted dining room, Lacy grabbed the bin of half-folded napkins and hurried to the kitchen. "Monty's here," she whispered to Pearl, who was frosting a cake.

Pearl nodded her understanding, continuing to swirl dollops of dark chocolate. Thinking she should have hidden in the storage closet instead of the kitchen, Lacy folded another napkin. Then another. Why didn't Pearl go out front?

Monty burst through the double swinging stainless steel doors. "Good morning, beautiful ladies." He leaned his guitar case against a wall. Then he embraced Pearl and kissed her cheek. "Hello, Mama."

Wanda turned from the pot of gravy she'd been stirring. "Lord love a duck if it isn't Monty."

In a flash Monty had an arm around Wanda's ample waist, giving her a side hug. "Wanda. My favorite cook in the world. After my mother, of course."

Wanda laughed. "Seems like old times, you hanging around the kitchen, acting a fool."

"Now Wanda, you know I'm not acting."

After laughing, releasing Wanda and moving within a few feet of Lacy, Monty's face grew serious. "Hello, Lacy. It's wonderful to see you."

She glanced at him. "Hello, Monty." Taking the napkin bin in her arms, Lacy stepped quickly to the kitchen doors. She tried to think of something more to say—something appropriate to the situation—but no words came. She hurried from the room. As soon as the napkins were stowed in the closet, Lacy returned to the dining room. It was time for the lunchtime crowd to start trickling in.

While serving water to her first customers, Lacy noticed Monty carry his guitar case to the storage closet and emerge without it. So true to form. He could sleep on a park bench, but his precious guitar had to be inside, out of the heat and humidity, in a temperature-controlled environment.

She was relieved yet strangely disappointed when Monty took a seat at a table outside her serving area. As she delivered a tray full of salads, Lacy noticed he was no longer sitting alone. Patty Chesterfield was sitting across from Monty. In town two days, and somehow he'd found an attractive, unattached woman to share lunch with. And to think, she'd been worried about him. Lesson learned all over again, she thought. *No more sympathy for that alley cat.*

For the first time in years, Lacy got orders confused. When she apologetically returned a plate of fried chicken to the kitchen, explaining the customer specified "gravy on the side", she saw Wanda and Pearl whispering with each other. Then she dropped an empty tray, sending it skittering across the floor. The next thing she knew, Pearl put an arm around her shoulder. "Why don't you take a break, Lacy? Sit down and have a glass of tea. I'll take care of your area for a while."

Lacy started to protest, but when she burst into tears she realized Pearl's advice was sound. "I'm sorry," she said, taking a seat on the stool at the back of the kitchen. "You know how I am." Wanda handed her a plastic cup with sweet tea and lots of crushed ice—just the way Lacy liked it. "I'm sorry," she repeated to Wanda, wiping her eyes with the paper napkin wrapped around the cup.

"You'll be all right, honey. Just take a little rest, like Miss Pearl said." Wanda patted Lacy's shoulder and returned to cooking.

Attempting to pull herself together, Lacy grabbed a cup of shaved ice and ducked into the restroom. She washed her face with a paper towel and rubbed ice around her eyes. Then she t inside a stall, humiliated that she'd broken down in front of other people. She was angry with Monty, but even more upset with herself. She hated being a cry baby, but her tears always came easily when she was upset. After a few minutes, she washed her face once more, set her jaw, and went to the dining room to continue doing her job.

Chapter Twelve

Try as he might, Monty couldn't concentrate on Patty's conversation with Lacy coming in and out of the dining room. The years had been kind to his wife, still as beautiful to him as the day when she smiled and handed him crayons in second grade. Whatever possessed her to fall in love with him? And to stick with him when all he could think about was making music and hanging out with his band? He knew he could not erase the misery he'd caused, but only God knew how desperately he wanted to make up for the years the locusts devoured. After Lacy disappeared into the kitchen, Monty realized Patty was staring at him with an expectant look.

"Tell me again where this house is located," Monty mumbled.

"Like I said, one street over from your mother. The corner of her backyard touches the corner of this home's lot. If you're athletic enough to jump over the fence, it's only a few seconds from your back door to hers."

Monty kept an eye on the swinging doors that led to the kitchen. Maybe Lacy would sit down with him after the lunchtime rush. If nothing else, they could talk about Monica's upcoming wedding. Anything to get a dialog started with her. "All right. That sounds fine."

"I thought that's what you'd say." Patty smiled. "You'd be crazy not to jump on this deal, with them hiring you to house sit instead of having to pay rent. Meanwhile, I have breathing room for a home in that area to come on the market. I'm sure by the time the Johnsons return from Colorado I'll have the perfect place for you."

Monty watched his mother emerge from the kitchen, delivering orders to Lacy's tables. That struck him as peculiar, but Pearl always did have her own way of doing things. He wondered if Lacy was all right. Keeping his vision focused on the kitchen doors, Monty asked, "Now when did you say I can move in?"

A coil of irritation wrapped itself around Patty's words. "As I mentioned *just a moment ago*, the sooner the better. The Johnsons want you to get comfortable with their animals' routine before they leave. And they're anxious to get away from the Texas heat."

While Patty rattled on, Lacy emerged from the kitchen. Monty watched her pass out tickets to diners who were finished with their meals. Was it his imagination, or had she been crying? It took all of his self-control not to go over there, take her in his arms, and ask what was wrong. When she turned toward him, he tried but failed to read her face. He made little circles on the table with his index finger. Maybe Lacy was worried about Pearl. Or Monica. Or things he knew nothing about, having been missing in action for a decade.

"Here's a card with the Johnsons' phone number," Patty said. "I'll send them a text and let them know you'll take the job. I'd suggest moving this afternoon if possible." When the server laid their ticket on the table, Patty scooped it up and stood. "No charge?" She stared at the bill, then put it down. "Oh, that's right. Your mother owns this restaurant. Well, I owe you one. I always take my clients out to eat. It's a tax write-off."

Monty rose and shook hands with Patty. "Thank you for everything. I'm looking forward to getting out of the motel."

"I can't blame you for that. Stay in touch." With those words, Patty hurried away.

Taking one last gulp of tea, Monty spread the napkin over his plate and scooted his chair back. Then he felt a hand on his shoulder.

"Don't rush off." Pearl sat her coffee cup down at Patty's place, and took her chair.

Monty readjusted his seat. "Is Lacy all right?"

"She'll be fine. Where are you living?"

Monty looked around the room, searching for Lacy but not finding her. "At the moment I'm in the Highway Motel, but—"

"I figured you were in some dump like that," Pearl interrupted. "You know I bring in extra part time help during the summer months when the tourists flock to the lake, mostly hiring local kids who need a job during the school break."

"I'm glad you're still doing that."

"The new labor crop is coming in to start work Tuesday afternoon. I want you to work the evening shift with the kids."

Shaking his head, Monty began to protest. "Mama, you and everyone else in Polson's Crossing seem to think I came home because I'm down on my luck, but that's not it at all. In fact—"

Pearl cut him off with a wave of her hand. "Lacy needs your help." Although she drank from her coffee cup, Pearl's eyes never left Monty's face.

"She does?" He looked around the room again, spotting Lacy at the cash register, accepting money from lunchtime stragglers.

Keeping her voice low, Pearl said, "I don't know how much longer I'll be able to work. A lot depends on how much surgery and chemo and all that hooray I have to do. Lacy knows the business backwards and forwards, but she could use someone to lean on while she takes on the responsibility of owning the Roadhouse."

Before he made a decision about working at the Roadhouse, Monty thought about his conversation with Pastor Tom. "How do you think Lacy would feel about having me here?"

"We talked it over a couple of days ago and she agreed I should offer you a job."

He watched Lacy disappear through the kitchen doors again. "In that case, when do I start?"

"As you know, we're closed Sunday and Monday. I'd like you to be here from four in the afternoon until ten pm, Tuesday thru Saturday, beginning next week. That gives you time after we stop serving dinner to help Lacy close up. If you have to stay longer to keep her from being alone here at night, keep track and I'll pay you overtime." Pearl narrowed her eyes and cocked her head. "If you meant what you said about wanting to help me get through this cancer thing, take care of Lacy and your girls. That's the best thing you can do for me."

Monty took the coffee mug from his mother and gently took her hands in his. "It's a deal. I'll move out of the hotel and get all of my personal business squared away before Tuesday. You can count on me, Mama. I won't disappoint you."

Chapter Thirteen

It took Monty less time to pack his belongings than to check out of the motel. The desk clerk was not inclined to accept an out-of-town check. Exasperated, Monty took a wad of twenty-dollar bills from his wallet to pay for his short stay. When the young man printed a receipt and apologized, Monty grinned. "Don't worry. You're in good company. No one in this town wants to take my checks. In fact, you're one of the few who is willing to accept my cash."

Before occupying the home he'd agreed to house sit, Monty decided to open a local bank account and obtain a credit card. He passed some branch banks with unfamiliar names, but drove on to the Polson's Crossing National Bank just off the square. He didn't bother locking his loaner car, since he'd arranged to leave his guitar in the Roadhouse store room. If thieves wanted to steal anything else he had, they were welcome to it.

"I'd like to open an account," he advised the teller through iron bars that had been there as long as Monty could remember.

"Take a seat in the waiting area and someone will be right with you."

Apparently, a few things did change over the years in Polson's Crossing. No longer could one begin banking without proper identification and a personal interview in an ante room. Monty sat for a while, enjoying the air conditioning as well as the mid-century architecture. When the wait dragged on, he considered giving up. As he stood to leave, a woman wearing a tailored suit asked him to step into her office. The process seemed almost as tedious as the negotiations for buying a car. Monty remembered why he'd vowed never to take a job that involved sitting behind a desk, filling in forms.

A half hour later, the bank officer's shocked face somewhat compensated for the time taken up by process. "Yes, sir. We'll make the first transfer right away. There will be a delay of a day or two before you are able to write a check for more than ten percent of your balance." The woman glanced at the amount Monty was requesting from Nashville, and lifted her eyebrows. "I wouldn't expect that to be a hardship."

"No, ma'am. I don't think so." Monty accepted a cold bottle of water, but explained he didn't have time for the suggested meeting with an investment counselor.

After cruising slowly down Pine Street checking house numbers, Monty parked in front of number 227. He sat for a moment, taking in the traditional red brick two-story house with big white colonial columns in front. The lawn was neatly trimmed, and a white picket fence encircled the front yard.

As soon as Monty opened the gate, a golden retriever barked and charged at him. Monty squatted. "Come on over here and let's be friends." The dog complied, wagging his tail. "That's a good boy." After briefly petting and patting, Monty went to the front door with his new canine buddy trotting behind him.

Monty knocked, reaching to rub the golden retriever's ears while he waited.

"Hi, I'm Janie. I see you've already met Goldie. Come on in." She held the door open while pushing the dog away. "No, Goldie, you stay outside."

"Good afternoon, Janie. Patty said she'd call and let you know I'm ready to start house sitting."

Janie was tall and thin, with bright red hair and freckled skin. She didn't look much older than Monica. "I'm glad you're here. We were planning to go to Colorado for the summer, but Dexter—that's my husband, Dexter— he got a call this morning that his mother had a stroke. So, we've repacked, and we're on our way to North Carolina. Now that you're here, we can leave first thing in the morning." She raised her voice. "Dexter, our house sitter is here." Returning to a normal volume, she asked, "What did you say your name is? I'm sorry. I have too many things on my mind."

"It's Monty. I understand. What can I do to help?"

Dexter appeared in the stairwell. "Good deal. I'm ready to start packing the van after dinner." Dexter had dark auburn hair atop his spare, lanky frame. He crossed the living room and shook hands with Monty. "Good to meet you. You're a life saver. Did Janie give you the low down on the animals?"

"For goodness sake, Dexter, he just got here," Janie yelled from the next room. "I haven't even shown him where to hang his clothes yet. I'm late picking up the kids from the pool. Where are the keys?" she asked, hurrying to her husband's side.

Dexter tossed Janie a key ring from his pocket and raked his hands through his hair. "I hope we have everything. I hate all this rushing around." He clapped Monty on the shoulder. "You're a godsend. It was a huge relief when the real estate lady told us you're an avid animal lover."

I am? Surprised by his new label and uncertain how he got it, Monty smiled and said, "I met your dog Goldie on the way in, and we seemed to hit it off just fine."

"Oh, yeah, Goldie loves everyone except the cat. Janie, where do you want Monty to sleep?"

"In the spare room downstairs tonight and after that wherever he wants to." Janie barged out the front door. Monty heard the van squeal from the driveway.

"I'm sorry," Dexter said. "Janie and I spent all week organizing all our camping gear and the sudden change in plans has us in an uproar. The guest bedroom is over there." He waved toward a hallway. "You can bring your stuff inside. Enjoy the peace and quiet while you can, because when the kids get home there won't be any more of that." Dexter bounded up the steps, two at a time. "I'll be upstairs if you need anything."

Feeling as if he was wading through the aftermath of a tornado, Monty went in search of the guest room. He passed by a formal dining room stuffed with a folded tent, suitcases, and a clump of cardboard boxes. At the end of the hallway, he seemed to emerge through a time portal into a spacious bedroom from another century. The ice blue walls and pastel color scheme whispered tranquility, while a reading nook lined with bookcases invited Monty to curl up among the cushions and relax. In contrast to what he'd seen of the rest of the house, this room was in perfect order. The scene reminded him of pictures he'd seen on the covers of house decorating magazines in the grocery store checkout line.

A few quick trips to the car, and Monty had his clothes arranged in the spacious walk-in closet. He opened the plantation shutters, allowing a flood of sunlight to brighten his room. Before long, a cacophony of high-pitched voices heralded the arrival of the Johnson children. The copper-clad ceiling above Monty's head creaked to the rhythm of hurried footsteps upstairs, accompanied by Janie's shouts.

Monty turned from the window to see a boy with flame-red hair standing at the entrance to his bedroom. "Are you going to take care of Mr. Munch?" The boy held a small ball of fur in his hands.

"Is that Mr. Munch?" Monty crossed the room, hoping he didn't have to touch the rat-like creature.

"Yes." The boy grinned, revealing a gap instead of two front teeth. "He's a guinea pig. He likes lettuce."

"That's nice. Salad is good for you. What's your name?"

"River Breeze Johnson, but I go by River. Mr. Munch has to stay in his cage most of the time. He has to stay away from Sweetie."

"Sweetie?"

"She's my sister's cat."

A disembodied voice floated from the vicinity of the hallway. "River Breeze, where are you?"

The boy's eyes widened. "I gotta go now."

"Bye," Monty said with a smile. A dog, a cat and a guinea pig. More than he'd bargained for, but manageable.

Chapter Fourteen

"I'm going to go out and grab something to eat," Monty told Dexter. "I'll be back before dark."

"Don't you want to eat dinner with us?" Janie called from another room.

"Yeah, no need to spend money going out," Dexter agreed. "Hey, honey," he shouted. "What are we having tonight?"

Janie ducked her head inside the door frame. "I don't know. It's your turn to cook."

"It is?" Dexter looked perplexed. "I guess I lost track in all the confusion. You spent a fortune at the grocery store. There must be something in the fridge we can have tonight."

"It's all right." Monty said, dodging away from a girl with bright red pigtails who ran through the room. "I'll fend for myself." He was tempted to make a dash for the door, which probably wouldn't seem out of place. Everything in this household seemed to occur at maximum speed. How many kids did they have? He thought four, but there might be a set of twins confusing the headcount. Monty closed his eyes and forced out the dangerous do-unto-others question, "Can I bring you anything?"

Janie continued the conversation as if Monty had not spoken. "I didn't get any people stuff at the supermarket. I just stocked up on pet food so Marty would have enough to last all summer if need be."

"My name is Monty." Why bother correcting her? No one was listening. "I could bring something back from Bob's Burger Barn."

Youthful cheers arose from throughout the first floor of the house, but Dexter frowned. "Janie doesn't allow our kids to eat fast foot. It makes them hyperactive."

Janie stepped all the way into the room, hands on her hips. "Well, this is an emergency, Dexter. Don't be so hidebound."

"It's your rule, Janie, not mine." Dexter snapped. "I've never seen any harm in an occasional hot dog or hamburger."

"You could have said something before now," Janie fussed, elevating her voice a decibel. "Willow, go find my purse and bring it to me."

"That's all right," Monty instinctively patted the pocket of his jeans. "I have money. Are hamburgers okay? How many?"

"No," Dexter protested. "Janie, can't you keep up with anything?" He pulled out several crumpled bills and pressed them into Monty's hand. "Seven of everything, hamburgers, sodas, and fries. Thank you."

As Monty left the house, he heard a child yelling, "Mama, are we going to eat hamburgers? Oh boy, Raven, we're having hamburgers for supper."

Uncertain whether or not he was included in the seven, Monty decided to increase the order to feed at least eight people. Only one table was occupied in Bob's Burger Barn when Monty stepped up to the counter. Scanning the menu hanging from the ceiling, he said, "I'd like eight hamburgers, eight large fries, and eight lemonades."

"Yes, sir," the unshaven young man squeaked in response. "Will that be dine in or take out?"

Monty was amused by what he took to be the clerk's wit, but did his best to swallow his laughter when he saw the earnest anticipation on the young man's face. After taking his time to look around at the deserted tables, Monty struggled to keep his face straight. "Take out." Since he hadn't thought about the logistics of carrying liquids in the car, he set the cardboard drink carrier behind the driver's seat, bracing it with bags of sandwiches and French fries.

Arriving at 227 Pine after driving at no faster than 10 miles per hour, Monty eased over the prominent hump in the graveled driveway. He didn't have to wonder how to get the food indoors. Stair-stepped children with hair in every imaginable shade of red rushed the car, clamoring to carry sacks. "Be careful, and don't run," he instructed them, passing out bags to little pairs of outstretched hands.

"Pipe down," Monty heard Janie saying as he brought the mostly-still-full drink tray into the kitchen. "You'd think you kids never had a hamburger before, the way you're carrying on."

"We had them almost every day at camp," the tallest child declared between bites. "I love them."

"That's Raven." Leaning against the cabinet, Dexter pointed a French fry in the direction of the auburn-haired boy who'd just spoken. He dipped the fry into a glop of ketchup. "Willow." Dexter put the potato strip in his mouth after waving it toward the girl with carrot-colored braids down to her waist. "The twins, River and Brook." He patted the strawberry blond toddler in Janie's arms. "And Aspen."

"Children," Janie said, "This is Maury. He's going to take care of our pets while we're gone."

"Actually, my name is Monty. You have a beautiful family."

"Thank you." Janie smiled and tickled Aspen. "We think so."

"I showed him Mr. Munch already, and I told him guinea pigs like lettuce," River announced proudly. "I can show you his cage where he lives."

"Eat your dinner." Dexter coated another fry with ketchup. "I'll show Monty how to care for all of the animals this evening."

Brook tugged at Monty's shirt sleeve. "Do you like snakes?"

Chapter Fifteen

That night Monty lay in the massive bed, staring up at the high ceiling and wondering what in the world he'd gotten himself into. Raven's dog, Willow's rabbits, River's guinea pig, Aspen's ailing cat, and worst of all the black snake whose wire mesh cage occupied most of Brook's bedroom. "Now and then the cat brings us a bird or field mouse she's killed," Dexter had explained. "You can feed them to the snake as a treat, as long as you make sure they're dead first."

Monty was the first person awake and up in the household the next morning, searching unsuccessfully in every kitchen cabinet for coffee. When Janie came downstairs a half hour later, he asked, "Where do you keep your coffee maker?"

Her eyes grew wide and her eyebrows shot upward. "We don't drink coffee. You look so healthy I assumed you didn't put toxins into your body. There may be some old herbal tea bags in the pantry. Help yourself to whatever you find."

"I believe I'll go out and have some breakfast."

Janie opened the refrigerator and stared at its interior. "Whatever. Take your key. I'm sure we'll be gone long before you get back."

Dexter stumbled into the kitchen, still wearing pajamas. "I thought we were going to get on the road early."

"We were." Janie slammed the refrigerator door. "But you forgot to set the alarm."

"Since when is that my job?" Dexter took a cereal box from an upper cabinet. "Do we have any milk?"

"Since you bought that clock radio with all those confusing buttons on it. And you told me not to buy any more milk because it would spoil. I'm making pancakes for breakfast."

Dexter sat at the table with his head in his hands.

Seeing a chance to wedge into the conversation, Monty said, "You guys have a good trip. I'm going to eat breakfast out and run some errands."

"Right." Dexter spoke but didn't change his position. "We'll check in with you when we get to my Mom's, and you already have the phone number there. Janie and I will be back in town as soon as we can. We don't have any choice but to be back before school starts, since we both signed contracts to teach again next year. If the washing machine poops out, or lightning strikes a tree, just use your own best judgment. We're fine with that. Like I said before, make yourself completely at home."

Monty remembered something. "What do I do if one of the animals gets sick or hurt?"

"No sweat," Dexter waved a hand. "Take it to the vet and we'll settle up when Janie and I come home."

"Good deal." Monty put a hand on Dexter's shoulder. "I hope your mother makes a full recovery." As he passed through the door, Monty added, "Have a safe trip."

Janie nodded, continuing to stir batter. "Dexter, did you remember to get a bottle of syrup?"

Monty stopped to rub Goldie's fur on the way to the car. "You and me, buddy. We have to take care of business with this weird collection of animals." With a grin, he added, "Maybe I'll get a song out of this menagerie."

His first stop was Pearl's house around the corner. Checking his watch, Monty calculated he was arriving at about the time his mother got out of bed, unless she'd changed her routine.

Pearl opened the door fully dressed. "Monty, come on in." She held the screen while he entered. "New car?"

"It's a temporary loaner from Jimmy. I'm on my way to breakfast at the Pancake Patch. Do you want to go with me?"

With a glance at her watch, Pearl said, "I was just about to fix something to eat. Are you sure you don't want to stay in and let me cook?"

"I'm sure." Monty leaned down and gave her a peck on the cheek. "Don't you think it's about time someone served you a meal for a change?"

"I'll drive. Let me get my purse."

"Mama." He gently put a staying hand on her shoulder. "Let me take you."

"All right, Son. Let's go. I'm hungry."

Sitting at the familiar restaurant, enjoying breakfast chit chat with his mother, Monty wondered how many such occasions he'd forfeited by being absent for the past ten years. "You know the house behind and kind of catty-cornered from you? The one with the rabbit hutch in the backyard?" he asked, scooping a bite of huevos rancheros with a tortilla chip. "I'm living there for a while."

Pearl sliced open a biscuit and stared at it. "The cook needs to use a tad more shortening." She applied a pat of butter. "The Johnsons' house? I wouldn't think they'd have room for a renter, with all those young'uns running around."

"I'm house sitting, taking care of their house and the animals while they take a trip to North Carolina." He took a pen from his shirt pocket and wrote on a napkin. "Here's the phone number at the Johnson's house and my new cell number. I want you to promise you'll call me if you need anything, no matter that time it is."

"That's sweet." Pearl tucked the napkin into her handbag.

Monty pulled another paper napkin from the dispenser. "I'd like to have your number. And Lacy's, too, if you don't think she'd mind if I call the girls."

"I think Lacy would be happy for you to get in touch with your daughters." Pearl reached for the napkin and scribbled numbers on it. After pushing the napkin toward him, she asked, "Monty, tell me honestly. What's going on?"

84

"It's really pretty simple. Like I said the other day, Mama. I've committed my life to Jesus, and I'm doing my best to figure out and do what pleases Him." Monty folded the napkin and slipped it into his pocket. "I can understand why you're skeptical, given all that's happened in the past. But stay with me, give me some time, and I hope you'll see that I've changed."

"You're not going to drop out of sight in a few days?"

"No, Mama. This is for real. I guarantee it."

"And there's nothing you want from me?"

"I didn't say that." Monty pushed his plate away and reached across the table. "I want you to let me help you beat this cancer thing." He chewed his lip and studied their clasped hands. "If you're willing, I'm asking you to do something else for me." He took a deep breath and raised his eyes to meet Pearl's. "Help me put my marriage back together."

"I gave up a few years back and quit asking God to reconcile you and Lacy. I'll start up praying for that again." Pearl nodded, as if in agreement with her own statement. "You do understand, we're asking the Lord for a miracle."

Monty cocked his head and smiled. "The last I knew, He was still in that business."

85

Chapter Sixteen

Monty returned to the Johnson's house encouraged. In his estimation, Pearl was a great prayer warrior. As he turned onto Pine Street, the Johnson family's van streaked by, moving too fast through the residential area. So much for their early start.

With his tail wagging non-stop, Goldie came running as soon as Monty pulled into the driveway. It had been a long time since a brief absence brought about such an enthusiastic welcome home, and it was a nice feeling. He knelt and patted Goldie's furry back. Something sparkly caught Monty's attention. "What on earth?" He picked a ring out of the grass. "I'll bet your owners will be glad we found this." Monty gave the dog's ears one last rub before using the Johnson's spare key to go inside.

Monty closed the front door and stood amazed. It was as if a cyclone had swept through, distributing a layer of children's toys and clothing over the pre-existing clutter of the Johnson home. He spent a moment regretting the complaints he once registered about Lacy's compulsive neatness. He dismissed the thought, having already vowed to accept his wife's quirks without criticism if he ever had another chance.

Still holding the ring tightly in his left fist, Monty scanned the living room for a storage place. He reached over his head for a blue cut glass bowl on the top shelf of the crowded bookcase. As he dropped the ring into the shallow container, it suddenly occurred to him that Lacy never had a diamond ring. He'd pawned a guitar to buy her a plain gold band for their wedding, but she deserved so much more. Polson's Jewel Box, that was the place for good jewelry, or used to be. Their store was right on the square if they hadn't moved. Maybe he could do some business with them.

Monty wandered toward the backyard to begin the daily animal care routine Dexter showed him the day before. First, he gave the rabbits fresh food and water. Finding no new babies, he assumed Dexter overstated the frequency of their breeding. Next Monty took care of the guinea pig, reminding himself it was a child's pet even if it was a rodent. He brought Goldie inside the house, watched him eat, and then brushed the dog's teeth, exactly as Dexter Johnson had demonstrated.

Taking care of Sweetie the cat was the next item on Monty's mental checklist. He went to the bathroom where Sweetie's pills were stored. "Here, kitty, kitty," he said, mimicking Dexter's singsong rhythm. Sweetie jumped lightly to the countertop, hunched down and began to purr. "Nice kitty." Monty smoothed her fur with one hand and opened the medicine cabinet with the other. When he popped open the plastic pill container, Sweetie jumped to the floor and skittered away.

Monty called Sweetie again, but this time she did not respond. Thinking he must have frightened the cat, he walked through the downstairs rooms searching for her. He had no success, not surprising considering how many hiding places there were amidst the disorder. Monty decided to tackle the worst chore of all, taking care of Brook's snake. He'd get back to the cat.

Monty quickly added fresh water while the black snake remained motionless in the opposite side of the wire mesh cage. "Sorry, fellow, Dexter said you eat on an every-other-day schedule." He double checked the latch, not at all sorry to leave Brook's bedroom and the reptile behind him. Maybe he'd get used to the routine in a few more days, and not be so put off by the pet snake.

Luck was with him as his footsteps creaked along the upstairs hallway. Happening to glance into the master bedroom, he spotted the tip of Sweetie's orange tail sticking out from under the bed. He slipped softly into the room and closed the door behind him. When he flipped up the corner of the bedspread, Sweetie retreated to the other side. Monty wondered why there was a spare curtain rod in the corner, but he gratefully took it under the bed with him in an attempt to herd Sweetie close enough to grab her.

Ten minutes later, sweating and frustrated, Monty finally caught hold of the cat's hind legs and pulled her into his arms. "You're a slippery little feline," he muttered as he descended the stairs. This time he closed the bathroom door to prevent another escape. After numerous unsuccessful attempts to administer the little white pill by poking it inside the cat's cheek, Monty gave up. Instead, he ground the pill into a fine powder and sprinkled it on Sweetie's food. She responded by sniffing around it and then making elaborate covering-up motions with her paws as if her food bowl was a litter box.

Admitting defeat, Monty phoned the veterinarian listed in Dexter's notes. Her advice was to give the cat fresh food and forget about the antibiotic until the following day. "If the kitty still won't cooperate tomorrow, bring her in to my office and I'll administer her medication," the vet told Monty.

He'd hardly hung up when the telephone rang. "Johnson's residence," Monty answered, not knowing what else to say.

"Hey, Monty, this is Dexter."

"You can't be in North Carolina already?"

"No, no. We're at a service station on I35. Janie lost her wedding ring somewhere along the way, so we've been backtracking. I thought I'd check on the animals while I have a break from driving."

"I found a ring next to your driveway this morning," Monty cut in. "It has five square-cut diamonds in a row."

"Oh, thank heavens. That's it." Dexter began to shout, "Janie. You left your ring at home. Why didn't you tell me to call Monty sooner?"

Monty heard Janie's voice. "If you hadn't been in such a hurry to get on the road, I would have noticed my ring was missing."

Monty reported on his conversation with the veterinarian about the cat, which didn't seem to ruffle Dexter at all. Deciding to cash in on the good will generated by recovering Janie's ring, Monty asked, "Say, I'd be glad to stow away all that camping gear that's sitting in your dining room, if you'll just tell me where you want it."

Dexter did not seem to take offense. "That would be great. You can put that stuff anywhere you can find space. Janie never stores anything in the same place twice." His volume increased suddenly, "No Brook, don't touch that. Hey, I got to go. We'll be in touch."

Monty grinned and shook his head. Instead of hanging up the telephone, he took out the number Pearl gave him for his daughters. He wasn't sure how to get to know them again, but he could start with a phone call. He considered asking if they'd like to go to a movie. However, on second thought, that seemed too impersonal. Maybe the girls would like to go shopping. Yeah, that was the ticket, shopping.

Chapter Seventeen

When the Roadhouse opened on Tuesday, Lacy had a hard time concentrating on the morning preparation routine. She stared into space while the industrial mixer combined the ingredients for pie dough. She'd spent most of the weekend wondering what prompted Monty to show up in Polson's Crossing after a ten-year absence.

"Are you all right?" Wanda asked.

Lacy smiled. "Yeah, I'm fine." When she took the bubbling apple pies from the oven, there was enough of a lull in kitchen activity for Wanda to carry on without assistance. Lacy always looked forward to the morning break, when she and Pearl shared coffee, business discussions, and personal chit chat.

"The invasion force lands this afternoon." Lacy spread manila folders in the space between her coffee cup and Pearl's. "Five new kids plus the three who were here last summer. Cindy, Monica and Julio. Oh, and Monty, of course."

Pearl did not touch the folders. "What are you thinking about assignments?"

"That's usually your department," Lacy said. When Pearl didn't comment, she continued. "Julio is a hard worker, but very quiet. If he'd interact with people more, I'd put him on the cash register. We could assign four of the kids to wait tables and put one in the kitchen to fetch and carry for Wanda. Then there's Monty. I don't know about him."

After Lacy finished talking, Pearl stirred her coffee for a moment as if it required her full attention. "I've been thinking we need someone to help out in the smokehouse. Leonard is getting on in years, and he could hang it up anytime. Julio can help him with the lifting and learn how to run the smokehouse while he's at it."

"That's a great idea." Lacy nodded and made a note in Julio Chapa's folder. "Maybe the young man will be interested in working for us full time in the fall if he doesn't go away to school. Do you have any other ideas?"

"Well, you could assign Monty to the cash register. He has no problem talking to people." Pearl tapped folders as she talked. "Monica in the kitchen. That will put a different kind of experience on her resume in case she needs it, and it doesn't hurt that she and Wanda are thick as thieves. Put the rest of the crew waiting tables and bussing until we see if they stick with us. If they don't all quit after the first week, we'll pick one of them to run the register and let Monty entertain the crowd with his singing."

"Pearl, you're a genius." Lacy was always amazed by the old woman's ability to match personalities with jobs. "You nailed it." She made more notes before arranging the folders into a neat stack and pushing them aside.

"Monty has been by to see me a couple of times," Pearl said, as calmly as if continuing to discuss restaurant work. "He's house sitting at the Johnson place, practically in my backyard."

"I thought I saw him in the crowd at graduation, but I may be mistaken." Lacy swept hair from her forehead. "And Sunday he was at church. Pearl, there's something wrong. Monica told me Monty promised to take her and Cindy shopping. I'm sure he won't actually do it. I can't stand the thought of him breaking my girls' hearts." *Like he did mine.*

Pearl smiled. "Monty was at church on Sunday? Wouldn't you know he'd be there the one time I missed. Praise the Lord. That's an answer to prayer."

"Forgive me for saying this, Pearl." Lacy dropped her eyes. "I think he's putting on an act. There's probably more to his homecoming than meets the eye."

"He tells me he's been saved, and that's he's changed." Pearl stared through the window toward the empty parking lot. "Monty's my son, Lacy. I have to give him another chance and hope he's telling me the truth."

"Yes, of course you do. I get that." Lacy did not share her private suspicion that Monty was back in Polson's Crossing with one goal. After thinking long and hard, she'd decided her ex-husband wanted his mother's assets, including the Roadhouse. Why couldn't Pearl see that she was being manipulated? She's old, and sick, Lacy thought, and Monty is her only child. Although she couldn't totally put herself in Pearl's shoes, she knew she'd make any sacrifice—perhaps even believe flimsy lies—to assure Monica and Cindy's welfare. "I hope he doesn't end up disappointing you."

Rubbing a hand across her chin, Pearl replied softly, "So do I." She cleared her throat and drained her coffee. "I may or may not be in tomorrow. It all depends on how tired I am after the trip to the doctor." She took a paper napkin and swiped at the surface of their table. "Now that we have

93

the assignments all settled, I guess I'll go open up the register. It won't be long before the lunch crowd hits."

Lacy refilled her cup and sat gazing out the window but seeing nothing. How could she operate the Roadhouse without Pearl to lean on? Maybe it would be better to let Monty have it without a fight. But what if he refused to let her keep her job? Where would she go? How would she make a living? She hadn't finished high school and she'd never worked one day anywhere other than Pearl's Roadhouse. The idea of looking for employment at almost forty made her shiver, even though she was sitting in the sunlight. Was it possible Monty really had straightened up? What if the girls wanted to spend their free time with him instead of her? What if he remarried and her daughters adored his new wife? She put her head down on her arms. Too many what ifs.

Chapter Eighteen

"Mom, come see Monica's wedding dress." Cindy bounced up and down on the balls of her feet. "You won't believe how gorgeous it is."

Lacy dropped her groceries on the kitchen table and joined her daughters in the bedroom they shared. The girls stood near an exquisite, full-length wedding gown hanging from the top of the closet door.

"Have you ever seen anything so beautiful?" Monica pulled at the hem, causing the dress to sway and shimmer.

"Oh, my." Lacy moved nearer and rubbed the fabric of the skirt with the back of her hand. "It feels so smooth."

"It's silk, Mom." Monica gazed up at the dress with bright eyes.

"One hundred percent *peau de soie*," Cindy squealed. "Don't you love it? I think it's gorgeous. Monica said I can wear it when I get married, too."

"Let's hope that's a lot of years from now." Lacy edged her hand upwards to the price tag dangling from a seed pearl. She turned the yellow rectangle over and gasped. "Monica, honey, we can't spend this kind of money. This dress is more than we agreed on for your whole wedding budget. It's lovely, but you'll have to return it." She let the tag slip from her fingers. "I'm kind of surprised the credit card company let the purchase go through."

Instead of the reaction Lacy expected, Monica smiled. "It's okay, Mom. I didn't use your credit card."

Cindy blurted, "Daddy bought it." She clapped a hand over her mouth.

Lacy glared, first at Cindy, then at Monica. She did her best to keep her voice calm. "Your father can't afford that dress any more than I can."

"He wrote a check, and the bridal shop took it." Monica pressed her lips together firmly for a moment, while staring at her toes. Then she lifted her chin. "Another thing, Mom. I asked Daddy to give me away at the wedding." After a short silence, she added, "He agreed."

"Well, then." Lacy brushed nonexistent lint from the front of her shirt. "I guess that's all been settled behind my back. It's late, and I'm tired. I'm going to take a shower and go to bed. One of you put up the groceries." Departing from the room, she tossed a final remark over her shoulder. "I'm sure you know you can't depend on your father to show up at your wedding just because he said he would. So be prepared."

Monica's voice trailed down the hallway after Lacy. "But he promised."

Lacy closed the bathroom door and used both hands to brace herself on the vanity. *Lord, what am I going to do when Monica's wedding dress gets repossessed?* She stood in the shower long after her body was clean, as if the warm water would wash away old memories. How elated she'd been twenty years earlier, marrying Monty after her junior year at Polson's Crossing High School. Her mother tried to

96

convince her to wait, but she didn't listen. She and Monty were so in love, and Lacy was certain they would live happily ever after. Her heart ached for her own lost dreams, but also because she was afraid Monica was repeating the same mistakes she'd made. At least her daughter had her high school diploma.

Still, Lacy reminded herself, if things had been different, she wouldn't have her two precious children. Determined to be upbeat, she put on her gown and housecoat and joined her girls in the living room. As seemed to happen all too often since Monty came back to Polson's Crossing, the conversation stopped when Lacy walked in. Nevertheless, she settled next to Monica on the sofa and nodded toward the television. "What are you watching?"

Cindy's tuxedo cat meandered into room and jumped into his owner's lap. "We were just talking. I wasn't really paying attention to the TV," Cindy said, rubbing her kitty's ears.

"Me neither." Monica clicked the television off.

Searching for a way to break the silence, Lacy asked, "Is your dress going to need any alternations?"

"They nipped the waist in a little while we waited. It doesn't need anything else." Monica tossed her mother a sidelong grin. "Do you want to see how it looks on me?"

Cindy jumped up, dumping the complaining Fluffy onto the floor. "Yes. Come put your dress on, Monica. Let Mom see how awesome it is."

Forcing a smile, Lacy said, "I'd love to see you in your wedding dress."

"Wait here, Mom, and no peeking." Cindy was already in the short hallway. "Monica can model it for you."

Lacy was happy to sit on the sofa and rest after a long day at the Roadhouse followed by a stop at the supermarket. She stretched her neck and then rubbed her feet. Monica reminded her so much of herself at eighteen, with her ambition singularly focused on marrying her high school sweetheart. She could only hope Philip Pearson proved to be more mature and responsible than Monty. Despite herself, Lacy's mind dredged up memories. How could she *not* have fallen in love with handsome, charming, full-of-fun Monty?

Her thoughts were interrupted by Monica, whirling into the living room in her wedding dress, complete with a sparkling tiara.

"What do you think?" Cindy followed her sister, gleefully carrying the long, trailing train. "Isn't this dress the most supercalifragilisticexpialidocious thing you've ever laid eyes on?"

"Oh, Monica." Lacy's moist eyes prevented her from focusing for a moment. How grown up her daughter was. How like her father she looked, with those china blue eyes and wavy blonde hair.

Cindy settled next to Lacy on the sofa. "I hope those are happy tears."

Taking hold of her daughter's hand, Lacy said, "Yes, with a little sadness mixed in because my babies are growing up. Monica, you're going to be the most beautiful bride this town has ever seen."

Monica giggled and scrunched her shoulders. "I hope Philip feels that way."

"He will," Lacy assured her.

"For sure," Cindy agreed. "And if he doesn't, Daddy will rip off his epaulettes and put him in front of a firing squad."

"You have seen way too many old movies." Monica gathered the front hem of her skirt in her hands. "Come on, grab my train so I can go take off my beautiful dress."

Chapter Nineteen

Sweetie arched her back and charged sideways on her toes toward Goldie, hissing and switching her tail. "Calm down," Monty said. "Don't you know cats are supposed to be afraid of dogs?" The golden retriever cowered in a corner of the room. When Monty rolled a ball into the dining room, Sweetie tore out after it, her attention directed away from Goldie's presence, as expected. Monty tapped his thigh. "Come on, fearless superdog, let's go brush your teeth."

As soon as he completed the animal care routine for the day, Monty sat on the only living room chair not covered with a layer of clothing to phone his agent, Carson Henry. "This is Monty. I have a new address for my mail." He poked at a toy truck with his toe while giving Carson time to record the information. "I also have a couple of songs about ready to send you, "Three Generations of Trouble" and "Cleaner Than a Hound's Tooth.""

Carson chuckled into the phone. "Let's hope the big guys like them. It beats me where you get the inspiration for your lyrics. You must have a wild imagination."

Gazing down at Goldie, Monty replied, "You wouldn't believe me if I told you. Do you have a date for my next release?" The silence lasted a heartbeat too long. "What's wrong?"

"That new kid Wayne Houston has already recorded it. So, it won't be long. But you know how it goes, Monty. A guy comes to Nashville, never been away from home before, signs a contract, and suddenly he has more money than sense."

"Yeah, I know that story better than anybody. Look, it was tough for me to get used to the idea of other people singing my songs instead of me. Now that the deal's done and I see how well it can turn out, you can't let this Houston kid mess everything up for you and me as well as himself. You're not just my agent. You're my business manager, too. You're supposed to look out for me. What are you going to do?"

"I'm well aware of my responsibilities. However, I represent Wayne Houston also. The best thing would be to get him out of town for a few weeks, give him time away from the bad company he's been running with." Monty heard papers rustling before Carson continued, "He refuses to go home to his folks' place in rural Tennessee. If he keeps partying like he has been, the news hounds are going to sniff him out and there's no telling what kind of blunders he'll make."

Monty rubbed Goldie's back with his bare toes. Without thinking things through, he asked, "Has Wayne ever been to Texas?"

"No. He's barely nineteen years old, fresh off the farm, never been anywhere. He's not a bad guy, just young and impressionab—say, that's not a bad idea. I'll talk to him about, what's the name of that town? Oh, I see it, Polson's Crossing. He can hang out with you for a little while and get his head together. I think he might listen to you."

"I'm not exactly a sterling example." Monty wasn't sure he should have hinted that Wayne could stay with him, and he certainly hadn't expected Carson to jump on it so enthusiastically. "Even here in the hinterlands, there's some possibility country music fans will know who Wayne is."

"I doubt it." Carson actually sounded excited, for him. "Only a few people outside of Tennessee know his voice, and he has an ordinary-looking face. I don't think he can grow a moustache, but I'll get his hair dyed. No one in Polson's whatever will ever know the difference. I'm excited about your plan. Where's the nearest airport?"

Monty hung up wondering, again, what he'd let himself in for. He wanted to help Wayne Houston if he could, and not strictly for financial reasons. If he could use his own bad decisions to save a younger man from the same pitfalls, maybe his years of wrong living weren't a total waste. All he had to do was get Dexter Johnson's clearance for a house guest, which he expected to be no hurdle. He glanced around and sighed before gathering an armful of children's clothes and trudging up the stairs.

Within a couple of hours, Monty had the living room of the Johnson home as presentable as the dining room he'd decluttered over the weekend. Standing with his hands on his hips, he surveyed his handiwork for a few minutes with satisfaction. Then it was time to get ready for work. He was excited about his job at Pearl's Roadhouse because he'd be near Lacy. Although she'd avoided him at church Sunday, she'd have to communicate with him at the Roadhouse. Maybe, God willing, she'd see that he was not the same old Monty, so slippery he could dodge raindrops in a cloudburst. He could only hope and pray.

Monty did his best to tame the waves in his blond hair. Since Lacy used to say blue made his eyes look like pieces of sky, he chose a pale blue shirt. How could his palms be sweaty in a cool house, immediately after a shower? He remembered to park in the back of Pearl's Roadhouse, leaving the front and side lots for customers. Wanda didn't seem surprised when he cut through the kitchen to go into the dining room. "Hey, Monty. Good to see you," was all she said. However, her warm smile made him feel welcome.

"Hello, honey. You're early." Pearl hugged him and gestured toward a long table. You can wait over there with Julio. Help yourself to something to drink first if you like."

Monty took his time meandering around tables to the drink dispensers, hoping all the while to catch a glimpse of Lacy. He scooped ice into a plastic glass and pushed it under the sweet tea nozzle. *If it's plastic, it can't be glass. And if it's a glass, how can it be plastic?* He gave up on spotting his ex-wife and took a seat next to a muscular young man with dark hair and eyes. "I'm Monty." He thrust his right arm forward to shake hands.

"Julio." He had a good, firm grip.

"Is this your first summer to work at the Roadhouse?"

"No, sir. I was here last year."

Monty almost groaned, realizing he looked old enough for this fellow to address him as sir. "So you've just graduated this year, right?"

"Yes, sir."

They were soon joined by several girls who'd come in the front entrance. Then Monty saw Monica heading his direction, followed by Lacy and Cindy. Monty felt a wave of guilt wash over him. Of course, Lacy had to go and pick up their daughters for work. He should have offered to bring the girls with him. He needed to get them another car. He should have been there to take responsibilities off his wife's shoulders in so many ways. He wouldn't blame Lacy if she hated him. He could only hope she didn't.

Chapter Twenty

Pearl took Cindy and the other new servers aside to explain their duties, while Lacy sat down next to Monica. She flashed her incredibly beautiful smile that always made Monty's heart do flip-flops. "You've all worked here before. So, you already know how Pearl wants us to treat our customers."

"Monty, Pearl and I would like for you to take care of the cash register. It's the same old mechanical monstrosity you used as a teen-ager. It's an antique now, but Leonard keeps it in good working order." She looked into his eyes, making his pulse quicken. "Keep the money straight, resolve any problems with bills. You know the drill."

Monty's mouth felt dry. "Yes, ma'am."

Lacy rolled her eyes toward Monica. "Sweet girl, you're in the kitchen helping Wanda prepare food. She'll show you what to do."

"Cool. I'll hone my cooking skills before the wedding."

"Julio." Lacy turned from Monica to the young man across from her. "We want you to be Leonard's helper and start learning how to run the smokehouse. As you know, Leonard does a lot of different things. Any of the handy man work you can pick up from him will be a plus. Does this sound like something you would be willing to do?"

Julio replied, "I will do whatever Miss Pearl wants."

"We're all set then. Find Pearl or me if you have any questions." Just like that, Lacy was out of her chair and gone, leaving a faint scent of lilacs behind her.

Monty took some consolation in having a conversation with Lacy. Even if it was brief and impersonal, it was a start. Maybe the ice will melt when she sees I'm dependable, he told himself. He stood, put a hand on both Monica's and Julio's shoulders, and said, "You're going to do great. Good luck."

As Monty slid his chair into place under the table, Julio spoke to Monica, although he did not look at her. "You mentioned a wedding. Who is getting married?"

At the register, Pearl counted out money to Monty. He re-counted it according to the standard Roadhouse procedure before tucking bills into compartments in the wooden cash drawer. "How did things go between you and Lacy?" Pearl asked.

"About like I expected. It will take time." He dumped coins into their appropriate cubes. "How do you think she'd take it if I offer to give the girls a ride to work with me? That would save her a round trip every day."

Pearl zipped the money bag. "Why are you asking me? Talk to Lacy."

"Good advice. I'll do that. Thanks."

By the time the first wave of early eaters ordered, Monty suspected the dining service was moving too slowly. Sure enough, he noticed Lacy started helping to wait tables. When she passed near his work station, Monty spoke her name. "Lacy." She looked at him expectantly. He asked, "Do you want me to help out the servers?"

"Yes. Do the drinks and salads." She rushed away.

Monty quickly washed his hands, smiling at his image in the bathroom mirror. He said a prayer of thanks for a chance to demonstrate his new-found reliability to Lacy. Remembering to keep an eye peeled so patrons didn't wait to pay bills, he delivered glasses of ice water to anyone who took a seat in the dining room. Salads required him to match table numbers to the diagram by the kitchen doors. In between times, he took it upon himself to remove dirty dishes from unoccupied tables.

Shortly after eight o'clock, the hectic pace slowed enough for Monty to return full time to the cash register. A few minutes before ten, he started counting out the day's receipts. Meanwhile, he noticed Pearl talking with the wait staff in a far corner. He'd been in those meetings as a youngster, when Pearl gently but firmly instructed the servers how to pick up the pace without making patrons feel as if they were being rushed.

While Lacy wiped the drink bar, Monty saw his chance to speak with her alone. "Hey, Lacy, I'll be happy to drop by and pick the girls up on my way to work. It would save you a trip, and your house is on my way."

Her hands stopped moving, but Lacy didn't look at him. "Why are you so concerned about my daughters all of the sudden?"

"I guess it does seem out of character for me." Taking a deep breath, Monty added, "Since accepting

Christ as my Savior, a lot of things have changed with me. I want to reconnect with the girls if you'll allow me to."

After a moment, Lacy resumed swiping the dishrag back and forth. "Cindy won't care one way or the other. I don't know about Monica. You'll have to ask her. It's all right with me if they want to ride around with you."

Monty gave her a big smile and an eyebrow shrug. "Thanks. I'll talk to them."

After he and Pearl tallied up the day's intake and reconciled it to the tickets, Monty found Monica cleaning up in the kitchen. "How did it go, kiddo?"

"Great. Wanda's going to show me how to make gravy tomorrow. Philip will be so impressed."

"You know what they say about the way to a man's heart going through his stomach, isn't that right, Wanda?"

"If you say so." Wanda shrugged. "It never seemed to work out that way for me."

"That's because you hide behind those stainless-steel doors." Monty leaned against the sink. "Fellows out front wonder who's back here cooking up all that yummy food, but they're not allowed to come in here and find out."

"That's for sure. The last thing we need is a bunch of gawkers underfoot in my kitchen." Wanda laughed and removed her apron. "I'll see you two tomorrow." She nodded toward Monica. "Take care of that young'un. She's a keeper."

"You betcha." Monty turned to face his daughter. "How about a ride to work tomorrow?"

"I don't have a car. Mom has to come and get me." Monica dried her hands. "Do you want me to ask her if she'll pick you up?"

"No, Monica. I'm saying I'll come by and get you and Cindy on my way over here. That way your mother won't have to make an extra trip home to bring you to work."

"Oh. Okay. I mean, if you really want to."

"Of course I do." Monica's indifference cut Monty to the quick. He hated having one of his little girls doubt her importance to him. "Now, let's help get this place closed up so we can get home at a decent hour."

Chapter Twenty-One

When Monty arrived at his temporary home, he thought he saw movement near one of the wicker rocking chairs on the darkened front porch. As he drove over the bump in the driveway, his headlights illuminated Goldie and a human form. His first thought was that one of the Johnsons' animals had caused a problem in the neighborhood.

"Evening," Monty said to his visitor. "Are you looking for someone?"

The lanky figure stood and glanced at a slip of paper. "Mr. Montgomery? Mr. Henry sent me. I'm Wayne Houston."

As Monty stepped onto the porch, his eyes adjusted to the dim light. "Montgomery is my song writer pen name. My real last name is Chapman. You can call me Monty. Carson Henry didn't waste any time, did he?"

"No, sir." The man-sized youngster had the face of a teen-ager. Luggage and a guitar case leaned against a two-story porch pillar, while Goldie sat touching the fellow's pant leg. "Mr. Henry found a trucker hauling a load to Austin, Texas, and put me in the cab with him."

"How'd you get from Austin to Polson's Crossing?" Monty unlocked the door and gestured for Wayne to come inside.

"Mr. Henry told me not to say a word to anybody until I got to this address. That wasn't too hard until I got to Austin because that trucker, he listened to political talk shows on the radio all the way from Nashville, nonstop." Wayne sat his suitcase in the living room. "I figured I couldn't buy a bus ticket without talking. So, I hitchhiked the rest of the way."

"You had to speak when someone stopped to pick you up, didn't you?" Monty settled onto the sofa.

"No, I made me a sign that said "Polson's Crossing" on it. If somebody asked a question, I made hand motions like I couldn't talk."

"I don't think that's exactly what Carson meant when he told you to keep your mouth shut."

"Anyway, I got here." Wayne grinned, adding, "The last thirty miles were kind of rough. I wish I could have told the farmer that let me ride in the back of his pickup just how bad he needs to replace the shocks on his truck. After he dropped me off in the town square, I showed some old geezer the piece of paper with this address on it He gave me directions, and I walked on over. Nice house you got here."

"Thanks, but it's not mine. I'm staying here to take care of the place and feed the pets while the family is out of town." He took a good look at Wayne in the light. "I hope you didn't pay much for that dye job."

Wayne brushed his hair back with one hand. "That trucker Mr. Henry found was in a hurry to get on the road out of Nashville. I used a bottle of something I got at a drugstore to dye my hair. I think I got more stuff on the bathroom floor in Mr. Henry's office building than I got on me. It kind of looked like a crime scene in there, but I got

111

my hair nice and red, you know, to kind of disguise myself."

"It's red." Monty clapped Wayne on the shoulder. "I'm not so sure about the nice part. Are you hungry?"

"Starving."

"Come on back in the kitchen and we'll see what we can rustle up. Pickings may be a little slim tonight, but tomorrow you can eat at the best restaurant in the great state of Texas." Monty patted the Johnson's dog following at Wayne's heels. "Did you hypnotize Goldie? He acts like he belongs to you."

"So that's his name. Goldie. I've always had a way with dogs."

After Wayne devoured a mound of cornbread mixed into an enormous quantity of milk, he pushed away from the kitchen table. "Mmm, good. Cornbread and milk reminds me of home. What's the night life like around here?"

"There's an all-night bingo parlor just across the county line, on the way to Watson's Lake." He tried not to smile at Wayne's woebegone face. "And a few beer joints that stay open until midnight. You need to be able to defend yourself in a knife fight to hang out there." Monty glanced at his watch. "Anyway, those places are all the way across town. By the time you walked over there, they'd be about ready to close."

"Did you say walk?"

"Yeah." Monty put the milk carton in the refrigerator. "I've had a long day and I'm ready to hit the hay. And there's no way I'd let you take my buddy's car to some sleazy dive."

Wayne crossed his arms and rubbed his biceps. "Couldn't go without you anyhow. Mr. Henry said I can't go places by myself. I have to go with you or somebody you pick. Aren't there any high-class nightclubs here?"

"Not that I'm aware of. This weekend, I'll take you to a place where there are lots of pretty girls, though."

"Yee ha. Now you're talking. What kind of joint is it?"

"A church." Ignoring Wayne's obvious disappointment, Monty dampened a dishcloth and wiped the table. "There are a bunch of bedrooms upstairs. A guinea pig lives in one, and a snake in another. It's possible you'll find a cat wandering around. Her name is Sweetie, although I can't imagine why. She pretty much has the run of the house. Anyway, figure out where you want to sleep and put your things in there. There's a linen closet in the hallway where you can find clean sheets and towels."

Wayne followed Monty from the kitchen. "What kind of snake?"

"According to the owner of this house, not poisonous. That's all I know."

"Which room is he in? Or is it a she?"

"Up the stairs and to the right, last door on the left. As to whether the snake is male or female, I don't know. I don't think I *want* to know."

Grabbing a suitcase, Wayne headed up the stairs. Instead of avoiding Brook's room, the young man went directly to it. "Hey there, handsome. What's shaking in this hick town?"

For an instant, Monty wondered if someone had sneaked into Brook's room. Then he realized Wayne's conversation was directed to Brook's pet snake. He watched the upstairs bedroom door close, shook his head, and went to bed.

Chapter Twenty-Two

The following morning, when Monty returned from checking on Pearl, he met Wayne descending the stairs. Goldie trotted close behind him. "I wondered where that pup was," Monty said by way of greeting.

"Morning." Wayne stopped, sat on a stair, and hugged the golden retriever. "Goldie kept me and Big Boy company last night. I hope that's okay."

"I don't see why not." Monty shuffled toward the kitchen. "Every other animal known to man lives in here. Who's Big Boy? The snake?"

"Yeah. His name's on the back of his cage."

As they shared a breakfast of cereal, Monty thought how good it felt not to eat alone, even if his companion was a mixed-up kid half his age. "Here's the routine," he told Wayne. "First thing in the morning, I always walk around the block and check on my mother. Then I take care of the Johnsons' pets, which you can help me do after we finish eating. When the chores are done, we have free time until I go to work at Pearl's Roadhouse."

Wayne poured more milk into his cereal. "You have a job? Mr. Henry told me you made a pile of money writing songs."

"No one in Polson's Crossing knows that yet, and I'm starting to like it that way. People treat you different when they think you're a celebrity. A whole lot of folks act like they think you're a great guy when all they want is to get their hand in your pocket or share your limelight. You get in trouble or run out of money, and all of the sudden you're out of friends, too." Monty replaced the top on the sugar bowl. "Does any of that sound familiar?"

"Yeah, a little."

"Grab the lettuce and carrots out of the fridge and we'll feed the rabbits first." Monty loaded his bowl and spoon into the dishwasher. "Later on, we'll drive over to the drugstore and get some of that comb-through dye to try and tone down your hair. Then we can tune up our guitars and make some music."

Wayne jumped up and shoved his bowl away. "Got it."

"Don't forget to pick up your dishes. Everything is strictly self-service around here."

Later that morning, Monty phoned his agent. "I thought you'd want to know Wayne got here safe and sound. He hitchhiked from Austin to Polson's Crossing—which is kind of risky—but it all worked out."

"He *what*?"

Monty took some satisfaction from the surprise in his agent's voice.

"He couldn't figure out how to buy a bus ticket without talking, and he was following your instructions not to say a word to anyone."

After muttering a curse word, the agent asked, "Where is he now?"

"Taking a shower."

"Don't let him out of your sight any longer than you absolutely have to. He's woefully unsophisticated, as I suppose you've already discovered."

"I'll do what I can, but Wayne's a grown man. He's not going to want to tag along after me for very long."

To Monty's surprise, Carson actually chuckled. "Wayne's naïve, but he's not stupid. He'll do whatever you say because I told him if he gave you any trouble I'd see to it that he never works as a singer again."

"You don't mean that, do you?"

"Just keep him on a short leash. Excuse me. I need to take another call."

Monty stared at the phone, realizing he was no longer connected. Carson Henry was never warm in their previous business dealings, but he was now exhibiting a mean streak that Monty found distasteful. He leaned back in the easy chair to sort out what to do. Of course—pray! Would he ever develop Pearl's seemingly automatic response of prayer when facing a dilemma?

Descending the stairs two at a time, Wayne asked, "Where can I get a big, sturdy cardboard box?"

"I don't know, maybe at a storage company. Why?"

117

"We need a place to put Big Boy while I clean up his living space."

Monty realized he was gawking. "You're saying you actually plan to take the snake out of his cage?"

"Well, yeah." Wayne grinned. "There's lots of bedding bark stored in the linen closet. It looks to me like Big Boy's man cave needs cleaning up. Didn't the home owners tell you about all of that?"

Scratching his head, Monty admitted, "Maybe Dexter did mention fresh bedding every week or so. I should have written down some notes. How do you know so much about taking care of snakes?"

"Growing up on a farm, I always had a few critters around, to keep me company. Most reptiles are nice and quiet and don't take a lot of fussing with. Now a four-legged animal like a skunk—"

"Never mind." Monty held up a hand. "Remind me to get you a box when I take the cat to the vet to get her pill. Just make sure that slithering snake never gets loose."

"Okay, sure, whatever you say." Wayne's smile revealed a gap between his front teeth. "You know, people think snakes are slimy, but they really aren't."

"I'll take your word for it."

Wayne cocked his head and raised an eyebrow. "You're not scared of Big Boy, are you?"

"Just make sure he stays upstairs in his cage where he belongs."

Chapter Twenty-Three

Monty told Wayne to wait until both of them were present to feed Sweetie the cat. "I'll grab her while she's eating, before she has a chance to run away. She seems to have caught on to going to the vet for her pill every day. I think she enjoys making me hunt her down."

"What's so special about the pill that she can't get it at home?"

Monty rolled his eyes. "Have you ever tried to give medicine to a cat when she doesn't want to take it? I did my best, but there was no way."

Wayne cocked his head and stared at Monty for a moment. "Cats are tricky rascals. You have to sort of nudge them along instead of pushing. Want me to corral Sweetie for you?"

"Sure. I'd be interested in seeing how you get that ornery kitty into her cage. It's in the utility room."

When Monty finished shaving, he noticed Wayne strumming his guitar on the living room sofa. At his feet, a towel was draped over the open cat carrier.

Wayne looked up and flashed his gap-toothed grin. "Have you ever noticed how cats want to get in the way when you're trying to do something?" He played a riff. "I'm betting old Sweetie can't resist checking me out if I ignore her."

Sure enough, in less than a minute Sweetie wandered into the living room and hopped up on Wayne's lap. She tried to insinuate herself behind the guitar. When that didn't work, she crawled onto the back of the sofa and put her paws on Wayne's shoulder. As soon as he sat his guitar aside and rubbed her ears, Sweetie jumped to the floor. When the cat sniffed at the carrier, Wayne grinned. "Watch this." He picked Sweetie up, sat her in his lap, and restrained her with one hand. "If she thinks she's not supposed to get inside there, you can't keep her out."

In no time, Sweetie was munching a treat inside the cat carrier. "Do you want me to try to give her the pill?" Wayne asked.

"Knock yourself out. The bottle's on the bathroom counter."

Monty didn't know whether to be relieved or irritated when Sweetie swallowed her medication without a struggle. "Pesky cat," he muttered to Wayne. "I'll let the vet know we won't have to bring her in today."

That afternoon, after making music on the Johnson's back porch for a while, Monty set his guitar aside, stood and stretched his arms. "It's time for me to get ready to go to work."

Wayne played a chord. "What am I supposed to do here all by myself all night, with nobody but the animals to keep me company? I might as well be back on the farm in Lawrenceburg if that's all I'm going to do. And besides, if you're not home, how are you going to keep me from going out and partying?"

121

Monty settled into his chair. "Look, Wayne. My only role in this situation is to give you a place to stay for a little while. If you want to risk getting crossways with Carson Henry, that's between you and him. I'm not going to try to control where you go and what you do. You can make choices that mess up your career if you want to. I'm happy to give you advice when you ask for it. Otherwise, you're on your own, my friend."

With a frown, Wayne strummed his guitar. "Okay, I'm asking. If you were me, what would you do?"

"Knowing what I know now? I'd make peace with God. Figure out why you were put on this earth and then get busy doing it. Settle down, find a nice, Christian girl, get married, and raise some kids." Monty stood and put a hand on Wayne's shoulder. "That ought to be enough to keep you busy for a while."

"Yeah, well, I guess what I wanted to know is what would you do *tonight*."

Suppressing a smile, Monty said, "Watch a movie, read a book, give Goldie a bath." He hesitated after opening the back door. Would he want to sit home by himself in a strange town? *Treat others the way you want to be treated.* "Or you can go to work with me if you don't want to be alone. You can have a good dinner at the Roadhouse, and my mom might let you sing a song or two if you ask her nicely."

When Wayne resumed playing his guitar, Monty went inside to shower and dress. He wondered how long it would take for his houseguest to get restless and take off. Although he didn't mind helping the young man, he had no plans to become a babysitter. He stared into the mirror after shaving. No matter how he tried to deny it, he couldn't shake the nagging feeling it was up to him to keep Wayne out of trouble. Responsibility. Wasn't that something he'd prayed for help to develop, seeking to be the kind of man his family could depend on? Wayne Houston wasn't anything close to Monty's idea of an answer to prayer, but Pearl always said the Lord moved in mysterious ways. "Maybe you need to be more careful what you ask for," he said to his own reflection.

When he walked into the living room, Monty was surprised to find Wayne sitting by the door, wearing a fresh shirt, guitar case beside him, patting Goldie's head. "I'm ready to go," he announced.

"My middle name is Wallace," Wayne said as Monty backed out of the driveway. "That's my mother's family name. It wouldn't really be a lie if I said I'm Wayne Wallace, would it?"

"I guess not." Monty drove down Pine Street, hoping Wayne was a slow eater. He hoped he wasn't going to be saddled with keeping the young man entertained too much of the evening.

"Say, Monty, how much is a chicken fried steak at this place we're going to? I may have to ask to borrow some money if it's more than ten dollars. That's all the cash I have left."

"The Roadhouse takes checks and credit cards." Monty waited at a stop sign for a pickup to cross in front of them.

"All I have is a ten-dollar bill. I wouldn't even have that if I hadn't had a twenty stuffed down in my shirt pocket when Mr. Henry took my wallet."

"Are you saying you came all the way from Nashville with only twenty dollars?"

"Yeah." Wayne hunched down in his seat. "I spent a little here and there for snacks. So now all I have left is a ten and some change. Mr. Henry took everything else."

Noticing a car waiting behind him, Monty turned onto Main Street. "What do you mean, everything else?"

"My wallet with all my money and credit cards in it, my phone, and my checkbook. He made me turn it all over him for safekeeping."

"Did he tie you up or hold a gun on you?"

"No, nothing like that. He just made me—"

"If he didn't use force, then he didn't make you do anything. He said what he wanted and you gave it up."

"I had to." Wayne's head was turned away, as if he was watching the Polson's Crossing scenery go by.

Monty made the loop around the town square, then turned north toward Lacy's house. "No, Wayne, you chose to submit to what Carson Henry told you."

"Well, what else could I do? I signed a contract."

"Does your contract say anything about Carson Henry having the authority to take your credit cards?"

"I don't think so. But I was scared I wouldn't get to sing your songs."

"There's something you need to understand, Wayne. Carson talks tough, but he needs you a lot more than you need him. Anyone can learn how to do business, but musical talent is God-given. You have to comply with your contract, and it's a good idea to listen to Carson's financial advice. But you don't have to let him bully you."

Continuing to face the window, Wayne mumbled, "Why can't everybody be nice?"

"Good question, but that's not how the world operates." Monty turned into Lacy's neighborhood. "I have to make a stop and pick up my kids. You can hop in the back with Cindy. Monica can sit up here with me."

"I didn't know you had a family. I mean, besides your mother."

Monty grinned. "Yep. An ex-wife that I'm hope to take the 'ex' off of, and two sweet little girls."

Wayne gave out a quiet whistle and quickly opened his car door when Cindy and Monica came outside. "Little girls?" he sputtered. Leaping from his seat, he simultaneously held open a front and back car door. "Hello, ladies," he said.

"Hello." Monica slid into the front seat.

"Hey, Dad." Cindy bounced into the back. Before Monty had a chance to introduce anyone, he heard his daughter say, "Hi. I'm Cindy. Who are you?"

"Wayne's a friend of mine from Nashville." As he backed out of the driveway, Monty caught a glimpse of Cindy's curious face in the rearview mirror.

"What happened to your hair?" Cindy's question caused Monica to sink lower in the front seat.

"I dyed it," Wayne answered.

Monty smiled and turned onto the main road out of the neighborhood.

"Apparently you don't know you always have to dye your eyebrows when you do your hair," Cindy said. "Otherwise, you end up looking like the top of your head doesn't go with the rest of you."

"The red didn't work like I thought it would. So, I tried a dark comb-through dye that *someone* told me to use to cover over everything."

"I had a friend like that once. She brought some spray-on hair dye stuff to school. We went in the bathroom and gave each other pink and blue highlights. I thought it looked pretty good, but Mom made me wash it out as soon as I got home. You remember Cheyenne, Monica. She got in trouble for saying Miss Worsham—that was our history teacher—had manifest destiny hips, because they looked like they were going to spread all the way across the continent. Cheyenne's dad got transferred and they moved

126

to Florida last year. I really miss her. Hanging around with her made me look good, kind of like a model kid."

Monty and Wayne laughed, but Monica wore a pained expression. "Cindy, please," she said. "Don't talk so much."

"Oh, I forgot I'm not supposed to make you laugh. We have to walk around with sad faces, in deep mourning."

Cindy's words sparked Monty's curiosity, particularly since he detected no sorrow in her voice. He glanced at Monica. "You're awfully quiet today."

Monica sniffled.

"That's because she's decided Philip doesn't love her anymore." Cindy leaned into the space between the front seats. "Isn't that right, Monica?"

"Please, Cindy."

While Monty pulled into a Roadhouse parking slot, wondering what to say, Wayne charged into the lengthening silence. "Who's Philip?"

"Monica's fiancé. The love of her life until he doesn't do whatever she wants. Then he's public enemy number one, guilty of high crimes against humanity." Cindy hopped out of the car, closely followed by Wayne.

Monty put a hand on Monica's arm. "What happened, honey?"

Monica began to cry. "Oh, Daddy," she choked out, "I never want to speak to Philip again as long as I live." After a few sobs, she bolted from the car and ran inside without a backward look.

Watching the door of the Roadhouse slam behind his daughter, Monty puffed his cheeks and blew a stream of air upward. "Just like her mother," he muttered. "We should have named her Lacy junior."

Monty cut through the kitchen, determined not to be distracted by the aromas wafting from Wanda's stove. When he emerged into the dining room, Pearl caught him by the arm. "Two of the new school kids didn't show up today. You're a mind reader, bringing that young man with you."

With his thoughts still locked onto Monica, Monty squinted at Pearl. "Who? Wayne?"

"Yeah. I asked him if he wanted a job. He said 'yes, ma'am' and I put him right to work." Pearl smiled. "He seems like a nice kid."

"Right." The stubborn hair Monty raked away with his fingers fell back across his forehead. "Where's Monica?"

"In there." Pearl gestured with a tilt of her head toward the women's restroom. When Monty took a step toward the door, Pearl added, "Lacy's with her."

Although he was frustrated by his daughter's retreat into the one place he could not invade, Monty's mind slipped into gear. "What did the doctor tell you?"

Pearl shrugged. "Surgery, and then we'll see what comes next."

"Surgery? You're having an operation? When?" Monty felt as if he'd been punched in the gut. His mother was never sick. She didn't catch colds, and never missed work—at least not that he knew of. Now she had cancer. It didn't make sense.

"In a couple of weeks. We'll talk about all that as soon as there's time. Right now, I need to finish getting things organized for the dinnertime rush." Pearl turned toward the kitchen. "Don't worry," she said over her shoulder. "Remember who's in control."

Monty leaned on a dining room chair, trying to block out thoughts of a place nearby where he could get some whiskey. He wasn't up to dealing with his family's issues, and no one wanted his interference anyway. He'd been out of the picture so long, the women he loved learned to cope without him. They'd all moved on without him in their lives, even his mother.

Gripping the back of the chair so hard his hands hurt, Monty warred with himself. *I won't get drunk. I'll merely have an adult beverage to calm my nerves.* No. If I leave now, I'll never come back. *Sure I will. I can stop after one or two and come back to work as if nothing out of the ordinary happened.* That's a lie and you know it. *They won't even notice I'm not here. Nobody cares anyway.* Jesus cares. *Help!*

Monty didn't realize he'd said his one-word prayer aloud until Wayne waved a hand back and forth in front of his face. "Are you all right, man?"

129

"Huh? Yeah, sure. I'm fine." Monty blinked. "Nice apron."

"On the job less than an hour and I already got me a uniform and a title. Just call me Mr. Cleanup." With a wide smile, Wayne rolled the bussing cart forward.

Monty slowly released his death grip on the chair back, took several deep breaths, and strode resolutely to the cash register.

Chapter Twenty-Four

After following Monica into the well-appointed sitting room that led to the Roadhouse's restroom, Lacy sat on the sofa with her arms around her weeping daughter. "What's the matter, sweetheart? Is Philip sick? Has he been in an accident?"

Monica's words were punctuated with hiccups. "He didn't come to graduation and now he's not coming to the wedding."

Obviously, a wedding was not possible without the groom. "What do you mean? What happened?" She snatched a tissue from the side table and put it into Monica's hand.

"They're having an inspection I think he called it." After dabbing tears from her cheeks, she began to cry harder. "He told me his commander said no one can be gone until after it's over, and that won't be until the end of August."

"Then you'll just have to change your wedding date. August isn't that far off."

"But, Mom. Everything is all arranged. I mean, you have the church booked, and the flowers ordered, and the cake, and, oh, just everything. Why can't Philip come home like he said he would and get married on the fourth of July the way we planned?"

Lacy smoothed her daughter's hair. "He's in the military, honey. He can't pick up and leave if he's been told to stay. We can reschedule everything."

"Everybody's going to think Philip got cold feet. I'll look like a fool."

"People will understand the situation. We'll have corrected invitations printed up. Cindy and I will help you get them addressed and sent out right away." *I wonder what the printer will charge for a rush order. Thank the Lord Monty paid for the wedding dress.* "Now wash your face and go help Wanda get ready for dinner. Everything is going to be all right."

In a few minutes, Monica returned from the lavatory looking presentable. Pausing at the restroom exit, she turned toward Lacy and said, "How can I ever forgive Philip for doing this to me? Maybe I should call off the wedding until Christmas, and let *him* see how it feels to be disappointed."

Knowing how unlikely her daughter was to follow through on her threat, Lacy said, "Fine with me, but make up your mind before I talk to the printer." After Monica left in a huff, Lacy continued to sit on the sofa to gather herself, preparing to go nonstop for the rest of the evening. She fluffed a sofa pillow and remembered she'd shed quite a few tears herself in this very room over the years. However, her own hurts seemed much easier to bear than those of her kids. Pearl's illness, graduation, a wedding, and Monty's sudden reappearance threatened to overwhelm her. It didn't help that her oldest daughter was a drama queen. *Monica approaches every situation only in terms of how it impacts her, exactly like her father. I should have named her Monty Junior.*

Chapter Twenty-Five

Monty caught Cindy's eye and head-motioned her to the cash register. "What's up with your sister?" he asked.

"The Air Force won't let Philip come home until August is almost over. Naturally, Monica decided that means he doesn't love her. If he did, he'd go AWOL or jump off the Washington Monument or picket the Pentagon on the national news." With tented eyebrows, Cindy flashed a big smile. "She ought to be more insouciant."

"What does that mean?"

"I'm not sure," Cindy replied. "But it's a really cool sounding word, isn't it? I saw it in a book and Tommy Copeland told me how to pronounce it. This is the first time I've been able to work it into a conversation. Tommy was in my French class last year. He plays drums, but I like him anyway. As a friend, I mean." Her eyes widened. "Uh oh, the guy at table seven is giving me *the look*. I'd better go refill some tea and water glasses. Customers drain them pretty fast in this hot weather."

As soon as he had a chance, Monty slipped into the kitchen.

With a quick glance in his direction, Wanda asked, "Want to taste my spaghetti sauce?"

"I'll take a rain check. Have you seen Monica?"

"She went for a walk out back." Wanda continued stirring the contents of a huge pot on the stove. "I expect she's okay."

Try as he might, Monty could not corner his mother or wife during the dinner time rush. About a half hour before closing time, the crowds began to thin. Monty swept his eyes around, searching for Pearl or Lacy.

It wasn't long before Wayne's voice filled the dining room. Some of the remaining patrons stopped eating and moved closer to the music, while others seemed unaware they were being serenaded. One young couple waltzed onto the small dance floor, leaving ice cream to melt over their untouched slices of warm pecan pie. Monty used the excuse of refilling water glasses to roam through the dining room. At last he caught a glimpse of Pearl's white head inside the party room. Slowly rolling the drink caddy by the doorway, he saw Lacy and his mother engaged in deep conversation. Were they deliberately avoiding him by retreating to an out-of-the way spot, or merely avoiding their customers?

Feeling like a gate-crasher, Monty leaned against the door frame, smiled, and did his best to look casual. "Is this a private party or is anyone invited?"

The conversation between Lacy and Pearl stopped instantly. Were they annoyed or simply surprised by his interruption? Monty tried to read their impassive faces while the silence dragged on. Finally, Pearl cleared her throat and said, "We were just talking."

Monty lingered in the doorway. Pearl's words were not exactly an invitation. He briefly considered asking if he could join the discussion, but decided not to offer up an opportunity to turn him down. He quickly slid into one of the two vacant chairs at the four-seat table. "It appears the wedding has to be rescheduled." He glanced toward Lacy, who seemed to be fascinated by her own folded hands.

"Yes," Pearl answered after a long pause. "I reckon that's the deal."

Monty waited for the conversation to continue. In the background, Wayne finished an old Hank Williams tune and started another. Maybe a question would get things going. Anything to dilute the tension he felt in the air. "Is Monica okay with a delay?"

Pearl chewed her top lip. Her eyes flicked toward Lacy and then back to Monty. "Monica will be fine once she's had time to settle down. She's just a bit flighty. Getting married is a big step." Pearl scooted her chair back and stood. With a light caress of Lacy's shoulder, she said, "Time for me to think about closing down for the night. You two can hash this out without grandma."

Not knowing what to say, Monty decided the best approach was to wait for Lacy to speak. The waiting wasn't easy. He wondered if Lacy recalled how he hated the silent treatment. When he couldn't take it any longer, he motioned toward the drink cart outside the party room doorway. "Want some tea?"

Although she didn't answer his question, at least Lacy broke her silence. "Why are you here?"

"Well, Monica was crying on the way to work, and I figured you and Mom were—"

135

"No." She shook her head. "Not why are you in this room. I mean why are you in Polson's Crossing? Why now?"

"I've been planning to come home for months, as soon as I wrapped up my unfinished business in Nashville. When I heard about Mom's cancer, I knew it was time." This was a talk he'd wanted to have with Lacy. So why was it so hard to push out the words? "But even before that, I was getting ready to move back home." He took a deep breath and didn't allow himself to look away from Lacy's pretty face. "I want to be part of our girls' lives." Unable to continue to bear up under her piercing gaze, dropping his eyes to the table. "Yours, too, if you're willing to allow me back in."

Her voice was not angry. In fact, Lacy displayed no emotion at all. "Just like that?" She twisted a ring on her right hand. "After ten years?"

"Lacy, I'm sorry it took me so long to wake up and realize what a fool I've been. I know 'sorry' isn't enough, but it's all I know to say. I want to help Mom through her cancer, and I don't know, maybe I can do something to help you, too."

She squeezed the bridge of her nose between a thumb and ring finger for a long moment before facing him. "I could have used some help when I was working full time and trying to get my high school equivalency certificate. Or when both of the girls had strep throat and Pearl got pneumonia. And the day I found out Monica was sneaking away from school every day after I dropped her there in the morning. But it's too late now, Monty. What do you really want? The Roadhouse? Isn't that why you showed up now, to make sure you get your hands on Pearl's assets if she…if something happens to her?"

Feeling as if he might throw up, Monty leaned back in his chair. "Lacy."

"No." She held up her hand as a shield against his words. "Let me finish. I'll give you the Roadhouse. I don't have the strength to fight you for it. In fact, I'll go see Pearl's attorney and put that in writing if you want me to. Then you can drop the knight-in-shining-armor act and go back to doing whatever it is you do in Nashville."

"I don't want the Roadhouse, Lacy. If you think back, you'll remember I've never wanted to be a restaurant owner. I'll work here until my dying day if that's what Mom or you need, but it's not my cup of tea and never has been."

Monty struggled to keep his mind organized to answer each of Lacy's points. "I admit I'm no saint. We both know that, but I *am* now a Christian. I'm doing my best to live up to that name. My plan is to settle here in Polson's Crossing and try to get back something precious I lost." He reached for her hand, and then thought better of it. It was better not to touch her without permission. "I regret every minute I wasn't here for you and our daughters. There's nothing that will change the past. All I can do now is make sure I never disappoint you again. Not you or Mom, or Monica, or Cindy, either. Most of all, my goal is to live in a way that pleases my Lord and Savior. You may not believe this now, but I hope someday you will."

Lacy rested her head in her hands. "It's been a long day, and I'm too tired to think anymore. All we can worry about right now is getting through Pearl's surgery and Monica's wedding."

"All right." He hoped he was included in the 'we' Lacy mentioned. At least he'd had a one-on-one conversation with her about something more meaningful than napkins and table assignments. Would the love of his life ever forgive him? All he could do was let the matter rest in God's hands.

Chapter Twenty-Six

A few days later, when the noon rush quieted, Lacy withdrew to her tiny office. She tried to concentrate on the invoices to be paid, but her mind kept wandering. She signed checks to food suppliers, and then leaned back and stared at the ceiling. She'd repeatedly suggested automating the Roadhouse's accounting, but Pearl didn't trust computers. Maybe it was time, as the owner, to pursue that thought. Lacy puffed her cheeks and blew air at the stack of bills.

As soon as she finished putting stamps on the envelopes, Lacy spread out the huge fill-in calendar stored beside her desk. There was a note clipped to the top page, reminding her of the date for Pearl's surgery. Even though she doubted Monty would do more than put in a brief appearance at the hospital, Lacy decided not schedule him to work that day. Naturally, she and her daughters would be at Pearl's side until she disappeared into the surgical suite. Later they would be waiting for her when she came out of recovery. That left the problem of designating someone to be in charge of the Roadhouse during her absence.

Lacy tapped her pen against her teeth, considering the possibilities. Leonard could fix anything, and he was a wizard at smoking meat. However, he knew nothing about managing a restaurant. Wanda resisted all attempts to delegate any authority to her. "I'm the cook," she told Pearl and Lacy after serving as the temporary manager for one day several years ago. "I don't know what goes on outside the kitchen door, and I'm too old to start learning it now. When you two have to be gone at the same time, somebody else has to be the straw boss from now on." Other long-term employees made it clear they felt the same way.

With a sigh, Lacy set the calendar aside. It wasn't as if filling in was a heavy responsibility. She only needed someone to handle any customer complaints and resolve whatever minor issues that might arise. Maybe she'd ask Pearl's opinion over coffee tomorrow. The thought of making independent decisions from now on left Lacy feeling strangely unsure of herself.

She spent a few minutes going over her to-do list for Monica's wedding. It shouldn't take long to nail down a new date for the arrangements, once Pearl's surgery was behind her. Although she'd had her doubts about turning Monica loose with the keys to Monty's old car, it was a relief not to have to take her daughters everywhere. With an extra auto in the driveway, the girls were able to drive to and from work, plus take care of a lot of errands. She was somewhat concerned the car would be repossessed, leaving the girls stranded, but she'd decided to cross that bridge when she came to it.

Lacy laid her index finger next to the list where the word "florist" appeared. She dreaded dealing with grouchy old Mrs. Applegate. With a sly smile, she made a note to ask Monty to take care of changing the date for the floral arrangements. He'd offered to help. Let him find out how much fun it was to listen to an hour's worth of complaints before any discussion of flowers could proceed.

Against her will, Lacy's thoughts lingered on Monty. He must be desperate to take ownership of the Roadhouse, even though he claimed otherwise. What other reason could he have for continuing to maintain the façade of a solid citizen? The girls and Pearl seemed so willing to believe Monty's story that he'd changed. Lacy felt a pang of sympathy, realizing how hurt they were sure to be when he disappointed them. And how in the world did he manage to buy a new car, only working part time at the Roadhouse? Probably that twenty-four karat smile, backed up by a pile of convincing lies. No one understood better than she how easy it was to let Monty's charm overcome common sense. *I can't keep my daughters from risking their hearts on him, which they seem to insist on doing. Not me. Never again.*

The pattering sound of the Roadhouse's tin roof told Lacy last night's rain had returned. If it kept up, there would be fewer customers than normal this evening. After checking the time, she pulled a magazine from the bottom drawer of the desk. She was flipping through the pages, lost in thought, when Monty rapped on the frame of the open door.

"May I interrupt you?"

Lacy jumped. She slammed her magazine shut and folded it to hide the cover. "You're early."

"I went to look at some vacant buildings on the way to work, and it didn't take as long as I expected. I didn't mean to startle you."

"No problem." She slid her book back into its storage place and closed the drawer. Why did being alone with Monty make her anxious? She should invite him to sit in the lone visitor chair, but purposely did not. "What's up?"

"The roof is leaking, fortunately not in the dining room. It's under control for now, but you probably need to get a roofer to look at it."

For the first time, Lacy looked at Monty. "Your shirt's wet."

"Yeah." He glanced downward. "I got caught in the rain downtown."

Downtown? Buildings? Lacy was curious, but restrained herself from asking for more information. She didn't want to know too much about Monty's shady dealings. "I'll talk to Pearl and get in touch with someone to look at the roof." She turned back to the desk opened the folder sitting on its top. "Are you still willing to help rearrange Monica's wedding?"

"Sure." Monty took a step inside the doorway. "But last I heard the wedding was off."

"No, it's on. You're just getting a taste of Monica's dramatics. I know my daughter. She's going to marry Philip."

"If you say so. How can I help?"

Chapter Twenty-Seven

It was still dark when Lacy and her daughters made their way from the parking garage to the hospital. Humidity hung heavy in the damp morning air, adding to a sense of pre-dawn gloominess. The clack of their footsteps on the hard floor echoed through the silent hallways. As soon as they entered the surgical waiting room, Monty sprang from a brown vinyl-covered sofa to greet them. Lacy scouted the room with her eyes during the father-daughter hugs. Before there was any chance of physical contact with her ex-husband, she settled into a recliner as far away from Monty as she could get in a room the size of four ping pong tables.

"Coffee?" Monty asked. He offered Lacy a tall paper cup. "I assume you still like it black?"

Lacy nodded and accepted the drink. To her surprise the coffee was steamy hot. It tasted wonderful sliding down her throat. "Thank you."

"They just took Mama back." Monty nodded toward a set of double doors. "After they get her IV started, we can go in and visit until they take her to surgery." He turned to Monica, who'd taken up a seat near Lacy. "Help yourself to some coffee."

Wordlessly, Monica trudged across the room. She returned and slumped into her chair, drank a swallow of coffee, and sat with her head bowed over her cup.

"Is there enough for me, too?" Cindy chirped.

"Sure, there is." Monty smiled. "That thermal server holds a gallon, and I filled it all the way to the brim. I brought breakfast tacos and cinnamon rolls, too."

"Oh, yum. How did you know I was starving? We didn't have time for breakfast this morning."

Lacy winced at Cindy's revelation. She expected Monty to throw out a sarcastic remark about her lack of mothering skills. Instead, she heard him say, "Your digestive system probably needs a while to wake up before you start bombarding it with food. Nothing works right at this uncivilized hour of the morning."

Cindy dug into the cooler. Without asking for preferences, she sat a napkin-wrapped taco beside Lacy Then she delivered a cinnamon roll to Monica. She took one of each for herself and plopped beside Monty on the couch. "They'll be comatose until sunrise," she said, with a nod toward her sister and mother. "By seven o'clock, they'll begin to recover their power of speech, only to have it disappear all over again sometime around midnight. Tomorrow morning, they'll be zombies again."

"Good tacos," Cindy said after swallowing her first bite. "I don't know how I escaped the curse of the silent mornings." She cast a sidelong glance at Monty. "Maybe I take after you."

Lacy lifted her head, interested to observe Monty's reaction. Much to her surprise, he was beaming at Cindy. "Your mom's a far better role model, kiddo."

A tall woman dressed in green scrubs burst through the double doors. "Family of Pearl Chapman?"

Lacy followed her daughters through the stainless-steel doors. "Check it out, Monica." Cindy nudged her sister's arm. "We look like a real family. You, me, Mom, and Dad, all marching along together. Pretty cool, don't you think? We should take a picture."

Lacy glanced backward to see if Monty caught Cindy's remark, but his face showed no trace of emotion. Maybe he hadn't heard. Lacy wished she hadn't either. *Cindy's such a dreamer, just like her father. Always reaching higher than she can climb.*

The four of them crowded around the hospital bed, everyone's backside pushing against the tan curtains that marked off individual spaces in the large room. Cindy and Monica went to one side of the bed, leaving Lacy to stand next to Monty.

Pearl's bed was adjusted so that she was almost sitting upright, tilted back at a slight angle. "Good morning, girls." She smiled. "Oh, Lacy, bless your heart. I know what a sacrifice it is for you to be out and about before sunrise. Thank you for coming."

Monty took Pearl's hand, the one that didn't have an IV needle taped to it, leaned, and kissed his mother's cheek. He straightened, still clinging to Pearl's hand. "I love the shower cap. It reminds me of the hairnet you used to make me wear in the kitchen."

"Yes," Pearl replied with a broad smile. "It makes what the young folks call a 'fashion statement' with this lovely hospital gown."

145

Monica dabbed a tissue to her eyes. "I think you look beautiful, Grandma." She punctuated her statement with a sniffle.

"Don't cry, honey," Pearl admonished gently. "Everything is going to be fine."

"Right." Cindy side hugged Monica. "Because if you start with the tears, pretty soon Mom will too."

"I'm not crying." Monica wiped her nose.

The five of them chatted amiably with each other while technicians, the anesthesiologist, and the surgical team bustled in and out of the curtained area. Eventually, a green-gowned technician unlocked the wheels of Pearl's hospital bed. The same woman who'd escorted them from the waiting room pushed back the privacy curtains.

Recognizing they were being dismissed, Lacy tucked the bedcover over Pearl's feet. "We'll see you in a little bit."

"Wait." Monty held up a hand. "Let's pray together."

While Monty prayed, Lacy couldn't help thinking how sincere he sounded. She used to be able to discern when he was being dishonest. He must have improved his technique over the years in Nashville.

"The doctor will come and talk to you when your family member is in recovery," the tall woman explained as she steered the four of them back toward the waiting area. "The surgery normally takes two to three hours."

"This is the hard part," Monty said as they joined a handful of other people in the previously deserted room. "The waiting."

"Yes," Lacy agreed. "I'll have one of the girls call you when Pearl comes to if you like."

He turned toward her with an odd expression, one she couldn't read. "I'm not going anywhere until Mom's surgery is over and I have a chance to talk to her doctor. I'll call and let you know what he says if *you* need to leave."

Lacy wavered. Was Monty trying to dismiss her? Did he want to impress Pearl by being the only family member there when she woke up? Maybe she should go home.

Monty took his phone from a pocket and swiped at the screen. As if he could read her mind, he said, "I'm sure Julio can manage the Roadhouse for one day."

Chapter Twenty-Eight

Monty sat at the end of the plastic-covered sofa and drummed his fingers on the arm rest. He watched Lacy open her tote bag and take out a book, while both Monica and Cindy tapped at their phones. He stood and stretched. He paced around and read all of the notices posted on the waiting room bulletin board. In an attempt to force himself to settle, he stood staring out the window.

He became aware of Cindy's presence next to him. "Great view of the parking lot, huh?" Her voice was softer than usual. "Only I wish they'd put the dumpsters closer to the window. They lend a sort of *je ne sais quoi* to the whole scene, and as a form of folk art, they really deserve to be showcased better."

Putting an arm loosely on his daughter's shoulder, Monty nodded in agreement. "Yeah. They should paint them a nice, bright color to draw attention to them. Shocking pink maybe, or day-glow orange."

With a chuckle, Cindy briefly leaned her head against his shoulder. "It's so cool that you get my jokes." She glanced at her phone and jumped. "Monica, Christy Bailey and Billy Joe Stapleton broke up. Can you believe it? Wow, I thought they were a forever couple. Last I heard, Christy was expecting an engagement ring for her birthday." With that, she plopped into the nearest chair, thumbs flying. "I have to see if Olivia knows about this."

Monty thought he brought enough food for a three-day siege. Soon, however, there was nothing but a few bottles of water left in his cooler. The pimento cheese sandwiches he'd brought for lunch were gone along with the breakfast leftovers and a sleeve of fig newtons. Although the food had no taste, he couldn't stop nibbling as he paced back and forth.

Everyone looked toward him with anxious faces when his phone jangled. He stepped to the far corner of the room, where two floor-to-ceiling windows met. "Hello?" His own voice sounded as if it belonged to someone he didn't know.

"Monty? This is Patty Chesterfield. I've located another commercial property downtown for you, and it's perfect. Can you meet me there in a half hour?"

"It's not about Mom," Monty announced to Lacy and the girls before turning to the windows and lowering his voice. "Patty, I'm at the hospital right now, waiting for my mother to come out of surgery. I can't leave until I talk to the doctor. After that, I don't know what my schedule will be."

"That's too bad." Patty's disappointment was evident. "I'm sorry to hear about your mother. This place isn't on the market yet, but the seller is willing to give you a preview since–oh, well, I guess you have enough on your mind right now. But, do call me as soon as you get a chance. This is a choice location, and I expect there will be multiple offers as soon as the 'for sale' sign goes up."

"I'll be in touch as soon as possible." Monty jingled the coins in his pocket with his left hand. "Maybe we can get together this afternoon." Feeling like a caged animal, he tucked his phone away and paced around the room.

"They said two to three hours," Lacy mumbled without lifting her eyes from her book. "It has only been an hour and a half."

Feeling the room closing in on him, Monty stepped outside the waiting room. He considered the options, and then turned into the longest visible hallway. Some exploration revealed he could circle through the connecting halls and return to where he started without turning around. On his second pass by the waiting room, he found Cindy standing at the doorway. She fell into step with him.

"It's nice to have company," Monty commented. He didn't add that he felt Lacy and Monica would be glad to see him leave the hospital and let them keep the vigil without his interference.

Cindy smiled. "Yeah, the silent statues can't stand being talked to in the early morning, and I can't ever remember to keep quiet. You know what I mean?"

"Exactly." Monty thought how many times he'd irritated Lacy by wanting to pick up the threads of a previous evening's conversation before she'd had her first cup of coffee. If he was honest, he'd have to admit he'd sometimes done so purely to needle her. After turning the corner into a new expanse of hallway, he asked, "How are Monica and Philip getting along these days?"

With a cut of her eyes in his direction, Cindy exhaled noisily. "Last night she hung up on him. Then when he called back, she didn't answer. I hope I get to wear my bridesmaid's dress, because if I don't Mom will make me save it for prom next spring."

"The separation makes it hard on them, with Monica here and Philip in D.C."

"Not necessarily." Cindy rolled her eyes. "They broke up a bazillion times before he graduated. Then they'd get back together after Monica decided he'd groveled long enough."

Monty's assumptions about Monica's relationship with Philip were beginning to crumble. "What did they argue about?"

"Like, one time he stood in the hall and talked to a girl Monica doesn't like. And then he wanted to go to a tractor pull and she didn't want to go. She got uber mad though when he went with some guys instead of taking her out to a movie she wanted to see. Let me see, another time, they had a big row over who should be nominated for homecoming queen. You know, normal stuff, like you and Mom used to fuss over when you lived with us." Cindy's phone buzzed. "It's Olivia!" she announced before sprinting away with the phone pressed to her ear.

Monty stood and watched Cindy disappear around a corner. *Lord, what have I taught my daughters about love and marriage? What a mess I've made of everything. Help me make things right again somehow.*

When he circled by the waiting room entrance, Monty decided to go inside and try to be calm. He sat next to Monica, wondering how to begin a conversation about her upcoming wedding. Before he found the right words, the phone in his pocket started to vibrate.

Pearl's doctor came through the double doors that led to the surgical area. "Family of Pearl Chapman?"

"I'm Pearl's son." Monty grasped the doctor's outstretched hand. "The rest of her family," he added, gesturing toward Lacy and the girls.

The four of them stood in a tight knot around the physician. "Things went well," he said, removing his green cap and wiping his brow with it. "In a few days we'll get the pathologist's report on the lymph nodes and surrounding tissue. My office will phone you with the results. Mrs. Chapman can go home tomorrow or the next day." He held out a card. "Call and make an appointment for me to see her in two weeks." He glanced at his wristwatch. "She's in recovery now. Someone will come and get you when she wakes up."

Before Monty finished tucking the card into his wallet, the doctor had disappeared through the double doors.

Chapter Twenty-Nine

Later, Monty could not remember the sequence of events over the next few days. Everything moved too fast and at the same time seemed to drag. He took a sleeping bag from the Johnson's camping gear and slept on the floor beside Pearl's bed after she came home from the hospital. He hadn't realized how tense he was until the doctor's office called to give him the optimistic news from the pathology lab. There was no cancer in Pearl's lymph nodes and 'the margins were clear'. He choked out, "Praise God," and hurried to pass on the good news.

Monty spent as much time as possible with Pearl while continuing to work the evening shift at the Roadhouse and running essential errands while she slept. Somehow, he managed to squeeze in his assignments for Monica's wedding preparations. He was grateful for Wayne, who took over management of the Johnson family's menagerie of animals. Wayne also seemed to find rides to wherever he wanted to go, relieving Monty of the responsibility to haul him around.

A few days after she came home from the hospital, Pearl sat in her rocking chair, soaking up the morning sun. "What do you want for lunch?" she asked.

"I was thinking about warming up the chicken noodle soup we had night before last," Monty replied.

"That sounds good." Pearl nodded. "I'll heat it up and make some cornbread to go with it."

"But Mom—"

She held up a hand. "I appreciate you taking such good care of me. But I'm not going to lay down and be an invalid. You can spend the night in your old bedroom if you want to, but you don't need to sleep on the floor anymore. In fact, I don't see why you don't go home and get on with your life." She picked up her crochet.

"I'll sleep in my old room or on the couch tonight, and then we'll see how things go. Right now, I have an appointment to look at a place that's for sale downtown. As soon as the girls get here, that is."

"For goodness sake, Monty. I don't need babysitting." She peered at him intently. "What kind of place? Are you thinking of going into business?"

"More or less." Monty grinned. "Pastor Tom says Polson's Crossing has needed a rescue mission for some time. The real estate agent who hooked me up with the Johnsons has found something she says is perfect, but we have to make an offer right away or risk losing it."

Pearl snorted. "They say that every time they show a house. Be careful you don't get roped into something you regret." She slipped on her reading glasses and consulted the crochet pattern book before adding, "Before you go, you can call the church office, thank them for their concern, and let them know my friends don't need to 'happen by' when you go to work every afternoon. I'd have to be dense as mesquite wood not to see what's going on."

Monty grinned and ducked his head. "Okay, I get the message. I knew you'd never put up with me hiring a nurse, and your Sunday school class insisted on helping. Do you want me to ask the girls not to come over?"

"No need to go overboard." Pearl smiled, pushed her reading glasses to the top of her head, and resumed her crochet. "I'm happy for my granddaughters to come over any time."

Ten minutes later than the time they were supposed to arrive, Monica and Cindy pulled up to the curb in Monty's old car. He met them in the front yard and, after giving each daughter a quick hug, hurried off to rendezvous with Patty Chesterfield. On the drive downtown, he wondered why the realtor instructed him to meet her on a street corner. He parked in a public lot and stood with his hands in his pockets, wondering if Patty had given up on him and left.

In a few minutes, Patty appeared as if from nowhere. Looping her arm through his, she suggested, "Let's take a walk. We may be getting the horse before the cart by looking at this place. We have something to talk about before any commitments are made."

"Fine with me." They turned toward the Rialto, the old downtown theater where Monty spent many pleasant Saturday afternoons as a boy. "Where are we going?"

"I found out from a friend that this property will be coming on the market soon." Patty slowed their pace as they passed an upscale shoe store. "However, I promised absolute discretion. Agreed?"

"Sure," Monty answered. "But why all the secrecy?"

"The sellers are very concerned about how their building will be used after they move out." Patty turned her face from the shoe display to Monty. "Are you familiar with Holy Trinity Church?"

"Yeah. It's a beautiful old—wait!" He spun toward her. "Is that the building that's for sale?"

"It is, or more correctly it may be soon. I know of someone who wants to put a nightclub in the downtown area. Another group of investors plans to build luxury downtown condos, meaning they plan to tear down whatever they buy and use the land for new construction. Neither of which appeals to Holy Trinity." Patty sighed. "So here we are."

Monty looked up at the steeple that rose above the red brick exterior of the old church. What a loss it would be to Polson's Crossing if this beautiful house of God was torn down to make space for a modern building. He pulled open one of the heavy wooden doors to allow Patty to enter ahead of him.

After stepping inside, Monty surveyed the interior of the sanctuary. A large oscillating fan quietly stirred the morning air. The sunlight filtering through the old stained-glass windows cast an atmosphere of worship over the empty pews. He knew instantly that his prayers for a suitable mission site had been answered.

Patty tilted her head toward the figure of a man at the altar. "Reverend Buckley," she mouthed.

Monty made his way to the altar and knelt beside the pastor. Not wishing to disturb a prayer, Monty closed his eyes and silently offered thanks for being led to this location.

After a moment, Reverend Buckley said a quiet "amen" and leaned back, still on his knees. He was younger than Monty expected, powerfully built, with skin of polished ebony. The men introduced themselves to each other and shook hands, while Patty lingered near the entryway.

"I understand you're interested in acquiring this church building." His eyes bored into Monty.

"Yes, sir."

An air of calm authority radiated from the quiet man of God, commanding Monty's respect. "Come with me. I'll show you around while you tell me why you're interested in Holy Trinity." Rev. Buckley sprang lightly to his feet, offering a hand to help Monty rise.

"Before we begin the tour, I want you to know we have filed papers to have this place declared an historic site. If the state ever gets around to approving our request, you will not be able to make changes to the building's exterior. Also, there's a small graveyard out back, which cannot legally be disturbed." Buckley cocked an eyebrow. "Are you still interested?"

"Yes, more than interested. May I ask why you are considering putting your church house up for sale?"

For the first time, Rev. Buckley smiled. "Very few people live downtown nowadays. The members of this congregation have just about all migrated to the suburbs. Our last downtown member, Miss Louella Jefferson, is now in hospice. Most everyone else lives out in the direction of the lake." He opened a door. "This is the fellowship hall,

157

and the kitchen is at the rear. The deacons and the business committee agreed that when Miss Louella passes, the church should relocate near the community we now serve." He looked around. "We believe the Lord is leading us to a gathering place with an after-school program, close enough for neighborhood kids to walk to church. That kind of thing."

"This is perfect. With some folding chairs and tables, this fellowship hall would be a great dining room. The kitchen is exactly right, and already up to date." Monty ran his hand over the smooth stainless steel of the kitchen counter.

He noticed Patty tossed him a frown. She gave her head a slight 'no' shake. "A building of this age is bound to have hidden issues," she warned. "The electrical may not be up to code, and old plumbing is notoriously unreliable."

Reverend Buckley motioned toward a hall. "Let me show you the classrooms." As Patty passed through the doorway, he turned to Monty and said, "We have maintained the church faithfully over the years. I can't say nothing will ever break, but we are blessed to have members who've used the knowledge of their various trades to keep the building in excellent condition."

After a tour of the classrooms, the nursery, a next-door parsonage, and the administrative offices, Monty could hardly contain his excitement. He could sense Patty's disapproval of his obvious enthusiasm, guessing she'd planned to use the age of the building as a negotiating point.

"Pastor Buckley, Holy Trinity fits a mission's needs perfectly. The kitchen and sanctuary wouldn't need any renovation at all. With a little work, the classrooms can be converted into dormitory rooms." Monty glanced at Patty, whose lips were pressed tightly together. Nevertheless, he couldn't stop himself from saying, "I'm prepared to make an offer right now. What is your asking price?"

Monty expected Reverend Buckley to be as excited as he was. Instead, the pastor's voice was calm. "Do you have time to step into my office and chat?" Without waiting for an answer, he led the way.

In the small office, Monty and Reverend Buckley settled onto a worn but comfortable love seat. Patty claimed a wing-back chair and sat with her arms crossed.

"I'd like to hear more about your plans," the pastor said, his brown eyes piercing Monty.

Chapter Thirty

After Monty recounted his Nashville conversion experience, Reverend Buckley asked him how he'd chosen Polson's Crossing. Although he hadn't planned to discuss his personal life, Monty found himself opening up to the pastor's warmth.

Reverend Buckley reached across the space between them and rested his massive hand on Monty's shoulder. "I feel led to pray. Will you join me?"

Monty nodded and bowed his head, still too overcome with the emotional drain of pouring out his heart to speak again.

With his deep, resonant voice, the pastor began, "Lord, Brother Chapman is obeying your command to seek first the Kingdom of God and Your righteousness. Now I ask that you add to these things the renewal of his marriage…"

Monty lost himself in his own prayer for the success of the mission. It wasn't until he heard Reverend Buckley's resounding "amen" that he opened his eyes and tuned back in to his surroundings.

The pastor ran his fingers along the edge of his tie. "The mission you described is precisely what many in Holy Trinity's congregation want to undertake. I've opposed the idea because we don't have to resources to go into a building program and operate a mission simultaneously." He smiled and shook his head. "The Lord moves in mysterious ways."

"Pastor Tom has the same concern about resources," Monty admitted. "He has lined up a few dedicated folks to work on getting the mission going, but it seems that only a small percentage of our congregation will put any effort into doing things."

"You are a member of Tom Gillespie's congregation?"

Monty's affirmative nod brought a smile to Reverend Buckley's broad face. "I know Tom from the ministerial council. He's a good man." The pastor stroked his chin. "I'll give him a call. Holy Trinity is not in a position to help you financially right now, but manpower is another matter."

"That sounds wonderful." Monty noticed Patty making something of a production of consulting her wristwatch. "I guess we've taken enough of your time, Reverend Buckley."

Both men stood and shook hands. Buckley said, "With God nothing is impossible."

"We'll be in touch," Patty murmured, hurrying toward the exit.

Outside, Monty stopped and surveyed the old church. "I remember walking by this old church when I was just a kid. I never dreamed then what was in store. I'm so pumped!"

Patty walked ahead. "Let's grab a cup of coffee." Without waiting for Monty to agree, she entered the next doorway they came to.

As they sat waiting for their number to be called, Monty asked, "Can you do the formal part of making an offer on the Holy Trinity building this afternoon?"

"I'm sorry to rain on your parade, but there are a couple of big issues we have to discuss before you take off running." Patty studied the nails of her left hand intently before making eye contact with Monty.

He smiled, still euphoric that he'd found the perfect facility. "Lay it on me."

"The first show stopper is money."

"That's the least of our worries." Monty stood when the barista called out number fifteen. "I'll go get our coffees. Do you want any cream or sugar?"

"No." Patty's bottom teeth clawed at her upper lip. "Thanks."

When Monty returned with steaming cups of coffee, Patty spoke before he'd settled into his chair. "I reviewed some credit reports this morning. Oakwood Community Church can't possibly qualify for a loan to buy the Holy Trinity building."

"The church isn't the buyer. I am."

She closed her eyes as she sipped her coffee. "Your personal credit history would never—"

"Patty," Monty interrupted. "I plan to pay cash."

She stared at him, expressionless. After a long silence, she repeated, "Cash. You just happen to have a few hundred thousand dollars in your pocket."

"No, I'm not carrying that much money around in my wallet. I may have to rearrange a few things, but by the time you can get the paperwork done, I'll have a cashier's check for the full amount made out to Holy Trinity."

"I'm sure I can negotiate a lower price for a cash sale," Patty said.

"No." Monty shook his head. "Holy Trinity needs enough money to buy a piece of land and put up that temporary building Reverend Buckley mentioned. I'm happy with their asking price."

"Assuming you do have the money." She sounded distinctly unconvinced. "There's another show-stopper."

"Well, we both heard what Pastor Buckley said about nothing being impossible with God." Monty leaned back and smiled. "What's the problem?"

"Buckley is very influential at Holy Trinity, but he doesn't have the final say. You haven't dealt with their deacons and business committee, but I have. Some of their families have been members of that church for four generations. The emotional ties are unbelievable. They have memories of their children being baptized there, and a good number have relatives in the graveyard. They want the new building in another location, but at the same time they're never going to stand for tearing down their old home church."

163

"Who said anything about tearing it down? All I want to do is convert the classrooms into bedrooms. The exterior will still be the same." Monty scratched his head. Patty wasn't making sense. "Reverend Buckley said they were thinking about doing the same thing I want to do. Where's the issue?"

"What's to keep you from re-selling the property to someone else as soon as the ink is dry on your deed? Maybe to the people who want to put up the high rise?" Patty folded and unfolded her napkin. "I suspect that's why they're campaigning for the historical site designation, to preserve the old church building. The deacons may try to slow roll the sale until the state makes a decision, and no one knows how long that may take."

"Don't you think they will believe my intention is to use the church as it is? And that I have no plans to sell it?"

"I'm sure Reverend Buckley is convinced. But what if the mission folds up after a few months? What if you walk in front of a concrete truck—God forbid. Your wife might decide to liquidate your assets, including the church property."

"I don't have a wife," Monty protested.

"All right then. Suppose you get married and lose your shirt in a nasty divorce. I'm just saying stuff happens. Situations change. These guys know that."

"I see your point." Monty twirled his coffee cup, trying to put himself in the congregation's shoes. "But I'm not sure what to do about it."

"In a week or two, I expect they'll ask you to meet with some representatives from Holy Trinity, and possibly after that the whole congregation. Think about how you can reassure them about the future of the building when, and if, they decide to sell it to you."

"I'll pray for words of wisdom," Monty promised. "And don't forget, I'm still looking for a house to live in."

"Right." Patty slipped the strap of her handbag over a shoulder and stood. "No doubt you'll want to finalize your financial arrangements, too. I'm pretty sure the Holy Trinity business committee will be interested in knowing a great deal more about your cash offer."

Monty drove home whistling a tune, with the words of a song about an old church building taking shape in his mind. When he arrived home, he found Pearl sitting on a tall stool in the kitchen, supervising while Monica and Cindy mixed pastry dough.

Chapter Thirty-One

"What would you do if I said I wanted to head back to Tennessee?" Wayne stirred sugar into his cereal bowl without looking up at Monty. "I've saved up enough money from working at the Roadhouse to pay for a bus ticket."

"That's entirely your decision," Monty replied. "I don't know what I would have done without you the past couple of weeks. I had my hands full with Mom's surgery and all. The Johnson menagerie would have gone hungry if it wasn't for you taking care of them."

"You should never starve an animal."

Monty grinned at Wayne's sincerely shocked expression. "I didn't mean that literally. I'm trying to say thank you for your help."

"Yeah, well, I guess I'm the one to say thanks." Wayne picked at his Cheerios. "You and your family and the guys at the church have all been really nice to me. I've been studying my copy of the contract I signed with Mr. Henry. Now I know what I agreed to do and not do."

"So, you're going to plunge back into singing with a different outlook?" Monty gazed out the window at his mother watering flowers in her backyard, not paying full attention to the earnest young man across the table.

"I've been doing a lot of thinking, and I feel different about a lot of things. That's for sure. The only thing I don't know is what I want to do. You know what I mean?"

"Not exactly."

"See, I've always loved singing. Like at the Roadhouse. It's nice to just kick back and sing what I want to while people are clapping and dancing and having a good time. I love that. But sitting in a recording studio with all the wires going every which way and people griping about time being money isn't much fun. Plus, there's this girl…"

Monty let the kitchen curtain drop and turned to focus his full attention on Wayne. "A girl? I hope she's in the church youth group."

"Yes, she is. She really helped me sort things out, maybe more than anybody else." His voice grew soft. "I think I may be in love."

"And now you're going to take off and leave her behind?"

"Yeah." Wayne hoisted Sweetie into his lap and begin to rub her fur. "There's business I've got to take care of back home. I'd like to take her with me, but she just laughed at that idea. She said I could call her when I decide to grow up and make something of myself and maybe she'll talk to me then."

"Smart kid," Monty said. "That's probably what my wife should have told me a few years ago."

Wayne put away the milk and rinsed his bowl and spoon with one hand, balancing Sweetie on his shoulder with the other. "I guess I'll go start packing my duds. If you wouldn't mind dropping me off at the bus station on your

167

way to work, I'll get on the road this evening." He lingered in the kitchen doorway for a moment. "I'm sure going to miss all of the animals. Big Boy and Goldie most of all."

Monty finished his breakfast, offering up a silent prayer that Wayne would do well in life. He suspected Carson Henry would be sorry he'd sent the young man to Polson's Crossing. He may have grown up more in the space of a few weeks than Carson bargained for. Monty wondered about the length of Wayne's contract, knowing the agent would insist on every jot and tittle being fulfilled.

"That's it," Monty said aloud, snapping his fingers. "A contract." When Patty Chesterfield didn't answer her phone, he left her a voice mail. He'd suspected for some time that she thought he was a little nutty. If not, the message he left would definitely convince her.

When Pearl's porch light went out, Monty leapt over the back fence and knocked on her back door. "I noticed you were up and thought you might want some company."

"Come on in." Pearl smiled. "Have you had breakfast?"

"Yep, but I could drink some of your good coffee and watch you eat." Monty planted a kiss on Pearl's cheek.

"What do you hear from the Johnsons?" Pearl asked as they sat at her kitchen table. "Are they ever coming home?"

"They check in every week or so." He cradled his coffee mug in both hands. "I'm pretty sure they'll let me rent the downstairs bedroom for a while if they get back before I buy a house."

"You really do mean to buy a house and settle in?"

Monty loved the light of hope in his mother's eyes. "No doubt about it. I'm home for good."

Pearl listened intently as Monty talked about his plans for a downtown mission. When he finally wound down, she asked, "How are things at the Roadhouse?"

"Fine. Everyone misses you, but Lacy assures us you'll be back as soon as you're up to it." Monty watched as his mother focused her eyes on buttering a biscuit. When she took an unusual amount of time with the task, he sensed something was going on. "Is there something on your mind, Mom?"

"You know me too well." She smiled and fidgeted with her silverware. "I've been working since I was a teenager, and I've always loved the Roadhouse."

The silence dragged out while the old wall clock ticked. "And?" Monty prompted her.

"I just don't know if I want to go back to work. No, that's not true. I *know* I don't want to."

"You've always said you were never going to retire. What changed your mind?"

"This little brush with cancer has given me time to do a heap of praying and thinking. I'm not getting any younger, and I sort of have a yen to travel. I've always

169

wanted to see the Grand Canyon. I hear folks talk about going on cruises and I think that might be nice, too." She pushed her plate away and folded her napkin. "I guess you think I'm crazy."

"No, Mom. I think you're way overdue to stop and smell the roses in life. Where do you want to go on your cruise? The Caribbean?"

"Oh, I don't know. Just being on a big old boat out on the ocean sounds so peaceful I don't know as I'd care where it was headed to." Pearl had a faraway look on her face. She sipped coffee, slowly positioning her cup back on its saucer before saying, "I just don't know how to break this to Lacy. She isn't real sure of herself, and depends on me to help her make decisions at the Roadhouse."

"I wish I could say I'll take care of Lacy, but I don't know if she will allow me do that." Monty picked up Pearl's dishes and took them to the sink. "I'd sure love to." He stared out the kitchen's back window. Wayne was taking each rabbit out of the hutch one-by-one, giving each little ball of fur a cuddle. "Wayne is going back to Nashville this evening. He confided in me he's sweet on a girl from Polson's Crossing, but he's leaving anyway so it must not be anything serious."

Pearl broke out in the heartiest laughter Monty had heard from her since before her surgery.

"What's so funny?" Monty dropped the kitchen curtain into place.

"Oh, nothing." Pearl giggled and waved a hand. "Wayne's a good boy and I love his singing. I hope Lacy doesn't get all tied in a knot over finding a new busboy."

"Julio has dug up replacements for other people who quit. He can probably find someone to clean up tables."

"Another fine young man, Julio. Leonard says he catches on to everything right quick."

"Yeah, the Roadhouse doesn't get many employees as good as Julio. I'd like to see him lighten up a little, though. He's always so serious. Want me to warm up your coffee while I'm up?"

Pearl nodded a yes and held out her cup.

After Monty returned to his kitchen chair, his mother reached across the table and patted his hand. "You haven't asked for my opinion, Son, but I'm going to give it to you anyway. It's going to take a lot for Lacy to trust you. You know the old saying, 'once bitten, twice shy'. If you want her back, you will have to be patient. Convince her you are back in her life for good, with no drinking and no running around."

"Do you think she could ever love me again?"

Pearl hesitated before saying, "I don't she ever stopped."

Chapter Thirty-Two

Monty turned over and squinted at the grandmother clock on the bedroom wall. Four fifteen. It wasn't like Wayne to be up so early, making a racket in the kitchen. He nestled into the coziness of the bed and started drifting back to sleep. Suddenly he remembered Wayne left for Nashville yesterday afternoon. He propped himself up on an elbow, listening. What kind of intruder had the nerve to use the microwave oven?

He fished on the floor for his slippers. Finding only one, he abandoned the search and ran toward the kitchen barefoot. As he rushed down the dark hallway toward the kitchen light, Monty realized he had nothing to defend himself with. Too late to worry about that. He burst into the room with a shout, "What's going on in here?"

River, Brook and Raven Johnson sat glum-faced at the kitchen island. Dexter stood by the stovetop, his wooden spoon suspended in midair. "Oh, did I wake you?" He turned to silence the pinging oven timer. "I should have let you know I was coming home, but things happened so fast and there was so much chaos I just wasn't thinking clearly. Sorry, man."

Monty rubbed his face with both hands and smoothed his hair back as best he could. "I thought your house was being robbed." He yawned and put a pod into the coffee maker.

"That's a nifty machine." Dexter motioned toward the coffee maker with his wooden spoon. "You must have bought it after we left, because *she* would never allow us to have coffee in the house."

172

"Yeah." Monty silently encouraged the brown liquid to hurry into his waiting mug. "I can't do without my morning coffee."

"I think I'll have a cup, too." Dexter stirred a pot on the stove. "If you'll show me how that thing works."

"I'll brew it for you." Monty savored several swallows of coffee before popping in another pod for Dexter. "How's your mother doing?"

"She's home, but she still has a long way to go. Thank God my Dad is able to take care of her now."

Monty nodded. "Where's the rest of your family? Still sleeping?"

"My sons are my family now," Dexter announced. "*She* has the girls. No telling where they are or what they're doing. And I couldn't possibly care less."

"It sounds like you've had a rough time." Right before the words tumbled from his mouth, Monty stopped himself from suggesting he and Dexter have a stiff shot of whiskey to start off the morning. *Lord, will I ever stop thinking that way? When will I learn to depend on You instead of alcohol?* "What do you want in your coffee?"

"I don't know." Dexter looked perplexed. "I've never had it before."

"Lots of cream and sugar." River sat with his elbows on the island, his chin resting in his hands.

"Okay," Dexter said. "Like he said, lots of cream and sugar. How do you know about coffee, River?"

"Meemaw watches cooking shows on TV," Brook said in a monotone.

Monty waited in silence while the brewing machine did its work. Now that the Johnsons—some of them—were home, it was time to ramp up his effort to find his own house to live in. He glanced at the time display on the oven. In a mere five hours Patty Chesterfield would open her office. The realtor would simply have to make time for him in between her other clients and his appointment with Pearl's lawyer.

"I'll bet Mr. Munch missed you." Monty put a hand on River's bright hair. "He'll be glad to see you this morning."

"He's not dead?" River perked up noticeably. "Willow told me you would probably kill all our pets while we were gone."

Monty suppressed a smile. "They're all doing fine. Sweetie is over whatever she had, and at last count you have eight new bunnies."

"Oh, wow." River said.

Raven turned toward Dexter. "Daddy, can we keep the new bunnies?"

"All of the animals are staying here with your mother and the girls." Dexter bent almost double, peering into the bottom shelves of the open refrigerator. "Do you have any soy milk?"

"No," Monty answered. "Nothing but two percent cow's milk." Apparently, food he'd brought into the house was now community property.

"We're not taking Goldie with us?" Raven knelt on the floor to hug his dog.

"What did I just say?" Dexter demanded. "Didn't I say *all* of the animals are staying behind?" He pulled the milk carton from the fridge. "I suppose I can have dairy just this once."

"Goldie has been my dog for three years," Raven protested.

River began, "But Mr. Munch…"

"Shut up," Dexter ordered. "Quit whining like your mother."

Monty finished off his coffee in the kitchen's tense silence. It was clear the Johnson's marriage was in serious trouble. What he wanted to do was go back and sleep for a couple of hours, then pack his clothes and move into a motel. Instead, he brewed another cup of coffee, and prayed for wisdom to know what to do. Maybe he could catch Pastor Tom and see if he had time to talk with Dexter this morning. That is, if Dexter was interested.

"The kitchen looks good," Dexter commented, bringing his coffee and sitting across from Monty at the table. "Did you repaint in here?"

"No, I wouldn't paint anything without getting your permission first." What Monty had done was scrub the kitchen thoroughly. As long as he could remember, Pearl had insisted on a spotless kitchen, both at home and at the Roadhouse. He figured it must be in his genes to operate the same way.

Dexter looked the white cabinets up and down. "Something looks different." He rubbed his eyes. "I'm going upstairs to get some sleep. Boys, you should probably do the same."

"We slept in the car," River mumbled.

"It's up to you." Dexter yawned. "Just don't get rambunctious and wake me up. I'm dead on my feet."

The sound of Dexter's footsteps ascending the stairway faded away. Fighting the impulse to depart to the peace of his bedroom, Monty instead picked up the breakfast dishes and pots Dexter had left haphazardly strewn everywhere. After he loaded the dishwasher and wiped down the stove and countertops, he brewed another cup of coffee. The boys ate in silence, picking at their food.

"It's your fault," River said quietly. "You asked for raisins in your cereal."

"No," Brook disagreed. "Willow shouldn't have read the raisin box out loud."

"Mom would have found out about the preservatives anyway." Raven laid his fork aside. "Mr. Monty, do I have to clean my plate?"

176

Taken aback, Monty replied, "I don't make the rules for you. Your parents do. What would they say?"

"I don't know." Raven turned toward Brook. "Do you?"

River piped up, "They'd get mad and have a fuss about it."

Monty thought Brook had the saddest little face he'd ever seen. A jolt of guilt rammed its fist into his gut. He could imagine his daughters having a similar conversation once upon a time.

Following some whispered discussion, River finished the scrambled eggs and wrapped his remaining half slice of toast in a napkin.

"Are you guys going to help me take care of your animals as soon as the sun comes up?"

All three boys rewarded Monty's question with a smile.

"I want to see the baby rabbits," Brook declared.

"Me, too." River hopped down from the island stool. "Let's take Goldie and go out back."

"Quietly," Monty reminded them as they raced away. Knowing he couldn't go back to sleep after three cups of coffee, he rummaged through the refrigerator for something to toss into the Johnsons' slow cooker for lunch.

Chapter Thirty-Three

"Let me check my calendar," Patty said. "I have appointments all day. Tomorrow doesn't look too good, either." After a brief pause, she added, "I'm showing a ranch on the other side of the highway in a half hour. I could possibly squeeze in a late lunch at your mother's restaurant today, say around one? I have some new listings you'll find interesting."

"Okay. One o'clock works. See you then." Monty clicked to disconnect the call, relishing his new car's hands-free option. He'd bought the car with a loan from the bank. Immediately after taking delivery of his new vehicle, he drove to the bank and paid off the loan in full. It was what locals called a 'goat rope', but it made Jimmy Glassman happy.

Within a few minutes, he was sitting in a waiting room that had the aura of an old-fashioned funeral parlor. The sofa and chairs had been reupholstered, but Monty was certain he recognized them from the last time he'd been in Darrell's office, more than twenty years ago.

A young woman wearing huge glasses sat behind a wide desk, strategically placed to block access to a door marked 'private'. After asking Monty's name, she punched some buttons on a device that looked like the product of a telephone's marriage to an aircraft console. "Mr. Mabry will be with you shortly," she said, before concentrating her attention on a stack of file folders.

Before Monty could settle into an easy chair, the private door opened. Darrell Mabry stood in the doorway.

Other than a few additional wrinkles and a transition from brown to white hair, the attorney's appearance was unchanged. He even wore the same kind of clothes Monty remembered—a dark, conservatively cut suit, starched white shirt with cuff links, and a striped silk tie. "Hello, Monty. It's good to see you again. Come on in."

"Nice to see you too, Darrell." The two men shook hands. Monty sat in a leather chair facing the attorney's polished wood desk.

Darrell put his elbows on his desktop and laced his fingers into the shape of a pup tent. "I must remind you that I represent your mother."

"I know that." Monty was puzzled. "She's not involved in the two things I need to get done today."

"Good." The attorney leaned back and smiled for the first time. "What's on your mind?"

"I'm negotiating to buy Holy Trinity Church's building." Monty grinned at Darrell's quizzical look. "A group of us plan to set up a rescue mission there. Some members of the Holy Trinity congregation are concerned about what happens if the mission folds. They don't want their former church turned into condos, or worse."

"I see."

"So, I want a contract that returns ownership of the church building and the land it occupies, free and clear, to Holy Trinity Church if it ceases to be used as a place of worship or a rescue mission."

The attorney wrote a note on his yellow legal pad. "You'll need some time to get started before this provision kicks in. Now, who would be responsible for the mortgage payments if the property reverts to the original owner?"

"There won't be a mortgage," Monty replied. "I am paying cash. Oh, and add something that requires Holy Trinity's approval of any substantial changes to the building's appearance in advance."

Darrell wrote more notes. "What happens if this Holy Trinity congregation disbands? It does happen."

The question took Monty by surprise. "They've been around for more than a hundred years, and they're growing." He'd never considered the possibility the attorney raised. "I suppose the contract would no longer be in effect. It just goes away if there's no Holy Trinity church. I also want them to have veto power over any loan that would use the church house or land as collateral."

"Suppose the church leadership changes and, say, the new managers dislike your mission operation. They could litigate to regain their building."

"I'm willing to trust those things won't happen." Monty leaned back and smiled. "That's about it."

"Do you realize the position into which you are placing yourself?" Mabry cocked an eyebrow ever so slightly. "You will be putting a considerable amount of money into a property, and yet you may easily lose ownership."

"I know what I'm doing," Monty insisted. "And I completely understand that I am going ahead against your best advice." He thought there must be a course in law school about keeping the same facial expression regardless of what anyone says. Or maybe Darrell Mabry was a poker player.

The attorney flipped to a clean sheet of paper on his legal tablet. "You mentioned having two items?"

"Yes. I want to give up any and all claims on Pearl's Roadhouse. I understand my mother is in the process of selling the place to Lacy, my ex-wife."

"Actually, I believe the sales transaction is complete and the deed recorded. I would see no need for--"

Monty interrupted, "My statement is to lay the issue of ownership to rest permanently, just so there's never any doubt. You might say it's for everyone's peace of mind."

"I see. Your requests will take a bit of research. I'll get back to you in a few days," Darrell said.

Monty went on his way, whistling a tune he'd written years ago. He was glad to escape from the conversation about legal mumbo jumbo. Still, he was willing to do whatever it took to convince Holy Trinity of his good intentions and lay Lacy's suspicions to rest. With a glance at his car's clock, he realized he was not going to be on time for his one o'clock appointment.

As soon as Monty walked into the Roadhouse, he saw Patty Chesterfield waving at him from a booth. "I'm sorry to be late," he said.

181

Patty waved off Monty's apology. "No worries. I have some great homes for you to check out."

A waitress who'd worked at the Roadhouse since Monty was in high school approached the table immediately. "Hey, Monty. Can't get enough of this place?" She pointed at the closed menu in front of him. "Do you need more time?"

Monty chuckled. "Hi, Betsy. Unless you changed it this morning, I believe I can recite the whole menu from memory."

Nodding toward Patty, the waitress asked, "What'll you have, sweet thing? Are you going to get adventurous, or stick with the tried and true?"

"I have enough adventure without trying." Patty handed over her menu. "I'll have my usual. BLT, no mayo, and coffee."

Betsy wrote on her order pad. Without consulting Monty, she said, "And for the gentleman, fish tacos and lots of sweet tea." She stuck her pencil behind her right ear. "Right?"

"I had my heart set on a watercress sandwich," Monty said with a grin. "But since you've already written it down, I'll settle for tea and tacos."

Patty pulled a stack of flyers from the depths of her enormous tote bag. "I brought pictures of a variety of listings, since you don't seem to have a clear idea of what you're looking for."

"Maybe I'll know what I want when I see it." Monty accepted the flyer Patty held out to him.

"There's some beautiful new construction further out." Patty moved from her seat across from Monty and slid into his side of the booth. She tapped a nail on the top flyer. "This one has a fabulous lake view, its own boat dock, a pool, and a separate guest house."

"Nice." Monty barely glanced at the picture. "But I don't want to be that far from my mother." He scooted away, putting a few inches of space between himself and Patty. "Why don't we stick with the neighborhood where I am now?"

"No problem." She lifted the corner of her sandwich and rearranged the lettuce. "Homes in that area are few and far between, however, and often need updating."

Chapter Thirty-Four

Earlier that same day, Lacy was delighted to see Pearl's car in the Roadhouse parking lot. The last few weeks without her mother-in-law's presence had been difficult. Maybe now that Pearl was back everything could settle into the old routine.

As soon as the first-thing-in-the-morning chores were under control, Lacy grabbed a cup of coffee and made her way to the sunny table where Pearl sat gazing out the window. "Good morning," she said, sounding remarkably cheerful even to herself.

"Good morning, Sunshine." Pearl smiled.

"You don't know how glad I am to see you sitting in your normal spot." Lacy took her usual chair. "I'm sorry I haven't been by to see you this week. I forget how busy things get around here in August. Everyone flocks to the lake before school starts. How are you feeling?"

"I get tired way too easy. But as long as I get a good night's sleep and my afternoon nap, I perk along pretty good for an old woman. How about yourself?"

"I'm okay I guess."

Pearl lifted an eyebrow. "Just okay?"

Lacy hesitated. She'd promised herself she wouldn't burden Pearl with restaurant business. However, there was no one else who understood the difficulties of keeping the Roadhouse running smoothly. She'd been so stressed she was even tempted to ask Monty's opinion on operational issues lately. "You know how it goes. As soon as a problem gets solved, two more pop up in its place." She took a deep breath. It felt good to admit her inner turmoil instead of pretending to have everything under control.

"What's going on?"

The calm strength in Pearl's voice opened the floodgates. "A few days ago, Leonard came into the office and suggested putting Julio on full time so he could cut his own schedule down to a day or two a week." Lacy rubbed a hand back and forth across her forehead. "I'm pretty sure Leonard is about ready to retire, and I can't blame him. But what will I do if he and Julio both leave? Where would I find someone to keep the juke box going? Not to mention that cranky chiller."

Pearl nodded. "Have you talked to Julio about taking over Leonard's job permanently?"

"No," Lacy admitted. "Julio is so quiet and shy. I never know what to say to him. Plus, he keeps busy all the time. I've never seen him take a coffee break."

"He graduated from high school this year, didn't he?"

Lacy nodded. "Yes, he was in Monica's class. She told me he was a straight A student. That makes me think he's going to college in September."

"I doubt it. He's not working for spending money like most of the kids we hire. His mother is a single parent, and he has a couple of younger sisters he helps support. Anyway, that's what Leonard said."

"Oh." Lacy took a sip of coffee. "Maybe I'll ask Leonard to catch Julio when he comes in this afternoon and send him to see me."

"Or maybe you could wander out to the smoke house about the time he comes to work and have a friendly chat out there." Pearl smiled. "That might be easier for a shy kid than reporting to the principal's office."

"Great idea." Lacy wondered if Pearl was officially back to work, but she wasn't sure how to approach the subject delicately. "Are you regaining your strength?"

"I'm not bouncing back like I did when I was your age, but I feel good most of the time. I'm plumb spoiled to having my afternoon nap." After a brief silence, Pearl asked, "Are you excited about Monica's wedding? It's not that far off now."

"Oh yeah." Lacy wondered if she should attach any meaning to the abrupt change of topic. "It's going to be beautiful, Pearl, just like a fairy tale. And you'll never guess who's coming." Lacy reached across the table to grasp Pearl's wrist. "Your Cousin Fanny. She and her whole family."

"I know. She called me last night. I haven't seen Fanny in years, not since she took off for West Virginia. I'm trying to get them to stay here for a week or two. There's no point driving all that way and then turning around and going home right away. Elmer's retired now. He and Fanny can stay as long as they like. Her son and daughter-in-law have jobs, though, and Fanny doesn't want her grandkids to miss the first week of school." Pearl finished the last of her coffee. "It will all work out somehow. I have to get those upstairs bedrooms straightened up, because I invited them to stay with me while they're in town."

"That was nice of you. The girls and I can help."

"No, honey," Pearl said. "I appreciate the offer, but you've got enough on your plate with the wedding and all. I'll piddle around and take my time. If I get in a tight, I'll ask Wanda's niece to come over and work for me a couple of days." She yawned. "I think I'll head on home now. I just dropped by for a social visit."

Lacy watched Pearl make her way toward the kitchen. She walked slowly, more like an old woman than the energetic dynamo who'd dominated the Roadhouse for decades. Lacy toyed with her empty mug, turning it around several times. For the first time, she considered the reality that her mother-in-law would not be able to work many more years. In a few weeks, Monica would be living somewhere else, Cindy would be back in school, and the summer help, including Monty, would be laid off. Even though she tried to avoid talking to him, she looked forward to seeing her ex-husband at the Roadhouse each evening. What would he do without the income from the part time job? She briefly contemplated letting him stay on when the other summer employees left. Would that be an admission she wanted him nearby? If so, that might encourage him to think they could patch things up. She stared, unseeing, through the front window.

"Are you all right?"

Lacy jumped as Wanda's voice penetrated her reverie. "Yes, I'm fine." She grabbed the mugs from the table. "I just lost track of the time."

Wanda smiled. "Miss Pearl looks good," she said, pushing a cart of freshly-baked pies toward the display case. "Considering."

"Yes, she does." Lacy didn't agree with her own words. She actually thought her mother-in-law looked old and tired, and she suspected Wanda thought so, too. To be honest, she felt worn out herself. She wanted to be excited about being her own boss, making some changes and implementing her own ideas at the Roadhouse. Instead, the responsibility of making final decisions weighed heavily on her shoulders. What if she made bad choices? What if she bankrupted the restaurant? Maybe she should get out while the getting was good, and sell the Roadhouse to the big corporation that had its eye on the place. She sighed and pushed the chairs into place around the table where she'd sat with Pearl. *Too much to think about. Maybe things will be clearer after Monica's wedding.*

At lunchtime, Lacy caught sight of Monty sitting with Patty Chesterfield, the two of them with their heads close together. *That rotten alley cat.* She retreated to the kitchen. What a fool she was to buy into Monty's family man act, when all the while he was keeping company with Patty. Why was she worried about laying him off? He could eat out of garbage cans and sleep on park benches for the rest of his life as far as she was concerned. Lacy pulled pots from the dishwasher, slamming them noisily into place. Out of the corner of her eye, she saw Wanda observing her with hands on hips.

She clanged the last pan into its storage shelf and whirled to face Wanda. "What?"

The cook took a step toward Lacy.

She ran out the back door, knowing if Wanda hugged her she risked breaking down in tears. Lacy stood outside the back doorway, wondering what was wrong with her. Maybe she was going into early menopause. Or dementia. Or plain vanilla insanity. There were chores she should be attending to, but she didn't want to go back inside the Roadhouse while Monty was there with that woman. And to think, later this afternoon he would come to work and try to be nice to her like nothing was wrong. Squaring her shoulders and taking a deep breath, she wandered toward the smokehouse. This was as good a time as any to find out what Leonard knew about Julio's plans.

Chapter Thirty-Five

Monty tried to concentrate on the flyers describing homes outside his preferred area, despite Patty's brushing her hand against his more than once.

"This is everyone's dream." She pointed to a picture of a rambling ranch house shaded by a stand of sturdy oaks. "I'd give my eye teeth to live there. In addition to the fabulous home, you get five acres of land."

Monty had retreated as far as he could against the wall. When Betsy brought their food, he decided it was time to take control of the situation. "Why don't you go back and sit across from me, Patty? I need lots of space when I eat."

With a smile, she moved to occupy the space across from him in the booth. She suggested he consider renovating a house in his mother's neighborhood. There was also the possibility of demolishing an older home and going for new construction.

Monty's mind wandered. He'd noticed a marked change in Patty's attitude toward him after he'd assured her of his ability to pay cash for the Holy Trinity church building. In addition to Patty, Darrell Mabry and the business committee of a sizeable church now knew he was negotiating to buy a piece of high-priced property. Jimmy Glassman had sold him a car. He'd put a substantial amount of money into his local bank account. Polson's Crossing had grown since he was a boy, but it was still small enough to provide fertile ground for gossip. He realized he needed to open up to his mother, before she started to hear rumors.

"I'll think about the options," Monty said, when he noticed Patty was waiting for him to respond to something she'd said. "Meanwhile, if anything pops up in my Mom's neighborhood, be sure to let me know."

Patty tilted her head to gaze at him from beneath her eyelashes. "We should definitely stay in touch."

There was a time when he would have pounced on Patty's unspoken offer, but no more. Now if only he could stop wishing for a drink whenever things became uncomfortable.

On his way home, Monty stopped off at his mother's house. Pearl smiled when she opened her front door. "Come on in." She stepped aside to allow him passage. "I was just thinking about you."

"Good or bad?" he asked, stooping to plant a quick kiss on her cheek. He took a deep breath. "Your house always smells like a bakery."

"Those house decorating magazines Lacy reads say your house should smell like flowers or some such nonsense. Nothing beats an oven full of bread if you ask me. I was just mulling over what good care you took of me after my operation."

"You took pretty good care of me for a lot of years. Turnabout's fair play, they say."

"Well, I just want you to know how much I appreciate you." Pearl settled into her platform rocking chair. "Help yourself to some of that pumpkin bread I just pulled out of the oven if you're hungry."

"No, thanks." Monty sat on the end of the sofa closest to his mother. "I just had a late lunch."

"Did I tell you Fanny and Elmer are coming to Monica's wedding? They're bringing their kids, and they're going to stay with me for a week or so."

"That's great." Monty thought for a moment. "I can't remember how many years it's been since I saw them."

"Me, neither. I'm so glad they decided to come." Pearl picked up her ever-present crochet. "I noticed the Johnson kids in their backyard this morning, messing with those rabbits."

"Yeah, that's why I was talking to Patty—you know, the real estate agent—at lunchtime. I'm looking for a house, and I want to stay in this neighborhood if I can."

"You could always move in with me."

"Thank you, Mama." Monty was deeply touched by his mother's offer. "But I need a place of my own, somewhere with space for the girls anytime they want to come over and a soundproofed studio where I can make music in the middle of the night if the mood strikes."

"Just so you know you're welcome."

"I appreciate that. More than you know. Now if you think you'll be lonely…"

"Oh, no," Pearl said quickly. "Not at all."

Monty watched Pearl's hands moving rhythmically across the rows of crocheted lace. He cast about for a way to direct the conversation toward what he wanted to reveal. "Did you hear Holy Trinity Church is moving out of downtown? They're going to relocate out nearer the lake."

"Yes, Marge Freeman dropped by the other day. She told me they're worried about what will happen to the old church building. Seems like someone said a buyer wants to tear it down and build something else on that corner."

"A group from my church plans to turn Holy Trinity's building into a downtown rescue mission."

"Lord knows Polson's Crossing needs something like that. Have you seen the homeless people sleeping on the sidewalks downtown?" She continued making stitches without looking down at her work. "Is Holy Trinity giving you their old church?"

"No, Mom. They have to sell out to finance their new building. I'm buying the Holy Trinity building for the mission."

Pearl laid her crochet aside and peered at Monty. "That's a full city block of pricey downtown real estate. Where are you going to get that kind of money?"

"I'm selling some apartments I own in Nashville." Without waiting for Pearl's reaction, Monty charged on. "Did you ever hear the song, "Barely Hanging on in Old Nashville Town?"

Pearl nodded. "It played on the jukebox at the Roadhouse until I knew the words by heart."

"I wrote that, and a few other songs you'll hear if you tune your radio to a country music station, under the pen name of M.C. Montgomery. My agent is meaner than a junkyard dog, but he's a genius when it comes to making money. He persuaded me to invest most of what I've made writing songs. And, well, here I am, able to get the rescue mission started, and still live comfortably for the rest of my life if I never make another dime."

Pearl didn't appear to be as surprised as Monty expected her to be. "Well, what do you know? My little boy went to Nashville and hit the big time, just like in the movies." After a moment, she picked up her handwork again. "I figured something was going on when you bought them fancy wheels. Jimmy Glassman's a fine man. He might even give you something to drive if you needed it, but it would be a used car, nothing like what you got." Pearl rocked back and forth, her lips pressed into a thin line.

"I hope you're not upset at me for not telling you this the day I arrived back here in Polson's Crossing."

"No," Pearl answered. "I might not have believed you then anyway." She continued to rock.

Something was clearly bothering Pearl. Monty scratched his hair back. "Are you disappointed that I gave up on a singing career?"

"No, of course not. I'm proud of what you've accomplished." Pearl stacked her crochet into her lap and

194

sat with her hands folded. "Since you've come clean with me, I believe this is a good time for me to let you know what's on my mind, too."

Chapter Thirty-Six

"How would you like to buy this place?"

"What?" Pearl wasn't making sense to Monty.

"You said you want to buy a house in this neighborhood. Why not this one? The living area could use some updating, but I had the kitchen redone a couple of years ago. There's a nice, big bedroom downstairs and four more upstairs for the girls and, someday, their families to sleep over. The backyard has plenty of room for a pool if you want to go to the trouble of having one put in."

"Wait." Monty put up his hands to stop his mother's sales pitch. "You've never mentioned selling your house before today. Do you need money to pay your medical bills?"

"No. My insurance took care of everything." Pearl smiled and looked around. "I don't need this big house. And like I said the other day, I want to go see some places I've never been to. Running a restaurant is pretty demanding. Now that I'm giving it up, I don't want to be tied down any more."

"Traveling is fine, but you need a place to come home to eventually."

"I've decided to live out by the lake. It's so peaceful out there. I love the idea of having my coffee on the back porch, looking out over the water." She leaned back, causing the rocking chair to move with her. "Doesn't that sound like a little piece of Heaven on earth?"

Was his mother losing her grip on reality? Although his thoughts were racing, Monty told himself to proceed with caution. Pearl could be extremely determined once she'd made up her mind about something. "Don't you think you'd be lonely, out there all by yourself? The Wilsons and D'Amicos have lived next door to you for decades. Wouldn't you miss Dora? And Esther?"

Pearl pursed her lips and took a deep breath. "Maybe I forgot to mention that I've been keeping steady company with a very nice man." She exhaled. "He's asked me to marry him, and I'm going to do it."

Struck speechless, Monty sprang from his seat on the sofa. He ran both hands through his hair, pushing it backward, despite its unwillingness to remain there. He paced back and forth, not knowing what to say or do.

Pearl resumed her crochet as if nothing significant had been said. "Sit down, Son, and calm down. People fall in love and get married all the time."

"People Monica's age, maybe. Not yours. Please tell me this isn't someone you just met on the internet." Monty perched on the edge of the sofa, not certain he could remain seated.

"Oh, fiddle faddle. You know I don't have a computer and wouldn't know how to use it if I did." She grinned. "I've known Leonard for years. We see each other every day at the Roadhouse. Used to, anyway."

"Leonard? Leonard Berry?"

"None other." Pearl's face fairly glowed in the afternoon sunlight. "After we get back from Niagara Falls, we plan to live in his house at the lake."

"Mom, you've been alone for a long time. Are you sure you can do this?"

"Twenty-eight years, to be exact. And, yes, I'm sure." She leaned forward, reaching across the space between them to put a hand on Monty's knee. "I hope you approve. But anyway, my mind is made up."

"Have you set a date?"

"No. We're getting a license tomorrow, but I don't want to land on top of Monica's big day. Once her wedding is over, we'll have a quiet ceremony in Pastor Tom's living room and that will be that."

Still trying to process his mother's shocking news, Monty asked, "Have you told Lacy?"

"No, I went to the Roadhouse this morning, intending to let her know I wasn't coming back to work and then I was going to tell her about the plans Leonard and I have made." Pearl shook her head. "I couldn't bring myself to do it. She was too frazzled. Maybe I made a mistake turning the Roadhouse over to her. I wanted her and the girls to be financially secure. Now I wonder if I shouldn't have sold out and given her the money instead." After pausing for a moment, Pearl brightened. "You and Leonard and I are the only ones who know we're getting married, but we're not trying to keep it secret. Feel free to tell anyone you want to."

"Not me." Monty waved the idea away with a hand. "I'll let you be the one to explode this bombshell." A recent memory popped into his head. "I should have known something was going on between you two when Leonard started driving you to your medical appointments."

Pearl flashed her mischievous grin again. "You should spend some time in the little office next to the smokehouse. That's where the action is at the Roadhouse."

"Speaking of the Roadhouse, I've got to run home and get ready to go to work." Monty bent over Pearl and kissed the top of her head. "I love you, Mom. I wish you and Leonard many years of happiness together."

"Thank you. That is my prayer."

He stood straight. "You may as well go ahead and put a 'for sale' sign in your front yard. There's no reason for me to stay in this neighborhood if you're not here."

"That's too bad." Pearl sighed dramatically. "I was hoping to unload my old furniture on you along with the house."

Monty climbed into his car for the short drive around the block to the Johnson house, wondering what Lacy had been 'frazzled' about, as his mother put it. He should have asked, but the surprise of his Pearl and Leonard's upcoming marriage left him too stunned to think straight. He chuckled, realizing he was going to have a step-father. He'd always liked Leonard. He was a decent, dependable, easy-going man. Things were going to work out for his mom. He was sure of it. Now, if only the romance floating in the air would inspire Lacy.

Lacy. His heart beat a little faster at the thought he would see her at the Roadhouse this evening. Before long, he and the other temporary summer hires would be laid off. He pushed that thought from his mind. "With God nothing is impossible," he reminded himself as he pulled into the driveway.

Monty assumed the car parked in front of the Johnson's house belonged to someone visiting a neighbor. However, as soon as he opened the front door, he realized that was not the case. All five Johnson children sat in the living room. Their solemn faces contrasted starkly with the angry voices flying out of the kitchen.

"Hey, kids," Monty said, wishing he could grab them up and hug away their hurt.

The children mumbled greetings, most of them not making eye contact with him. Monty hurried toward the kitchen. He heard Janie yell, "Give it to me and I'll take my girls and go. Then you and that little witch you like so much can do whatever you want. But if she ever so much as touches one of my boys--"

Janie stopped in mid-sentence when Monty walked in. Her hand was suspended in midair, with an index finger almost touching Dexter's nose. "Hi, Morty."

Deciding it wasn't worth telling Janie she had his name wrong, Monty kept his voice calm. "May I suggest you continue your conversation in the backyard?"

"What about the neighbors?" Dexter asked.

200

"Wouldn't that be better than having your children hear you?" Monty moved across the room and opened the door that led to the back porch. To his relief, the Johnsons meekly exited the house. They continued arguing, but not at their previous volume.

"Just give me my ring," Janie said.

Dexter stood with folded arms. "Why? So you can sell it? Besides, it's not your ring. I bought it. It should just about pay the fee for my divorce lawyer."

"And what am I supposed to do? Starve my kids to get an attorney? Is that what you want? Me and your girls going ragged and hungry so you can have your floozy?"

As soon as he could, Monty interrupted the stream of vitriol. "I have to get ready to go to work. Maybe the two of you can call a truce for the evening."

"I will if he will," Janie announced. "Right now, I'm going to see about my kids." She brushed by Monty and stomped into the house.

Dexter muttered, "See what I have to put up with? She's impossible."

Laying a hand on Dexter's shoulder, Monty said softly, "The other woman isn't worth breaking up your marriage."

Dexter scowled. "You don't need to stick your nose into our business." He paused, before adding, "There is no other woman"

"Your wife seems to think there is."

"Janie is the problem. I can't do anything to please her. She's always carping at me."

Monty handed Dexter Pastor Tom's business card. "Do me a favor. Take your wife and go talk to this guy. At least you'll have the satisfaction of knowing you made an effort to work things out."

After accepting the card, Dexter poked it into his pocket. "I don't think Janie will go."

"You don't know for sure unless you ask her." Monty opened the door to go inside. "I can only tell you if I had it all to do over again, I'd make any sacrifice to hold onto my wife and daughters. But I didn't. I walked away, and I'd give everything I own if I hadn't."

All the way to work, Monty thought about the Johnson family. He doubted they'd find the diamond ring on the high bookcase shelf, not amid the hundreds of nooks and crannies in their large house. Surprisingly, neither Dexter nor Janie had asked him where the ring was. He hoped that meant something within them resisted going through with a divorce. He thought he should have talked to the couple about how Jesus could change their lives, instead of relating his own regrets to Dexter. He consoled himself he'd done the best he could, and then he prayed for divine intervention to straighten things out between the Johnsons.

It wasn't until he walked into the back door of the Roadhouse that Monty realized he'd driven by several places that sold liquor without giving any thought to stopping for something to numb the anguish he felt over the Johnsons and their children.

Chapter Thirty-Seven

One more traffic light and Monty would have been late to work. As it was, he raced through the kitchen door exactly on time. The first thing that caught his eye was Monica's tear-stained profile. He went to the stove where she stood stirring a pot of white gravy. Monty put his arm around his daughter and gave her a side hug. "What's the matter, honey?"

Monica sniffled. "I don't want to talk about it."

"Everything will be all right," he said with a conviction he did not feel. "I love you."

Monica nodded, reaching for a pepper mill.

With another squeeze, Monty went into the dining room. From near the private party room, Lacy tossed him a stern look, which he supposed had to do with walking in a minute or two after his shift started. As soon as he'd completed counting out the day cashier, he motioned Cindy to the register. "Your sister is in tears again. Do you know why?"

"I believe the issue *du jour* is the result of a remark Philip made during a phone conversation. It must have been totally egregious, because Monica won't tell me what he said, just that she's going to break up with him forever this time." Cindy rolled her eyes toward Lacy's back. "Mom told her to decide right now, this very day, whether the wedding is on or off. Because if it's off, Monica has to tell you and Grandma and Cousin Fanny in person. I mean, I think Mom would let her call Cousin Fanny, instead of going to West Virginia to say it to her face. Then she has to handwrite a real letter to every one of the wedding guests and tell them, you know, that she really wants to marry Philip even though he's criminally insane but unfortunately she's been diagnosed with Ebola and can't. Or, like, some other reasonable explanation why she's not going to float down the aisle in that gorgeous wedding dress you bought her. And then she has to go to college and be a nurse."

Monty had difficulty keeping his mind on work that evening. "I'm sorry," he said the customer who'd been standing at the register for an undetermined time. He counted twice, but later realized he had given the man ten dollars too much change.

As soon as he could, Monty ducked into the kitchen. "Where's Monica?" he asked Wanda.

"Out back." Wanda wiped her hands on a towel. "Julio came in and told her she has a flat tire." When Monty took steps toward the back door, Wanda added, "It's getting fixed."

Leaning out of the door, he saw Julio fitting a tire onto the rear axle of the car while Monica stood nearby. "It looks like Julio has everything under control."

"He usually does. I'm sure going to miss having him around." Wanda expertly arranged vegetables on plates of chicken fried steak. "If you're loose from the front counter, I could use some help plating up these orders."

"I'm sorry, Wanda. There's no one at the cash register. I was so worried about Monica I took an unauthorized break." He was about to open the stainless-steel double doors that led to the dining room when Wanda's words soaked in. "Where's Julio going?"

"He has a job offer at the high school, some kind of maintenance apprentice I think he said."

"Oh." He pushed on the door. "If things slow down, I'll come back here and help you."

"When things slow down, I won't need you."

Monty blew the cook a kiss and hurried away. The first sight that met his eyes was Lacy at the front counter, processing a customer's credit card.

"I'm sorry," he said to Lacy after the customer left. "I noticed Monica was crying and I went to check on her."

Lacy didn't make eye contact. "It's okay." She pulled out her register key and rested both hands on the counter. "What did Monica say?"

"I didn't talk to her." Monty fitted his key into place. "She's in the back parking lot, watching Julio fix her flat tire." He couldn't shake off a gnawing feeling something wasn't right. "We need to talk about her and the wedding."

"I'm listening."

"Not now. Can you meet me someplace where we can have a private conversation, just the two of us?" When she didn't immediately say no, he added, "How about breakfast tomorrow morning at The Grill?" Then he remembered how Lacy hated early mornings. "Better yet, we could drop by there tonight, after closing up, and have a late dinner."

Lacy shook her head. "No, we can talk here after closeup. We can have privacy in my office."

"All right." He'd prefer a more comfortable setting, a place where they could both relax and enjoy being served a meal. He reminded himself to be grateful she hadn't refused him altogether, which he'd feared.

An hour later, Cindy rolled the drink cart to the tables nearest the front counter. "Mom wants to know if you'd like to sing for the customers when the dinnertime rush is over." Cindy wiggled her eyebrows. "If you play your cards right, you could get a mandolin player who can sing backup and harmony."

Monty smiled. "And relieve that mandolin player from evening cleanup."

"Well, there is that. People are driving Mom crazy asking why Wayne isn't here anymore." She leaned closer. "Monica wants to know if you can meet her in the smokehouse office *tout de suite*. Meaning now if possible."

"Why?"

Cindy wrinkled her nose. "I'm not supposed to know why, only I do. But Monica said I could have her pink sweater and wear her pearl earrings with it if I keep my mouth shut for once. So, you know how it is. I really really love that sweater." She drifted away, leaving Monty puzzled.

Sensing a vibration, Monty checked his phone. He realized he'd failed to notice an earlier text from Monica asking him to come to the smokehouse. "10 Minutes," he replied. Monica could easily leave the kitchen long enough to chat with him at the front counter. Why all the cloak and dagger stuff?

Monty glanced back at his messages. The latest was from Carson Henry's agency, notifying him of preliminary work being done to produce his song, 'Three Generations of Trouble'. I nailed that one, he thought. *My wife hardly speaks to me, my mother is going into her second childhood, and now my daughter wants a secret meeting.* He sighed and put his phone aside to take a customer's money.

Right on time, Lacy took over the cash register for Monty's break. Normally he went to the kitchen to grab a snack and visit. This evening he scooted quickly through the kitchen and toward the back exit, tossing Wanda a salute as he navigated around the long stainless-steel island. The cook responded with raised eyebrows and a nod of her head. Out of the corner of his eye, Monty noticed Julio was unloading the dishwasher. He briefly wondered how Wanda persuaded him to do kitchen duty, but quickly refocused his thoughts on Monica.

Chapter Thirty-Eight

Hardly anything about the smokehouse office suggested a business operation. There was no desk, only a small table against one wall, sporting a checkerboard set up and ready to go. Here and there, chairs too worn or outdated to be used in the dining room sat in random order. A vinyl-covered recliner that had seen better days occupied a corner. The only decoration gracing the cedar plank walls was an oversized calendar hanging from a sturdy ten-penny nail.

Monica looked up without smiling when Monty entered the room. Before he had a chance to speak, she said, "Daddy, I've made a mess of everything."

"What do you mean by everything?" He sat next to Monica and slipped an arm over her shoulder.

"Don't give me any sympathy or I'll start to cry." She edged away.

Monty dropped his arm and sat with his hands in his lap. "Do you want to talk about what's bothering you?" It felt like a lame question, since she'd asked him to meet her. However, he didn't know what else to say to draw her out.

"How long do you think people should stay married before they get a divorce?" Monica turned her face toward him.

Looking into her blue eyes was like looking into a mirror. He was concerned that lecturing would push his daughter away, but a big alarm was going off in his head. "Honey, if you're thinking about divorce, you need to back up a step or two." How could he get through to her? "I know I've set a terrible example for you, always arguing with your mother, and then leaving her to raise you as a single parent. But marriage should be for life. If you don't want to be with Philip for keeps, then you can't marry him. Maybe you need to wait a while, until you're sure."

"The wedding is only ten days away," Monica said in a monotone. "I have the reprinted invitations in my car. Your car. All addressed and stamped." She took a deep breath. "Mom thinks they've already been mailed. I drive by the post office every day, but I just can't put those envelopes in the mail. That makes everything seem so--I don't know--final."

"Nothing is final until you stand before God and take your wedding vows," Monty assured her. He thought he'd whipped the alcohol demon, but now it was hitting him hard. How he'd love a drink to calm his nerves. *Lord Jesus, help me.* "Do you love Philip?"

"In a way. All through school, he was there to take me places, and talk things over. How can I break his heart now by calling off our wedding?" Monica rubbed her face with both hands. "I should have said no when he asked me to marry him. I so wish I had."

"I don't know Philip, but I'm sure he'll be hurt if you break your engagement. You have to take the long view, honey. Both of you will be a lot better off if you call a halt now than if you get hooked up in an unhappy marriage."

Monica sniffled and brushed at an escaping tear. "I guess I'll have to go to college, and I don't want to. I'm sick of school. I want to find the right guy, get married, and have a home and kids. I don't want to be a nurse, and I never did, ever."

"You must have felt differently last year, when you applied to go to college."

"No." She shook her head and took a deep, noisy breath. "As long as I can remember, Mom has made it clear Cindy and I have to get an education. Which, for Mom, means getting a college degree. She wouldn't let me alone until I chose a profession that requires going to school. I didn't know what to pick. One day I saw a movie about Emergency Rooms and I said, 'maybe I can be a nurse'. That was it. From then on I was going to State and getting my R.N., no doubt about it as far as Mom was concerned."

"Why haven't you told her how you feel?"

"I've tried a few times. You know how she is when she has her mind made up." Monica dabbed at her eyes with a crumpled tissue. "Sometimes I wouldn't turn in my homework so my grades wouldn't be good enough to get accepted to college. I kept hoping State wouldn't approve my application, but they did. When Philip asked me to marry him, I though how much easier everything would be if I left town. So, I said yes and Mom shifted into mother-of-the-bride mode. I know she's spent a ton of money on wedding arrangements, and Cousin Fanny is driving here from West Virginia, and I'll be a big disappointment to you and Mom and Grandma and everybody." The flood of tears finally broke through as Monica began to shake and sob.

Monty pulled his grown daughter into his lap and cuddled her the way he had when she was a little girl with a skinned knee. "You've never been a disappointment to me, baby. You never will be because I'll always love you. We'll figure all of this out, and it will be okay." He knew Monica's situation was mostly of her own making. Hadn't he been there and done that himself so many times? Nevertheless, something deep inside hurt in sympathy with his daughter's pain.

She nestled against him, wetting the shoulder of his shirt with her tears. "What am I going to do, Daddy?"

"If you don't want to marry Philip, you have to tell him. The sooner the better. You can't let him get on a plane and come home without knowing his wedding is canceled."

"I'll call him first thing tomorrow morning. I don't want to wake him up tonight." Monica wrapped her arm around his neck. "Will you tell Mom for me?"

"No, honey." Much as he wanted his little girl to feel better, Monty knew this was something she needed to do herself. "I'll go with you if you like, and I'll hold your hand. But your mother deserves to hear this from you." He stroked Monica's hair. "Part of growing up is taking responsibility for your actions and making things right with people when you know you've done wrong."

"She's going to be mad." Monica stood and wiped her eyes again.

Monty had to be honest. "Probably, but you can understand why. She's worked hard getting everything ready for a nice wedding. But you know she loves you with all her heart, and she only wants the best for you always.

My advice is to get this revelation over with as soon as possible. The longer you wait, the worse it will be."

"I guess you're right. I mean, I know you are," Monica agreed. "Breaking the news to Philip seems easier than trying to explain to Mom." She tossed her wet tissue into the rusty bucket that served as a wastebasket. "I'd better get back in the kitchen. I asked Julio to cover for me for a few minutes. He and Wanda probably wonder what happened to me." In a flash she was gone.

Monty took advantage of being alone to pray for his family before leaving the smokehouse office. When he cut through the kitchen, Monica was chatting with Julio and Wanda as if everything was all right. Lacy was no more distant than usual when he returned to the register. To his relief, she didn't ask why he'd taken extra time for his break.

Chapter Thirty-Nine

Lacy sat at her desk, doing her best to digest an article on cloud-based computer applications. Once the Roadhouse's financial operations were automated, she'd tackle Pearl's inventory system. Food orders were currently based on a stack of handwritten three by five cards, which only Pearl could accurately interpret. The immediate challenge was to figure out what kind of equipment and software to buy. She leaned back and laced her hands behind her head. Maybe this was something she shouldn't take on until after the wedding. Once the vacation rush was over. When things quieted down and the summer help was laid off. She sighed and put the mind-boggling literature aside.

Through the office window that provided a view of the dining room, Lacy watched Monty adjust microphones and speakers. As his mellow voice filled the air, she opened her bottom desk drawer. She leafed through the latest issue of her favorite magazine, devouring page after page of exquisite home designs. She was so absorbed the sound of the office door opening made her jump.

"I'm sorry," Monica said. "I didn't mean to startle you."

"That's okay. I was just doing some paperwork." She buried her magazine under a stack of folders. "What's up?" She patted the seat of the visitor chair, indicating Monica should sit. "Or is this a social visit?"

"I'm not sure what to call it." Monica slowly settled into a sitting position. She took a deep breath and lifted her chin "Mom, you said I should decide if my wedding is on or off." She took a deep breath, but did not break off eye contact. "It's off. Permanently. I'll call Philip in the morning and tell him."

Lacy sat in shocked silence for a long moment. "Are you sure that's what you want to do?"

"Yes." Monica balled her hands into fists, then opened them and splayed her fingers. "I feel at peace for the first time in weeks." She put a hand on Lacy's wrist. "Please try to understand, Mom. I don't want to marry Philip. I want someone who treats me like I'm special, and Philip doesn't. He acts like I'm a pal, a buddy, which I am and have been for years. But I want something more than that from my husband." She bowed her head. "I know I'm disappointing you. I'm sorry."

"Honey, I don't want you to get married to please me. If it's not right, don't do it." She glanced through the window over Monica's shoulder at Monty, sitting on a tall stool, singing an old tune. "We can't help who we fall in love with." *My impractical little princess. Exactly like her father.* Lacy relaxed into her office chair, refocusing her eyes on Monica's face.

"There's a ton of work to do to cancel all of the arrangements and uninvite the guests." Lacy took a lined tablet and picked up a pen. "I may have to take a couple of days off work." Without thinking, she added, "I wish Pearl was here."

"About the guests," Monica said.

"Yes?"

"I haven't mailed the invitations. They're still in my car."

"What?" The phrase 'herding cats' popped into her mind. Pushing down her irritation, Lacy said, "Steam the stamps off and save them, then." "I suppose that's one item off the list. Fanny and Elmer are leaving West Virginia day after tomorrow, though. You have to call them after you talk to Philip in the morning. And then you can get busy gathering up your things to move into the dorm at State."

"I don't want to be a nurse, Mom." Monica's voice was soft. "And I don't want to go to college. It would be a waste of your money."

"Monica, we've been over this a thousand times. I'm not going to have you sit home and watch old movies all day. If you don't go to school, how do you plan to support yourself?"

"Why can't I keep working here at the Roadhouse? I love to cook, and Wanda needs help."

"If Wanda needs something, she's perfectly capable of telling me that herself." *This kid has to face reality.* "What if you manage to get a job at a fast food place or as a waitress at The Grill? Then what? Do you want to spend your life standing on your feet all day, struggling to make ends meet?"

"If you won't help me, maybe Daddy will. Or Grandma. Or I'll just be homeless and die." Monica slumped for a moment, then straightened in her chair. "Anyway, I'd rather starve than go live in a stupid dormitory and spend four more years in school."

216

Lacy combed her fingers through her hair in frustration. "It's easy to talk about starving when you haven't tried it. You're going to college, and that's that."

Rising from the chair, Monica said, "I have to go and help get the kitchen cleaned up." At the door, she paused and halfway turned around. "I'm sorry, Mom. I want you to be proud of me, but I just can't do it."

Lacy rested her head on the desk. She didn't want to embarrass herself by crying in front of her employees, but she couldn't keep a few tears from falling. As quickly as she could, she dried her eyes and did her best to pull herself together. Monty was singing "Amazing Grace", which was always the last song of the evening. Maybe she could dart into the restroom and wash her face in cold water before anyone noticed her red eyes.

Lacy reached for the intercom button for the smokehouse office. She assumed Leonard and Julio were long gone. Therefore, her plan was to leave a message. To her surprise Julio answered her buzz. Lacy hoped her voice did not betray that she was upset. "I have to be gone from the Roadhouse for a day or two. I would appreciate it if you would keep things going in my absence. I'll call Leonard and Wanda tomorrow and let them know you're in charge.

"Yes, ma'am," Julio answered. "I will be happy to look after things for you."

Lacy wondered why she kept talking, but she couldn't hold everything inside. "Monica has decided to cancel her wedding. I'll be running around, undoing all of the arrangements I've made. If I get it all done tomorrow, I'll be in Thursday. It all depends on how things go."

217

Julio's voice was filled with concern. "Is Monica sick?"

"No. It's nothing like that." She doodled on her writing pad. "She has decided the wedding is a mistake."

"Oh."

He doesn't know how to react to this turn of events any more than I do, Lacy thought. After giving Julio some instructions and thanking him for stepping in, she made some 'to do' notes. Conflicting emotions battered her. She was angry at Monica for not mailing the wedding invitations. At the same time, she was relieved they hadn't gone out. Despite her determination to give both of her daughters a college education, something deep inside admired Monica's surprising display of spunk. She briefly considered going by Pearl's house on the way home. No, it was too late. Pearl was probably in bed. She couldn't allow herself to dwell on the empty feeling of having no one to confide in.

Chapter Forty

Monty watched Lacy hurry into the restroom while he sang the last verse of "Amazing Grace." Catching a glimpse of her thundercloud face, he suspected Monica had informed her the wedding was not happening. Monty put his guitar into its case and folded the music stand, shifting his eyes every few seconds to the restroom door.

A couple who'd been dancing to his music earlier came up to compliment Monty on his 'lovely voice'. He tried to be gracious without engaging in an extended conversation. He'd hoped to prepare Lacy for Monica's decision to call off her wedding, but the discussion he'd planned was obviously moot now.

Shaking off the music fans as quickly as he could, Monty locked his guitar in the storeroom. Cindy swept by. "Goodnight, Dad. Monica told me she's leaving on the dot whether I'm in the car or not. She might even mean it this time. So, I gotta go. See you tomorrow."

"Good night, sweetheart."

One by one the late shift employees tossed their aprons into the big rolling hamper and made their way out the back door. Monty stationed himself at a table near the restrooms, waiting for Lacy to appear. As the minutes ticked slowly, his concern grew. Did she slip out without him noticing somehow? Not likely. Was she sick? She'd fainted once when she was pregnant with Cindy. Was she lying on the bathroom floor, unconscious, suffering, needing help?

Julio emerged from the kitchen. "I have to go and pick up my sister. You and Miss Lacy are the only two people left. Will you see that she gets to her car safely? She's parked next to you."

"Sure, Julio. I'll be glad to. Good night." *Nice kid, Julio. Responsible. Lacy should offer him a raise and try to keep him at the Roadhouse. Her business, not mine. If Lacy doesn't come out after five more minutes, I'm going in.*

The time limit Monty set was up. He stood, intending to pound on the bathroom door, when to his relief he heard the water start running. Shortly thereafter, the sound stopped and Lacy emerged into the dining room. "Who's here?" she asked.

"Just you and me." As always, her tears melted Monty's heart. "I promised Julio I'd escort you to your car." He walked toward her. Unable to resist, he put his hands on her shoulders. "Everything is going to be all right, Lacy."

To Monty's astonishment, she leaned into his chest. "Oh, Monty, I've tried so hard with the Monica, but nothing's turning out the way I planned."

Wrapping his arms around her, He felt a rush of conflicting emotions. He hated to see Lacy cry, but holding her felt marvelous. "You've done a wonderful job raising the girls. Monica isn't in jail, or pregnant, or hooked on drugs. She's just headstrong."

"I know. Once she makes her mind up, there's no reasoning with her. She reminds me so much of you."

Monty was glad Lacy couldn't see his face. *Me? No way! She's your clone.* "I guess I can have a closed mind sometimes." *A few years ago, Lacy's comment would have been the beginning of a three-day argument. Thank You, Lord, for putting a guard on my mouth.*

Lacy took a step backward, removing herself from his arms. "I'm sorry. I got your shirt wet."

"It will dry."

She nodded. "I need to go."

Monty didn't want to end this bittersweet moment. "Have you had dinner?"

"Too much was going on." Lacy swiped a tissue under her eyes. "I must have forgotten about lunch, too. Maybe that's why I'm feeling shaky."

"Let's go out to the kitchen. I'll make us scrambled egg and bacon sandwiches. Is that still your favorite?"

"Yes." She sniffled. "But the girls will be worried about me."

"Maybe you should call them." *She didn't say no.* Before long, Monty was bustling around the kitchen. He was happy to find pans, spatulas, and seasonings stored in the same locations he remembered, despite the numerous kitchen updates Pearl had done over the years."

"I'll grab the plates." Lacy took two dinner plates from a wire rack and sat them next to the stove.

"Thanks," Monty said. "The short order cook will have your chicks on a raft ready in a jiffy, topped off with three slices of Arkansas t-bone. Why don't you just relax?"

"You know, I think I will sit down and rest a minute." She stacked the plates next to the stove and took a seat on one of the high stools tucked under the island's overhang. "I don't know why I'm so exhausted."

"Your body needs fuel." Within a few minutes, Monty served her food. He took two bottles of water from the small employee refrigerator, prepared his own plate, and sat beside Lacy. "Shall we say grace?"

"Yes. Of course." She hastily put down her half sandwich.

Monty hesitated briefly, hoping Lacy would offer her hand for the prayer. When she did not, he went ahead and gave thanks for their food.

After devouring most of her sandwich, Lacy paused long enough to say, "Monica is about to drive me crazy. Why didn't she tell me she never mailed those invitations?" She took a swig of water. "I shouldn't have put her in charge of recording the RSVPs. I'm taking tomorrow off to start undoing all of the arrangements I've made."

Monty silently prayed for the right words before he began to speak. "Maybe not mailing the invitations is a blessing in disguise. What I mean is, no one has to be to disinvite anyone."

"That's one way to look at it." Lacy took another bite.

"The rehearsal dinner was to be here at the Roadhouse, right? That's a quick one to check off the do list."

"I've already ordered the meat." Lacy paused a moment. "I can run a special on prime rib to take care of that."

"And Cindy is the bride's maid. I'm sure she can find something to do with her dress."

"No doubt." Lacy exhaled noisily. "That only leaves changing the Roadhouse work schedule, canceling the church and fellowship hall, the cake, the flowers, the photographer, the musicians, the reception, and probably a hundred other details I can't remember right now."

"Maybe if we take it one thing at a time, and split up what has to be done? We'll divide and conquer." Monty stretched his arm to take Lacy's hand, caught himself, and awkwardly shifted his motion to pick up his water bottle. "What's the worst thing that can happen? Somebody delivers a cake and there's no one there to eat it."

"You make it sound so easy."

Monty took time to consider his reply. "I don't mean to minimize the work you've put into the wedding. But this is doable. You can get through it, and I'm more than happy to help." He decided to broach something that had been on his mind, hoping not to touch off an explosion. "I'm not so sure Monica is mature enough to be getting married anyway. That's what I wanted to discuss when I asked you to take some time for us to talk privately."

Swallowing the last of her sandwich, Lacy folded her napkin. "You have a point." She pressed the napkin's crease with a finger. "She and Philip don't seem to get along very well." With a sigh, she added, "Part of the whole thing is that it's so embarrassing. You know how people love to gossip in Polson's Crossing. And now, on top of everything else, your daughter says she's not going to college. All of the sudden, she doesn't want to be a nurse anymore." Lacy sighed. "I've always wanted the girls to have opportunities I never had. Choices, and above all an education.

"It could be that Monica will change her mind about school after a while. Even if she gets started next semester or next year, that's not so bad." Monty doubted Monica was going to relent, but he hoped with time Lacy would adjust to the change to her plans. "Besides, a lot of people have good lives without getting a college degree. Look at Jimmy Glassman and his car empire. And you, owner of all this." He waved an arm around.

"This will always be Pearl's Roadhouse," Lacy mumbled.

Something about hearing his mother's name caused an idea to leap into Monty's brain. He snapped his fingers. "Hey, wait a minute. We may not need to cancel anything." He quickly began to run through a mental list of the wedding plans. He leaned forward. "Has Mom told you that she and Leonard are getting married?"

"No, but I'm not too surprised."

"You're not?" Monty was amazed that Lacy so easily accepted what he considered to be a stunning turn of events.

"No," Lacy replied calmly. "He's been in love with her for years. Pearl has changed since having cancer. I think she has decided to enjoy life instead of working all the time, and I say more power to her. But what does that have to do with—." Lacy's eyes grew wide. "Are you thinking about Pearl and Leonard using the church and everything?"

"Why not? I know neither one of them likes fancy affairs as a rule, but I remember how starry-eyed Mom was when she talked about wedding dresses and such." Monty started to clear away their dishes. "Would you like a piece of pie?"

Lacy stacked their plates. "No, I need to get home. Talk this over with Pearl as soon as you can, because I have to get busy backing out of things if she's not game."

"I'll text you tomorrow as soon as I have an update."

"Not too early." Her face relaxed into an expression that almost passed as a smile. "You know how I feel about mornings."

After helping Lacy lock up, Monty watched her drive away before starting his car. How many times had she driven home in the dark, only to get up the next morning and do it all over again? He understood why his ex-wife was so determined to give their daughters an education.

Monty parked on the street, leaving the driveway open for the unpredictable comings and goings of the Johnson family. If he didn't find a house in the next day or two, he'd have to make some temporary arrangements elsewhere. He unlocked the front door with one hand while rubbing Goldie's ears with the other. After this emotionally draining day, he looked forward to a good night's sleep. Then he'd get up early and try to be gone before the Johnsons woke up tomorrow morning.

Walking the familiar route through the dark house, he noticed an intermittent whistling sound. The source became apparent the moment he flipped on the bedroom light. Dexter Johnson was tucked into Monty's bed, sound asleep and snoring away. Monty made himself as comfortable as he could on the living room sofa, spread an afghan over his feet, and settled in for the night.

Chapter Forty-One

It was well past midnight when Lacy pulled into her garage. She'd neglected to let the girls know she was running late. Obviously, they hadn't sat up worrying about her. Creeping by the closed door of their dark bedroom, she wondered if they were avoiding her. That wasn't too surprising, since lately every conversation between her and Monica ended in an argument. Normally talkative Cindy had turned strangely quiet, seeming to disappear within herself whenever the atmosphere turned hostile.

Despite being exhausted, Lacy could not fall asleep. She tried to read, but could not concentrate. She snapped off the light and stared into the dark ceiling, while recent events played through her mind. *This constant quarreling has to stop. It won't be long before both of my daughters are out on their own. I don't want Monica to look back on her last few months at home as an unpleasant memory. Starting tomorrow, no matter what Monica says, I'm not going to take the bait. Regardless of her foolishness, I'll only give her advice when she asks. I'm going to get back to being the mom who cheers her girls on instead of nagging them. Surely Monica and Cindy understand that I've always acted out of concern for their welfare.* She curled into the fetal position and drifted into a fitful sleep.

The next morning, Lacy awoke to the jangling sound of the alarm she'd forgotten to reset the night before. She sat up in bed, debating whether to go back to sleep or give up and go in search of coffee. Coffee won. She yawned and reluctantly put her feet on the floor. The girls' bedroom door was open, the twin beds made. A note on the kitchen table told Lacy her daughters were eating breakfast out and catching a movie before their evening shift at the Roadhouse. *They're staying away from me.*

Lacy sat at her kitchen table, savoring her first cup of coffee. If it turned out she didn't have to run around to caterers and florists this afternoon, she wanted to do something fun on her day off. Something different, maybe even exciting. She traced a doodle on the table with her index finger. Her life consisted of taking care of her daughters and working. Her interaction with other people took place at the Roadhouse and at church. Other than family, the people she encountered were more acquaintances than real friends.

After pouring a fresh cup of coffee, Lacy went to her bedroom and retrieved a sketch book from the bottom of the old cedar chest. She flipped slowly through her drawings. For some unexplained reason, she'd never been able to throw them away. She rummaged further into the depths of the chest, locating pencils. While the house was quiet and empty, she wanted to fill one of the blank pages.

Lacy showered and dressed, and then spread her drawing materials on the kitchen table. How she'd missed her hobby. She was so absorbed in her new sketch she didn't notice her daughters were home until they entered through the kitchen door.

"We thought you would be gone to work," Cindy blurted. "Are you sick, Mom?"

"No. I'm fine. I just decided to take a day off." Lacy hastily closed her sketch book and smiled. "I thought you were going to breakfast and a movie."

"We were, but, uh…" Cindy tossed a pleading look toward Monica.

Her daughter's loss for words told Lacy more than she wanted to know.

"You never take a day off." Cindy sat next to Lacy and put a hand on her shoulder. "Are you sure you're okay?"

"I'm sure."

Monica filled a coffee cup and leaned against the kitchen counter. "What's that?" Her eyes were fixed on the back of Lacy's tablet.

Lacy slid a caressing hand across her sketch book and hesitated. She wondered if the girls intended to deceive her with the note about going to a movie. Would it be any more honest to offer some pretense about herself? "Don't you remember how I used to draw pictures of old houses?" She turned the pad over and opened to the first page. "If I get time today, I may start adding to my collection."

Cindy leaned and stared at a drawing of Pearl's house. "This is beautiful, Mom. It looks like a picture on a Christmas card. You even got the dormers and the roses and everything."

Lacy squirmed, not knowing what to say. She was uncomfortable with someone, even her own daughter, looking at her pictures. Regaining her focus, she did her best to keep her tone casual. "How did Philip take the news?" She glanced at Monica. "You did talk to him, didn't you?"

"That creep!" Monica gulped coffee. "Yes. I called him, and I'm never going to speak to him again as long as I live. What a loser. How did I ever think I could marry a pig like him?" She rinsed her cup and sat it in the sink. "I'm going to take a shower."

Waiting until Monica stomped away, Lacy turned toward Cindy. "I guess he didn't take the breakup very well."

"On the contrary." Cindy smirked. "Of course, I only heard one side of the conversation, but the problem is that Philip didn't go crazy and beg Monica to change her mind. Which she wasn't going to do, but the least he could have done was carry on and pretend to be disappointed even if he wasn't. Monica said she'd kill me if I ever told this next part, so act surprised if she lets it slip." Cindy leaned toward Lacy and lowered her voice. "It seems old Phil has already written Monica a letter backing out of getting married. It should be in today's mail, and that's why we decided to come home instead of going to the movie. Monica wants to watch for the postman so she can read Philip's letter and burn it before anybody else ever finds out about it." She leaned back and smiled. "She wanted to break up, but she wanted to be the breaker, not the breakee. So naturally, she's totally steamed at Philip for not being heartsick over her."

"What am I going to do with that girl?" Lacy experienced a twinge of guilt for her complete understanding of Monica's reaction. She felt the vibration of her cell phone in the pocket of her slacks. Her caller ID read 'Monty'. Leaving Cindy leafing through her drawings, Lacy walked toward her bedroom.

"Good morning." Monty's voice was, as always, cheerful. "I hope I didn't call too early."

"No," Lacy responded. "I've been up a while."

"Good. Mama's all in for using the wedding plans. She talked to Leonard, and he said whatever she wants to do is fine with him. Why don't we meet for brunch at *Le Colibri* and iron out the details? Say about 11:30?"

Le *Colibri* advertised themselves as an elegant bistro, and they were known to be the most expensive restaurant in Polson's Crossing. Lacy had never been there. However, the idea of eating a meal at a trendy place appealed to her today. She and Pearl and Monty could settle all of the wedding arrangements with one conversation in pleasant surroundings, and she would have the rest of the day to play. "All right. I'll meet you there."

She wandered back to the kitchen, considering whether she should change clothes. Monica and Cindy were at the table, falling silent as soon as Lacy appeared. She gathered her pencils into their box. "I'm meeting some people for brunch," she announced. "Do you think this outfit is all right for *Le Colibri*?"

"I've never been," Monica mumbled, fluffing her hair with a towel.

Cindy cocked her head and looked Lacy up and down. "You look perfect, Mom. *Le Colibri* is an awesome restaurant, but nobody really dresses up here in good old laid-back Polson's Crossing. Jerry took me to eat dinner there right before we broke up. Or was it Owen? Anyway, one of the clarinets. The name means 'the hummingbird' in

231

French. I looked it up. Oh, yeah, it was Jerry, because I remember him saying you have to eat like a bird there. Actually, a human-sized hummingbird would need about 70 times as much food as we do. They gobble up half of their body in weight in sugar every day. So, who are you having lunch with?"

Both girls looked at Lacy with expectant faces.

"Brunch, not lunch. Some friends of mine." Lacy smiled and stacked her ruler and pencil case on her sketch book.

"But you don't have any--" Cindy clapped a hand over her mouth for a moment before saying, "You don't have a lot of brunch dates."

"No, I don't." Lacy picked up her drawing supplies. "By the way, I plan to do some sketching afterward and I may not be home before you leave for work." She grabbed her handbag. "Don't worry about me. I'll see you tonight. Ta ta."

It probably wouldn't be long before the girls knew she'd gone out to eat with Monty and Pearl. For the moment, however, she rather enjoyed leaving them mystified. It felt good to depart the house with a smile on her face for a change, instead of regretting things she'd said to one or both of her daughters.

Chapter Forty-Two

Monty succeeded in packing his belongings into his car and leaving before the Johnson household awakened. Then he cooked breakfast for himself and his mother at her house. Pearl was surprisingly excited about a church wedding. Based on hearing one side of a phone conversation, Monty could tell Leonard was pleased with the idea as well.

After breakfast, he sat in Pearl's living room and made an afternoon appointment with Patty Chesterfield. He also chatted briefly with his Nashville agent Carson Henry. Finally, he decided it was late enough to call Lacy. He punched her number, praying she wouldn't insist on doing their business over the phone. He was elated when she confirmed their meeting. He puttered around his mother's house for a while, replacing light bulbs and emptying the trash. Finally, he could restrain himself no longer. He dropped by Darrell Mabry's law office to pick up his affidavits on the way to brunch.

Despite all his activity, Monty was early. He surveyed the available tables, and made arrangements with the hostess to seat him and Lacy near a window overlooking the downtown streets. Then he paced back and forth, avoiding the plush sofa provided in the waiting area. *Le Colibri* was too fancy for his tastes. He much preferred the blue-collar atmosphere of places such as Bob's Burger Barn and Pearl's Roadhouse. However, he'd chosen the bistro in the hope Lacy would like it. He glanced around at the elegant décor, wondering if he should have put on a tie. He had a suit stuffed in the trunk of his car, somewhere among the rest of his clothes. He hadn't worn that suit since his first meeting with Carson Henry, and was thankful he didn't need to get it pressed for his mother's wedding. Pearl and Leonard wanted a casual cowboy theme, which suited Monty just fine.

Lacy smiled and glanced around after following a group of three women into the tearoom. "Hello, Monty. Where's Pearl?"

"Hello." He resisted the temptation to kiss Lacy on the cheek. "Mom's home phoning all her friends, inviting them to her wedding."

"I thought she was joining us for brunch, to make decisions on arrangements."

"No." *Did I leave that impression somehow?* "She told me whatever we decide suits her, and Leonard said he doesn't care as long as Pearl has the wedding she wants."

"Oh."

Monty followed the hostess and Lacy to the table for two he'd selected earlier. As soon as they were seated, a server wearing a dark suit appeared. "*Bonjour*, and welcome to *Le Calibri*. My name is Marcel, and I'll be taking care of you."

Monty turned his attention to Lacy as soon as the server left the leather-bound menus for their perusal. "How are the girls this morning? Is Monica suffering any pangs of regret?"

"No, she's all right." Lacy tapped the folders she'd sat on the table. "If you've decided what you want, we can get down to business."

"Sure." *What I want is for you to give me some hope we have a future together.* "I trust you won't be embarrassed if I order in English." *Did I detect a quick smile? Please soften her heart to see that I've changed, Lord.*

"I have a hunch our waiter wouldn't know what you said if you order in French. If I'm not mistaken, he's Otis and Modena McIntosh's youngest son and his name is Buford, not Marcel." Lacy flipped open the top folder. "Monica talked to Philip. I'll check with her to make sure she calls Cousin Fanny as well." She opened another folder. "The rehearsal dinner is planned for the Roadhouse. I've already taken it off the calendar, and I'll sort out the food issue."

"Actually, Pearl and Leonard don't want to call it a rehearsal dinner, but they do want to throw a celebration party for a bunch of their friends. Let's keep the menu you planned for Monica." He kept a straight face, adding, "I've heard the food at the Roadhouse is pretty good, even if their menu is all in English."

Lacy smiled briefly. "Well, that takes care of the rehearsal dinner. I'll need a headcount a couple of days before, but Pearl knows all about how that works." She opened another folder. "Now, let's see. The church."

Taking advantage of Lacy's pause, Monty said, "Mom's okay with everything you've arranged. The same cake, flowers, photographer, and reception. I need to talk to Pastor Tom anyway. I'll let him know that we want him to officiate, but for a different couple."

"I'm sure he will insist on a counseling session with Pearl and Leonard."

"Okay." Monty was glad to have something to write down. "I'll make a note so he and I discuss that. Then I'll let Mom and Leonard know." He wrote another line. "I have a shopping date with the girls day after tomorrow. We'll get a bridesmaid's dress for Monica. Cindy already has hers, and Mom wants both of them to stand up with her. Cindy's dress is kind of fancy for a cowboy wedding, but the girls probably won't mind looking like princesses at the ball." The next topic was delicate. He took a deep breath. "Can you let me know what you've spent on the wedding so I can reimburse you?"

Lacy looked at him with a surprised face. After a long moment, she said, "I have all the numbers."

"Of course you do. I've always admired how organized you are."

"I'll get the information to Pearl."

"No, Lacy. *I* will take care of this. Surely you don't think I'd expect my mother to pick up the tab for her own wedding."

Lacy tucked her top lip over the bottom one, the way she did when she wasn't sure what to say. It was an endearing gesture that made him want to climb across the table and wrap her in a bear hug. Instead, he waited for her response.

At last she said, "I'll fix up an itemized list for you."

"All I need is the bottom line." He doodled on his pad. "You know how I am. If you give me a piece of paper I won't know where it is ten minutes later."

Marcel—or was he really Buford?—returned to take their brunch order. Monty realized he hadn't paid attention to the menu. When Lacy opted for the Eggs Benedict, he quickly said, "I'll have the same." Two breakfasts in one day wouldn't be the end of the world.

Lacy rearranged the silver-topped salt shaker and pepper mill sitting in the center of their table. "Maybe we should split the cost of the wedding. I don't imagine Pearl would choose so much what she calls 'folderol' if left to her own devices. Besides, she's been really good to the girls and me." Lacy realigned her silverware. Without looking at Monty, she added, "You know, your mother practically gave me the Roadhouse. I'm sure some people think it should be yours."

"Polson's Crossing has grown a lot since I left, but one thing hasn't changed. Half the town will state their opinion on things they know nothing about, and everyone else will listen and then talk it to death." *Help me say this right, Lord.* "I think Mom had a great idea, handing the Roadhouse over to you. It was her property, and she had every right to dispose of it any way she wanted to. Not to mention how hard you've worked to help her keep it going." He took out the envelopes tucked into his writing pad. "To show that I mean what I say, I had Darrell draw up and notarize a statement." He held out one of the envelopes. "You can keep this in case there's ever any question about ownership."

Lacy slowly put forth a hand to take the envelope. She opened it as if she expected a jack-in-the-box to leap from it. After a long look at Monty, she unfolded the paper. A frown began to form as her eyes moved over the page. "What's all this about a church building? This doesn't make any sense at all." She thrust the affidavit and its envelope back toward Monty.

One glance at the page told Monty he'd confused the two statements. "I'm sorry, Lacy. I gave you the wrong one. Like I said, you know me and paperwork." He opened another envelope and verified the words before handing her the affidavit relinquishing all claims to the Roadhouse, henceforth and forever more. "This one is for you."

Lacy took the paper from him. Her face softened, and she put a hand across her throat. It was a long time before she spoke. "You didn't have to do this." She folded the statement neatly and tucked it back into the envelope.

"I wanted to."

Chapter Forty-Three

Lacy fought hard to keep her composure. Monty had made a kind gesture, but nothing that warranted tears. She'd always hated that she cried so easily. A sad TV show or movie, even a sentimental commercial could bring tears to her eyes. An effective strategy she'd learned was to shift her attention. Slipping Monty's official-looking affidavit into a folder, Lacy asked, "What's going on with you and a church building? Are you taking up the ministry?"

She thought what she'd suggested was funny, but Monty didn't laugh.

"Not exactly." He leaned forward, his big blue eyes glowing. "Holy Trinity Church has outgrown their building, and there's no room to expand downtown. The congregation has decided to move out nearer to the lake. I'm negotiating to buy the facility and turn it into a rescue mission. Do you have any idea how many homeless people there are in Polson's Crossing now? I see men sleeping behind dumpsters and on park benches. It breaks my heart that we don't have a place of refuge for them. So Pastor Tom and a group of guys and I decided to do something about it."

"I see." Same old Monty, always dreaming miles beyond his reach. He might possibly lay the groundwork to start a mission. Then he'd disappear when he discovered hard work was involved. She nibbled at her food. "Their Hollandaise sauce is pretty good. The eggs are done perfectly, but the English muffin is tough. I don't think it's as fresh as it could be."

"I agree." Monty flashed his devastatingly handsome grin. "You'd never see such a thing at Pearl's Roadhouse. I understand the new owner is just as persnickety as the old one."

Lacy couldn't keep from returning his smile, although she'd promised herself all of her dealings with Monty were to be at arm's length. "Pearl taught me how to serve top quality food. In fact, she taught me everything I know about the restaurant business. I'll always be grateful to her for all she's done for me."

"Mama's a smart woman. I wish I'd listened to her more. It would have kept me from making a lot of bad decisions."

Lacy relaxed slightly and sipped at her second cup of coffee. It was unusual to hear Monty admit to being wrong about anything. He had always been so glib at justifying his actions. "What do you think of her remarrying after all these years of living alone?"

"Mama's pretty set in her ways, but I'm sure Leonard knows that by now. She's making a lot of big changes in her life all at the same time. I hope she doesn't regret giving up her house, but I'm not going to offer any advice unless she asks. And she hasn't." Monty's face was somber. "Mama and Leonard may not have a lot of years together. He will always have health issues from exposure to Agent Orange, and then there's her cancer episode." Monty gave his cute eyebrow shrug. "Mama says they're going to accept every day as a gift without worrying about what tomorrow may bring. I agree that's how we are supposed to live. It's Biblical."

Another surprise, Monty acknowledging the truth of the Bible. But then, he'd always had an extraordinary ability to tell people what he sensed they wanted to hear.

There was a lull in the conversation while they ate. Lacy accepted the server's offer of a coffee refill. With the wedding arrangements fairly well wrapped up, she looked forward to a leisurely afternoon. It had been so long since she'd had nothing pressing to do, she hardly knew how to handle the free time.

Lacy paid scant attention as Monty spoke more about his plans for a mission. If she didn't know him, his enthusiasm would have convinced her he was actually going to pull it off. "I can't wait to get the mission going. My priority today, though, is to find a house to live in."

"Oh?" Poor, unrealistic Monty, nursing another fantasy. Did he honestly think any mortgage company on Planet Earth was going to approve a home loan for him? "I thought you were all settled in right near Pearl."

"The family I have been house sitting for came home unexpectedly. I've seen chaos before, but these folks practice it as an art form. Plus, they have enough animals to start their own zoo." Monty grinned. "You know how fond I am of reptiles and rodents."

In spite of herself, Lacy chuckled at the idea of Monty in the same house with a snake or a mouse.

"Now I'm one of those homeless guys I mentioned. Except for the guitars locked up in the Roadhouse store room, all of my physical possessions are riding around town with me." He brushed his hair back, only to have a

241

stubborn lock flop back over an eyebrow. "I have an appointment to look at some places this afternoon, but I'm not too optimistic. I'll probably end up in a hotel or sleeping in my car."

"Yeah, home loans have really tightened up since the big crash a few years ago." Lacy couldn't help feeling sorry for him. How would her daughters feel if she let their father live on the streets? "Monty, if you need your job at the Roadhouse, I'm willing to keep you on."

"That's very kind of you, Lacy. You don't know how much I appreciate your offer. I'm sorry I made that crack about sleeping in my car. It was an ill-advised attempt at humor." He stared at her with a look she could not interpret. If it wasn't Monty, she'd call it sincere. "If you ever really need me at the Roadhouse, or anywhere else for that matter, I'll be there for you." He cleared his throat, giving every impression of being almost overcome with emotion. He'd honed his technique in the years since he left Polson's Crossing. "I expect to work at the mission full time." He ducked his head. "And I don't plan to give up my songwriting job."

Did his delusions never end? "Monty, mission work never pays much, if anything. As for songwriting, we both know how impossible it is to make a living in the music business." How many times had she tried to convince him of that?

Monty waved off the server's offer of a coffee refill, but he gladly accepted more ice water. "Did you ever hear the song 'Barely Hanging on in Old Nashville Town'?

Lacy rolled her eyes. "How could I not? People still play it at the Roadhouse all the time."

"I wrote that."

His mental condition was worse than she'd realized. "The juke box label says it was written by M.C. Montgomery." Perhaps she could persuade him to see a psychiatrist.

"Did you ever see a picture of M.C. Montgomery? Let me answer that. No, you haven't, because *Monty Chapman* Montgomery doesn't do publicity photos. Not that my fans have been clamoring for one. They want to see the singer, not the writer." He smiled. "You know that kid who worked for you a few weeks this summer, Wayne? He's recording my next release. I'm hoping it's enough of a hit to set up an endowment for the rescue mission."

Lacy slowly drained her fourth cup of coffee, mentally turning Monty's words over and over in her head. He was the same man she'd gone to school with, dated, and eventually married. He was the father of her children. And yet, at this moment he seemed like a total stranger. "Is that how you got the money to buy Monica's wedding dress? And that fancy new car?"

He nodded. "Yes. Everyone has issues. I certainly do, but right now money isn't one of them."

Her mind was in overload. He didn't need his job at the Roadhouse, after all. Then why did he work so hard? What made him go out of his way to be helpful? What was his agenda? Knowing Monty, he had one. Sooner or later she'd figure out what it was.

243

Chapter Forty-Four

Monty wasn't sure if it was the coffee or him being honest with Lacy, but she did seem more relaxed by the time the waiter brought dessert. The business partner façade gave way to a softer, though still somewhat aloof, atmosphere.

"Monica is determined not to go to college this fall," Lacy said. "She wants to keep working at the Roadhouse."

Lacy sat swirling her coffee, giving Monty the impression he was expected to comment. "Are you going to let her stay?"

"I don't know. She told me Wanda needs help in the kitchen. I've thought that same thing for a long time. But if I let Monica keep her job, it's like I'm agreeing with her choice not to go to school." She drew a deep breath. "And I just hate it."

"Is there any chance she'll change her mind?"

"I don't think so." Lacy shook her head.

"Then she's going to need to find a job somewhere. The Roadhouse pays better than any other restaurant in Polson's Crossing. That's assuming she stays here in town."

Lacy's eyes grew wide. "She wouldn't move away?"

"I don't know her plans." Monty shrugged.

"I suppose you think I should give your daughter a full-time job at the Roadhouse."

Monty knew in times past he would have jumped in with both feet, telling Lacy she was a heartless mother unless she kept Monica on the payroll. Then he'd try to guilt her into giving the girl a big raise. He held back his opinion, saying, "That's your decision."

"I'll think it over." Lacy tucked her top lip over the bottom one for a moment. "At least I could keep an eye on her at the Roadhouse."

"If it matters, I'll support you, whichever way you go."

"Thank you, Monty."

If only he'd realized years ago that he should respect Lacy's point of view instead of trying to steamroll her. He knew his superior attitude was the spark that touched off so many harsh words between them.

"Say, I have an idea. You used to love checking out houses. Why don't you go with me to look at some homes this afternoon?" He watched for a reaction, but she recaptured her poker face.

"Where are you looking?"

"I started out wanting to be near Mama, but now that she's moving to the lake, I'm not sure where I want to live." Monty held out his hand for their bill when the server was still a few feet from their table. "I have a sneaking suspicion Patty will try to steer me toward the biggest price tags without worrying about the houses that go with them."

"I appreciate the offer, but I have other plans." Ice cubes were floating in her voice again. "If you'll excuse me, I have to be going. Thanks for brunch."

"It was my pleasure. Thank you for sharing it with me."

Without waiting for him to pay, Lacy gathered her things and quickly disappeared. Monty watched her hurry away, wondering about the plans she'd mentioned. Was she seeing someone? She had every right to do so, but the thought squeezed the breath out of him. He flipped the page on his writing tablet and scribbled, "Will she ever give me another chance?"

On the way to Chesterfield Realty, Monty used his hands-free car phone to make an appointment with Pastor Tom the following day. He breezed into the office, hoping to find a suitable house immediately. "Hey, Patty. What do you have for me?"

The realtor smiled and put on her reading glasses. "You're not going to believe this. I have two fabulous homes in your preferred neighborhood." She clicked a remote control to activate a big screen mounted on the wall beside her. "Now this one is choice, just listed today. It won't be on the market long."

Monty was taken aback to see an image of his mother's house appear. "No need to go and look at that one. It belongs to my mother. I grew up there. Four bedrooms, three bathrooms, separate formal dining room, recently remodeled kitchen, well maintained, and way too many rose bushes in the yard."

"Oh." It only took a moment for Patty to regain her composure. She clicked to a different picture. "You'll recognize this home also. The Johnsons are only asking--"

"No way." Monty held up a hand to stop Patty's spiel. "I have every hope the Johnsons will rethink their situation and withdraw their listing."

Looking over the top of her spectacles, Patty frowned. "You seem to be more knowledgeable of this particular neighborhood than I am." She clicked to another image. "The area nearer the lake is really hot right now. I have this new construction that ticks all of your boxes. The builder is known for quality work. Let's take a virtual tour." With that comment, a video took over the screen, with a guided tour through the interior of the house."

"Beautiful, but it looks as if I could lean out of the kitchen window and shake hands with my next-door neighbor without either one of us going outside. And it has a cookie cutter look to it."

The next video featured a trip down a tree-lined driveway leading to an isolated ranch house. Without addressing Monty's objections about the previous listing, Patty said, "Here's a fantastic home that sits on a hundred acres of land."

"I don't want to live on top of my neighbors," Monty commented. "But I'm not interested in living out in the country either."

Monty left Patty's office thoroughly frustrated. Until now, he'd thought money was the only obstacle standing between a buyer and his dream house. After viewing dozens of virtual video tours, he concluded he leaned toward older places because they had a charming warmth. Still, he wanted a modern kitchen and bathrooms. Patty advised him he had the choice of waiting for an updated older home to be offered for sale, renovating an existing structure to his liking, or choosing a plan and waiting for a new home to be built. Regardless of what he selected, it was clear a wait was involved.

Where had the day gone? Monty realized he had only an hour before his evening shift at the Roadhouse began. That wasn't enough time to check into a hotel. For sure he didn't want to be late on a day when Lacy was off. She'd probably think he had a case of the mice playing while the cat was away. He'd have to wait and find a place to sleep after the Roadhouse closed for the evening. Wait, wait, wait. Everything he wanted to get done seemed to lead to a roadblock.

He turned toward the Roadhouse, wishing for a beer to counteract his frustration. What a disappointment. He thought he'd eliminated such thoughts from his mind forever, but here it was again. *Will I ever be free from this demon?* He prayed all the way to the Roadhouse.

Chapter Forty-Five

Lacy parked on the town square and walked through the adjacent residential neighborhood, stopping frequently to study the architectural details of the old houses built before she was born. She took pictures from different angles of the two places she decided to sketch, a stately old Victorian and a sturdy craftsman. Although she frequently wished for more free time, now she couldn't think of anything she really wanted to do. Maybe she should have accepted Monty's offer to go and look at houses for sale. Despite being an unreliable scoundrel, the man was always loads of fun to be with. No, she couldn't tolerate Patty Chesterfield fawning over him all afternoon.

Instead of leaving town after snapping pictures of houses, Lacy walked right by her car. All of the trendy stores were in the newer section of Polson's Crossing, but a few old establishments hung on around the square. She wandered into Mamie's New York Fashions and perused the racks. There was a time when she would have given her eye teeth for a dress from Mamie's. Now that she could afford to have one, there was nothing in the store she wanted. A white-haired woman asked if she could help find something, a gift perhaps? Lacy politely declined and left.

Polson's Jewel Box had an attractive display of rings, necklaces, and bracelets. Lacy gazed through the window for a long while, before strolling into the book store next door. Although most of the shelves now held magazines and newspapers, she'd loved this shop since she was a little girl. She spent a half hour choosing a mystery novel and three design magazines.

Lacy passed by the tattoo and nail salon, Watson's Café, the campy five and dime, and a musical instrument shop without entering. After completing her stroll around the square, she decided to go home and draw. She found her house empty and quiet. A text she'd failed to notice earlier told her the girls were going out for pizza with friends before work. Crazy kids, spending their money on food when they could eat free at the Roadhouse.

She spread out her project on the kitchen table, neatly arranging her sketch pad, pencils, a small tee square, and a miniature set of metal rulers she used to guide curves. Brushing away the unbidden memory of receiving her rulers from Monty one Christmas, she located her photo of the Victorian style house and began to draw its elegant outlines. Lacy hardly noticed the passage of time until the waning sunlight broke her concentration. She stood and stretched and admired her finished work.

Satisfied with her drawing, Lacy packed her materials and stashed them in her bedroom. She wandered through her small house, flipping on a few lights, pondering what to have for dinner. She was making toast for a sandwich when her phone jangled. She answered immediately, assuming something at the Roadhouse demanded her attention. Instead, a man's voice said, "Ms. Chapman?"

"Speaking." Maybe it was time to change her phone number. Too many people had this one.

"Hello, this is Steve Thornton. How are you this evening?"

"I don't participate in surveys or polls, and I'm not interested in whatever you're selling."

"Very wise of you," Steve said smoothly. "I noticed that you are the new owner of Pearl's Roadhouse. I was wondering if we could get together and talk over my company's interest in acquiring your property."

"No, thank you," Lacy switched the phone to speaker mode while she spread mayo on her toasted bread.

"We are prepared to make a generous offer," he persisted. "We would also consider leasing the property back to you for a time, allowing you to operate your restaurant under our ownership."

"I'm sorry, Mr. Thornton. Pearl's Roadhouse is not for sale." For some reason, she added, "Right now."

"Please call me Steve. I understand your position. May I contact you again in a few months, in case your circumstances change?"

All Lacy wanted at the moment was to end their conversation and enjoy her sandwich. "That would be all right I suppose."

"Great. Thank you. I'll look forward to speaking with you again."

Lacy leafed through a magazine while eating. She knew without being told that Pearl hoped the Roadhouse would stay in the family. However, it couldn't hurt to find out what Thornton meant by 'generous'. Maybe Monica would come to her senses and start college next year with

Cindy. What would they want with a restaurant after graduating with professional degrees?

A magazine ad for a contest caught Lacy's eye. 'Design your dream home' it challenged. The grand prize was a scholarship for a correspondence course in architectural design. She suspected a scam, but dog-eared the page anyway. It would be challenging to create a house plan, even if she stuck it in a drawer along with her drawings.

The hours dragged by after dark. Lacy was more than relieved when she heard her daughters pull into the driveway. She buried her magazines under a stack of bridal publications and threw open the door to welcome her girls home.

When they were settled in their favorite living room seats, she asked if Monica had remembered to call Cousin Fanny.

"I did," Monica said. "And--"

"They're coming to Polson's Crossing anyway," Cindy broke in.

Chapter Forty-Six

"Come in and sit down, Monty. How about a spot of tea?"

"Thanks for making time for me," Monty replied. "Tea would be great."

Pastor Tom closed the door of the tiny refrigerator that sat in the corner of his office. He handed a cold can of tea to Monty and pulled out a bottle of water. After taking a sip of water, the pastor settled into an easy chair next to Monty. "What's on your mind?"

"So many things I had to make a list." Monty took a slip of paper from his shirt pocket. "You're scheduled to do my daughter Monica's wedding here at the church next week. There's been a slight change in plans. Monica has broken off her engagement."

"I'm relieved. I talked to Philip on the phone and spoke with Monica and Lacy here in my office. I told all three of them, separately, they should step back from this wedding. My assessment is that neither Philip nor Monica is truly committed to the other."

"You hit the nail on the head, Pastor," Monty said. "However, there's another wrinkle. My mother and Leonard Berry are getting married. We're all hoping to have the ceremony here at the church, with you officiating, same time, same day, same reception in the fellowship hall, basically keeping all of the arrangements the same except for a different bride and groom."

"Pearl? And Leonard? Getting married?" Tom held his bottle of water suspended halfway between the end table and his mouth for a moment. "He has been chasing after Pearl for years, but I never thought he'd catch her."

Monty wondered why everyone else seemed to know Leonard had a thing for his mother, while he'd had no clue. "I never dreamed Mama would remarry. She's been a widow for a lot of years."

"It just goes to show, it's never too late. I'll call and set up a counseling session with Pearl and Lenny." Tom smiled. "I want to make sure these two youngsters realize what they're getting into."

"Good deal." Referring to his handwritten list, Monty said, "I've housesat for a family this summer, the Johnsons. They live near Mama, and I'm pretty sure they don't go to church anywhere. Now they're discussing divorce. They've already put their house up for sale. Will you talk to them? To tell the truth, I wouldn't want to live in the same house with either one of them, but they have five kids to consider."

"Once a couple starts down the road to a divorce, it's very difficult to turn them around, especially if they're not believers." Tom's face was solemn. "I'll be glad to talk with them, but don't be surprised if they refuse." He uncapped his water and took a swig before continuing. "My suggestion is to tell them your story, without glossing over anything. You probably have more influence with these folks than I do, because they know you."

"I'll see what I can do." Monty returned his reminder list to his shirt pocket. "That brings me to my other topic. He showed Pastor Tom the affidavit he planned to give the leadership group at Holy Trinity Church. They talked about plans for the mission, discussing the possibility of a special campaign to gather the bedframes, mattresses, and linens for the men's dormitory. "I may be the first homeless person the mission serves," Monty said, half-seriously. "I slept at the Highway Motel last night, but that place is depressing."

"Doesn't your mother have some spare bedrooms?"

"She does," Monty said. "I didn't want to wake her up last night, and I'm not crazy about living in her house while it's up for sale. I'm not the neatest guy in the world. He finished his tea and stood. "I've taken up enough of your time. Thanks for everything."

Pastor Tom remained seated. "How are things with your wife and kids?"

"I'm developing a relationship with my daughters." Monty sank back into the chair. "As for Lacy, I don't know. Sometimes she seems friendly, and then she pulls back into her shell. It's like there's a fence between us, and I can't find the gate. At least she will speak to me now. I guess that's progress."

Tom nodded. "You're familiar with the Bible's description of love in the thirteenth chapter of First Corinthians?"

"Yes," Monty said. "It's one of my favorite passages."

"Then you know the first characteristic listed is patience."

"You're right. I never thought about the order."

"I could be wrong." Tom shrugged. "But I've always thought there's significance in patience being first, followed by kindness and then the rest of the list."

"Ending up with the promise that 'love never fails' as I recall."

"Right," Tom agreed. "Keep in mind, though, God's definitions of success and failure are different from ours."

"Yeah." Monty stood again, and shook hands with the pastor. At the doorway, he turned and said, "One more question. Am I ever going to stop being tempted by alcohol?"

"I don't know," Tom admitted. "Some people say they never wanted another drink after they quit. Others tell me they have to fight the urge every day."

Monty nodded. "I'm somewhere in the middle, I suppose. When I'm busy and things are going well, everything is all right. Then I get lonely, or down on myself, and I think a beer or a glass of wine would help me feel better. I know that's not true, because I don't have what it takes to stop at just one. As much as anything, I'm afraid someday I'll give in, even though in my heart I know that's a terrible thing to do."

"Now that you've identified the triggers, you can plan ways to avoid them as much as possible." Pastor Tom stepped forward and put an arm on Monty's shoulder. "Faith and prayer are vital to staying clean. You know, there are at least three hundred and sixty-five times where the Bible says in one form or another not to be afraid. That's one for every day."

"Thanks, Tom." Monty turned to leave.

"You can call me anytime, day or night, and we'll pray together or talk. Whatever you need," Tom assured him.

In the car, Monty checked his messages. There was a text from Wayne Houston, thanking him again for his help. Perfect timing, Monty thought. *I needed the encouragement of being of benefit to someone.* Much as he disliked the Highway Motel, he headed back there for a quick shower before going to work at the Roadhouse. There was an overpriced hotel downtown, and several motels around the lake. However, he wouldn't have time to move tomorrow. He had a breakfast meeting with the deacons and elders from Holy Trinity, and then he was taking his girls shopping. Maybe Patty could recommend a furnished apartment if she didn't find a house that suited him in a day or two. He had to get away from the musty smell and buzzing neon signs at the Highway Motel.

Chapter Forty-Seven

Monty walked out of his breakfast meeting with the leaders of Holy Trinity Church praising God. Things got off to a good start when Reverend Buckley informed the group Holy Trinity Church was officially being designated an historic site. He followed up by announcing the church had a full price cash offer from a prospective buyer.

There were numerous 'amens' after Monty was introduced and spoke about his plans to turn the church into a rescue mission. By the time he passed out copies of his affidavit guaranteeing the return of the building to Holy Trinity's ownership if the mission failed, there was no doubt in Monty's mind the deal was as good as done. He excused himself before Reverend Buckley called the meeting to order to consider and vote on accepting the offer.

Monty picked up his daughters for their shopping spree with a light heart. He reminded himself to let the girls do the talking instead of babbling on about his own hopes and dreams. He smiled when they came hurrying toward his car as soon as he turned into Lacy's driveway. They were probably much more excited about going shopping than being with their dad. Still, it felt good to be greeted with his daughters' enthusiasm.

Not far down the road, Cindy leaned into the space between Monica and Monty. "You know, Dad, I've been thinking my bridesmaid's dress is too fancy for Grandma's cowboy theme. Don't you agree Monica?" Without waiting for an answer, she burbled on. "I could save the dress I already have for prom next spring. That means nothing would be wasted. And then Monica and I could find something more suitable for Grandma's wedding. You know, more western-looking. What do y'all think?"

Monty glanced at Cindy's perky face in the rear-view mirror. "I think you've come up with a scheme to wangle another dress out of your old man."

Monica rolled her eyes. "You're busted, Cindy."

Cindy sat back and adjusted her seat belt. "I mean, we don't want to be inappropriate on this auspicious occasion, since it's pretty sure our grandmother isn't ever going to get married again after this."

With a hearty laugh, Monty said, "That's what I thought for a lot of years, but look at her now. Do you have any idea where we would go to find a proper western bridesmaid's fashion?"

"Cowgirl Couture," the girls said in unison.

Monica added, "It's at the Lakeside Mall."

"I smell conspiracy," Monty said, turning toward the highway. "Why don't one of you call the blushing bride and see if she wants us to pick her up for a late lunch after we cut a swath through the mall?"

While Cindy chatted on her phone, Monty asked Monica, "How are you doing?"

"Good," she responded with a smile. "I thought at first Mom was going to throw me out of the house."

"And now?"

"She's still mad at me, but she's not yelling so much anymore."

"Okay, we're all set," Cindy announced from the back seat. "Grandma said she can't go anywhere because she's getting ready for Cousin Fanny and her family. So, she wants us to come over to her house for lunch. Dad, she said to tell you she's making banana pudding for dessert."

"I don't know how we can turn down an offer like that." Monty offered up a silent prayer of thanksgiving. This was the kind of day he'd hoped for when he moved back to Polson's Crossing.

Three hours, two dresses, and two pair of western boots later, Monty pulled into Pearl's driveway. She must have been watching for them, since she threw open her front door and opened her arms for the girls to snuggle into. After hugging and kissing each of her granddaughters, Pearl bearhugged Monty and pecked his cheek. "I'm so glad you called. I was wishing for someone to share lunch with, and Leonard's busy at work." She ushered them into her dining room, where the table was elegantly set with Pearl's good china.

"What's going on?" Monty asked. "I don't remember these dishes ever being outside the china cabinet."

Pearl removed her apron and set it aside. "I decided there's no point keeping stuff around unless I'm going to use it. This tablecloth belonged to my grandmother. She brought it over on the boat from Ireland. Now, sit yourselves down. Monty, you say grace and we'll have something to eat."

Monty passed a platter of sandwiches, followed by a bowl of potato chips, and a tray of assorted veggie sticks.

"What kind of chips are these?" Monica asked. "They're so crispy and delicious.'

"They're just plain garden-variety chips." Pearl took strips of raw zucchini, carrots, and celery before passing the vegetable tray along. "I made them this morning."

Monica stared at her grandmother. "You *made* the potato chips yourself?"

"You don't have to look so shocked, honey," Pearl answered. "There's not much to it. Use an iron skillet and make sure the oil is good and hot. And, of course, you need one of them mandolin doodads to slice the potato up real thin. I'll show you how to make them sometime."

"I'd like that." Monica lifted the top slice of bread on her sandwich. "Mmm, chicken salad. My favorite. I bet you made that, too."

"Sure did. I baked the bread this morning, too. It's sourdough."

"Oh, wow, this is too far over the top to be called lunch," Cindy chimed in. "We're having *dejuner*. That's French for lunch."

"Nothing French about this meal. It's pure Polson's Crossing." Pearl chomped a carrot stick before asking, "I guess you're still hung up on studying them Frenchmen in college?"

"No, ma'am." Cindy beamed. "I've changed my mind. I want to major in accounting."

"What happened to French history?" Monty asked.

"I looked up statistics on the best paying occupations and decided I want to be a CPA. I'm getting ready to apply for scholarships to some out-of-state schools."

Monty stared at Cindy for a long moment. This was the first time he'd heard any hint of his daughter wanting to go away to school. Finally, he said, "Are you sure you don't want to stay close to home?"

"The closest school I'm applying to is about a thousand miles from here." Cindy crunched a chip. "I checked it out on the internet. Needless to say, a scholarship is a long shot. If I don't get one, then I'll have to go to State. That's seventy-four miles from our house as the crow flies. I don't know why a crow would want to fly from here to there. If there are any crows in Polson's Crossing. they could catch a ride on top of a freight train or a semi and save a lot of energy."

Monty wondered if Lacy was in agreement with Cindy's plans. "How does your mother feel about all of this?"

"We talked about changing my major," Cindy replied. "I may not have mentioned going to an out-of-state school yet.

Pearl chuckled. "Any time I think I'm beyond surprising, someone in this family finds a way to prove me wrong."

"I know exactly what you mean." Monty raised his eyebrows and tilted his head toward Pearl, causing the girls to giggle.

"Dad bought us bridesmaids dresses and new boots for your wedding, Grandma," Cindy said breathlessly. "Do you want to see them?

Pearl smiled and said, "Okay, you girls put on your finery, and I'll model my wedding dress for you. Monty, you can take pictures of us."

Monty wondered what got into his mother. As a rule, she shunned frou-frou. Now she seemed as excited as his teen-aged daughters. What was it about weddings that seemed to capture every female's imagination? That train of thought brought him back to Lacy. If she ever said 'I do' to him again, he wanted to make sure they had a fitting celebration to mark their fresh start.

By the time he dropped off the girls, it was time for Monty to go back to the Highway Motel and get ready for work. He noticed two messages from Dexter Johnson and three from Janie. A notice from his bank let him know his personal financial arrangements were in order for his purchase of the Holy Trinity property. Just in time, too, because Patty Chesterfield's message said she'd set up closing for the following day. There were several email bids from contractors interested in renovating Holy Trinity to make it suitable for a rescue mission.

Before leaving his motel room, he sent one reply to both Johnsons, who'd asked when he could drop by their house and locate the ring they were searching for. There wasn't time to review the contractor bids. That would have to wait until later. He had to admit he was looking forward to completing his employment at the Roadhouse. There weren't enough hours in the day to spend time with his family, get the mission up and running, and work the evening shift.

Chapter Forty-Eight

"Haven't I seen you two somewhere before?" Monty kidded Monica and Cindy as the three of them entered the Roadhouse through the kitchen's back door.

"Miss Lacy's called a group meeting," Wanda said without turning away from the stove. "You'd better get a move on."

Miss Lacy? She must have inherited that title when she took ownership of the Roadhouse.

In the dining room, Lacy motioned for everyone to gather in the corner where she held meetings. "I have a few quick announcements before we get to work." When the employees clustered around her, she smiled. "I want to thank everyone for a great summer. All of you will find a bonus in this week's paycheck in appreciation for your hard work. I realize some of you have other plans." Her eyes rested on Monty. "But I'm hoping everyone comes back next year."

She drew a deep breath. "As you know, Miss Pearl had a health issue. She's recovering well, but she isn't coming back to work. She and Leonard are retiring and getting married. Those of you who aren't working Friday night are invited to what they're calling their wedding supper." Spontaneous cheering broke out, causing Lacy to pause until it died down. "Julio Chapa has decided to remain at the Roadhouse, replacing Leonard." There was more applause and a sprinkling of whistles. "Finally, my daughter Monica will be working full time in the kitchen as Wanda's assistant and understudy."

Monica began to cry. She moved next to Lacy and hugged her while everyone cheered again. "Thanks, Mom."

"Stop that, or you'll get me started, too." Lacy's warning was wasted. A single tear escaped from each eye.

Monty shook hands with Julio. "Welcome to the family."

Julio did a double take before displaying a broad smile, "Thank you, sir."

Wading through the crowd, Monty reached Monica and embraced her. "Congratulations. I hope you learn to cook as well as Wanda, but hopefully you won't be as bossy."

Monica laughed and wiped tears. "Thanks, Dad. I don't know why I cry when I'm happy."

"It's genetic." He released Monica to other well-wishers, and leaned toward Lacy, "I'm so proud of you," he whispered.

Lacy rewarded his comment with a bright smile. Then she dabbed at her eyes and said "Well, back to work," quickly disappearing in the direction of her office.

The dinner crowd showed the effect of the waning season. At eight-thirty, Monty retrieved his guitar, leaving Cindy in charge of the cash register. He sang country songs he'd loved since he was a child. Meanwhile, his mind wandered. He mulled over his plans for the following day. He'd promised to drop by the Johnson home before the appointment to close on his building. If he was going to vacate his motel room without paying for an extra day, he'd have to pack up and check out either late tonight or early in the morning. Then what? He hadn't made a reservation elsewhere, and he hadn't heard a peep from Patty about an apartment. It wasn't until he was closing his program with 'Amazing Grace' he realized he could sleep in one of Holy Trinity's buildings after he officially owned the property. The church's sanctuary had old-fashioned pews a man could catch a decent night's sleep on. Problem solved, at least temporarily.

At closing time, Monty helped Cindy count out the register. "I'm glad Julio decided to keep on working at the Roadhouse," he said as he opened the zippered pouch used for the Roadhouse's bank deposits.

"Me, too." Cindy took the twenties from the register and began to count them.

"I wonder what made him change his mind."

Cindy giggled. "Oh, my, I have to start over counting. You tickled my funny bone."

"How?"

"Dad," Cindy restacked the twenties into her left hand. "You need to take more smoke breaks."

Monty was puzzled. "You know I don't smoke, Cindy. I never have, and your mother I don't want you or Monica to start, either."

Cindy held up a hand. "Please. Not *that* kind of smoke break. That's the term for hanging out in the smokehouse office when we take our work break. Break. Smokehouse. Smoke break. Get it?"

"Yes, I get it. What does it have to do with Julio agreeing to take Leonard's job instead of going to work for the school?"

"The smokehouse is where you find out what's going on." Cindy giggled. "I'm pretty sure Julio isn't staying because of the nice office he's getting." With another laugh and a roll of her eyes, she said, "Haven't you noticed he has a monster crush on Monica?" She glanced left and right and lowered her voice. "Don't tell her I said that, or it will be bye-bye pink sweater." She hopped from the counter's stool and handed him the twenty-dollar bills. "If you'll count these for me, I'll run and help straighten up."

While he counted money, Monty wondered if Cindy was exaggerating Julio's attraction to Monica. Surely he would have noticed if there was any substance to Cindy's gossip. She was probably imagining the whole thing or embroidering it into something more interesting than it truly was.

The following morning Monty bounded out of bed, excited about the day before him. After gathering his few possessions, he checked out of the motel and grabbed a fast food breakfast. He drove to the Holy Trinity parking lot, although he did not yet have keys to the buildings. If he wasn't able to go inside the church, he would pass some time at the downtown library. He smiled, reminding himself Holy Trinity was no longer a church. As of today, it was officially a mission, a dream come true.

There was a car parked behind the church, which Monty was fairly certain belonged to Reverend Buckley. He tried the back door, but it was locked. No one responded to his knocking. As he walked along the sidewalk to toward the front of the church, an elderly man approached him. "Hey, buddy, can you spare some change?"

Monty took in the man's appearance. He hadn't shaved in a couple of days, and his clothing had seen better days. He had a trash bag slung over his shoulder, probably containing everything the man owned. With a rush of compassion, Monty offered his sack of food to the man. "I drank the coffee already, but here's some breakfast if you want it."

The old man accepted the bag. After peeking inside, he took out a bagel and dumped the other contents onto the sidewalk. "No good junk food," he muttered, and walked on.

"You're welcome," Monty said after the man disappeared around the corner. He cleaned up the sidewalk as well as he could and tossed the dusty remains of his breakfast into a trash can on the street corner. When he tried the front entrance to the church, it opened. Monty stepped inside the foyer, admiring the classic beauty of the architecture. He pushed through the double doors leading to the sanctuary and was met by the stunning sight of Reverend Buckley pushing a wide broom across an empty floor. What made him think there would be pews left for him to sleep on? Of course, Holy Trinity's congregation took their furniture with them.

"Good morning." Reverend Buckley stopped sweeping and swiped a handkerchief across his forehead. "We've had everything professionally cleaned, but I noticed a spot or two they missed."

"That's very nice of you." Monty went over and shook hands with the Reverend. "Everything looks great."

"Yeah." Buckley leaned the broom against a wall. "I know it's only a place, and we can worship God anywhere." His eyes moved around the interior. "But I'm sure going to miss this old church house. It holds many years of good memories."

"We're recycling," Monty said. "Her life as a neighborhood church is coming to an end, and she's being reborn as a rescue mission."

"Amen." Buckley took up his broom again. "I'd better finish up and change clothes. I don't want to be late to our closing."

Monty nodded. "I'd like to unload a few things from my car if that's all right."

"No problem." The Reverend pulled a chain from his pocket and separated the keys. "This is the master. It fits all of the church doors. The other individual keys are all labeled and laid out on the counter in the kitchen." He took out a smaller key ring. "These are for the parsonage."

Monty had explored every square inch of the church, but he'd never paid any attention to the parsonage.

Chapter Forty-Nine

Monty locked up and stood surveying the property that was soon to be his responsibility. The church building faced Main Street. A two-story house backed up to the parking lot. Since it was constructed from the same dark red brick as the church, he concluded the house must be the parsonage he was about to purchase. How did he manage to overlook that major detail?

When the key fit the house's back door, Monty's suspicion was confirmed. He stepped into a large, old-fashioned kitchen that reminded him of his mother's place. Poking around, he discovered the house was spotlessly clean and totally empty. His footsteps echoed on the worn wooden floors as he toured the upstairs. If he installed bunk beds, men could sleep in the four spacious bedrooms in the house until the dormitory was ready. Plus, he could camp out in the parsonage while managing renovations to the church building.

At closing, Patty Chesterfield pressed her lips together firmly for a moment after Monty informed her he was suspending his house hunting for a while. "I understand," she said, with a tight smile that did not reach her eyes. "I'll let you know if something irresistible comes on the market."

Monty nodded. "Sure. Okay." His mind was racing ahead of the formalities of the moment, cataloging the numerous errands he needed to get done before this evening's celebration dinner. Somewhere in the midst of ticking items off his do-list, Monty checked his messages. Cindy sent him a cartoon, Dexter Johnson told him to "come now", and his agent left instructions to call him. A voice mail from Pearl said Fanny and Elmer had arrived. He grabbed a sleeping bag and a few other necessities at a discount store and drove toward his mother's neighborhood. On the way, he gave his car the voice command to phone the Johnsons.

"I'm on my way to your part of town," Monty said. "I'll stop by your house if both cars are there. I want to see the two of you together."

"She's here," Dexter replied. "Come on over."

As soon as Janie ushered Monty into her house, he went to the living room bookcase. He stretched to take down the small glass bowl where he'd stashed the diamond ring he'd found in the front yard. Sitting at the cluttered dining table with Dexter and Janie, he held the bowl in his hands while sharing how he regretted his divorce. "Our kids suffered more than either one of us," he told them. "I'll never be as close to my girls as I could have been if I'd stayed around and raised them." While he told his tearful story of how accepting Christ turned his life in another direction, the Johnsons sat with stony faces. Finally, he urged the couple to have at least one counseling session with Tom Gillespie, but both were noncommittal. He'd already given them Tom's business card. Nevertheless, he tucked two more in the bowl with the diamond ring and left.

Time was getting away from Monty, but something other than visiting his mother would have to be put off until tomorrow. He parked at the curb in front of Pearl's house and made his way by the two huge recreational vehicles that filled her driveway. Instead of answering the doorbell, a male voice from inside said, "Come on in. The door's unlocked."

Monty stepped into the living room, where his mother sat in her platform rocker. Fanny, older but still recognizably Fanny, occupied the sofa. The ample fabric of her bright, shapeless dress floated outward in every direction. The man in the recliner must be Elmer. He wore a plain white tee shirt and plaid Bermuda shorts held up by a pair of old-fashioned red suspenders. Elmer's cowboy boots were more appropriate for winter than for a warm summer afternoon in Texas.

"My goodness, Monty." Fanny came and hugged him. "We thought you were the kids, coming back from the grocery store. Now that I think about it, it did seem like they were getting back awful early." Fanny stood back, holding him at arm's length. "Last time I saw you, you were just a little tow-headed kid. Look at you now, all grown up and good-looking as all get out."

Monty smiled down at his mother's cousin. "How come I've aged and you haven't?" he asked.

Fanny laughed and returned to the sofa. "You've learned how to flatter the ladies, I see."

After kissing the top of Pearl's head, Monty shook hands with Elmer. "You must be the man that stole Cousin Fanny's heart."

"That's me," Elmer replied with a glowing smile. "Excuse me for not getting up. I'm all stove up from our long drive."

The group chatted about the distance from West Virginia, with Fanny describing their unexpected stopover for a minor repair to their RV's engine. Meanwhile, Elmer dozed in the recliner.

"Which one of your RVs broke down?" Monty asked, more to participate in the conversation than from curiosity.

Fanny looked startled. "The only one we have. That maroon jobbie, sitting out there in the driveway."

"The silver one is mine." Pearl leaned forward in her rocker. "I figured since Leonard and I are going to see the country, we may as well do it in style. I'm too old to start flying around in airplanes."

"Did you get your RV from Jimmy Glassman?" Monty hardly knew how to cope with the changes in his mother.

"Sure did," Pearl answered with a grin. "He brought it over himself last night. Come on outside and I'll show you all the bells and whistles. This thing has more gadgets than a TV remote."

Fanny stood and stretched. "While you're doing that, I'm going to go out back and make sure my grandbabies don't tear up your flower beds." She glanced toward her sleeping husband. "I ought to wake Elmer up so he can sleep tonight." Without doing what she'd said, Fanny ambled toward the kitchen.

Holding the front door open for his mother to exit, Monty asked, "Are you ready for your wedding?"

"I'm as giddy as a teenager." Pearl waved a hand toward her RV. "Ain't she a beauty? You're going to think I'm crazy, but right now I'm saying cancer has been a blessing. It woke me up to realize there's more to life than work." She strode forward, opening the door to the silver vehicle. "Now if I can just get this house emptied out and sold, I'll be as carefree as a little bird."

"You're sure you want to get rid of your house?" Monty followed Pearl, stepping up into the huge RV. "No second thoughts?"

"Nope. Not a one. Leonard has already moved most of my clothes and grandma's buffet. He took the last load over to his place this morning, sentimental things like pictures, and my collection of recipes. Everything that's left is either going to be sold or hauled off to the junk yard."

"If you really mean that, I'll buy your furniture."

"You don't need to pay me." Pearl fluffed a pillow. "Pick out what you want and Leonard will help you get it where it's supposed to go." She settled at one end of the sofa. "I guess that means you found a house."

"Sort of." Monty sat beside his mother, looking around at the inside of the RV, feeling claustrophobic. "When I bought Holy Trinity, I got the parsonage with it. I was so excited about the church building I glossed over any talk about the house. Now I'm thinking I'll live in it while the renovation is being done." He turned toward Pearl and smiled. "As you can imagine, I need a lot of furniture to fill up that big, old parsonage."

275

"You're welcome to the whole kit and kaboodle, but it'll take more than Leonard's pickup to hold it all." She leaned her head back and closed her eyes. "Clearing out the house is about the last hard thing I have left to do."

"Here's an idea. I'll get a moving company to come and pick everything up after you and Leonard leave on your honeymoon. While you're gone, I'll get your house cleaned and staged and turn the keys over to your real estate agent. We'll call it even."

Pearl sat up and smiled. "Oh, honey, that would be such a load off my mind. If you do that, then Leonard and I can take off for Niagara Falls right after the wedding, without having to get this house ready to sell. You've got yourself a deal." She reached and laid her hand over his. "You're a good son, Monty. I've been meaning to tell you that for a while. I had my doubts when you first came home, but that's all in the past."

"Thank you, Mom. That means a lot to me." Monty had a glimmer of understanding why Lacy cried when she was happy. He felt he could dissolve into tears if he didn't get a grip. "Hey, I have wedding gifts for you and Leonard in my car. I'll go get them and you can open yours now."

Chapter Fifty

Leaving the Roadhouse in the middle of the afternoon to go home and dress felt peculiar to Lacy. She ran through a mental checklist for the evening's festivities. Cindy had done a good though greatly overstated job of decorating. With Monica's help, Wanda had preparations for the evening meal well in hand. She couldn't help worrying about the extra servers hired for this evening, but Julio assured her the temps would show up. Things were proceeding as much as possible according to the plan.

So why was she so jittery? She'd managed the Roadhouse independently for several weeks now. However, she'd always known Pearl was only a phone call away. Now her mother-in-law would be on the road, often out of touch, and on top of that taking Leonard away with her. Although Lacy was happy for the couple, she was uncertain about facing the future of the Roadhouse on her own. Maybe Monica's decision not to go to college wasn't such a bad thing after all, since she'd be at the Roadhouse when Lacy needed someone to talk to. She was so deep in thought she failed to notice the traffic light changed.

The next few minutes were a blur. Lacy later remembered realizing she couldn't stop in time to avoid rear-ending the pickup truck sitting still in front her. She couldn't recall the moment of impact, except for the awareness of a terrible crashing noise. She sat with her head leaning against the steering wheel, afraid to look up.

"Are you all right?" A man tapped on the window.

Lacy grabbed her handbag from the floor and opened her door. "I don't know. I think so. What about you? Are you hurt?"

"Banged up, but otherwise okay," he answered.

Stepping out of her car, Lacy became aware her knees hurt. "I'm so sorry. I just didn't notice you had stopped." For the first time, she realized her car was sandwiched between the pickup and an SUV. Apparently the driver behind her couldn't stop in time, either.

The man grunted. "The cops should be here before long. I called them before I got out of my truck." He took out his wallet. "I hope you people have insurance, because this is not my fault."

Lacy fumbled to find her driver's license while people steered their autos around the wreck and through the traffic light. Standing on the sidewalk, she took pictures of the accident and the other drivers' licenses and insurance cards.

After a few minutes, the man in the pickup observed, "My tailgate's messed up, but I think I can still drive my truck. I'm not so sure about you two. Your front ends are in pretty bad shape."

The third driver, who up to now had not spoken a word, said, "My brother-in-law works at a service station. He's coming to help me."

After ascertaining no one needed medical attention, the next thing the police officer wanted to do was get the vehicles out of the intersection. As the man in the pickup

278

predicted, Lacy's car wouldn't start. "You'll have to call a tow truck," the officer instructed her.

Lacy leaned against a light pole. She was barely clear-headed enough to know she wasn't operating at full capacity. She stared at the contact list on her telephone screen. She tried calling Monica, but there was no answer. A call to Cindy's phone went directly to voice mail. What now? Pearl? No one answered. She stared at Monty's name. He'd probably chew her out for causing an accident. There was no other immediate option.

"Monty? This is Lacy. I'm sorry to bother you, but I've been in a wreck and my car won't start and the girls aren't answering their phones."

"Are you hurt? Where are you?"

Lacy gave him her location. To her great relief, all he said was, "I'll be there in ten minutes."

The police officer was completing paperwork when Monty came trotting around the corner. Lacy did not resist when he hugged her close. It felt as if his lips brushed her forehead. "Are you all right?"

"I'll probably be sore tomorrow, but there's no real damage. Except to my car." She tucked her head under his chin, needing to feel safe.

Monty held her for a long moment, and remained by her side. "Anyone else hurt?"

"I'll live," the pickup driver said sourly. Looking at Lacy, he added, "You should be more careful."

"These things happen," Monty said before Lacy could respond. "That's why they're called accidents."

Lacy felt a rush of relief. How unlike Monty to defend her.

The police officer cleared his throat. "As I said earlier, these vehicles must be removed to clear the intersection immediately."

"But my car won't start," Lacy argued, fighting tears.

Monty immediately started making calls. "I'm parked about a block away," he said, after pocketing his phone. "I'll pull around and pick you up so we can follow the tow truck." He quickly disappeared around the corner.

Lacy sent messages to her daughters, letting them know she was running late. She saw no reason to upset them by sharing the fact she'd been in an accident. She'd tell them in person later, when they could see she wasn't hurt.

In a few minutes, Lacy saw Monty pull into the space previously occupied by the damaged pickup. After the third auto was hooked up and towed away, a flatbed truck squeezed into the lane next to the sidewalk. The truck's driver rolled down his window and yelled to Lacy, "Where do you want her to go, ma'am?"

"I don't know," Lacy replied. Even if she had a mental list of car repair destinations—which she didn't— she couldn't seem to organize her thoughts. Everything seemed as if it was happening to someone else.

Monty appeared as if from nowhere and asked, "How about Glassman's Body Works?"

Lacy wanted to sit down and, if she could, calm down. "Fine." She signed a form without reading it and followed Monty to his car.

"Are you sure you don't want me to take you to the ER?" Monty asked as he pulled in behind the tow truck.

"No," Lacy insisted. "I'll have some bruises, but nothing's broken or bleeding." She studied the shattered rear window of her mangled auto ahead of them. "Do you think they can fix my car?"

Monty glanced her direction. "It looks to me like it's totaled. The back and front ends are both mashed. Do you want me to take you to a car rental place?"

"Just take me home." She couldn't face doing business of any kind right now. Her auto was insured, but she hated the ordeal of car shopping. If only she'd seen that pickup slam on his brakes a few seconds sooner.

"The important thing is that you're okay. Thank God for that. Automobiles are replaceable. You aren't."

Lacy leaned back in Monty's front seat and shut her eyes. After he dropped her off at her house, Lacy began to recognize how sore she was. Her back and shoulders felt as if she'd been lifting weights all day. She ached all over, desperately wishing she could go to bed and skip the big wedding supper. Nevertheless, she took a shower and put on the new dress her daughters had chosen for her to wear for the occasion. Fortunately, it was long enough to cover the bruises on her legs.

While doing her best to arrange her hair over the bump on her forehead, Lacy heard her daughters arriving. "Mom?" Cindy did a double-take as she passed by the open bathroom door. "We didn't think you were home. Where's your car?"

"I had a fender bender, nothing serious." Lacy rolled a stubborn lock of hair around the barrel of her curling iron. "The car will be in the shop for a few days."

Monica had come to stand in the hallway, peeking around the door frame and her sister. "Are you okay?"

"I'm fine." Lacy kept her eyes on her reflection in the mirror. "Can I catch a ride with you to the dinner this evening?"

"No problem." Monica replied. "I have dibs on the bathroom as soon as you're done."

Cindy made a turn as if to go down the hallway, but then she leaned inside the door jamb again. "How did you get home?"

"Your father brought me." Lacy glanced toward the doorway in time to see her daughters exchanging knowing smiles. "Don't start with the smirks and giggles. Neither one of you answered my calls, and Pearl wasn't home either."

Chapter Fifty-One

Monty arrived early for the wedding supper. When Pearl walked in to the Roadhouse, he met her with a hug. "Where's your fiancé?" he whispered to her. "Did you get cold feet and decide to dump him?"

Laughing, Pearl replied, "He'll be here. He and Elmer are moving our new RV out to the lake. I didn't want to wait until tomorrow, with the wedding and all going on. Fanny is coming later with her kids. I hope this is the last time I ever have to come to a party by myself." She swept her eyes around the Roadhouse. "The old place sure looks grand, doesn't it?"

"It does. You're going to miss it."

"I'll miss seeing my friends every day, but not the work. I'm ready to hang it up." Pearl nodded toward the kitchen. "Let's go see what Wanda's up to before things get hectic."

"Wanda is cooking?" Monty was surprised.

"Yes," Pearl said as they made their way to the kitchen. "I tried to get her to relax and have dinner with us, but you know Wanda. She wants to make sure everything is done to perfection and then stay way in the background while everyone enjoys the fruits of her labor."

Monty pushed open one of the stainless-steel doors. Wanda was wearing her everyday work clothes, covered by her standard white apron. "How goes the fatted calf?" he joked.

Wanda turned and smiled. "Well look at you, Monty. You clean up pretty nice. I wouldn't have recognized you with your shirt tucked in and your hair combed." She motioned with a wooden spoon. "I'd hug you, but I don't want to mess up your party clothes."

Pearl skirted around the long kitchen island. "That excuse won't hold water with me." She gathered Wanda into an embrace.

"It won't be the same around here without you, Pearl." The sweet sincerity in Wanda's voice tugged at Monty's heart. The two women had worked together as long as he could remember.

As soon as Pearl stepped back, Monty gathered Wanda into his arms. "Promise me there won't be any pushing and shoving when Mom tosses her bouquet tomorrow. Remember, I have two daughters to marry off."

"Don't you worry about me getting in the way. The last thing I need is some old man to take care of." Wanda chuckled, but her watery eyes betrayed the depth of her emotions. She patted Monty's arm. "Y'all run on now. I've got work to do." She turned toward a slender young woman. "You can pull the rolls out of the oven and put them in the warmer, Lupe. I turned it on a while ago."

Monty wandered back to the dining room, leaving Wanda and Pearl reminiscing with each other. He noticed Julio was holding a meeting in the same corner his mother used as a gathering spot. He scanned the faces of the young people gathered around Julio. No doubt they were listening to the customer service pep talk he'd heard more times than he could remember. At the opposite end of the large room, musicians were testing microphones and adjusting speakers. He watched the four young men, reflecting they were nearer his daughters' age than his. A sense of nostalgia washed over him, as he remembered time spent working and making music here. The dining room looked pretty much the same as it always had, but somehow it didn't feel the same any more. "It's the passing of an era," he mumbled to himself.

A young woman stopped pushing the drink cart by him. "Excuse me, sir?"

Stirring from his reverie, Monty said, "Uh, welcome to Pearl's Roadhouse."

"Thank you, sir." She smiled and continued on her way.

A few guests started to arrive, Lacy and their daughters among them. Monty embraced his girls, but hesitated when he reached Lacy. He'd hugged every other female who'd come through the door, why not the love of his life as well? To his relief, Lacy accepted the brief contact without any obvious resistance. "Are you okay?" he whispered.

"Yeah." She glanced toward Monica and Cindy, who'd moved further into the room. "I told the girls I was in an accident, but I didn't mention how bad it was. I don't want anyone else to know. The spotlight needs to be on Pearl and Leonard tonight."

"Got it." Monty would have liked to continue his conversation with Lacy, but she walked away. He turned to welcome other party-goers.

285

The fiftyish woman in the blue shorts did not look familiar, but Monty put an arm around her shoulder anyway, while he shook hands with the man who appeared to be with her. "I don't think we've met. I'm Monty, Pearl's son," he said. "I'm so glad you were able to come tonight."

The man looked puzzled. "We're the Williamsons, Max and Earline." He nodded toward his companion. "We stopped by here last time we drove down to the coast."

The woman smiled. "We fell in love with the place. I told Max we had to plan our next trip to come through Polson's Crossing, because I wanted to come back and try the chicken fried steak. That's what Max ordered, and it looked so good."

"Wait a minute," Max said. "Everything's all decorated. This must be a private party."

Earline took a step back. "Oh, you're right Max. That must be why the sign was dark." She put a hand on Monty's arm. "I'm so sorry. We didn't know." She turned as if to leave.

"Where are you folks from?" Monty asked.

"Wichita Falls," Max answered. "Can you recommend a good place around here where we can have dinner?"

"This is the best restaurant for miles around. We have plenty of food, although the menu is prime rib tonight instead of chicken fried steak. We're celebrating my mom getting married tomorrow. Why don't you join us?"

Earline smiled, but Max looked uncomfortable. "Well, we don't want to be party crashers," he said.

"That's all right. Pearl wouldn't want you to be turned away after driving all the way from Wichita Falls. You can tell anyone who asks that you're Monty's guests."

"I don't know about that." Max back toward the entrance. "Most of these people are dressed up a lot more than we are. What do you think, Earline?"

"I think we'll never get another chance like this. I can't wait to get home and tell my friends what happened." Earline took Max's arm.

Monty motioned across the room. "Come on over and let me introduce you to the bride and groom."

Eventually leaving the Williamsons talking with members of Pearl's Sunday school class, Monty picked up a napkin and scribbled words that had been bubbling in his mind for weeks. The verse needed polishing, but it was a beginning. He'd add the napkin to his stash of lyric fragments when he got home tonight.

Lacy's Song

Give me one more chance

To prove my love

I'll treat you right

Sure as stars above.

I've really changed

I'll be so true

Just one more chance

Is all I ask of you.

As more people filed through the front entrance, he tucked the napkin into a pocket and went to mingle. He checked his vibrating phone and saw Carson Henry's name on the screen. He'd been so busy he'd forgotten to respond to his agent's messages. He'd have to remember to call him later.

Chapter Fifty-Two

"Your part is pretty simple," Tom Gillespie told Monty, who stood fidgeting in the church foyer. Your mother will face me in front of the altar, and you will be on her left. When I ask who gives this woman to be married, you say 'I do' and take your seat on the front row."

"It sounds like a job I can handle." Monty checked the wall clock. "Ten minutes to show time."

"Don't be too surprised if the distaff members of the party are a little late. Their finery takes time to get together. You're not nervous, are you?"

"A little bit. I worry that I'll step on the hem of Mama's dress or trip over my own feet. That kind of thing."

Tom smiled. "I always pray that I won't get my tongue tangled up or accidentally skip over one of the important questions to the bride or groom."

Monty peeked down the empty hallway. "Do things like that ever happen?"

"No, but the best man knocked over a candelabra and caught the bride's train on fire once. We only use battery-operated candles now." Tom sat in a wing-backed chair. "May as well relax for a few minutes. How are plans coming along for the mission?"

"Renovations start next week. I'm hoping for occupancy in no more than three months." Monty stopped pacing. "Did you get any response from the pastors' council?"

"Not as much as I hoped for," Tom admitted. "Most of the local churches have pledged their financial support, but getting commitments to speak once a month has been more difficult. I talked with a professor at State, though, and he's recruiting some of his students. You may have to feed them and put them up for the night after they come over and preach. With God's help, we'll get our dance card filled up." He smiled. "By the way, you're on the schedule the 17th of each month."

"Me? I'm no preacher."

"You don't have to preach, not in the traditional sense anyway. Pray, sing a song, read John 3:16 or give your testimony, and invite the men let God change their lives the way He did yours. You can do it." Tom crossed his legs and leaned against the back of his chair. "Wait until someone responds and make a decision for Christ after you've said your piece. It's a thrill like nothing else I've ever experienced."

Monty nodded. "I'm still discovering how exciting it is to be a Christian. I never realized that before."

A burst of giggles announced the arrival of the bride and her attendants. Monty embraced Cindy, Monica, and Pearl in turn. "I've never seen a more beautiful bride," he said. "Or cuter bridesmaids."

"I couldn't agree more." Tom arose, hugged Pearl, and opened the double doors leading to the sanctuary. "I'm going to go around and come in from the side with Leonard and his guys." He turned toward Monica. "When the men are all in place, I'll give you a quick nod. That's your signal to start proceeding down the aisle. Pearl, I'm sure you remember to start your walk when the organist tromps down on the opening notes of the wedding march, just like we practiced."

"I got it," Pearl replied, beaming. "Go and make sure Leonard don't run out the back door before you pronounce us husband and wife."

"No worries there. I've never seen a man more moonstruck than Len." Tom headed down the hallway with the parting words, "See you in church."

"Don't you love Grandma's dress?" Cindy gushed. "She's all fixed up with something old, something new, something borrowed and something blue. Well, her whole outfit is blue. But she almost forgot about something borrowed, until Monica loaned her those pearl earrings. They go perfectly with your wedding present, Daddy."

"I love this string of real pearls you gave me." Pearl lightly caressed her necklace. "It's the fanciest piece of jewelry I've ever owned. After Leonard puts that diamond ring on my finger, I'm going to be the most dolled up old lady in Polson's Crossing."

Monica adjusted the satin sash on her grandmother's ice-blue dress. "And Niagara Falls, and all the other places you are going."

Soft music directed the group's attention toward the front of the sanctuary.

"We'd better not miss our cue," Cindy said. "Otherwise, we'll never live down making Grandma late to her own wedding."

The girls were almost all the way to front of the church when Monty heard the unmistakable crashing notes of the introduction to the 'here comes the bride' melody. "You're on," he said to Pearl.

His mother smiled and took a deep breath. "I want you to walk with me." She held out her left hand.

Monty took a step back. "That's not how Pastor Tom told us to do this thing. I'm supposed to follow at a discrete distance."

"Phooey on all the should's and supposed to's," Pearl replied. "Tom won't care. That center aisle looks a mile long all of the sudden, and I need you to hold onto."

Without further argument, Monty placed Pearl's hand through the crook of his elbow and guided her down the aisle. He saw a brief look of surprise pass across Pastor Tom's face, replaced immediately with a broad smile. No doubt a minor change in protocol was less problematic than setting something on fire.

Monty was overjoyed to see Lacy sitting next to his reserved seat on the front row. He patted his pocket to make sure his handkerchief was at the ready, knowing Lacy always cried at weddings.

Chapter Fifty-Three

Monty stood in the parking lot of the Pancake Patch, watching the bulky RV maneuver onto the access road to the highway. He'd treated the newlyweds to a leisurely breakfast as a final sendoff to their honeymoon, and now he wondered why he suddenly felt so low. Everyone agreed the wedding was perfectly beautiful. At the reception, Lacy was cordial. She thanked him profusely for helping her get home after her car accident. His daughters were lovely and charming. He was about to go full bore to get the rescue mission ready for occupancy. Maybe his melancholy was the result of sleeping on the floor in the empty Holy Trinity parsonage, zipped into his newly-purchased sleeping bag. Whatever the reason, he'd learned not to wallow in despair when a dark mood struck him. He knew he needed to keep his hands and mind busy.

As soon as the back of the silver RV disappeared in the distance, Monty drove to his mother's house. The once inviting home now seemed cold and sterile, stripped as it was of Pearl's personal touches. The eerie quiet gave him the sensation of viewing a corpse. During his walk-through, he identified a few small items he could take with him in his car—TV trays, a throw rug, and a kitchen stool.

Back at the parsonage, Monty unrolled the worn rug in the living room and sat the two TV trays on it. When his phone vibrated, he answered without bothering to check the caller ID. "Good morning," he said with a cheerfulness he didn't really feel.

"Why are you avoiding me?"

"Hey, Carson. I'm sorry I haven't returned your calls. Things have been busy, and it just slipped my mind. How are you?"

"I'd be a lot better if I hadn't found out you sold your downtown apartment building. What's going on? Did you take a trip to Vegas and run up a gambling debt? Is some woman sweet talking you out of your hard-earned money? Or is it something worse? Blackmail? Drugs?"

Monty laughed at the absurdity of his agent's suspicions. "None of those things. When I told you Jesus turned my life around, I meant it."

"You wouldn't be my first client to get religion one day and lose it just as fast the next. You don't return my phone calls, and you're starting to dissipate the financial security I moved heaven and earth to acquire for you. Both are signs of a man getting into trouble. I need to know what you've been doing all summer down there in Podunk Crossing."

"Let's see, what has been going on since I last saw you? I babysat Wayne Houston and a houseful of animals for a while, my daughter broke off her engagement, my mother got married, and I bought a downtown church building. The town's name is Polson's Crossing, by the way."

"Back up. You bought *what*? Carson Henry's voice grew quieter. "What do you plan to do with a church, Monty? Are you going to start preaching? There's no money in it, not unless you get a TV show."

"Some guys from my church and I are setting up a rescue mission. We'll take in homeless men, give them food, clothing, shelter, and the gospel. Some rewards are way better than money, Carson."

"Well, that's great. My most popular songwriter is trading a profitable apartment building for a homeless shelter. Why don't you invest in something practical, like a gold mine on Mars?"

"You didn't like it when I was running wild. Now you seem to be unhappy I'm doing God's work. It's not like you to get all hot and bothered."

"Hot and bothered." Carson snorted. "You're starting to talk like you're from that hick town.

"Polson's Crossing *is* my hometown. Remember?" Monty was surprised and somewhat amused that he was keeping his cool while Carson Henry lost his. "By the way, I'm working on a song I think you'll like."

Carson went on as if Monty had said nothing. "And speaking of Wayne, what did you do to that kid? They're about to release what I think will be a gigantic hit, and now he's talking about taking time off from singing to go to college."

"Really? That's great. Good for him." So that was the real reason Carson was upset.

"Yeah. If he gets through school and works hard for the next thirty years, maybe he'll make as much as he would with a couple of recordings in the top ten. Songs you would be writing for him, I might mention." Carson cursed before continuing. "I have to take another call. Be aware I've told your financial advisor not to alter your portfolio without letting me know first." With that parting remark, he was gone.

Monty chuckled. He knew his agent had no control over what he did with his money. All Carson could do was keep tabs and lecture him. As long as the songs he wrote were popular, Carson would put up with anything. He sat on the stool he'd brought in to the kitchen and called Patty Chesterfield.

"Good morning," she said brightly. "Have you decided to resume your house hunting? I have a fabulous new listing with a view of the lake."

"Finding a house is still on my back burner. I'm hoping you can recommend a professional house cleaner and a staging company. I'm in charge of getting Mom's house ready to sell while she's on her honeymoon"

"Barton's is the best house cleaner around. I'll give you their number. I own the only staging company in Polson's Crossing. I'm doing model homes this week, and after that," Monty heard paper shuffling. "Let's see. The soonest I can fit you in is after the 20th of next month."

This was a development Monty hadn't counted on. "Thank you. That's too long a wait for me. I'll figure things out on my own."

After getting information on the house cleaner, Monty sat and toyed with an idea. Lacy always had an eye for design. She drew the layout of their house before they moved in, meticulously arranging each piece of furniture on a scaled graph. On moving day, she knew exactly where everything went, and the results were perfect. Maybe she would be willing to help him get Pearl's house looking its best. He didn't want to offend Lacy by offering to pay for her help. On the other hand, he didn't want her to think he was trying to take advantage of her. In any case, there was no way he planned to wait a month for Patty.

Meanwhile, he had to turn over a set of church keys to his contractor. He pocketed his phone and headed across the parking lot, eager to get the rescue mission renovation started.

Chapter Fifty-Four

Although she'd much rather have slept in, Lacy rolled out of bed early Monday morning. She fortified herself with two cups of strong coffee before phoning Glassman's Body Works. Just as she'd feared, repairs to her car amounted to more than the auto's value. She was speaking with her insurance company when Cindy came bounding into the kitchen.

"Good morning, Mom. Oh, sorry. I didn't notice you were on the phone." Cindy immediately began taking ingredients from the fridge.

"My car is a total loss," Lacy announced as soon as her conversation with the insurance agent ended.

"I'm sorry. I thought it was just a fender bender. But as long as nobody got hurt it's okay, right? Have you had breakfast?" With a glance toward the kitchen clock, Cindy added, "Of course not. It's way too early. I bought mushrooms at the store, and I'm going to make an omelet for Monica and me. Want some?"

"No, thanks." Lacy puffed her cheeks and exhaled. "You can top off my coffee, though."

"Yes, ma'am." Cindy whisked the cup from the table. "At Pearl's Roadhouse, we always treat customers like family. So, it makes sense at the Chapman residence that we treat family like customers." She smiled and sat the full cup by Lacy's hand.

"Thank you, sweetie. I always thought if there was a wreck it would be Monica behind the wheel," Lacy admitted. "Are you putting flour in your omelet?"

"No way. The flour is for a batch of Grandma's biscuits. They're Monica's fave. I have to be extra nice to her because she's using her day off to take me to get my school supplies. I have to get a gym bag and new athletic shoes, too."

"Good." Lacy sipped her coffee. "You can drop me off at a car dealership." If she didn't resolve her transportation issue today, she'd have to ask Monica to take her back and forth to work when the Roadhouse opened for the week on Tuesday morning.

"Okay." Cindy rolled the dough and expertly cut six plump biscuits. "Don't you think it puts you in a poor negotiating position if you go into a showroom without a trade-in? I mean, if they see you're on foot and you didn't arrive in your own car, they know you're stuck."

"It can't be helped, unless you and Monica want to go with me."

With a stricken look, Cindy countered, "Maybe you could find something on line? There are several terrific websites--"

"No," Lacy broke in, with a wave of her hand. "I have to kick the tires to know if I want to drive around in it for the next five years."

"Well, if you really want us to go along..." Cindy left the remaining words unsaid.

299

"That was a joke, Cynthia Pearl. You would be getting the salesman's life history and Monica would keep saying 'let's go home' every ten minutes. I'll handle this on my own."

"Didn't Grandma go with you when you bought the green machine?"

"Yes. She knows how to drive a hard bargain. But she's going to be gone at least a month, and I need wheels now."

Cindy turned to the stove and cracked eggs into the skillet. "Daddy's like Grandma in a lot of ways."

"Meaning?"

"Oh, I was just thinking. I'll bet he's pretty good at gaining an advantage when you're trying to make a deal."

Too good, Lacy thought. The day of the car accident was an emergency, but she was reluctant to ask Monty for another favor so soon. He'd renounced all claims to the Roadhouse. *He always has an agenda, and now he has manipulated my daughter into playing along with him. What is he up to?*

Monica strolled into the kitchen wearing a bath robe, toweling her wet hair. "Good morning," she mumbled.

"Perfect timing," Cindy announced. She sat two heaping plates on the table. "The biscuits will be out in three minutes."

Monica sat at her usual place. "Then you know next time to start your omelet four or five minutes later."

Cindy leaned against the counter. "She speaks, but she does not yet make sense."

"Ideally, everything should finish cooking at once. If not, you want your biscuits done first," Monica explained. "Breads hold their heat better than egg dishes. Something Wanda taught me." She draped the towel around her neck.

"That's the longest speech you've ever in your life made before noon. I don't think I was born to cook like you were." Cindy placed the skillet in the sink. When the timer sounded, she pulled the pan of biscuits from the oven. "These look pretty good, even if they weren't ready on the dot with the omelet." Without asking who wanted what, she served everyone two biscuits each. "Try these, Mom. Grandma says they're good for what ails you."

Lacy ignored her two allotted biscuits, certain they weren't going to cure the soreness from her recent car accident.

"Monica, Mom wants to go car shopping while you take me to get my stuff for school." Cindy sliced a biscuit open and poked at the middle with her knife. "Done all the way through, and hot enough to melt the butter. That's as good as it needs to be as I see it." She stopped talking long enough to eat a bite. "I heard the band is going to be in the Fiesta Flambeau parade in San Antonio next Spring. I hope we get to stay on the river walk."

"Another fund raiser is coming, I suppose." Lacy instantly regretted her comment. With Monica working instead of going to college, she was in a much better financial position than she'd anticipated at this point. Plus, now that she owned the Roadhouse, she had the potential for things to improve even more. So why did she have to sound so grumpy about supporting the band?

"Probably," Cindy agreed cheerily. "I hope we do car washes instead of those icky magazines. The candy bars and popcorn did pretty well last year, though."

"Car shopping?" Monica looked toward Lacy at the head of the table, as if Cindy's earlier statement finally penetrated her awareness. "You're getting a new car, Mom?"

"I totaled the green machine." Lacy lowered her eyes, but not before catching a piercing glance from Monica.

"Totaled?" Monica let the word hang in the air for a moment. "I thought you said you had a minor collision."

"I didn't want to get everyone upset right before Pearl's wedding."

Monica's raised eyebrow made Lacy feel more like the child than the parent. She felt a flush creeping up her neck. How many times had she lectured her daughters about a half-truth being as deceptive as a lie? The vibration of her cell phone offered such a welcome escape that she answered without checking the identity of the caller.

"Good morning." It was Monty's rich baritone voice. "I hope it's not too early to call. I'm in a bit of a situation, and I was wondering if you'd be kind enough to help me out?"

"Tell me more." Lacy stood and retreated to her bedroom, shutting the door behind her. Perhaps Monty was finally about to reveal the reason he'd returned to Polson's Crossing. She was curious to hear what kind of cockamamie scheme he'd cooked up this time.

"I'm getting Mom's house ready to sell. It needs something. I don't know if its paint or what, but it just isn't appealing somehow. You've always had an eye for how a house should look. I'm hoping you'll check it out and give me some advice on what to do so Mom gets top dollar. I'll come by and pick you up, and buy you breakfast as part of the deal, too."

Lacy hesitated.

"I understand I'll owe you big time if you do this," Monty said. "I'll come and work a shift at the Roadhouse without pay if that helps make up for asking this favor."

How could she refuse to do something to benefit Pearl? "I'm up and dressed, if you want to come and pick me up now. After we're done at the house you can take me car shopping. Oh, and bring some stick-on labels." Pearl's home was an easy fix. For years, Lacy knew it was overloaded with too much furniture. Her simple advice would keep her from being indebted to Monty for helping her negotiate for a car.

"Who was on the phone?" Cindy asked as soon as Lacy returned to the kitchen.

"Something has come up," Lacy said, purposely avoiding her daughter's question. "You two go on without me." She didn't sort out the reason, but she didn't want the girls to know she was spending time with Monty.

"But how will you--" Cindy began.

Monica cut in immediately. "That's fine. Come on, Cindy. Let's get a move on. We'll clean up the kitchen when we get home. See you later, Mom." She tossed Cindy an arch look.

"Stow the arrows in your quiver, Cupid," Lacy said as Monica exited. "It's not what you think."

Chapter Fifty-Five

"Did you bring the labels?" Lacy asked as soon as Monty opened the front door of Pearl's house.

"Sure did." Monty withdrew packets from his shirt pocket. "I bought several kinds. I wasn't sure exactly what you wanted."

Sorting through the choices, Lacy selected the colored dots. "These will work." She removed the plastic wrapping and made a sweeping gesture. "This is a big, spacious room, but it looks small because it's too crowded. I'm going to put a green dot on things you need to remove. Later I'll draw a diagram for placement of the remaining pieces."

Within an hour, Lacy had green-tagged half the furniture in Pearl's house. Monty watched her work with growing admiration. He'd never seen her so sure of herself, and he liked what he saw.

"I'll get a crew over here today or tomorrow to pull all of this extra stuff out," Monty said. "Are you ready for breakfast?"

"I'm sure you've already eaten." Lacy said.

"Yeah, but I can drink coffee and watch you eat."

"The sooner we get the car thing done the better. I brought a protein bar."

"Fair enough," Monty locked the door behind them. "Is Glassman's Auto World okay, or do you prefer another dealer?"

"Glassman's is good. They have the biggest inventory for miles around."

"What do you have in mind?" Monty asked on the trip to the car dealership.

"Reliable transportation," Lacy answered immediately. "I don't need anything fancy, just something to get me back and forth to work."

"New or used?"

"New if I can afford it. Gently used if not."

To Lacy's surprise, Monty asked all kinds of questions about accessory options, monthly payments, and color combinations. "Am I supposed to dicker with the salesman, or am I only there for moral support?"

"I'll pick out what I want. Your job is to negotiate a price that fits my budget. Just bear in mind, no lies."

"No problem." He glanced at her briefly. "I'll try not to embarrass you or the Lord in any way."

Lacy drummed her fingers on the arm rest, impressed by how sincere he sounded. "Pearl was with me when I bought what the girls called the green machine."

"All right, then. No worries. I'm teamed up with a graduate of the Pearl Chapman school of deal-making. We can improve on Mom's methods by texting each other. How this for a strategy? Pick out at least three acceptable cars, and don't eliminate anything you want. We can keep the conversation weird by talking about different options, and if things don't go our way we'll walk. I'll portray the bad cop, and you can play the good one."

"Got it." Lacy marveled at Monty's way of transforming a dreaded chore into a game, with the two of them playing against the car dealer's team.

Lacy meandered among the autos parked in front of the showroom while Monty went inside to make contact with a salesman. Normally she had difficulty with decisions, but the pressure was off when she wasn't forced into a single choice. By the time Monty brought Mike Freeman outside to meet her, Lacy had several good possibilities in mind.

"I'm pleased to meet you," Mike said when Monty introduced him to Lacy. "Monty tells me you're looking for a new car."

"It doesn't have to be new," Lacy replied, remembering Monty's suggestion not to be too eager. "That one's not too bad." She pointed to a blue compact.

After two hours and lots of haggling between Mike and Monty, Lacy was prepared to purchase a new cream-colored beauty with a matching interior. She could make the down payment and the monthly cost was within her budget. Still, Monty wanted Mike to knock off a few hundred dollars.

"She didn't ask for cruise control, and I don't think she should have to pay for it," Monty contended.

"It was installed at the factory," Mike explained.

"Why don't you take it off? Your mechanics can uninstall it here." Monty opened a bottle of water.

Mike seemed to be struggling to remain calm. "That's impractical. Think about the labor costs involved."

"Which is why you should toss it in for nothing. She doesn't pay for what she doesn't want, and you don't have to pay to remove the cruise control."

Mike swiped his hand across his eyes. "I don't see how that's possible. I've made the best deal I can for this car."

"Okay." Monty was so calm, as if he had the rest of his life to do nothing but discuss the price of side mirrors and cruise control. "Let's go back to the little blue compact, the used one. Now, if you can bring the cost down a few hundred dollars and include a warranty extension..."

"All right." Mike held up a hand. "No charge for the cruise control."

Lacy spoke up. "Deal." She was ready to escape from the oppressive room and breathe.

"Good," Mike said. "Let's do the paperwork. We can have the car ready for you tomorrow.

"No, she needs it this afternoon." Monty glanced at the time. "If you can't deliver it, let us know now while there's still time to do some business with the guys over in Watson's Lake."

"I'll check." The salesman bolted from behind his desk.

Monty smiled at Lacy and drank water. She silently returned his grin. After a few minutes, when Mike still hadn't returned, she said, "I haven't been to Watson's Lake in a couple of years. It's a nice drive."

"We can have a late lunch at Mama Manicotti's on the way," Monty responded. "I wonder if the Torelli family is still running the place."

"They were still in business last I knew." Lacy couldn't help enjoying this aspect of the game. She didn't believe the sales room was bugged, but Monty had warned her he thought it was.

"How long do you think it will take for you to do the layout of Mom's house?"

"Not long. I've been mentally rearranging Pearl's place for years. I already know exactly how I want everything to look. When do you think the movers can take the extra furniture out?"

"Tomorrow I hope." Monty tapped his phone. "I'll call now and set it up."

Monty was completing his call when Mike returned. "We'll have your brand-new car ready for you at five o'clock this afternoon, Mrs. Chapman," he said. "Now, if you'll sign the papers, we are all done."

Lacy removed the staple from the document Mike gave her. She handed each page to Monty after she read it.

Three pages in, Monty took out his phone and tapped the screen. "What's up with this interest rate, Mike? I though we agreed on zero per cent before we sat down in your office."

"Well, yeah." The salesman ran a finger around the inside of his collar. "But that was on the assumption you were paying the sticker price. I can't give you the big discount we talked about and give you zero per cent as well. I'm sure you understand."

"I see." Monty turned toward Lacy. "Are you a member of a credit union?"

"No." She thought fast. "But I can apply for an account at the one over by The Grill."

"Good." Monty shifted to face Mike. "We'll do the financing through the credit union."

Looking somewhat uncomfortable, Mike said, "They can't do any better than us on a car loan."

"That's not what *they* say." Monty held up his phone, screen out.

Mike's face reddened. "I suppose we could simply give you the car."

"That would be nice." Monty's calm answer almost made Lacy laugh out loud. Instead, she covered her mouth and coughed.

In a little less than an hour, Lacy signed the paperwork for the automobile she wanted, with a total price below her budget, and a comfortable monthly payment. "Thank you, Monty," she said as they left the dealership.

"Always glad to be of service," he said. "Now, how about that lunch at Mama Manicotti's? A round trip to Watson's Lake and a late lunch would put us back here at about the right time for you to pick up your car and keys."

"No, I need to go home and get a few things done before tomorrow." It was a lame excuse, and she suspected he knew it. In her euphoria at getting the car business done, she'd allowed herself to relax into Monty's charm.

He accepted her answer. "Okay. Shall I pick you up around four-thirty to go and get your new car?"

"No. you've done enough, getting me a good deal from Glassman's. I'll get Monica to take me back over there." Why didn't he show some anger? That would be so much easier to deal with than the look of disappointment that passed across his face. "I want to get that furniture layout to you as soon as possible," she said, hoping her explanation would soften the impact of turning down his offer.

"I really appreciate your helping me out with Mom's house." Monty pulled up to the curb in front of Lacy's house and stopped.

"It's nothing, really. Easy peasy." She turned to step out, but stopped to add, "Thank you again for running interference for me with the car salesman."

Chapter Fifty-Six

Monty loved the way Pearl's house looked when the furnishings were pared down and rearranged. Buyers responded the same way, too. Before the end of the first week, multiple offers drove the price up to give Pearl a nifty profit. "I'm tickled to death," Pearl said when Monty called his mother to make sure Patty had been in touch with her. "Thank you for putting the old house in order," Pearl said. "Patty told me it looked like a magazine cover when you got through with it."

"Not me," Monty replied. "Lacy chose what furniture to move out, and made a graph to arrange what was left. Then she brought over some dishes and things to give the dining room and bedrooms their finishing touches."

"That girl's a whiz," Pearl said. "Give her a big hug for Leonard and me." There was an awkward silence before Pearl continued. "How are things going with your mission?"

"Slower than I'd like, but good. We may have to replace more piping than we planned for." After talking for a while about the renovation, he asked Pearl if she was enjoying being a vagabond.

"We are having a ball. It's a good thing I didn't ever know how fine a thing it is to have a man around the house and be foot loose and fancy free to go touristing around the country," Pearl declared. "If I'd had any idea, I'd probably have closed up the Roadhouse and married Len years ago. We're going to hang around Niagara Falls for another week or two, and then we are off to West Virginia. As long as we're on the road, we decided to take Fanny and Elmer up on their invitation to come and visit. Elmer promised to take us fishing."

Monty ended the conversation thankful his mother was happy. No one had worked harder or deserved her retirement more. He allowed his thoughts to linger on the prospect of growing old with Lacy. He couldn't imagine her wanting to drive across the country in a recreational vehicle, but maybe in thirty or forty more years the idea would gain in its appeal.

The next few weeks raced by for Monty. Despite devoting long hours to the mission project, he made sure to spend time with his daughters. He occasionally cooked a meal for them at the parsonage, which he thought of as his temporary home. Although it was larger than Pearl's house, her furniture was sufficient to keep the place from looking bare. He installed two sets of bunk beds in each of three upstairs parsonage bedrooms, giving him the capacity to sleep twelve guests.

When the jangle of his phone awoke Monty in the middle of the night, he experienced an immediate jolt of apprehension. Monica. Cindy. Lacy. Pearl. Which one was hurt or in trouble? "Hello."

"Do you want Goldie and Sweetie?"

The muffled voice was familiar, but in his drowsy state, Monty couldn't match it with an identity. "What? Who is this?"

"Dexter Johnson. My boys and I are leaving town tonight. I gave the guinea pig and the rabbits to neighbors, and the snake died. My kids are driving me crazy about the stinking dog and cat because nobody wants them?"

"Do you know what time it is? Call me in the morning and we'll working something out."

"No," Dexter insisted. "If you won't take these animals, I'm dropping them off at the pound on the way out of town."

Monty sat on the side of the bed and gave Dexter directions to the parsonage. After completing the phone call, he put on pajamas over the underwear he slept in and turned on more lights. What was Johnson thinking, dragging his boys out of bed at this time of night? In a few minutes, he heard a knock at the kitchen door.

"Come in," Monty said as he swung the exterior door open. Goldie licked Monty's hand, while Sweetie began an exploration of the house.

"Thanks, Man. I owe you." Still at the threshold, Dexter turned away.

"Wait a minute." Monty stepped onto the back porch. "Have you been drinking?"

"I had a beer or two. You would, too, if you had to put up with Janie and her historics."

"I think you mean histrionics." Monty looked toward the Johnson van sitting in the driveway. "Are your kids with you?"

"Just the boys." Dexter slurred his words slightly. "The girls are Janie's problem now."

"You can't drive around drunk, especially with your boys in the car. Bring them inside. You can sleep here tonight and sober up."

"Why don't you mind your own business?" Dexter glowered at Monty.

"I have friends and neighbors and a couple of daughters driving around in Polson's Crossing. You could hurt one of them driving drunk."

"I'm not drunk, just a little tipsy."

"If you start up the motor, I'm calling the cops. We'll let them decide whether you're in shape to drive or not." Monty folded his arms and stood still, hoping he looked more confident than he felt.

Dexter hesitated for a long moment. Then he cursed and called out his boys' names. "Raven. Brook. River. Get inside."

The three boys filed into the kitchen without speaking. River leaned against the table, staring at the cookies displayed under a glass dome, while Brook knelt and hugged Goldie.

"The bedrooms are upstairs." Monty fought his anger at Dexter Johnson, aware at least a part of it was directed toward his former self.

"May I have a cookie?" River turned a pleading face up to his father.

Without waiting for Dexter's reply, Monty asked, "Have you guys had dinner?"

The boys looked at Dexter, seeming to await his reaction. "No, sir," Raven mumbled at last.

"Sit down." Monty tried not to sigh. "I'll fix some eggs. How about the animals? Have they been fed?" He knew the answer before Raven shook his head. Of course not. If Dexter starved his own kids, he wasn't going to take care of their pets.

Monty did his best to keep a conversation going, to avoid the tense silence that settled over the kitchen when he was quiet. "Do you boys know how to make biscuits? My mother had me cooking them before I was old enough to go to school, and I've always been glad I learned. Raven, would you look in the freezer and take out a couple of patties of ground meat? I'll show you how to brown them for Goldie. Brook, you and River find a bowl for Sweetie and pour her some milk. It's in the refrigerator."

After Dexter and his boys consumed an impressive amount of biscuits, scrambled eggs, bacon, and leftover lasagna, Monty sent them upstairs to bed.

The house was quiet when Monty's six am alarm sounded. He assumed the Johnsons were still sleeping, but when he glanced through the window he saw the van was gone. Upstairs, he found Sweetie dozing on one of the four rumpled bunk beds. "Everybody has a job here," he said, rubbing her fur. "Yours is to keep us mouse-free. Can you

317

handle it?" Sweetie closed her eyes and purred, which
Monty took as agreement.

Chapter Fifty-Seven

Monty turned the knob and pulled, but the back door to the Roadhouse wouldn't budge. After one more vigorous attempt, he decided his only choice was to go to the front entrance. He was descending the porch steps when Wanda flung the door open. "I thought I heard some kind of varmint scratching around out here." Her broad smile negated her disparaging words. "I figured it was a raccoon."

"Hey, Wanda." Monty scrambled inside. "Is something wrong with the door?"

"We've started keeping it locked." Wanda followed him into the kitchen. "Miss Lacy decided we needed to be a little more security conscious." She sighed. "That's the world we live in nowadays."

"Probably a good idea." Monty hugged Wanda. "You never know what kind of creature may try to get in here where it smells so good."

Monica turned from the stove and smiled. "Hi, Daddy."

"Hello, Sweetheart." Monty hugged his daughter and pecked her on the cheek. "What's cooking?"

"Sauce for today's special, spaghetti and meatballs."

"It looks delicious."

319

"It is," Monica agreed, pulling her wooden spoon through the thick sauce. "You should order it."

"Thanks for the tip." Monty had arranged a fixed menu for the first meeting of the mission's new executive board, but he saw no reason to burst Monica's bubble. "I'll see you later, assuming I survive all the speechifying."

Exiting the kitchen, Monty scanned the dining room. Since Lacy was nowhere in sight, he proceeded on to the party room. The tables were arranged into a U-shape, with places set for the twenty-six guests he expected.

Tom Gillespie was the first to arrive, wearing a dark suit and matching tie. Monty wondered if he'd made a mistake with his own casual attire.

"I may have to leave a few minutes before the end of the meeting," Tom explained. "Amanda volunteered me to speak at a women's tea, and I didn't notice the conflict in time to get out of it. She's always getting me into time crunches like that."

Monty clapped Tom on the forearm as they shook hands. "Be glad you have a wife to get you into trouble."

Tom nodded. "How are things with you and Lacy?"

"Hard to say." Monty shrugged. "I've tried everything I know. Each time I think we're making progress, she backs off. Maybe I'm fighting a losing battle."

"The Bible says when you've done all you can, just stand. If you're out of ammunition, that may be a sign to wait for the Lord to fight for you."

Monty made small talk with as many people as he could until it was time for the luncheon to begin. When everyone was seated, Tom Gillespie asked God's blessing on their food and the mission. After lunch was done, Monty stood and introduced the five people who'd agreed to serve as the board of directors. He thanked the pastors and churches who promised to support the mission in various ways. "Here's where we are today," he said. "The renovation is complete, giving us room to feed and house up to a hundred men a night. The paid staff will include security guards, a cook, and housekeepers, augmented by volunteers from your churches and others. We expect to get our certificate of occupancy by the end of the week. God willing, we'll have open house this coming Sunday afternoon and be open for business Sunday night." He recognized a long list of people who'd helped him survive the challenges of keeping the historical society happy while satisfying building codes. Monty glanced at his notes to make sure he mentioned everyone who'd worked on the mission's certification as a non-profit charitable organization, wading through a mountain of paperwork he knew he could never have completed. "Finally, I want to thank my pastor and good friend Tom Gillespie, without whose prayers, vision and organizational skills the rescue mission would never have been more than a dream."

Monty disliked leaving without at least saying hello to Lacy, but she was nowhere in sight when his luncheon broke up. Should he check the office? Perhaps the smokehouse? Reluctantly, he decided not to instigate a search. For the time being, he would abide by Tom's advice, although patience was alien to his nature.

Making use of driving time, Monty listened to his voicemail on the way back to the mission. He was happy to hear Pearl's voice flowing through the speakers. "Well, I reckon Len and I have worn out our welcome with Fanny and Elmer. And besides that, I have to get home and sign the papers to sell my house. You must have done a wonderful job getting the place ready. If you start answering your phone, I'll talk to you tomorrow. If not, we'll see you in a few days." There was a muffled conversation before Pearl added, "Leonard just reminded me of something. I don't rightly know what Cindy was so excited about this morning, but give her a big hug and tell her I'm proud of her and right happy she got whatever it was she was hollering about."

Monty wondered what his mother meant. He hoped to receive a call or text from Cindy if something important was going on in her life. He sat through a traffic light while Carson Henry's message gave him an update on songs that were in various stages of production. "I haven't seen a submission from you in a while," Carson added at the end. "I hope you're going to send me something good before the end of this month.'

"Subtle," Monty said aloud. His only recent inspiration was "Lacy's Song." The words needed tweaking, and he hadn't come up with a tune yet. Carson could benefit from one of Tom Gillespie's sermons on patience.

Chapter Fifty-Eight

The following Saturday dawned bright and clear, with a hint of crispness in the early morning air. Monty walked through the newly renovated facility with Goldie close behind, double checking to assure himself the mission was ready for their first guests the next day. Aside from the faint smell of fresh paint, everything was exactly as he'd envisioned it. He'd hoped to reduce the size of the sanctuary to create more bedrooms. However, opposition from all sides convinced him to leave it alone, at least for the time being. He sat in a folding chair in the back, praying for many men to pass through this room and be helped. A peaceful feeling came over him while he rubbed Goldie's ears and thanked God that he was able to be part of the mission.

On Sunday afternoon, clouds hid the sun from view. What Texans call a "norther" blew into Polson's Creek, announcing an abrupt end to the mild autumn days. Monty blamed the small trickle of visitors to the mission's open house on the cold drizzle that gathered force throughout the afternoon. His daughters suddenly had other obligations. At least Pearl was honest with him, saying, "It's too cold for Leonard and me to get out our old bones out of the house this afternoon."

The cook was supposed to arrive at four o'clock to begin preparations for dinner. When he hadn't shown up by four-thirty, Monty tried without success to contact him. "It's a good thing my mother made me learn how to cook for a crowd," he grumbled to Max, the security guard on duty. Since he'd done the grocery shopping, Monty knew what supplies he had on hand. He winced at the term 'soup kitchen' but he opted for the easy solution of chicken noodle soup for dinner. He consoled himself it wasn't a bad choice for a cold, rainy evening.

Around five-thirty, Tom arrived with his wife and kids in tow. Soon afterward, the evening's volunteers began to filter in. Monty had the food situation under control by then. He gave brief instructions to three women who seemed to know their way around a kitchen well enough to bake the sheet cakes he'd prepared from a mix. Meanwhile, Tom and Amanda had made assignments to the rest of the volunteers.

"It's time to open the doors," Monty told Tom. "Pray, brother."

"I have been." Tom pointed toward Monty and said, "Are you planning to wear that all night?"

Monty untied his white chef's apron and tossed it onto a chair. "Old habits." He sprinted to the front entrance, where the security guard Max was unlocking the door. Monty's heart leapt when he saw a line of men waiting to come inside. The miserable weather spoiled the open house reception, but it was driving homeless men indoors. "Lord, You are perfect in all of Your ways," he whispered.

After the men who checked in to the mission had showers, clean clothes, and dinner, they filed into the chapel. Amanda Gillespie played the piano while Monty led the ragtag congregation's singing. Tom's sermon was brief, simple, and filled with redemptive scriptures. Although no one came forward in response to the invitational song, Monty refused to let that put a damper on his joy. It was around midnight before he trotted through the rain to the parsonage, gratefully anticipating a hot shower and a good night's sleep.

By the next morning, the rain stopped, leaving a wintry cold suspended in the humid air. Monty wanted to send his overnight guests out with a hot breakfast. However, Tim Gillespie had convinced him not to attempt preparing two meals a day immediately. Max was guiding men through the mission's back exit with their packaged muffins and a small box of juice when Monty arrived. He stood back and watched for a while, praying for each man who passed by. When the last fellow walked out, Max locked the door and smiled. "Well, we made it through the first night."

"Did you get any sleep?" Monty asked.

"I caught a few cat naps, off and on, but I'm ready to get into bed and catch up."

"That sounds like a good idea." Monty clapped Max on the shoulder. "Great job. See you tomorrow."

Last night's volunteers left the kitchen spic and span. They'd even taken trash to the dumpster and emptied the dishwasher. Before long, housekeepers were busy stripping beds and mopping floors. The big commercial washing machine whirled soiled garments the men left behind. Goldie fell into step behind Monty as he walked throughout the building, making sure the mission would be ready to take in the homeless again by evening.

The days slipped by quickly and before Monty knew it, the mission doors had been open every night for a month. He had to admit, it wasn't smooth sailing. New issues cropped up every day, but he and his small staff were able to keep the operation going. One November evening, frigid temperatures drove a record number of men inside. The kitchen ran out of the chicken spaghetti casserole the new cook prepared. Ten men received the emergency ration of peanut butter and jelly sandwiches, but they did not complain. After the chapel service, there were several professions of faith. Not even the bite of wind-blown sleet bothered Monty as he hurried across the parking lot to the parsonage that night.

He slowed down to ascend the steep steps to the back porch. Inside the door, Goldie was barking. He was normally a quiet, placid dog, making Monty wonder if the noise of ice pellets against the windows had him upset. As soon as the door opened, Goldie squeezed outside. He brushed by Monty and stood at the corner of the porch, barking nonstop.

"Hush and come inside," Monty ordered. Goldie circled back and forth between the door and the side of the porch, staying out of reach and continuing to bark. Monty stepped to his right to grab Goldie's collar. When he did so, he saw the reason for the dog's agitation. Someone was out there, flattened against his house.

Monty leaned over the porch railing. "What are you doing here?" He regretted not adding security lighting around the parsonage. He sensed movement, but received no answer.

Turning up the collar of his coat, Monty descended from the porch and went to the side of the house. "You can't stay here." He strained to see who was in his yard. "If you need a place to sleep, you should have checked into the mission."

A human figure, wrapped in a blanket stepped forward. "The mission is only for men."

As his eyes adjusted, Monty realized there was a group of women and children huddled against the outside wall of the parsonage. He pulled his coat tighter. Even though his dormitory was full, he couldn't go inside the house and leave them there. "Come inside and warm up." He didn't have to say it twice.

Monty was relieved to learn the five women and eight kids crowded into his kitchen had eaten dinner, after which they said they lingered inside the fast food restaurant until the it closed for the night. He advised them to go to the only family shelter he knew of in Polson's Crossing, but the women told him they'd already tried it and found it full. Not knowing what else to do, he offered the parsonage's bedrooms for the night. After using all of the milk in his refrigerator to make hot cocoa, he grabbed his sleeping bag from the hall closet and trekked back across the icy parking lot to the mission with Goldie trotting close behind.

As soon as Monty stuck his key in the lock, Max jerked the door open. "Did you forget something?" he asked.

"More or less." Monty and Goldie hurried inside, while Max secured the entrance and re-engaged the alarm. "It seems I forgot how to say no."

Chapter Fifty-Nine

The voice was vaguely familiar, but Lacy couldn't connect it with a name or a face. "This is Steve Thornton. You may recall that we spoke last fall. I am in town for a few days, and I was wondering if we could get together and chat."

Now she remembered. Steve's company had tried for several years to convince Pearl to sell out to them. "The Roadhouse isn't for sale." Then she added, "Not at this time, anyway."

"Perhaps we could have a friendly discussion, nothing binding, in case at some time in the future you have a change of heart."

Lacy hesitated, switching the phone to her other ear. "I really don't foresee that happening."

"Perhaps I could drop by Pearl's Roadhouse one day this week. It would be nice for us to get to know each other, in the event we someday agree to do business."

"No." Lacy drew circles on the scratch pad in the middle of her desk. "I don't want to get my employees stirred up about the Roadhouse's future."

"I understand exactly what you're saying," Steve agreed. "How about joining me for lunch somewhere else? We could have a private discussion at *Le Colibri*. Do you know the place?"

"I've been there." Lacy stopped herself before adding "once."

"Great. How about Wednesday?"

"I suppose it wouldn't hurt to have a conversation." Lacy held up a hand to delay the waiter about to barge through her office doorway.

"Fine. I'll make reservations for us at *Le Colibri* for noon on Wednesday. I'm looking forward to meeting you."

Lacy hung up, motioned for the waiter to enter, and absently-mindedly scribbled her initials to approve an out-of-state check. When the server left, she covered her face with her hands and took a deep breath. For a moment, she let her mind run wild, wondering what she'd do if she received an astronomical offer for the Roadhouse, a sum so huge she couldn't afford to turn it down. Reality soon set in, and she returned to her bookkeeping. She really did need to make a final decision on how to automate her administrative tasks.

When posting the accounts was done, Lacy grabbed her cell phone to leave the office. The blinking light signaled she'd missed a call. She walked toward the Roadhouse dining room listening to Cindy's breathless voicemail. "Mom, I got it! I got it! I got a scholarship to the school I wanted. Aren't you thrilled? The counselor just told me. I'm trying to let everybody know between classes but I have to go to physics right now so I'll call you after school. Eeeeek! Love you. Bye." With one final squeal, she was gone.

Lacy tried her best to think which scholarship Cindy referred to as 'the one she wanted'. She couldn't recall her daughter being specific about a preference, simply mentioning in a casual way that she'd applied to several schools in various locations. Assuming there was little chance of a scholarship coming through from some far-flung place, Lacy chalked the applications up to Cindy's inclination to nurture big dreams.

Puzzled, Lacy detoured into the kitchen. "What's for dinner?" she asked, as if she didn't know.

Wanda lifted her eyebrows and continued to monitor the commercial mixing machine. Monica briefly glanced up from chopping carrots. "Hey, Mom."

"Did Cindy call you?" Lacy leaned against the island.

Suddenly animated, Monica used the edge of her knife to scoop carrot coins into a bowl of water. "Yes. I'm so excited for her. I bet you are, too."

"I'm happy to hear the word scholarship, but I didn't get any details." Lacy propped both elbows on the island's stainless-steel top. "Which college is making the offer? All she told me was that it was the one she wanted."

"East Tennessee State." Monica dumped two handfuls ice cubes to the bowl of carrots.

"That's a long way from here." Lacy stood straight and turned toward Wanda. "Were *you* aware Cindy wants to go to school in Tennessee?"

"Mm hum." Wanda nodded affirmatively, before turning off the commercial mixer and lifting the huge metal bowl onto the counter.

When Lacy turned back to face Monica, her daughter was peering into the open refrigerator. She slid the carrots in and took out a box of lettuce. The kitchen buzzed with food preparation. Monica separated and sprayed lettuce at the sink. Wanda banged scoops of dough into muffin tins, stopping only to turn on the exhaust fan.

Lacy put her hands on her hips. There was a time when she would have skulked out of the kitchen, recognizing that neither Wanda nor Monica wanted her there. Now she was the boss, and she wanted answers. She strode to the wall and flipped the switch to turn off the noisy fan. "All right, what's the big secret? What is it that I don't know about Cindy's choice of schools?"

Wanda washed her hands while Monica spread lettuce leaves on the counter. The two of them traded glances while Lacy stood waiting. "I believe I'll check on something out in the smokehouse," Wanda said at last. She patted Monica and ambled out the back door.

When a timer buzzed, Monica pointed toward the big ovens. "The pies will burn if I don't take them out." As she placed pecan pies on the island, the smell of freshly-based crust filled the air.

"I'm waiting for an answer, Monica." Lacy had decided she wasn't moving until she knew whatever it was her daughter knew. There had to be something afoot to drive Wanda out of the kitchen on a flimsy pretext.

"Just a sec." Monica adjusted the oven temperature. "This cornbread has to be ready by noon." She seemed to take a long time loading the muffin tins before turning to face Lacy with a big smile. "Cindy says they have fantastic

331

business and technology programs. She's been thinking about designing computer games, you know. And—"

"Stop." Lacy held up a hand. "She could do that right here at home."

"Well, she really liked the variety of courses ETSU offers. They can get all of their requirements—"

"They?"

"Yeah, I mean, you know, everybody can get whatever they need at that school."

The insight came to Lacy like a flash of lightening. "Is some boy involved in all of this?"

"Um, maybe you should ask Cindy about that."

Moving near to stand beside Monica, Lacy said, "I will. But right now, I'm asking you. Who is he?"

"Well, you remember that guy who stayed with Daddy last summer? Wayne Houston? The one with the pretty voice and the funny hair?"

"The *singer?*" Lacy could almost feel steam coming out of her ears. "I see your father's fine hand in this."

"I don't think Daddy knows about Cindy and Wayne," Monica said.

"Anyone who thinks I'm sending my daughter off to college so she can get mixed up with some here-today-gone-tomorrow musician has another think coming. Over my dead body." Lacy stalked out of the kitchen, leaving Monica wide-eyed.

Chapter Sixty

Monty gathered the notes for his mid-year presentation to the board. After six months of operation, the rescue mission was humming along successfully. He should have been on top of the world instead of on edge.

As usual, the board meeting was held in the event room at Pearl's Roadhouse. Pastor Tom arrived early, as he customarily did. When they shook hands, he stared at Monty intently and said, "You look tired, my friend."

"I haven't been sleeping very well," Monty admitted.

"Why is that?"

"I'm not sure. I seem to have a lot of trouble falling asleep. Then I wake up every half hour or so. Maybe it has to do with old age creeping up on me. I'm staring down that gun barrel of turning forty before too long." Monty riffled through his notes again, arranging the three by five cards on the podium for later. He took the chair next to Tom. "Part of the problem is that I really messed up with Lacy. She yelled at me and I yelled back."

"Do you want to tell me what happened?"

"Cindy wants to go to college in Tennessee, mostly because she wants to be near her boyfriend. Lacy thinks it's my fault Cindy is going with this young man because I gave him a place to flop last summer when he was going through a tough time. So Lacy called and started reaming me out for being the reason Cindy wants to go away. She said she wasn't paying for an out-of-state school for such a dumb reason and furthermore Cindy was never going to be allowed to be involved with a singer." Monty took a swig from the nearest glass of water. "I told Lacy she couldn't dislike every singer because she married one and he did her wrong. And then I went on to say she has to stop trying to control the girls' lives. It went downhill fast from there. We both said things we shouldn't have."

"Maybe you can kiss and make up." Tom grimaced. "Figuratively speaking."

"I doubt it. I get mad and blow off steam and then it's over," Monty replied. "Lacy simmers and boils for weeks. At this point, I've decided if she wants to hold a grudge so be it. She'll be furious all over again when she finds out I plan to pay for Cindy to go to college wherever she wants."

"Do you really think Lacy will object if you help Cindy financially?"

"I know she will. She uses the purse strings to make the girls toe the line. I love my wife, Tom, but I love my daughters, too. Lacy has to let go and let the girls start to make their own decisions as adults."

"Do you want to know what I think?" Tom asked.

"Shoot."

"You need a vacation."

Monty laughed. "Excuse me? Did I miss something? I thought we were talking about a totally different issue."

"It's all related. When was the last time you took a day off?"

Monty knit his eyebrows. "I work when I feel like it. There's no schedule for song-writing."

"When did you write your last song?"

"Oh, a few months ago. You know how busy I've been getting the mission going."

"You're not a song writer if you're not writing songs." Tom's tone was casual, but his eyes burned into Monty. "How many nights have you been away from the mission since it opened?"

"None," Monty confessed. "You know it's a seven-day-a-week operation."

"You mentioned having trouble sleeping and being irritable. Those are classic signs of exhaustion, usually accompanied by other symptoms such as difficulty concentrating. Do you want some advice, or shall I butt out?"

"Tell me what's on your mind." Monty shifted in his chair, expecting to dislike Tom's next words.

"Take at least two weeks when you don't go near the mission or handle any of its business." Tom held up a hand against an interruption. "Let me finish. Move away from the mission campus. Establish a regular work schedule that leaves you at least two days off after working five days. God knew what He was doing when He gave His people a day of rest every week, Monty. He doesn't want us to kill ourselves serving Him." Tom glanced up as two board members entered the room. "I have to speak with Reverend Buckley before our meeting. Think about what I said."

Monty tried to review the note cards for his speech, but he couldn't seem to keep his focus. Maybe Tom had a point about giving himself a break. He recalled how upset he'd been when the women he'd allowed to spend the night in the parsonage slipped out the next morning with every blanket in the house. He was working on forgiving their ingratitude when he found his underwear drawer was empty also, and then he exploded. Fortunately, no one but Goldie was there to witness his tirade. Only he and his God knew how badly he wanted to get drunk that morning. I have let myself get too tired, Monty confessed to himself. *How did Tom come to have much wisdom? He's not much older than I am, but I have to hand it to him. He's smart about people.*

The meeting exceeded all of Monty's expectations. The board members went on and on about their gratitude for the mission's excellent work among Polson's Crossing neediest population. Afterward, he cut through the kitchen to say hello. "I didn't see your Mom," he said to Monica, hoping not to sound too nosey.

"She had to run an errand downtown." Monica put a hand on his arm. "I think she's mad at you and Cindy."

Enraged would be more like it. "Yeah. Maybe we'll get back in her good graces before too long." Monty didn't

337

believe what he said, but he was determined not to criticize Lacy to their daughters.

Monica untied her apron. "I'll walk you to your car."

With a roll of his eyes toward Wanda, Monty followed his daughter through the kitchen exit. "And the problem is?" he said as they descended the back steps.

"Oh, no problem. Well, not exactly."

He waited for her to continue. When she didn't, he said, "However?"

"Daddy, I want to get my own apartment. I'm afraid Mom will fire me if I move out of the house, and then I won't be able to afford the rent."

"Have you talked to your mother about your plans?" Monty leaned against his car. "That seems like the thing to do."

"I was going to as soon as I had everything worked out. Now that I've saved up enough to make the deposit on an apartment, Mom's on the warpath because Cindy wants to go to college where Wayne is." She sighed. "I'm scared to mention moving out right now."

Putting an arm around his daughter, Monty said, "I know you think this is something you have to do right away, but moving into an apartment isn't urgent. If I were you I'd wait until your Mom simmers down, even if that means you move a month or two later than you planned." He pecked her on the cheek and opened his car door.

338

"Daddy?"

Monty sat in the driver's seat, his door still wide open. "Yes, honey?"

"If I end up being homeless, will you let me stay at the mission until I get another job?"

Monty got out of the car and hugged his daughter. "Your mother isn't going to let that happen, and neither am I. Just keep your head down, wait for the right time, and keep on doing a good job here at the Roadhouse."

Monica sniffled and wiped tears with her hands. "I guess I can sleep in Grandma and Leonard's RV if I have to."

On his way back to the mission, Monty phoned Patty Chesterfield to let her know he was ready to resume serious shopping for a house.

Chapter Sixty-One

"I'm delighted you agreed to have lunch with me," Steve Thornton said as soon as he and Lacy were seated at *Le Colibri*. "You are not at all what I expected. I thought you were a much older woman."

"You may have me confused with my mother-in-law, Pearl Chapman. She used to own the Roadhouse, but she retired last summer and sold the place to me." Perhaps a better description would be 'gave' rather than 'sold', but that wasn't any of Thornton's business.

"I spoke with Mrs. Chapman several times, but we never met." Steve moved his eyes from Lacy to the open menu in front of him. "We hoped she would allow us to make an offer on the Roadhouse when and if she disposed of it." He smiled and closed the menu. "But I understand family ties take precedence. The *coq au vin* is quite good here. You should try it."

When their server arrived, Lacy was ready with her choice. "I'll have the salad niçoise, please. Separate checks."

"Coq au vin for me." As soon as the server walked away, Steve said, "Tell me about yourself. How did you happen to end up in an out-of-the-way place like Polson's Crossing?"

"I've been here all my life. I was born in the old Memorial Hospital."

"You've never lived anywhere else, ever?"

"No, just here. What about you? I suppose business brings you here."

"Certainly it does," he replied instantly. "I'm in charge of acquisitions for the southwest area. I operate out of the Albuquerque office. I swing through here every now and then, searching out locations and properties for our various enterprises. I average being home about one week out of every six."

"Don't you get tired of traveling all the time?" A strange expression passed across his face, something Lacy couldn't read. "I don't mean to pry," she added.

"Not at all." Steve smiled at her for a long moment. "I enjoyed the travel at first. But now, I'm ready to settle down and stay put for a while. My being gone all the time is probably what broke up my marriage five years ago. Would you like some wine?"

"No, thank you." Why was he revealing his marital status? She chewed on that thought while Steve signaled the server and ordered himself a glass of white wine.

"You mentioned the other Mrs. Chapman is your mother-in-law." Steve leaned forward. "Is your husband in the restaurant business also?"

"Perhaps I should have said ex-mother-in-law." She shifted in her chair. Revealing even this generally known information to a someone she hardly knew made Lacy uncomfortable. At the same time, it was pleasant to talk with someone who seemed intensely interested in what she had to say. How she missed those morning coffee breaks with Pearl.

341

By the time they'd finished eating lunch, Lacy had talked about the breakup of her marriage to Monty. She hadn't planned to discuss her personal life, but Steve's sympathetic ear seemed to draw her out. "My ex-husband moved back to Polson's Crossing last summer," she heard herself saying, "and I really don't know why."

"So, you and your ex are business partners now." Steve took the last piece of bread from the basket sitting between them.

"Oh, no. Monty isn't involved in the Roadhouse at all. It's all mine." She noticed Steve smiled at this revelation. "He has immersed himself in running a men's rescue mission downtown, in the old Holy Trinity church."

"What a strange coincidence," Steve said. "I was interested in acquiring that church property at one time." He dabbed his napkin at his mouth. "However, the historic site designation made it impractical to pursue. How about some dessert? The cheesecake is topnotch."

"No," Lacy replied. "I'm stuffed. But don't let me stop you."

It occurred to Lacy that she'd been gone from the Roadhouse for a couple of hours, something she hardly ever did during business hours. Since her phone wasn't buzzing, she assumed things were running smoothly without her presence. With Julio in the smokehouse and Wanda in the kitchen, there was no reason why she shouldn't occasionally take a long lunch break.

Steve slowly devoured his cheesecake, drizzled at his request with raspberry coulis, while the two of them continued to chit chat. He took both checks when the server brought them. "Please," he said as Lacy reached for hers. "Let this be my treat."

She smiled and wrapped her hand around her water glass. "All right. Thank you." Why couldn't she allow a gentleman to buy her lunch?

"Lacy." Steve spoke her name, and then paused. After a moment, he continued, "I'd like to see you again. Socially, I mean. May I take you to dinner one day this week?"

"Dinnertime is pretty busy at the Roadhouse." Lacy had no doubt she was blushing. Maybe another sip of ice water would cool down her warm face. Finally she composed herself enough to say, "Sunday and Monday are my days off. We're closed then."

"Sunday night is perfect. I'm not leaving town until Monday morning. I'll pick you up about six-thirty." He took the credit card from the server and returned it to his wallet. "I'll need directions to your house."

Lacy drove back to the Roadhouse in deep thought. Why did she feel as if she'd been caught with her hand in the cookie jar? All she'd done was make a dinner date with a nice man. There were several things she wished she'd asked Steve during lunch. Was he still divorced? He had to be. Otherwise he wouldn't be asking her out, and besides he didn't wear a wedding ring. How old was he? Older than her for sure, maybe by as much as ten years. He wasn't nearly as attractive or as witty as Monty. Stop comparing every man to Monty, she told herself.

Her vibrating cell phone interrupted Lacy's concentration. At the next traffic light, she took her phone from her handbag, but then the signal changed to green. She drove on through several intersections, finally pulling into the Roadhouse parking lot before being able to check her messages. When she saw she had a text from Monty, she jammed the phone into her purse and hopped out of the car without reading further. Anything Monty had to say to her could wait.

Lacy breezed into the Roadhouse kitchen through the back door, reminding herself again to replace the lock with one that worked on punched-in numbers instead of a physical key. Instead of a greeting, Monica said, "Have you heard about the terrible thing that happened?"

"What are you talking about?" Lacy asked. "Can't I be gone more than an hour without something blowing up around here?"

"Pastor Tom had a heart attack. It sounds pretty bad."

"What?" Lacy collapsed onto a stool. "But he's so young."

"No, Mom." Monica countered. "He's forty-five."

344

Chapter Sixty-Two

Monty ran up the four flights of stairs. He doubted he would arrive any sooner than if he'd waited for the elevator, but he felt compelled to remain in motion. Gulping air, he followed the signs to the cardiac ICU.

Amanda Gillespie sat on a sofa with her back to the door, flanked by women Monty recognized from church. He stood with his hands in his pockets, not sure what to do.

"How is Tom?" a familiar voice asked.

Monty turned his head to see Pearl standing beside him. He put his arm around his mother and kept his voice low. "I don't know. I just got here."

Pearl gave him a squeeze before going to join the other women gathered around Amanda. Monty edged around the sofa and stood near the group. Like the other women, Pearl seemed to know exactly what to say and do. He played with the coins in his pocket, wanting to be of some use but uncertain what his role should be. Finally, Pearl spoke up. "Lead us in prayer, Monty."

Since everyone else was seated, the only practical way to form a prayer circle was for him to get on his knees. The group held hands, while Monty spoke. He forgot all about the other people in the room as he implored God to restore his friend and pastor to good health. When he said 'amen', he opened his eyes to the presence of two men who'd silently approached the group.

The man with the stethoscope looped around his neck, spoke. "Mrs. Gillespie?"

"Yes?"

"Would you come with me, please?"

Amanda began to rise. "Finally. I've been asking to see my husband."

"Let's go to my office," the other fellow, the one with a clerical collar, said.

The pastor's wife's face grew pale. She swayed slightly before drawing a deep breath. "I think I know what you have to say, Dr. Davis. These people are my church family. They can hear it with me."

The physician moved until he was directly in front of Amanda. "We did everything we could."

Amanda's voice was so soft Monty barely heard her whisper, "Tom's gone?" She sank to the sofa. "But I didn't get to tell him goodbye."

Monty felt numb, as if he'd been hit really hard on the head but the pain had not yet registered. He walked to a window and stared at the parking lot, struggling to process what happened. When he turned back to face his companions, the two visitors were gone. Weeping women sat with their arms around Amanda Gillespie, who shook with sobs.

Pearl head motioned Monty to the group and stood. "Leonard is on his way. You two can take care of getting Tom's car to their house. She's in no condition to drive." She handed him a set of car keys Monty recognized as Tom's. "The other ladies and I will pick up the kids and get

346

them and Amanda home." Pearl put an arm around Monty's waist and leaned against his shoulder. "Lord, please help this woman and her children get through this."

"Amen," Monty agreed. "Is there anything else I can do while I'm waiting for Len?"

Pearl glanced toward the sofa. "Get Amanda a bottle of water."

Monty wandered the hospital hallways like a zombie, finally purchasing a six pack of water in the gift shop. It occurred to him he should be praying, but he couldn't find any words. He was relieved when Leonard arrived. Monty drove Amanda's car home, while Leonard followed him and then took him back to the hospital. "I just talked to Tom yesterday," Monty said several times.

Leonard left Monty standing in the parking lot. Looking toward the sky, he shouted, "But we prayed." He drove to the mission, unable to organize his disjoined thoughts. What happens now to our church? Who is going to see after the Gillespie family? How can the mission carry on without Tom's vigorous support? Underlying all his other concerns, Monty hurt for the loss of the man who had become his close friend. He walked into the mission dormitory, remembering Tom Gillespie carrying in a stack of blankets he'd talked someone into donating.

It wasn't long before the telephone tsunami began. In between telling and retelling what little he knew, Monty called members of his Bible study group to let them know about Tom. Pearl relayed that Amanda had told her son and daughter about their father, and Leonard had returned the keys to the pastor's car. The mission's cook called in sick,

347

prompting Monty to order pizza delivery for the evening meal. Women from the church had things as much under control as possible.

"You must have been born under a lucky star," the next phone call began.

Monty was in no mood to talk to a telemarketer. "Who is this?"

"It's your agent, Carson Henry. If you talked to me more often, you'd recognize my voice."

"I'm sorry," Monty replied. "I'm having a rough day. A very dear friend of mine had a heart attack and passed away."

"Too bad." Carson didn't sound particularly sympathetic. "I never thought that crazy 'Cleaner Than A Hound's Tooth' was going to do much, but once every five years a novelty song catches people's imaginations. This one is selling like hotcakes."

"Good." The popularity of a song paled in comparison to matters of life and death.

"If that doesn't excite you, maybe this will," Carson continued. "A company that makes dog treats wants to use your song in their commercials. This could be big, Monty, bigger than 'Barely Hanging On'. You will be able to buy back your apartments, and maybe a couple more."

"Thanks, Carson, but I have something else in mind. I want to set up a trust fund."

"Oh, for your children?"

"No, to endow my rescue mission."

He was accustomed to Carson's abrupt termination of their conversations, but this was the first time the agent hung up without so much as a terse goodbye. Monty didn't waste any time worrying about Carson Henry. Instead, he answered the next call about Tom.

Chapter Sixty-Three

"Take care of things tonight," Monty told the young man he'd recently hired to help him run the mission. "I have to go to a meeting at my church."

"No worries. Me and Jesus got this." The body builder pose LeShawn struck only served to emphasize the puny muscles in his skinny arms.

"Right." Monty smiled and patted his pocket to verify his keys were there. He nodded at the security guard at the back exit. "Hold it in the road, Max. LeShawn's in the office if you need anything."

Ross Templeton shook Monty's hand as he entered the meeting room at the church. "Welcome to your first deacon meeting."

"Thanks," Monty replied. "I never expected to do this without Tom's guidance."

"None of us expected him to have that heart attack. You'll do fine."

Monty wasn't so sure. He listened while the others discussed the urgency of locating a new pastor, feeling he had no ideas to contribute. He was relieved to hear there was a retired minister who was willing to serve on an interim basis.

Ross seemed ill-at-ease as he spoke. "This man comes highly recommended. He worked over in Watson's Lake last year and the congregation there loved him. He can start right away, I mean like this Sunday." He paused and looked at his shoes.

"Is there a problem?" someone behind Monty asked.

"He needs a place to live while he's here with his wife, a grandson who's in a wheelchair, and two large dogs."

"We could fix up some ramps on the parsonage—" the man in the back of the room stopped speaking in mid-sentence.

Ross cleared his throat before continuing. "Tom's family is still living in the parsonage."

"Amanda told my wife she's looking for a job," someone volunteered.

"We can't pressure her to move immediately on top of everything else the poor woman has endured."

The ensuing discussion seemed to be going nowhere, when an idea struck Monty. He sat for a few more minutes, considering whether or not it would work. Finally, he spoke up. "Do you think the Gillespies would want to live in the old Holy Trinity parsonage?" Surprised faces turned toward him. "I'm staying there now, but I can move out right away and camp out in the rescue mission until I find a house to buy."

"That might work," Ross said cautiously.

"Is there any possibility Amanda would take the administrator position we just authorized for the mission?" Bob Brown, a member of the mission's board of directors, cocked his head toward Monty. "Unless you've found someone already."

"That's a great idea," Monty said. "If she'll do it, I mean." He thought for a moment, "You know, with her and her kids in the house instead of me, we could start taking in a few women who need shelter for the night."

After another round of discussion, Monty realized he'd been appointed to get the Gillespies moved as soon as they were comfortable doing so. Although he'd known Tom well, the pastor's wife—now widow—was merely an acquaintance. He hoped she was receptive to his idea. Not everyone wanted to be the housemother to a group of homeless women.

The following morning, Monty met Pearl and Leonard at the Grill. "I never knew of you to eat breakfast at ten in the morning before now," Monty teased Pearl.

"Leonard is teaching me how to live like a lazy old retiree," she replied.

Leonard smiled and slipped an arm around his wife. "I thought you were teaching *me*."

"Either way," Pearl said, "we both seem to be fast learners."

The three of them followed the hostess to a booth. After they'd ordered various combinations of pancakes and eggs, Monty discussed the possibility of offering Amanda

Gillespie a job at the mission. "I'm not exactly sure how to approach her," he confessed. "Any ideas?"

Pearl stirred her coffee, as she often did when deep in thought. "You probably ought to let her come to you."

"You mean call her and invite her to my office?"

"No," Pearl answered. "I mean get someone to tell her you're hiring and hope she'll be interested enough to follow up. Throw in the part about her moving into the house later on."

"What if I don't hear from her?"

"Then she doesn't want to work at the mission and things wouldn't work out anyhow."

Monty frowned with concentration. "That sounds like a big risk."

"Your mom is one smart woman," Leonard commented. "It pays to listen to her. She reads people the way other folks read books."

"Thank you, darlin'. I appreciate that." Pearl beamed at Leonard before unwrapping her silverware and inspecting each piece. "Amanda's got plenty of sense. If you just call her up and offer her a job, she'll suspect the deacons have cooked up some kind of a charity deal. You don't want to embarrass her like that."

The conversation was interrupted by the arrival of their food. After Leonard said grace, Monty poured warm syrup over his pancakes. He picked up his fork, but did not put it to use. "I heard Amanda is looking for a job, but I don't think it would ever occur to her to apply at the mission. If she doesn't stumble across the job announcement at the employment office, and I don't call her I don't see how your suggestion works."

Pearl ladled salsa liberally over her scrambled eggs. "I used to order poached eggs all the time, but restaurants don't know how to fix them anymore." She peered at Leonard. "I think I'll take one of them hams you smoked over to the Gillespie family this afternoon. Is that okay with you?"

"Honey, whatever suits you tickles me to death," Leonard replied.

"Newlyweds," Monty said, bringing sly grins to the wrinkled faces across the table.

"While I'm at Amanda's, I'll diplomatically bring up your job." Pearl buttered a piece of toast. She'll get the hint, but me passing the word won't put her on the spot like it would if you call her."

"Good plan." Monty agreed.

Chapter Sixty-Four

Lacy winced after plucking a hair. She turned to view another angle in the mirror, tweezers poised, searching for gray lurking among her dark locks. Satisfied she'd exorcised all tell-tale signs of aging, she dabbed color on her cheeks. A dash of lipstick and she was ready for her dinner date.

"You look nice," Monica said when Lacy walked into the living room. "Mm, you smell good, too. I've been going through our bookcase. We ought to give some of these away. I don't want to move them to my apartment, and I'm sure you don't want them." She pulled a child's book from the shelf. "I wonder why we haven't cleaned these out before now. Maybe we should have a garage sale."

"No, I have to keep that." Lacy took the book and opened it. "You and Cindy loved this story when you were little." She flipped to a page decorated with cats of various colors. "Take whatever you want and leave the rest." She clasped the slim volume to her chest. "I'll sort through them later. Where's Cindy?"

"I'm slaving over a book report." Cindy was sitting at the dining table. "Seniors are supposed to have fun and be exempt from homework and tests. Especially in the last six weeks of school. Somehow, my teachers failed to get the word."

"I'm going out for a while. Don't wait up for me," Lacy said.

"Okay," Monica mumbled, turning back to the bookcase.

"Gotcha." Cindy agreed. "No emergency phone calls to Amnesty International. Same guy?"

"Yes. He's picking me up in a few minutes." Lacy waited for some form of reaction, but both daughters seemed suddenly absorbed in their work. Although no one appeared to be interested, she said, "We're driving over to Watson's Lake for dinner and dancing."

With her back still turned, Monica spoke without enthusiasm. "Nice."

Cindy's head remained buried in her book.

Perfect timing, Lacy thought, realizing Steve was walking toward her front door. She opened it and slipped outside, tossing a quick, "See you later, girls," over her shoulder.

"You look lovely," Steve said, opening the car door for her.

"Thank you. I'm glad you think so."

"You'll like this place I'm taking you to." Steve drove slightly faster than Lacy preferred as he steered his sporty car through her neighborhood. After a moment of silence, he said, "Your daughters don't approve of me."

Lacy was certain his perception was correct. "Why do you say that?"

"You always hurry out the door without introducing me, and it seems to me you don't want me inside your house."

"You know how kids are."

"No," Steve replied, turning onto the access road to the highway. "I don't have any children. How are they?"

"They think their separated parents should get back together, no matter how unrealistic that is." Lacy wanted to change the subject, and passing the Roadhouse suggested a topic. "Pearl's Roadhouse looks strange with the lights off and no cars in the parking lot."

"It does indeed. Do you have any idea how much money you lose by not being open on Sunday? It's staggering. Not to mention the lost revenue that comes from not offering alcoholic drinks."

"Pearl used to say she'd rather shut the place down than sell beer or make her employees work on Sunday."

Keeping his eyes on the road, Steve spoke as if explaining arithmetic to a first-grader. "That archaic business model might have worked a hundred years ago here in the Bible belt." He glanced at her briefly, then smiled. "The place I'm taking you to in Watson's Lake was that kind of restaurant, stuck in the twentieth century, until we bought it out. You'll be impressed with the transformation."

Lacy's mind wandered while Steve talked about strategies for increasing restaurant profits. The girls were planning to watch a movie that evening. She hadn't asked about what it was, but she knew their tastes ran to romantic comedy. Were Monica and Cindy having a better time than she was, sitting at home eating popcorn and laughing? Ridiculous! She was out on the town, dating, having fun.

"You're very quiet this evening." Steve pulled into the parking lot of a building outlined in softly glowing blue neon. The prominent but tasteful sign read 'Bob's Hideaway'.

"I'm just taking in your ideas and mulling them over," Lacy replied. Well, sort of. Close enough. It wasn't a total lie.

"Good." He beamed at her for a moment before coming around to open the car door.

It took Lacy a while to adjust to the muted lighting inside. The ambiance, unlike anything in Polson's Crossing, reminded her of a movie scene. White table linens, china place settings, and stemmed glassware graced the tables surrounding a wooden dance floor. Instead of the country music she was accustomed to, the live band played a song she did not recognize.

After Steve convinced Lacy they should order the chateaubriand for two, he asked, "What do you think of Bob's Hideaway?"

"I've never seen anything like it," she answered. There was something in the air that made her eyes burn, probably cigarette smoke. As she'd hoped, Steve seemed to take her noncommittal statement as a positive endorsement.

A server arrived with a wine menu. After some discussion, Steve made a selection. The server fetched a bottle, opened it, and offered a small sample. With closed eyes, Steve sipped and nodded. "Excellent." The server smiled and filled their glasses.

"Can you imagine Pearl's Roadhouse re-created into a place like this?" Steve didn't stop talking long enough for her to answer. "Of course, the real knockouts are in our city locations. Someday I'd like to take you to see what we've done in Dallas."

The arrival of salads caused a brief lull in their conversation. As Lacy began to eat hers, Steve asked, "Is something wrong with the wine?"

She picked up a fork full of lettuce and then put it down. "I don't drink alcohol."

He stared at her, unbelief written on his face. "You're kidding me."

"No. I'm serious."

Steve leaned forward. "You don't enjoy an occasional glass of wine with dinner? Or a cold beer on a hot day?"

"No, I never do. Never have."

"Are you saying you've never in your life had even one drink of alcohol?"

"I tasted beer once. To be honest, it reminded me of cat pee."

359

He grinned. "How would you know that? I'm quite sure you've never tasted cat urine."

"It's a long story, but yes I have. My daughter's pet anointed my toast, which I bit into before I knew what happened."

Without a hint of a smile, Steve said, "Just take a little sip of the wine. I think you'll like it."

"No. Thank you." There was no reason to continue explaining, but she did anyway. "As I mentioned before, my husband's drinking was a factor in breaking up our marriage."

Steve sighed. "Just because your ex is a lush, that doesn't mean *you* can't enjoy a glass of wine now and then."

She didn't feel like engaging in a debate with Steve, but she was determined not to drink the wine. Instead, she smiled, took a swallow of water, and changed the subject again. "Are you originally from Albuquerque?"

"I respect your decision, but if you aren't going to drink this, I will. There's no point in wasting it." Steve slid her wine glass to the side of his plate. "In answer to your question, I was born and raised in Philadelphia. I like big city life. There are so many interesting things to see and do in a place like Philly." He drained his wine glass and took a swig from Lacy's. "You don't know what you're missing."

She wasn't quite sure whether Steve referred to her lack of interest in wine or her workaday life in a small town. Very likely, it was both. She was glad when they finished their meal and he asked her to dance.

Chapter Sixty-Five

Monty rolled up his sleeping bag and stashed it in the corner of his office. Thankful there was a small private bathroom attached to the office, he gathered clean clothes from the file cabinet and headed for the shower. In a few minutes he emerged as fresh as a man could be after sleeping on the floor.

Amanda Gillespie caught up with him in the hallway. "I've got to find time to go house shopping," Monty told her.

"Why can't you do that today?" She asked.

"Well, for one thing, I have to contact tonight's volunteers and make sure they don't forget it's their turn to help out.

"I've already taken care of that." She swiped the screen of her tablet. "I got phone numbers and email addresses yesterday and sent out group messages this morning."

"Good work." Monty opened the hallway door and followed Amanda to the kitchen counter. "Did you include Reverend Buckley? He's our preacher tonight if I remember correctly."

"LeShawn called him. We decided it was better to have a conversation and not rely on sending the Reverend a message." She laid her tablet on the kitchen counter. "I hope you don't mind if we went ahead and took care of contacting people."

"Mind? I'm thrilled. Anything else you guys want to do to make the mission run smoothly, go for it." He reached to turn on the coffee maker. "Hey, somebody make coffee already."

"LeShawn said you like to have a few cups to start the day." She swiped at her screen again. "Now if you really don't mind us making suggestions," Amanda looked at him before continuing.

Monty took a big gulp of coffee. "Shoot. What's on your mind?"

"In the three days I've been here, you've had to make a trip to the supermarket every day."

"Yeah," Monty agreed. "I hate spending so much time shopping, but a bunch of hungry men can put really put away the groceries."

"If you'll make up the menus in advance, we can order food on line and have it delivered each morning."

"That's what Mama always did at the Roadhouse. Of course. It only makes sense." Monty drank more coffee, feeling more than a little foolish that he'd never thought of having supplies delivered. "If I'm not careful, you and LeShawn and going to work me out of a job." He grinned. "And I'm okay with that. Anything else?"

"Yes." Amanda took a diet soda from the refrigerator. "My worst vice," she said, holding the can away from her as she popped the tab. "I have been thinking about some kind of incentive program for the mission's guests. Say, for example, you allow some of the women who spend the night at the parsonage clean it up the following day for either a small wage or points toward guaranteeing them priority for lodging that night. Tom…" After speaking her late husband's name, Amanda stopped talking and took a deep breath. Then she closed her eyes and continued. "Tom used to say we all need to have a purpose and to be accepted into a community. Rewarding the women for helping the mission would make them feel worthwhile, as if they're contributing instead of receiving charity." She brushed away a tear. "I'm sorry."

"No need to be sorry," Monty said. "I want to cry every time I think about Tom, too." He considered going and giving Amanda a hug, but decided against it. Technically, he was the boss and she was his employee. Maybe it was best to keep a professional distance. "We've had a lot of turnover in the housekeeping staff. If what you're proposing for the women works out, maybe we could do something similar with the men."

"Wouldn't that be great? By starting small with the women and the house, we can work out the kinks before expanding the program." She picked up her laptop. "I'll write up some procedures we can talk about at the next staff meeting. This is exciting."

Monty refilled his coffee cup and searched the kitchen drawers for something to write on. Within an hour, he had two weeks of dinner menus written out in long hand. Then he went in search of LeShawn. Ordering and tracking food supplies was a job his sharp young assistant could handle.

After a week of house hunting and finding nothing, Monty signed a short-term lease on a furnished downtown apartment. Surely in six months something would turn up. Patty seemed as frustrated as he was. "I never thought I would have to show so many homes to someone who has no neighborhood preference and no price limit," she said when he told her he'd decided to lease an apartment. Tapping a nail on her desk, she added, "I understand what you don't like in certain homes, but it's still not clear to me what you really do want."

On his way back to the mission, Monty tried to picture exactly what he was searching for in a home. He detoured to drive through his mother's old neighborhood. Pearl's house now looked completely different from the front. New landscaping, bright exterior paint, and a red front door left no doubt that the home had changed hands. The old house where he grew up had what Patty Chesterfield called 'charm'. Yet it was not the architecture that drew him in. Pearl's love filled her household with a warmth no floor plan could reproduce. He stopped for a moment, looking over the exterior changes. There was a time when approaching that doorway filled him with the anticipation that someone inside would be happy to see him. That feeling was what was missing in his life.

He returned to his car and circled the block. The 'for sale' sign was gone from the Johnson house, and the children playing in the front yard had no hint of red in their hair. He mourned that family's disintegration, despite their tempestuous lifestyle. Surely with some give and take, Dexter and Janie could have worked things out. Maybe he and Lacy could have, too, once upon a time. But now? Only God knew the answer.

The irony of his situation struck Monty. The success he'd wanted so desperately was now his, though not in the form he'd expected. Still, it wasn't enough. He'd trade his hit songs and their financial rewards for the ten years he'd lost with his wife and daughters. *No, I didn't lose those years. I threw them away.* What was that scripture Tom quoted frequently? Something about forgetting what was in the past and pressing on into the future. He'd have to look that up and read it again.

Monty took his time returning to the mission, mulling over the things he needed to do in the next few days. He had only a few possessions to transfer from the Holy Trinity parsonage to his new apartment. LeShawn and Amanda would have to take care of his adopted dog and cat, since his apartment strictly forbade pets.

He'd also promised to help Monica move into her tiny little house. He smiled, knowing his daughter was going to tease him when she found out he'd taken an apartment. He'd been the one who'd convinced her to invest in a house instead of renting. He knew his own words were going to be repeated to him and rather looked forward to the good-natured razzing he'd endure.

Chapter Sixty-Six

Lacy surveyed the girls' bedroom. How many lectures had she delivered on the subject of keeping this space neat and clean? Somehow today's lack of clutter brought no satisfaction with it. Monica bought her own house, and now Cindy was packing her things to go away to college. Lacy picked up a doll and cuddled it close. "Aren't you taking Baby?" she asked.

Cindy replied without stepping out of the closet. "Nope. I barely have enough room to get everything I need into the dorm. Maybe that's part of the college experience, to see how small a space we can survive in without developing anti-social behavior." She pushed empty wire hangers aside. "Are you sure you don't want me to take some of these things to Dad's mission?"

"No. I'll take care of that later." *After you're gone and my nest is empty and quiet, I'll need something to do.* "Are you sure you kept out the clothes you're wearing this week?"

"Pretty sure." Cindy you came and sat on the bed beside Lacy. "I can always raid Monica's closet if I forgot something. Now that you mention it, I should have packed my graduation dress so I could wear that ruffley thing she had on at church Sunday." Cindy put an arm around Lacy. "Thank you for being so supportive, Mom. I know you wanted me to live here and go to State, but I'll be back home after graduation. I promise."

Lacy leaned against her daughter. "Four years is a long time. You may change your mind if you fall in love with some young man from Timbuktu."

"I've already told Wayne if he wants to have a future with me, he'd better figure out how he is going to make a living in Polson's Crossing. That's why he's majoring in veterinary science and I'll major in business with a minor in marketing. He'll do the vet work and I'll take care of the business side of things. We've got it all planned."

More than a little surprised, Lacy turned to look at the woman-child she'd raised. "Are things that serious between you and Wayne?"

"Yeah." Cindy spoke softly. "I wanted to tell you that before now, but I was afraid you'd get upset."

Lacy winced. "What about his singing career?"

"Wayne understands he has to have a regular job if he wants me to hang around with him. Singing can be a hobby, or a second job, or whatever he wants as long as he has a steady income." Cindy put a hand on the doll Lacy was still holding. "Maybe I'll take Baby after all. She can sit on my bed. If the other girls tease me, I'll just tell them it's an old Texas tradition to keep your first doll on your bed in college."

Lacy struggled to keep herself from crying at the sight of the bare-looking room, now devoid of all personality. "As soon as Monica takes this furniture, I'm going to turn this room into a home office."

"Sweet." Cindy closed up the boxes stacked near the door. "You can work here instead of that little cubby hole at the Roadhouse. Wait!" she slapped her forehead. "Where will I sleep when I come home for a visit?"

"On the couch."

Cindy screwed up her face. "Yuck. That sofa is lump city. Okay, so here's a plan. Remind Monica that one of the twin beds is mine. She can store it for me but I get to sleep in it anytime I'm in Polson's Crossing. Problem solved."

At the Friday evening graduation, Lacy sat between Monica and Pearl at the high school athletic field, thinking nothing will ever be the same again after tonight. *Tomorrow we will load Cindy's things into Pearl's RV, and she and Leonard will take my baby a thousand miles away.* She passed a packet of tissues to Monica. When Cindy stepped forward to accept her diploma, everyone in their small family group clapped and cheered. Monty stood and added an ear-splitting whistle to his applause.

Afterward, Cindy's friends and their parents packed the event room at the Roadhouse. Even with most of the tables and chairs removed, there was hardly space to move amid the throng of people. A woman wearing a lilac dress turned toward Lacy and smiled, "You must be Cynthia's mother. I'm Lauren Smith, her English teacher. What a delight it has been to have your daughter in my class."

"Thank you. I'm very proud of her."

"You should be, and she's equally proud of you. She often speaks about your many business accomplishments and her father's compassionate efforts on behalf of the homeless."

"Thank you." *My business accomplishments? With all of my self-doubt and difficulty making decisions? And*

369

Monty? Compassionate? Is that how Cindy sees us? She chatted with other parents, and then realized Monty was standing beside her.

"What a great party," he said.

Lacy kept her voice just above a whisper. "You may not think so when you see the bill."

"I've already settled up with Julio." He smiled and gazed into her eyes in a way she found unsettling, but at the same time pleasant. "And I *still* think you did a wonderful job, not just tonight, but with Cindy and Monica. You're one terrific mom. If I didn't think you'd smack my face, I'd give you a big hug and a kiss."

"Oh, Monty, you're such a tease." She turned slightly and lifted her glass of ice water from the table, sipping at it to combat the sudden warmth flooding her face. Lacy feared he might do exactly what he'd said, and for an unguarded moment she hoped he would.

"Mama asked me to drop by your house Monday morning and be a beast of burden," Monty said. "Is that all right with you?"

"Sure. The girls and I can manage Cindy's stuff, but I'm sure Leonard would welcome some extra muscle to get Monica's bedroom set loaded up."

Monty groaned and squinted his eyes. "Oh, no. Are we talking about those twin beds Jimmy and I brought in the van with a big hot dog on the side?"

"The same one." Lacy smiled, remembering the day Monty referred to, and how she and Judy Glassman laughed about the two "weenies" driving the hot dog truck.

Chapter Sixty-Seven

When Monty arrived at Lacy's house on Monday, the driveway was filled by his mother's RV. He parked across the street and joined Cindy and Leonard in the front yard. "Good morning," he said. Surprisingly, his voice sounded normal to his ears. He couldn't quit thinking about the last time he was inside this house, the night he packed his clothes and took a taxi to the bus station. Lacy told him never to try walking through that front door again. However, she'd seemed pleased when he offered to come and help with Monica's move. He knew Lacy had a tendency toward overstatement when she was angry. She may even have forgotten the words that he'd grieved over for so many years.

"Good morning." Leonard shifted his mug of coffee to shake hands with Monty.

Cindy leaned into his hug. "Hey, Daddy. Isn't this exciting? I can't wait to get on the road. Or, actually, to get to Tennessee. They call it the volunteer state, you know. I've been reading about it."

"Are you sure you don't want to go on to Florida with your grandma and me?" Leonard's delivery was deadpan, but Monty knew him well enough to know the question was the old man's idea of a joke.

"No way. I have to immerse myself in the college experience. Meaning, I want to have twelve hours racked up by the end of the summer."

Monty couldn't resist teasing his daughter. "Twelve hours? You can do that over one weekend."

"Come on, Daddy. You know that's just how they talk about college credits." She rolled her eyes toward the front door. "I have a bunch of boxes that want to go to school with me. Hint. Hint."

The morning sun cooked the June humidity into steam in the short time it took Monty, Leonard and Cindy to stack her luggage and boxes into the RV's living area. Meanwhile, Pearl and Lacy meandered outside, drinking coffee and solemnly observing the work. "All right, loadmaster," Leonard said, taking Pearl by the hand. "Come and see if you approve."

Pearl smiled and climbed the steps of her RV. "If I can get to the steering wheel, we're in good shape."

Monty stood with Lacy and Cindy, remembering the day he and Lacy moved into this house.

"I'm thirsty," Cindy announced. "Monica promised to be here at eight. Since it's almost nine, she should be arriving pretty soon. Would anyone else like a cold bottle of water?"

"That sounds good to me," Monty answered. "Len and I can take the twin beds apart while we're waiting." He realized something was missing. "Do I need to go and rent a truck?"

"No. Monica said she's borrowing one." Cindy scurried inside.

Only an hour late, Monica pulled up to the curb in a shiny white pickup.

"Nice wheels," Monty said. "All that pickup needs is a big hot dog painted on the side."

Lacy laughed. "I was just thinking about that crazy truck."

"We sure had some good times," Monty said without making eye contact.

Monica did an effective zombie impersonation as she ambled from the pickup toward her mother. "Why on earth did we decide to do this so early?" she groaned.

Pearl emerged from the RV, followed by Leonard. "Because lifting and toting needs to be finished before it gets too hot," Pearl said. "And good morning to you, too."

"Good morning, everyone." Monica dispensed hugs all around. "Thanks for helping Cindy and me."

"I'll move the RV out of the driveway." Pearl followed her words by climbing back into the huge vehicle. "I'll park her around the corner."

"Aren't you going to wait until after Cindy's stuff is loaded?" Monica asked. When laughter exploded all around her, she looked puzzled. "What? Oh, I guess you did that already."

Lacy led the way inside her house. Following close behind his daughters, Monty heard Cindy ask Monica, "Are you going to tell them?"

"Later." Monica glanced around before leaning close and whispering something to her sister.

Within an hour, they had the heavy dresser, chest, twin beds, lamps, and cartons of bedding packed into the white pickup. No one seemed interested in Monty's offer to recruit muscle from the mission to deliver the bedroom furniture. His proposal made obvious sense because it would allow Leonard and Pearl to start their journey without further delay. Nevertheless, after much more discussion than Monty thought necessary, the consensus was for everyone to caravan to Monica's. After unloading the furniture, they'd all have one last meal together at the Grill before sending the travelers on their way.

Everyone pitched in, and it wasn't long before the six of them were sitting at a big round table at the Grill. Monty quickly took a seat next to Pearl when he suspected his daughters were attempting to maneuver him and Lacy next to each other. He appreciated their effort, as well as their motive, but knew his ex-wife well enough to know manipulation would only push her away.

Somehow, the conversation turned to reminiscences of bygone days at the Roadhouse. Pearl told of the server who slipped and sent a tray of five dinners flying across the dining room. As the chicken fried steaks went airborne, the server screamed an expletive never before heard in Pearl's domain. A busser decided the best way to clean up the mess was to sprinkle it with flour to absorb all of the liquid, resulting in what Pearl described as a "royal mess."

Not to be outdone, Monty recounted the time a big can of chili powder got mixed up with coffee grounds. He demonstrated the facial expressions of the breakfast customers who were more than a little surprised by their morning cup of java.

Leonard was usually a man of few words, but he shared his recollection of participating in a scheme to 'borrow' a school bus on Halloween when he was in eighth grade. "I heard there was a bunch of boys that put outhouses on the lawn of the high school principal, the mayor, and the chief of police that night," he declared. "There was a lot of suspicion, but they never found out for sure who did it.

"Leonard Berry!" Pearl exclaimed. "Were you one of those rowdy boys? If I'd known that I never would have married you."

"That's why we had to keep it quiet." Leonard didn't crack a smile. "Looking out for my future with the sweetest little bride in Polson's Crossing."

"That's pure baloney," Pearl answered, obviously pleased by Leonard's compliment. She fished near her feet and came up with her handbag. "I don't know when I've had so much fun, but we have to get going if we're going to make it to Dallas by this evening."

"Monica," Cindy said. "Isn't there something you want to say? Like an announcement you promised me you'd make before I leave for Tennessee so I don't have to miss it?"

Monica took a deep breath. "I'm engaged." She moved her left hand from underneath the table and held it out, flashing her ring left and right. "Julio and I are going to get married."

Amid a chorus of congratulations, Monica smiled and stood. "I have to get Julio's truck back to him so he can pick up his sister. I'll call you later, Mom."

Chapter Sixty-Eight

In the Grill's parking lot, Lacy hugged Cindy for the third time. She couldn't resist giving last minute instructions to be careful, study hard, and call home often. She stood with Monty as the big RV pulled away. "My baby," she said, brushing away a tear.

Monty made a motion as if to put an arm around her, but stopped short of actual contact. "Tell me something, Lacy."

She wasn't in the mood for a deep discussion, especially not while standing in a hot parking lot. "What do you want to know?"

"How long has it been since you had a double chocolate dipped ice cream cone?"

Lacy laughed at the sheer absurdity of his question. "Probably not since..." She stopped short of saying the last time she had an ice cream cone was with him. "I don't know, but it has been a very long time."

He inclined his head to the left. "There's a Dairy Queen right over there. How about it? Want to join me?" When she didn't reply immediately, he added, "I'm buying."

A sweet treat to top off her lunch was much more appealing than going home to an empty house. "Oh, why not?" She'd move the furniture around to make an office from the girls' old bedroom later.

Soon they were seated across from each other in a booth, appreciating the air conditioning. "I wish I'd asked when Monica plans to get married," Lacy commented. "I was so surprised I didn't think." She took a bite of chocolate shell, breaking through to the cold vanilla ice cream underneath. "I had no idea she was seeing Julio. Did you?"

"I didn't know they were dating," Monty replied. "But they see each other every day at the Roadhouse."

"I thought she'd get tired of working in the kitchen and enroll in college this fall. Obviously, that's not happening."

"There's nothing to keep a married woman from going to school, if that's what she wants to do." Monty took a bite from the top of his ice cream. "Julio's a good kid. They'll do all right."

"I like Julio, too. He's exactly the kind of young man I want for a son-in-law. Just not yet." She held back her complaint about Cindy being involved with Wayne. "Why can't Monica see how important it is to get an education? She could major in hospitality, and come back and take over the Roadhouse someday. I'd gladly give it to her."

"What would you do then?" Monty asked. "Let me put it another way, what would you like to do with the rest of your life, Lacy? I mean, if you could do whatever you wanted, no obstacles?"

"I don't know." She pondered the question while finishing off the chocolate coating and eating her ice cream down to the top of the cone. "Maybe something related to interior design."

Monty gave her a piercing look. "Why don't you do it, then?"

"You can't be serious." She pointed at the cone he was ignoring. "You're about to drip."

He caught the melting ice cream in the nick of time. "I'm dead serious. Why don't you go to State and get whatever credentials you need and open up your own design business?"

"Who would run the Roadhouse if I took off to be a coed?"

"You know, for the first few months after we opened the rescue mission, I felt like I had to be there twenty-four seven. I oversaw everything, food, housekeeping, worship services, security, the whole schmear. Tom Gillespie gave me some valuable advice. He told me to back off, and let other people assume some ownership." Monty used a paper napkin to wipe melted ice cream dripping down the outside of his cone. "He was right. Things run a lot smoother now that I've let go. I can't hold a candle to the things LeShawn and Amanda get done. My point, if I have one, is that you might be surprised what Monica could do with the Roadhouse, especially with Julio helping her."

"I don't think Monica's ready for that kind of responsibility. Besides, assuming I could find someone to manage the restaurant for me, do you realize I'd be more than forty years old by the time I got through four years of college?"

Monty pursed his lips for a moment. "So, Lacy, how old will you be in four years if you stay at the Roadhouse?"

"I have to go." She had to put some distance between herself and Monty before his crazy ideas started to take root. "Thanks for the ice cream."

Lacy drove home deep in thought. Although she knew it could never happen, she allowed her imagination to explore becoming an expert in curb appeal and load-bearing walls. Monty seemed to have straightened up his wild ways, but once a dreamer always a dreamer.

After she removed the drawers, her desk was light enough to slide down the hall on a throw rug. With the addition of the bookcase, two chairs, and a lamp, her new office was complete. Soon she had her house in order. As she'd anticipated, all of the rooms looked larger with less furniture in them. She plopped onto the sofa, pleased with what she'd accomplished.

Cindy called to report a safe arrival at an RV park outside Dallas. "What are you doing?" Lacy asked her daughter.

"Pops Leonard hooked everything up, and then Grandma and I cooked dinner and we invited all of the other RVers to bring their lawn chairs and join us. We sat around in a big circle. Grandma and a couple from Arizona told stories. Then I played the mandolin and we sang a bunch of old songs that you and Grandma like. They're still out there talking, but I'm going to read for a while and go to bed. I'm practicing sleeping on a sofa, but this one is newer than ours. Have you talked to Monica?"

"No. We've missed each other several times. I thought you were her calling me back when the phone rang." Lacy was relieved to know Cindy was tucked in for the night in Pearl's care. One more day before she was turned loose to fend for herself out in the world.

"She really loves Julio, and he's absolutely over the top crazy about her. She's the only reason he stayed at the Roadhouse instead of going to work for the school. When she broke up with Philip, that's when Julio decided to hang around. They are totally epic together. I can't remember if you're supposed to know all of that or not, but I guess it doesn't matter now that Monica has revealed they're engaged. Anyway, I hope you're not going to yell at her."

"I never yell." Lacy knew better, and she knew Cindy did also. Lacy tried Monica's number again after speaking with Cindy. When her call went to voice mail, she suspected her daughter was avoiding her. She turned on some classic country music and picked up the stack of magazines beside the sofa. One-by-one, she leafed through them, setting aside only a few to keep. Her eye fell on an ad for a now-closed competition to design a dream house, and she took the open magazine to her desk. She was not interested in entering a contest, but it would be interesting to play around with a sketch.

Lacy sank into her project. When her phone rang, she glanced at the time. One o'clock, an hour past her bed time. "Hello, Monica."

"Hi, Mom. Are you mad at me?"

"You're a grownup, honey. You're old enough to decide things for yourself. I've always liked Julio." Lacy closed her eyes and forced herself to remain calm. She'd promised herself she'd stop trying to control her daughters, and she truly wanted to. "I hope you're going to wait a while before you get married."

"We were thinking about Christmastime." Suddenly Monica's voice sparkled. "We don't want anything fancy, just a few family and friends at the Roadhouse. By December, we'll have enough money saved up to take a quick honeymoon, maybe over a long weekend. And then we'll set up housekeeping. I'm glad Daddy persuaded me to buy my house instead of renting."

She listened while Monica talked about her plans, determined to remain calm even if she couldn't yet claim to be enthused. They must have talked a while, because it was after two when Lacy brushed her teeth and climbed into bed.

Chapter Sixty-Nine

When Monty called his staff together two days later, blank faces stared up at him. "Good morning," he said. "I know it's unusual for me to have a meeting this early. I have good news to share, and I can't hold it in any longer." He helped himself to a cup of coffee and sat at the table. "There are details to work out and papers to sign, but the mission is being endowed with enough money to keep us in business for a long time, for the rest of my life and beyond. I'll work up a full report for the board meeting next week, but I wanted you to be the first to know."

Monty enjoyed his coffee until the excited chatter died down. "The first order of business is prayer. Let's give thanks to God, the One who has blessed this mission beyond everything we could ask or imagine." He'd expected to lead the prayer, but LeShawn beat him to the punch, followed by Amanda's eloquent expression of praise. Even Max offered up a few spontaneous words.

Monty told them how brushing Goldie's teeth led to the inspiration for a song. The song became an unlikely hit, and then a dog food company bought the rights to use it in their commercials. "That's all God, start to finish."

"When do you think we can afford more staff?" Amanda asked.

"Now if there's a need," Monty replied. "What do you have in mind?"

She smiled and nodded to her co-worker. "LeShawn can explain it better than I can."

"Long story short, State is willing to work with us on vocational training." LeShawn took a piece of paper from his shirt pocket. "Culinary arts, meaning running the kitchen and teaching residents commercial cooking. Housekeeping for sure, groundskeeping maybe, and later on if those work out, office skills." He smiled and refolded the paper.

"That's fantastic," Monty said after LeShawn outlined how the program was to work. "How did you come up with this?"

"Me and Amanda got to talking, about how we wished we could do more for the homeless folks than giving them food and a bed one night at a time," LeShawn answered. "One thing led to another."

"State will pay the teachers' salaries, with us providing funds for their travel and any books or educational materials they use here," Amanda chimed in. "Our guests will then constitute the majority of the labor force required to maintain the mission. Meanwhile, they'll be learning a trade."

Max spoke up, "These two have convinced me to do on-the-job training for four helpers." He shrugged. "It's not much, but local companies always have openings for security guards."

"You guys are amazing." Monty's voice choked with emotion. "You blow me away. LeShawn and Amanda, I think you should be the ones to present this plan at the next board meeting. I want them to see who's behind this absolutely brilliant idea. They probably get tired of listening to me talk all the time." What Monty didn't say

385

was having LeShawn and Amanda speak happened to fit nicely with his proposal to ask for across-the-board salary increases for the mission staff.

One by one, people excused themselves. Monty continued to sit at the table, mulling over the surprising twists and turns the mission had taken since his original concept for a short-term shelter.

Amanda went to the refrigerator and popped the top on a soda. "Breakfast," she said, holding the soda can in front of her. "Don't tell my kids. They'll rebel against oatmeal if they ever find out."

"My lips are sealed," Monty replied. "I'm on their side, though. I despise oatmeal. When my mother used to make it, I'd secretly flush it down the toilet and then steal cookies for breakfast."

"Really?" Amanda's face registered astonishment. "You're such a straight arrow. I had you pegged as the model child who never gave your mother an ounce of trouble."

Monty waited for a punch line, but realized after a moment her remark was sincere. "Actually, I was a rotten kid who grew up to be a selfish jerk until I became a Christian. I still say and do things I shouldn't, but at least now I try not to."

She stood by the table and sat her soda aside. "We all have our struggles of faith. I still question why Tom had to leave us."

"Tom didn't leave," Monty said softly. "He died."

"I hate putting it that way because it sounds so final." Amanda ran her fingernail around the rim of her soda can. "I'm so thankful for my work here. I literally love helping people, and this job came along at exactly the right time."

"I second that emotion, as the old song says. The mission gives me purpose and fulfillment. But I've learned it's not everything."

"Agreed. My priority right now is raising my children." She wrapped both hands around her soda and gazed into it. "How are things between you and Lacy?"

"Up and down, as always. Monday, we had ice cream cones together. That's what we did to celebrate special occasions, back in the day when ice cream was all we could afford."

"Just the two of you?" Amanda pulled out a chair and sat at the table again. "That's wonderful. Tell me what happened."

"After our family lunch for Cindy's sendoff, I asked Lacy if she wanted to go for ice cream. She surprised me by saying yes. We were having a nice, relaxed conversation when all of the sudden she bolted out of there like a scared rabbit, and I have no idea why."

"Did anything unusual happen right before she left?"

"No, we were just talking." Monty reflected for a moment. "I asked what she'd do if she could do anything. You know what she said? Interior design. I thought Lacy had a passion for the restaurant business because she worked so hard at it. But I never asked her before now."

"What would you have done different if you'd known?"

Monty rested his chin in one hand while he considered Amanda's question. "Probably nothing. When Lacy and I were married, I thought what I wanted was the only thing that mattered. The night I left she warned me there was no coming back."

"We all say things we don't mean. I wish I could have a few minutes with Tom to ask his forgiveness for words I said in anger. Maybe we'll have that conversation someday in Heaven. Or maybe what hurts us here won't matter anymore there." Amanda stood and tossed her drink can into the recycle bin. "I'd better get to work. You still have a chance with Lacy. Make the most of it."

Chapter Seventy

Lacy continued Pearl's practice of hiring students to help out during the summer rush. As always, a few quit after getting a taste of bussing tables. Nevertheless, the crop that stayed learned quickly and did good work. When she wasn't busy in the dining room, Lacy spent her time learning to use the computer program she'd purchased to automate various aspects of the Roadhouse's management. She liked the inventory and bookkeeping so much she decided to activate the human resources module as well. For the first time, she understood why her daughters could lose all track of time playing computer games.

The more she explored her new toy, the better Lacy liked it. Processing background checks on her new employees was a breeze, and the results came back almost instantly. One of the temporary high school students had been in trouble several times for shoplifting. He'd stopped showing up for work after the first day. Lacy was relieved she didn't have to make a decision on whether or not to keep the youngster employed. When she successfully added an applet to her phone to view reports remotely, she threw her hands in the air and shouted, "Yes!"

Lacy was about to leave her office when her cell phone vibrated. "Hello," Steve said. "I'm going to be in Polson's Crossing this weekend, and I was wondering if you'd like to have dinner with me."

"Steve, it's good to hear from you. This weekend?" This was the opening she'd been waiting for. "Would you like to go to church with me on Sunday morning?"

389

It was a moment before Steve responded. "I'll have to take a rain check. I won't actually be in town until Sunday afternoon. Maybe another time. I was thinking about going to a cozy little place on the highway past Watson's Lake for dinner and dancing."

Now it was Lacy's turn to hesitate. "I have a commitment for Sunday evening. I'm sorry, but I didn't know you were going to be in town." There were usually six to eight weeks between Steve's visits to Polson's Crossing, but he'd been in town only three weeks ago. Meanwhile, she'd decided to get more involved in church activities, not only to be of service, but also in the hope of making friends. Pearl's retirement and her daughters moving out of the house left her hungry for someone to talk to. But why did she sign up to volunteer at the rescue mission with her Sunday school class this coming weekend?

Steve's voice broke into her thoughts. "I really want to celebrate my birthday with you. Can't you rearrange your schedule?"

"That might be possible." She could always cancel going to the mission. Her fellow class members probably wouldn't complain if she didn't show up. They might not even notice.

"Good, because I'd hate to miss seeing you. You're very special to me, Lacy. I'm sure you know that. I'll pick you up at five."

Sitting back in her office chair, Lacy wondered what 'special' meant to Steve. He often held her hand, and the last two times they were together he kissed her goodnight. She found him to be decent company when he wasn't harping on buying the Roadhouse, but he drank more than she liked. She'd even suggested she drive home from their last date, an offer he appeared to have taken as a joke. Something—she wasn't sure what—held her back from confiding her innermost thoughts to him.

On Sunday morning, Lacy caught up with her Sunday school teacher after class. Her mumbled excuse about something unexpected coming up sounded lame even to her own ears. She halfway hoped Mrs. McFee would object and say how desperately the class needed her help, but she merely patted Lacy's arm and said, "I understand."

Steve arrived right on time, dressed to the nines, as usual. "You've rearranged your furniture," he said, stepping inside her front door. "It looks nice."

"Thank you." Lacy didn't explain that no longer having her daughters in the house was the reason for the change. She picked up her wrap and slipped outside.

It took almost an hour to reach the restaurant Steve selected. No doubt they were going to another one of the places he could brag about acquiring. Lacy tuned out his discourse on the improvements he'd like to see at the Roadhouse. Over dinner, he again brought up the subject.

"Someday I may sell the Roadhouse," Lacy said. "But not until my youngest daughter finishes college."

"Isn't she a freshman this year?" Steve stopped eating and stared at her. "Why, you're talking about four or five years from now."

"Yes. At least. And maybe not then. Everything depends on my situation at the time."

"But Lacy, you can't wait that long." He seemed somewhat agitated. "What about us? What about our plans?"

She threw him a questioning look. "Plans?"

Steve seemed to calm down. "I'm in line for a promotion to one of our regional offices, probably Dallas. I won't be traveling all the time then. I'm hoping you'll come with me, put Polson's Crossing in your rearview mirror and see how the other half lives."

"Come with you?" What, exactly, did he have in mind?

"Yes." He reached for her hand. "Nailing down the Roadhouse would seal the deal for me. It's the final acquisition to guarantee I get the regional manager position. We can buy a nice house and just kick back and enjoy life."

"I'll have to give that some thought." Lacy's heart was racing. *He doesn't want me. He doesn't even really want the Roadhouse. All he's after is a big job in Dallas. Why did it take me so long to catch on?*

"Of course." He smiled. "But you can't take too long. I need to finalize our terms right away because the timing of putting all of the pieces together is critical." He held up a hand. "I know. You said three or four more years. That's doable. Now that you've agreed to sell us the Roadhouse, I can set up a deal where you manage it, under

392

our ownership of course, for up to two years, with an option to extend in increments of one year afterward. You can have your cake and eat it, too. You can continue doing your thing here while I get settled in Big D, and then you can join me as soon as you're ready." He released her hand and emptied his wine glass. "Oh, Lacy, you've made me so happy."

"I haven't agreed to anything yet."

"I understand we still have specifics to iron out." He held up his wine glass to catch the server's eye. "Selling price, for example, but I assure you our offer will be above fair market value. Nevertheless, we've agreed in principal." When the server approached, Steve ordered a bottle of champagne. "Let's celebrate."

Stunned, Lacy sat and fumed, wondering if her anger was obvious.

When the server poured each of them a champagne glass full of bubbly, Steve said, "I know you don't normally drink, but this is a special occasion." He lifted his glass and said, "To us."

"Lacy folded her fingers around the stem and lifted her glass to meet Steve's. She touched the glass to her lips without drinking. Much as she wanted to throw the drink in his face, she reminded herself she in a place where she knew no one, depending on a con man to get her safely home.

"Isn't this exciting?" Steve fairly glowed.

Lacy nodded. "I'm overwhelmed." She faked a laugh. "Will you excuse me? I need to visit the restroom."

"Certainly." Steve stood and held her chair. "Hurry back," he whispered in her ear.

The first thing Lacy did was pour her champagne into the lavatory and toss the stemmed glassware into the trash. She went into the last stall and sat on the toilet, trying unsuccessfully not to cry. She couldn't decide whether she was more furious with Steve for being a cad or with herself for stupidly falling into his trap. If they'd been in Polson's Crossing, she'd walk out. But they weren't. Whatever she had to do, she vowed not to leave this restaurant with Steve.

Cindy was in Tennessee. Pearl and Leonard weren't back from Florida. Typically, Monica didn't answer, and a recording said her voicemail was full. Lacy scrolled through her contacts, feeling nauseated, knowing she had only one option left. Before she could back out, she pressed a finger over Monty's name.

Chapter Seventy-One

Monty took out his vibrating phone and checked to see who was calling. It figured. Anyone other than his agent would know better than to call him in the middle of the evening chapel service. He put the phone back into his pocket, only to feel the vibrations begin again. This time it was a text. "Urgent. Pick up the phone," it read. "I know you're there."

With a sigh, he stepped outside. Before he could carry out his intention to call Carson Henry back, the phone vibrated again. "Hey, Carson."

Monty's ears burned from a string of curses. From a few normal words, he pieced together the understanding that he was a stupid, idiotic liar. Once upon a time, those would have been fighting words. When Carson took a breath, Monty said, "It's always good to hear from you, but I have lots of better things to do than listen to foul language. I admit I can be stupid, even idiotic, but I haven't told you any lies that I know of in a couple of years now. What's up?"

"You're married." Carson Henry spoke those words as if they identified a criminal.

"I wish I could say that's true. Maybe someday it will be," Monty looked through the window in the sanctuary door, enjoying the sight of so many worshippers. "Right now, I'm divorced."

"Have you ever heard of someone named Lacy Ann Gibson?"

"Sure, Lacy Ann Gibson Chapman. She's my ex-wife."

"That's not what the records show. We're trying to finalize this trust you want, which may I add is utter lunacy, and my financial eager beaver dug up the fact that you're married to this woman. She filed for divorce nine years ago, but no final decree was ever issued."

Monty felt his face break into a smile. "You're kidding."

"I wish I were. Don't you realize the position you're in? Texas is a community property state and you've reestablished your residence there. This woman owns half of everything you have. She can easily convince a sympathetic judge she should have half of everything you've *ever* earned, which thanks to me is considerable. I'll remind you that you've already spent a big chunk of that money. You aren't able to do anything until this gets straightened out. That is, unless, Mrs. Chapman agrees to sign off on your trust, which would distinguish her from every other female I've ever known. You'd better get your house in order, and lawyer up, fellow. This won't be pretty."

"Oh, man." Monty said. "This is probably just a recordkeeping problem. If it isn't, it's the best news I've had in months. Imagine, Lacy is my wife."

"Did you hear anything I said?" Carson screamed. "I don't know why I bother listening to tapes and reading lyrics. From now on I'm going to refer artists to a shrink and refuse to represent them unless they're certifiably insane. You guys with talent are all idiots. Just go turn

396

yourself in at the nearest looney bin and I'll talk to you tomorrow."

Monty smiled when Carson hung up on him, thinking how cool it would be if he and Lacy were actually not divorced. He tried to calm his excitement, realizing his agent probably had bad information. When his phone vibrated again, he assumed Carson wanted to rant about his woeful stupidity again.

Monty pressed the 'talk' button without checking the caller ID. "I concede I'm either stupid or crazy or both. Was there anything else, or shall we leave it at that?"

"Monty?"

He recognized the voice at once. "Lacy?"

"I know it's a lot to ask, but I'm in trouble. Will you come and get me? I'll tell you the whole story when you get here."

"I'm on my way." He headed for his car without stopping to tell anyone he was leaving. "Where are you?"

Monty broke the speed limit getting to the restaurant. When he walked in, he knew Lacy was still in the women's restroom because she was texting him from there. "I'm here," he responded to her last text. "You can come out now."

He hurried across the dining room to meet Lacy and give her a bear hug. "Are you all right?"

"I am now," she answered. "Please take me home."

Steve met them before they reached the door. "What's going on?" he asked.

Lacy glared at him. "Monty is taking me home."

Shifting his eyes to Monty, Steve said, "What's the meaning of this? Lacy is *my girlfriend.*"

Monty looked Steve up and down. "She's my wife, which trumps girlfriend any day of the week. If you'll excuse us."

"Wife?" Steve scowled at Monty. "Then that means you're co-owner of Pearl's Roadhouse."

Monty saw no reason to go into details about his disclaimer of rights to the Roadhouse at this time. "You might say that."

"My apologies, Mr. Chapman. You deceived me, Lacy. You should have told me you're married." With those words, he turned away.

Meanwhile, Monty and Lacy got into his car and left. For a few miles, Lacy said nothing and did nothing but cry. When she quit sobbing, she said, "Do you know how much I hate bursting into tears when I get really mad? It makes me come across like some wimpy damsel in distress."

"We're all wired in different ways. You got the tear gene." Monty kept his eyes on the road. "There's nothing weak or wimpy about you, Lace." He hadn't used that pet name for her in far too long. "You run a successful business and you raised two amazing daughters by yourself. I think you're pretty wonderful."

"Thank you, Monty. That means a lot." After a few miles of silence, Lacy asked, "Don't you want to know how I got myself into such a mess?"

"Only if you want to tell me." She didn't speak up right away. He continued, "I must say, I was impressed when the waitress came into the bathroom looking for you and you fended her off by making up that story about being sick. Quick thinking."

"I was telling the truth. After our first call got dropped, I lost my dinner. When Steve sent the waitress to check on me, I had plenty of evidence to demonstrate I was sick. I was never in my life so happy to throw up."

Monty smiled. "The Lord works in mysterious ways."

"That creep Steve Thornton pretended to be interested in me because he wants the Roadhouse." Lacy sniffled. "And I fell for it. The oldest trick in the book. What a fool I've been."

"Don't be so hard on yourself. We all get conned now and then. Just tonight, my agent called me a stupid idiot."

"Why would he say that to you?"

Monty cut his eyes toward Lacy, hoping to register her reaction to her next words. "He thinks I've set myself up for a woman to take me to the cleaners big time."

"Oh." Lacy turned her face to the window.

All the way from Polson's Crossing he'd prayed for Lacy. Now he asked for wisdom for himself. Was this the time to drop his information bomb on her? She'd had a rough night. Maybe he should wait. On the other hand, she didn't give him many opportunities to have a long, personal conversation. A phrase popped into his head, 'no time like the present'. He shook it off, but the words bubbled to the top of his mind again. He took a deep breath.

"Carson Henry—that's my agent—advised me to hire an attorney to fend off your claim on my assets."

In his peripheral vision, he saw the speed with which Lacy's head turned from the window toward him. "*My* claim? You're not making sense."

"Carson figures I owe you a bundle of money."

"If I was going to sue you for more child support, I'd have done it long ago. The girls are grown now."

"No, it's not about child support. I'm setting up a trust for the mission. A financial wizard did some preliminary research and concluded we're still legally married, meaning half of everything I have is yours." Monty expected a quick denial. Instead, there was only silence.

Minutes ticked by before Lacy said, "He may be right. About our divorce, I mean." She put a hand almost to his arm and quickly withdrew it. "I never got a copy of the final decree. I'm not sure one was ever issued."

"If it wasn't, you're entitled to half of what I have. If you'll agree to the mission trust, you can have everything else, and welcome to it."

"I'm not interested in your money, Monty. Ironically enough, I thought you came back to Polson's Crossing because you wanted to get your hands on the Roadhouse. What *do* you want? The other day you asked me about my dream. What's yours?"

"I have just about everything I need and most of what I want, with only one exception." He stopped to gather his courage.

"What is that?"

"You, Lacy. To have and to hold from this day forward, in sickness and in health, for better for worse, for richer for poorer, so long as we both shall live."

"What about making it big as a singer?"

"I'd be very happy to write more hit songs. If it happens, it happens. If not, so what? Jesus changed everything about my approach to life, including my purpose and priorities." Monty wished he could see her face, but the light inside the car was too dim. "We were good together once. With God's help, I think we can be again. Give me another chance to make you happy. I promise to give it my best shot."

She didn't respond immediately. Then, "We *were* good together, weren't we?" She paused before adding, "What about our divorce? We don't know for sure if we're married or not. Don't you want to find out?"

401

"I just want us to be married *now*. We can have a fancy church wedding where you wear a full-length gown and I put a sparkling big diamond ring on your finger. We'll build a house you design, and go from there."

"That all sounds fine, but let's be practical. What about your mission? And the Roadhouse? There are so many issues we'd have to deal with."

"All I know is I love you and the Bible says love never fails. I'm willing to step out on faith and solve whatever problems arise as they come along. Are you?"

She kept him waiting for a breathless moment before whispering, "Maybe."

Monty was happy and hopeful when he pulled into her driveway. The streetlight illuminated Lacy's profile against the window of his car.

"I really don't like extravagant weddings," she said. "All the planning and running around when Monica was engaged to Philip cured me of that idea permanently." She slightly bowed her head. "I wouldn't mind a nice ring, though."

Reaching across, Monty opened the glove box. "I've been carrying this around for months. If it doesn't fit or you don't like the style, Polson's Jewel Box will reset the stones." He opened the ring box and held it out to her. "Lacy Ann Gibson Chapman, will you marry me?"

THE END

EPILOGUE

On the fourth of July, Lacy and Monty Chapman renewed their vows in the same little Oklahoma town where they eloped twenty years earlier. Lacy is a professional architect while Monty oversees the Tom Gillespie Memorial Foundation and continues writing songs. Their children and grandchildren are the delight of their lives.

Monica and Julio were married at Christmas, as they'd planned. They successfully converted the Roadhouse from a restaurant into an event center for private parties and weddings. The change allows them to spend more time with their four sons.

Cindy married a radiologist who now practices medicine in Polson's Crossing. They live with their daughter near Pearl's lake house.

Wayne Houston and his wife own an animal health clinic in Nashville. "Cleaner Than A Hound's Tooth" was Wayne's only hit recording.

Pearl and Leonard had five happy years together before Leonard passed away.

Not long after Monty and Lacy's reunion, a manufacturer of aircraft parts broke ground for a factory and distribution mega center two miles from Pearl's Roadhouse.

If you enjoyed reading this book, please consider posting a review. Your opinion matters!

Other books by Carlene Havel:

A Hero's Homecoming

Baxter Road Miracle

Evidence Not Seen

Here Today Gone Tomorrow

Parisian Surprise

A Sharecropper Christmas

Texas Runaway Bride

Books by Carlene Havel and Sharon
Faucheux:

Daughter of the King

Song of the Shepherd Woman

The Scarlet Cord

Made in the USA
San Bernardino, CA
04 July 2019